THE BEST
HORROR
from Fantasy Tales

Forgotten lands of time-lost lore
Astound the senses, lifting high
Nacreous towers to a sky
That dreamers swear they've known before—of yore.
And warriors grim ride mighty steeds,
Sore pressed by runes of devilish source,
Yet never once avoid the course
That augers destinies of deeds—and dooms.
And galleons with scarlet sails
Loom out of misted oceans deep;
Ensorcelled oarsmen, fast asleep,
Sail on through sun and rain and gails—in Fantasy Tales!

BRIAN LUMLEY

THE BEST HORROR
FROM FANTASY TALES

Edited by STEPHEN JONES and DAVID SUTTON

Carroll & Graf Publishers, Inc.
New York

Selection, Afterword and Author Notes copyright © Stephen Jones and
David Sutton 1988

Introduction copyright © 1988 by Ramsey Campbell.

First Carroll & Graf edition 1990

Carroll & Graf Publishers, Inc.
260 Fifth Avenue
New York, NY 10001

Library of Congress Cataloging-in-Publication Data

The Best horror from fantasy tales / edited by Stephen Jones and
    David Sutton.—1st Carroll & Graf ed.
        p.   cm.
    ISBN 0-88184-571-X : $17.95
    1. Horror tales, English.   2. Horror tales, American   I. Jones,
Stephen.   II. Sutton, David, 1944–
PR1309.H6B47   1990
623'.0873808—dc20   89-78358
                                                        CIP

Manufactured in the United States of America

ACKNOWLEDGEMENTS

FANTASY TALES copyright © 1978 by Brian Lumley. By permission of the author.

THE FORBIDDEN copyright © 1985 by Clive Barker. By permission of the author.

DREAMS MAY COME copyright © 1939, 1978 by H. Warner Munn. By permission of the literary executor.

THE DARK COUNTRY copyright © 1981 by Dennis Etchison. By permission of the author.

DEAD TO THE WORLD copyright © 1982 by Allen Lucas. By permission of the author.

THE GENERATION WALTZ copyright © 1984 by Charles L. Grant. By permission of the author.

DON'T OPEN THAT DOOR copyright © 1940, 1979 by Frances Wellman. By permission of the author.

THE FROLIC copyright © 1982 by Thomas Ligotti. By permission of the author.

THE SORCERER'S JEWEL copyright © 1939, 1967 by Robert Bloch. By permission of the author.

THE STRANGE YEARS copyright © 1982 by Brian Lumley. By permission of the author.

RED copyright © 1986 by Richard Christian Matheson. By permission of the author.

EVER THE FAITH ENDURES copyright © 1978 by Manly Wade Wellman. By permission of the literary executor.

EXTENSION 201 copyright © 1979 by Cyril Simsa. By permission of the author.

THE LAST WOLF copyright © 1975 by Karl Edward Wagner. By permission of the author.

TONGUE IN CHEEK copyright © 1984 by Mike Grace. By permission of the author.

IN THE X-RAY copyright © 1949 by Fritz Leiber. By permission of the author.

THE BAD PEOPLE copyright © 1984 by Steve Rasnic Tem. By permission of the author.

A PLACE OF NO RETURN copyright © 1981 by Hugh B. Cave. By permission of the author.

THE TERMINUS copyright © 1985 by Kim Newman. By permission of the author.

THE GREEN MAN copyright © 1983 by Kelvin Jones. By permission of the author.

THE VOICE OF THE BEACH copyright © 1982 by Ramsey Campbell. By permission of the author.

CONTENTS

ILLUSTRATIONS

Individual copyright is retained by the artists

For Jo and Sandra
with all our love,
for putting up with
this 'hobby' for
more than ten years.

INTRODUCTION
Ramsey Campbell

I began collecting in this field in the mid-fifties, just when it seemed its magazines were a dying breed. Now and then the odd journal would appear and vanish: *Phantom*, edited by 'We at the Web' from Bolton, and voted 'best book of its kind available in this country today' by the Leicester Psychic Science Institute, survived for sixteen issues; *Weird World*, published by Gannet Press of Birkenhead, managed only two, and sank shortly after announcing a 'grand short story competition' which would pay each lucky winner a guinea once their five-thousand-word story was published. As obscure were Gerald G. Swan's *Weird and Occult Miscellany*, whose back cover with its advertisements for studies of torture seemed to make some disconcerting assumptions about its readership, and a one-shot whose title I believe to have been *Screen Chills and Macabre Stories*, which reprinted Robert Bloch's 'Notebook Found in a Deserted House' under the title 'Them Ones', rather to Bloch's surprise, I suspect. But though *Phantom* latterly lifted a good deal of its contents from *Weird Tales*, none of these journals could make up for the demise of that most famous of supernatural horror magazines.

In the sixties Robert A. W. Lowndes, a fine editor, tried to do so with a family of magazines, *Magazine of Horror, Startling Mystery Stories* and others. These not only reprinted stories and art from the pulp magazines but preserved a continuity by encouraging new writers; within a few months Lowndes wrote an editorial about one of my stories and published a tale by a teenage reader, Stephen King. On top of all this, the magazines included advertising in, shall we say, the tradition of the pulps, complete with coupon to fill in: 'Yes, I would like [insert number] LIFE SIZE GLAMOUR TOPLESS Go-Go Party Girls to come and live with me.' But even such advertising couldn't sustain the magazines beyond the early seventies, and for a while the field, as far as short stories were concerned, looked more moribund than ever.

Soon things changed, not least because that teenage reader of Lowndes' magazines made a name for himself. It's ironic, though, that in the midst of the explosion of horror fiction that followed King and Herbert and Ira Levin and *The Exorcist*, some aspects of it were still known only to the cognoscenti. I mean the little magazines of the field. Of these, *Fantasy Tales* has won more awards than any other magazine. I can't say I'm surprised, for when I saw the first isue back in the summer of 1977, I felt that *Weird Tales* had risen from its grave.

Part of this impression has to do with the illustrations, individual though they are, and in particular with the blurbs on the contents page. The latter aren't so easy to bring off as you might think. An anthologist who seemed ubiquitous fifteen years ago had a try, in a book which included a story of mine about litter that becomes animate. The blurbs on either side of mine were 'What do you eat after you've finished your mother's eyeball?' and 'When boys refused him, he cut them apart and laughed!', but the worst the anthologist could find to say about my tale was 'Trapped by malevolent bottles, napkins and straws!' I rather think the editors of *Fantasy Tales* have more sense of what they're doing and the tradition from which it derives. Only a sprinkling of pulp-style advertisements ('Throw Away That Truss', 'Glands Control Your Destiny', 'Learn To Mount Birds', 'Tombstones Direct To You', 'Ear Noises?', 'Nose Trouble?' 'Ruptured?' 'Piles?' 'So Nervous You Can't Sleep?',) could render the magazine more authentic.

However, this is by no means to say that *Fantasy Tales* is simply an attempt to pastiche the pulps; rather is it the magazine *Weird Tales* might have been if it had survived. While the magazine pays tribute to its roots by publishing material such as the stories by Leiber, Garfield, Bloch and Wellman, and Wagner's fine tribute to one of Ray Bradbury's preoccupations, it is at least equally strong in more contemporary terms: see, for instance, the tales by Barker, Grant, Ligotti and Tem. I think it deserves especial praise for taking risks. One example may suffice. It published Dennis Etchison's 'The Dark Country', though that is in no sense a fantasy, and this adventurousness was repaid when Etchison's became the only story so far to win both the British Fantasy Award and the World Fantasy Award.

I'm proud to have been associated with the magazine as a contributor over the years, and now to help introduce it to a wider audience. May this book give its readers as much pleasure as I always experience when I see a new issue of *Fantasy Tales*.

Merseyside
March 1988

'Do you believe in me? . . . I am Rumour'

THE FORBIDDEN
Clive Barker

Illustration by John Stewart

Already a respected playright (with such genre titles as The History of the Devil, Frankenstein in Love *and* The Secret Life of Cartoons), *Clive Barker made an impressive debut as a horror writer in 1984 with the publication of the first three* Books of Blood *collections. Since then a further trio of* Books of Blood *has appeared (in myriad permutations and deluxe editions) plus two novellas,* The Hellbound Heart *and* Cabal, *and a pair of acclaimed novels,* The Damnation Game *and* Weaveworld. *He has written the screenplays for the films* Underworld *and* Rawhead Rex *(the latter based on his* Books of Blood *story), and more recently, he wrote and directed the hit horror movie* Hellraiser *and executive produced its sequel,* Hellraiser II: Hellbound. *'The Forbidden' was published concurrently in the fourteenth issue of* Fantasy Tales *and* Volume 5 of Books of Blood. *A piece of modern urban horror that owes much to the influence of fellow horror writer Ramsey Campbell, the story won The British Fantasy Award in 1986.*

LIKE a flawless tragedy, the elegance of which structure is lost upon those suffering in it, the perfect geometry of the Spector Street Estate was only visible from the air. Walking in its drear canyons, passing through its grimy corridors from one grey concrete rectangle to the next, there was little to seduce the eye or stimulate the imagination. What few sapl-

1

ings had been planted in the quadrangles had long since been mutilated or uprooted; the grass, though tall, resolutely refused a healthy green.

No doubt the estate and its two companion developments had once been an architect's dream. No doubt the city-planners had wept with pleasure at a design which housed three and thirty-six persons per hectare, and still boasted space for a children's playground. Doubtless fortunes and reputations had been built upon Spector Street, and at its opening fine words had been spoken of it being a yardstick by which all future developments would be measured. But the planners—tears wept, words spoken - had left the estate to its own devices; the architects occupied restored Georgian houses at the other end of the city, and probably never set foot here.

They would not have been shamed by the deterioration of the estate even if they had. Their brain-child (they would doubtless argue) was as brilliant as ever: Its geometries as precise, its ratios as calculated; it was *people* who had spoiled Spector Street. Nor would they have been wrong in such an accusation. Helen had seldom seen an inner city environment so comprehensively vandalized. Lamps had been shattered and back-yard fences overthrown; cars, whose wheels and engines had been removed and chassis then burned, blocked garage facilities. In one courtyard three or four ground-floor maisonettes had been entirely gutted by fire, their windows and doors boarded up with planks and corrugated iron.

More startling still was the graffiti. That was what she had come here to see, encouraged by Archie's talk of the place, and she was not disappointed. It was difficult to believe, staring at the multiple layers of designs, names, obscenities, and dogmas that were scrawled and sprayed on every available brick, that Spector Street was barely three and a half years old. The walls, so recently virgin, were now so profoundly defaced that the Council Cleaning Department could never hope to return them to their former condition. A layer of whitewash to cancel this visual cacophony would only offer the scribes a fresh and yet more tempting surface on which to make their mark.

Helen was in seventh heaven. Every corner she turned offered some fresh material for her thesis: *'Graffiti: the semiotics of urban despair'*. It was a subject which married her two favourite disciplines—sociology and aesthetics—and as she wandered around the estate she began to wonder if there wasn't a book, in addition to her thesis, in the subject. She walked from courtyard to courtyard, copying down a large number of the more interesting scrawlings, and noting their location. Then she went back to the car to collect her camera and tripod and returned to the most fertile of the areas, to make a thorough visual record of the walls.

It was a chilly business. She was not an expert photographer, and the

2

late October sky was in full flight, shifting the light on the bricks from one moment to the next. As she adjusted and readjusted the exposure to compensate for the light changes her fingers steadily became clumsier, her temper correspondingly thinner. But she struggled on, the idle curiosity of passers-by notwithstanding. There were so many designs to document. She reminded herself that her present discomfort would be amply repaid when she showed the slides to Trevor, whose doubt of the project's validity had been perfectly apparent from the beginning.

"The writing on the wall?" he'd said, half smiling in that irritating fashion of his, "It's been done a hundred times."

This was true, of course; and yet not. There certainly were learned works on graffiti, chock-full of sociological jargon: *cultural disenfranchisement; urban alienation*. But she flattered herself that *she* might find something amongst this litter of scrawlings that previous analysts had not: Some unifying convention perhaps, that she could use as the lynchpin of her thesis. Only a vigorous cataloguing and cross-referencing of the phrases and images before her would reveal such a correspondence; hence the importance of the photographic study. So many hands had worked here; so many minds left their mark, however casually: If she could find some pattern, some predominant motive, or *motif*, the thesis would be guaranteed some serious attention, and so, in turn, would she.

"What are you doing?" a voice from behind her asked.

She turned from her calculations to see a young woman with a pushchair on the pavement behind her. She looked weary, Helen thought, and pinched by the cold. The child in the pushchair was mewling, his grimy fingers clutching an orange lollipop and the wrapping from a chocolate bar. The bulk of the chocolate, and the remains of previous jujubes, was displayed down the front of his coat.

Helen offered a thin smile to the woman; she looked in need of it.

"I'm photographing the walls," she said in answer to the initial enquiry, though surely this was perfectly apparent.

The woman—Helen judged she could barely be twenty—said: "You mean the filth?"

"The writing and the pictures," Helen said. Then: "Yes. The filth."

"You from the Council?"

"No, the University."

"It's bloody disgusting," the woman said. "The way they do that. It's not just kids, either."

"No?"

"Grown men. Grown men, too. They don't give a damn. Do it in broad daylight. You see 'em...broad daylight." She glanced down at the child, who was sharpening his lollipop on the ground. "Kerry!" she snapped,

3

but the boy took no notice. "Are they going to wipe it off?" she asked Helen.

"I don't know," Helen said, and reiterated: "I'm from the University."

"Oh," the woman replied, as if this was new information, "so you're nothing to do with the Council?"

"No."

"Some of it's obscene, isn't it?; really dirty. Makes me embarrassed to see some of the things they draw."

Helen nodded, casting an eye at the boy in the pushchair. Kerry had decided to put his sweet in his ear for safe-keeping.

"Don't do that!" his mother told him, and leaned over to slap the child's hand. The blow, which was negligible, began the child bawling. Helen took the opportunity to return to her camera. But the woman still desired to talk. "It's not just on the outside, neither," she commented.

"I beg your pardon?" Helen said.

"They break into the flats when they go empty. The Council tried to board them up, but it does no good. They break in anyway. Use them as toilets, and write more filth on the walls. They light fires too. Then nobody can move back in."

The description piqued Helen's curiosity. Would the graffiti on the *inside* walls be substantially different from the public displays? It was certainly worth an investigation.

"Are there any places you know of around here like that?"

"Empty flats, you mean?"

"With graffiti."

"Just by us, there's one or two," the woman volunteered. "I'm in Butts' Court."

"Maybe you could show me?" Helen asked.

The woman shrugged.

"By the way, my name's Helen Buchanan."

"Anne-Marie," the mother replied.

"I'd be very grateful if you could point me to one of those empty flats."

Anne-Marie was baffled by Helen's enthusiasm, and made no attempt to disguise it, but she shrugged again and said: "There's nothing much to see. Only more of the same stuff."

Helen gathered up her equipment and they walked side by side through the intersecting corridors between one square and the next. Though the estate was low-rise, each court only five storeys high, the effect of each quadrangle was horribly claustrophobic. The walkways and staircases were a thief's dream, rife with blind corners and ill-lit tunnels. The rubbish-dumping facilities—chutes from the upper floors down which bags of refuse could be pitched—had long since been sealed up, thanks to their efficiency as fire-traps. Now plastic bags of refuse were piled high in the corridors, many torn open by roaming dogs, their contents strewn across the ground. The smell, even in the cold weather, was unpleasant. In high summer it must have been overpowering.

"I'm over the other side," Anne-Marie said, pointing across the quadrangle. "The one with the yellow door." She then pointed along the opposite side of the court. "Five or six maisonettes from the far end," she said. "There's two of them been emptied out. Few weeks now. One of the family's moved into Ruskin Court; the other did a bunk in the middle of the night."

With that, she turned her back on Helen and wheeled Kerry, who had taken to trailing spittle from the side of his pushchair, around the side of the square.

"Thank you," Helen called after her. Anne-Marie glanced over her shoulder briefly, but did not reply. Appetite whetted, Helen made her way along the row of ground floor maisonettes, many of which, though inhabited, showed little sign of being so. Their curtains were closely drawn; there were no milk-bottles on the doorsteps, nor children's toys left where they had been played with. Nothing, in fact, of *life* here. There *was* more graffiti however, sprayed, shockingly, on the doors of occupied houses. She granted the scrawlings only a casual perusal, in part because she feared one of the doors opening as she examined a choice obscenity sprayed upon it, but more because she was eager to see what revelations the empty flats ahead might offer.

The malign scent of urine, both fresh and stale, welcomed her at the threshold of number 14, and beneath that the smell of burnt paint and plastic. She hesitated for fully ten seconds, wondering if stepping into the maisonette was a wise move. The territory of the estate behind her was indisputably foreign, sealed off in its own misery, but the rooms in front of her were more intimidating still: A dark maze which her eyes could barely penetrate. But when her courage faltered she thought of Trevor, and how badly she wanted to silence his condescension. So thinking, she advanced into the place, deliberately kicking a piece of charred timber aside as she did so, in the hope that she would alert any tenant into showing himself.

There was no sound of occupancy however. Gaining confidence, she began to explore the front room of the maisonette which had been—to judge by the remains of a disembowelled sofa in one corner and the sodden carpet underfoot—a living-room. The pale-green walls were, as Anne-Marie had promised, extensively defaced, both by mirror scribblers—content to work in pen, or even more crudely in sofa charcoal—and by those with aspirations to public works, who had sprayed the walls in half

5

a dozen colours.

Some of the comments were of interest, though many she had already seen on the walls outside. Familiar names and couplings repeated themselves. Though she had never set eyes on these individuals she knew how badly Fabian J. (A.OK.) wanted to deflower Michelle; and that Michelle, in her turn, had the hots for somebody called Mr Sheen. Here, as elsewhere, a man called White Rat boasted of his endowment, and the return of the Syllabub Brothers was promised in red paint. One or two of the pictures accompanying, or at least adjacent to these phrases were of particular interest. An almost emblematic simplicity informed them. Beside the word *Christos* was a stick man with his hair radiating from his head like spines, and other heads impaled on each spine. Close by was an image of intercourse so brutally reduced that at first Helen took it to illustrate a knife plunging into a sightless eye. But fascinating as the images were, the room was too gloomy for her film, and she had neglected to bring a flash. If she wanted a reliable record of these discoveries she would have to come again, and for now be content with a simple exploration of the premises.

The maisonette wasn't that large, but the windows had been boarded up throughout, and as she moved further from the front door the dubious light petered out altogether. The smell of urine, which had been strong at the door, intensified too, until by the time she reached the back living-room and stepped along a short corridor into another room beyond, it was as cloying as incense. This room, being furthest from the front door, was also the darkest, and she had to wait a few moments in the cluttered gloom to allow her eyes to become useful. This, she guessed, had been the bedroom. What little furniture the residents had left behind them had been smashed to smithereens. Only the mattress had been left relatively untouched, dumped in the corner of the room amongst a wretched litter of blankets, newspapers, and pieces of crockery.

Outside, the sun found its way between the clouds, and two or three shafts of sunlight slipped between the boards nailed across the bedroom window and pierced the room like annunciations, scoring the opposite wall with bright lines. Here, the graffitists had been busy once more: The usual clamour of love-letters and threats. She scanned the wall quickly, and as she did so her eye was led by the beams of light across the room to the wall which contained the door she had stepped through.

Here, the artists had also been at work, but had produced an image the like of which she had not seen anywhere else. Using the door, which was centrally placed in the wall, as a mouth, the artists had sprayed a single, vast head on to the stripped plaster. The painting was more adroit than most she had seen, rife with detail that lent the image an unsettling

6

veracity. The cheekbones jutting through skin the colour of butter-milk; the teeth—sharpened to irregular points—all converging on the door. The sitter's eyes were, owing to the room's low ceiling, set mere inches above the upper lip, but this physical adjustment only lent force to the image, giving the impression that he had thrown his head back. Knotted strands of his hair snaked from his scalp across the ceiling.

Was it a portrait? There was something naggingly *specific* in the details of the brows and the lines around the wide mouth; in the careful pictur-ing of those vicious teeth. A nightmare certainly: A facsimile, perhaps, of something from a heroin fugue. Whatever its origins, it was potent. Even the illusion of door-as-mouth worked. The short passageway bet-ween living-room and bedroom offered a passable throat, with a tattered lamp in lieu of tonsils. Beyond the gullet, the day burned white in the nightmare's belly. The whole effect brought to mind a ghost train pain-ting. The same heroic deformity, the same unashamed intention to scare. And it worked. She stood in the bedroom almost stupified by the picture, its red-rimmed eyes fixing her mercilessly. Tomorrow, she determined, she would come here again, this time with high-speed film and a flash to illuminate the masterwork.

As she prepared to leave the sun went in, and the bands of light faded. She glanced over her shoulder at the boarded windows, and saw for the first time that one four-word slogan had been sprayed on the wall beneath them.

'*Sweets to the sweet*' it read. She was familiar with the quote, but not with its source. Was it a profession of love? If so, it was an odd location for such an avowal. Despite the mattress in the corner, and the relative privacy of this room, she could not imagine the intended reader of such words ever stepping in here to receive her bouquet. No adolescent lovers, however heated, would lie down here to play at mothers and fathers; not under the gaze of the terror on the wall. She crossed to examine the writing. The paint looked to be the same shade of pink as had been used to colour the gums of the screaming man; perhaps the same hand?

Behind her, a noise. She turned so quickly she almost tripped over the blanket-strewn mattress.

"Who—?"

At the other end of the gullet, in the living-room, was a scab-kneed boy of six or seven. He stared at Helen, eyes glittering in the half-light, as if waiting for a cue.

"Yes?" she said.

"Anne-Marie says do you want a cup of tea?" he declared without pause or intonation.

Her conversation with the woman seemed hours past. She was grateful for the invitation however. The damp maisonette had chilled her.

"Yes . . ." she said to the boy. "Yes please."

The child didn't move, but simply stared on at her.

"Are you going to lead the way?" she asked him.

"If you want," he replied, unable to raise a trace of enthusiasm.

"I'd like that."

"You taking photographs?" he asked.

"Yes. Yes, I am. But not in here."

"Why not?"

"It's too dark," she told him.

"Don't it work in the dark?" he wanted to know.

"No."

The boy nodded at this, as if the information somehow fitted well into his scheme of things, and about-turned without another word, clearly expecting Helen to follow.

If she had been taciturn in the street, Anne-Marie was anything but in the privacy of her own kitchen. Gone was the guarded curiosity, to be replaced by a stream of lively chatter and a constant scurrying between half-a-dozen minor domestic tasks, like a juggler keeping several plates spinning simultaneously. Helen watched this balancing act with some admiration; her own domestic skills were negligible. At last, the meandering conversation turned back to the subject that had brought Helen here.

"Them photographs," Anne-Marie said, "why'd you want to take them?"

"I'm writing about graffiti. The photos will illustrate my thesis."

"It's not very pretty."

"No, you're right, it isn't. But I find it interesting."

Anne-Marie shook her head. "I hate the whole estate," she said. "It's not safe here. People getting robbed on their own doorsteps. Kids setting fire to the rubbish day in, day out. Last summer we had the fire brigade here two, three times a day, 'til they sealed them chutes off. Now people just dump the bags in the passageways, and that attracts rats."

"Do you live here alone?"

"Yes," she said, "since Davey walked out."

"That your husband?"

"He was Kerry's father, but we weren't never married. We lived together two years, you know. We had some good times. Then he just upped and went off one day when I was at me Mam's with Kerry." She peered into her tea-cup. "I'm better off without him," she said. "But you get scared sometimes. Want some more tea?"

"I don't think I've got time."

"Just a cup," Anne-Marie said, already up and unplugging the electric

8

kettle to take it across for a re-fill. As she was about to turn on the tap she saw something on the draining board, and drove her thumb down, grinding it out. "Got you, you bugger," she said, then turned to Helen: "We got these bloody ants."

"Ants?"

"Whole estate's infected. From Egypt they are: Pharoah ants, they're called. Little brown sods. They breed in the central heating ducts, you see; that way they get into all the flats. Place is plagued with them."

This unlikely exoticism (ants from Egypt?) struck Helen as comical, but she said nothing. Anne-Marie was staring out of the kitchen window and into the back-yard.

"You should tell them—" she said, though Helen wasn't certain whom she was being instructed to tell, "tell them that ordinary people can't even walk the streets any longer—"

"Is it really so bad?" Helen said, frankly tiring of this catalogue of misfortunes.

Anne-Marie turned from the sink and looked at her hand.

"We've had murders here," she said.

"Really?"

"We had one in the summer. An old man he was, from Ruskin. That's just next door. I didn't know him, but he was a friend of the sister of the woman next door. I forget his name."

"And he was murdered?"

"Cut to ribbons in his own front room. They didn't find him for almost a week."

"What about his neighbours? Didn't they notice his absence?"

Anne-Marie shrugged, as if the most important pieces of information—the murder and the man's isolation—had been exchanged, and any further enquiries into the problem were irrelevant. But Helen pressed the point.

"Seems strange to me," she said.

Anne-Marie plugged in the filled kettle. "Well, it happened," she replied, unmoved.

"I'm not saying it didn't, I just—"

"His eyes had been taken out," she said, before Helen could voice any further doubts.

Helen winced. "No," she said, under her breath.

"That's the truth," Anne-Marie said. "And that wasn't all'd been done to him." She paused, for effect, then went on: "You wonder what kind of person's capable of doing things like that, don't you? You wonder." Helen nodded. She was thinking precisely the same thing.

"Did they ever find the man responsible?"

9

Anne-Marie snorted her disparagement. "Police don't give a damn what happens here. They keep off the estate as much as possible. When they do patrol all they do is pick up kids for getting drunk and that. They're afraid, you see. That's why they keep clear."

"Of this killer?"

"Maybe," Anne-Marie replied. Then: "He had a hook."

"A hook?"

"The man what done it. He had a hook, like Jack the Ripper."

Helen was no expert on murder, but she felt certain that the Ripper hadn't boasted a hook. It seemed churlish to question the truth of Anne-Marie's story however; though she silently wondered how much of this— the eyes taken out, the body rotting in the flat, the hook—was elaboration. The most scrupulous of reporters was surely tempted to embellish a story once in a while.

Anne-Marie had poured herself another cup of tea, and was about to do the same for her guest.

"No thank you," Helen said, "I really should go."

"You married?" Anne-Marie asked, out of the blue.

"Yes. To a lecturer from the University."

"What's his name?"

"Trevor."

Anne-Marie put two heaped spoonfuls of sugar into her cup of tea. "Will you be coming back?" she asked.

"Yes, I hope to. Later in the week. I want to take some photographs of the pictures in the maisonette across the court."

"Well, call in."

"I shall. And thank you for your help."

"That's all right," Anne-Marie replied. "You've got to tell somebody, haven't you?"

"The man apparently had a hook instead of a hand."

Trevor looked up from his plate of *tagliatelle con prosciutto*.

"Beg your pardon?"

Helen had been at pains to keep her recounting of this story as uncoloured by her own response as she could. She was interested to know what Trevor would make of it, and she knew that if she once signalled her own stance he would instinctively take an opposing view out of plain bloody-mindedness.

"He had a hook," she repeated, without inflection.

Trevor put down his fork, and plucked at his nose, sniffing. "I didn't read anything about this," he said.

"You don't look at the local press," Helen returned. "Neither of us do.

10

Maybe it never made any of the nationals."

"'Geriatric Murdered By Hook-Handed Maniac'?" Trevor said, savouring the hyperbole. "I would have thought it very newsworthy. When was all of this supposed to have happened?"

"Sometime last summer. Maybe we were in Ireland."

"Maybe," said Trevor, taking up his fork again. Bending to his food, the polished lens of his spectacles reflected only the plate of pasta and chopped ham in front of him, not his eyes.

"Why do you say *maybe*?" Helen prodded.

"It doesn't sound quite right," he said. "In fact it sounds bloody preposterous."

"You don't believe it?" Helen said.

Trevor looked up from his food, tongue rescuing a speck of *tagliatelle* from the corner of his mouth. His face had relaxed into that non-committal expression of his—the same face he wore, no doubt, when listening to his students. "Do *you* believe it?" he asked Helen. It was a favourite time-gaining device of his, another seminar trick, to question the questioner.

"I'm not certain," Helen replied, too concerned to find some solid ground in this sea of doubts to waste energy scoring points.

"All right, forget the tale ·" Trevor said, deserting his food for another glass of red wine. "· What about the teller? Did you trust her?"

Helen pictured Anne-Marie's earnest expression as she told the story of the old man's murder. "Yes," she said. "Yes; I think I would have known if she'd been lying to me."

"So why's it so important, anyhow? I mean, whether she's lying or not, what the fuck does it matter?"

It was a reasonable question, if irritatingly put. Why *did* it matter? Was it that she wanted to have her worst feelings about Spector Street proved false? That such an estate be filthy, be hopeless, be a dump where the undesirable and the disadvantaged were tucked out of public view— all that was a liberal commonplace, and she accepted it as an unpalatable social reality. But the story of the old man's murder and mutilation was something other. An image of violent death that, once with her, refused to part from her company.

She realized, to her chagrin, that this confusion was plain on her face, and that Trevor, watching her across the table, was not a little entertained by it.

"If it bothers you so much," he said, "why don't you go back there and ask around, instead of playing believe-in-it-or-not over dinner?"

She couldn't help but rise to his remark. "I thought you liked guessing games," she said.

He threw her a sullen look.

11

"Wrong again."

The suggestion that she investigate was not a bad one, though doubtless he had ulterior motives for offering it. She viewed Trevor less charitably day by day. What she had once thought in him a fierce commitment to debate she now recognized as mere power-play. He argued, not for the thrill of dialectic, but because he was pathologically competitive. She had seen him, time and again, take up attitudes she knew he did not espouse, simply to spill blood. Nor, more's the pity, was he alone in this sport. Academe was one of the last strongholds of the professional time-waster. On occasion their circle seemed entirely dominated by educated fools, lost in a wasteland of stale rhetoric and hollow commitment.

From one wasteland to another. She returned to Spector Street the following day, armed with a flashgun in addition to her tripod and high-sensitive film. The wind was up today, and it was Arctic, more furious still for being trapped in the maze of passageways and courts. She made her way to number 14, and spent the next hour in its befouled confines, meticulously photographing both the bedroom and living-room walls. She had half expected the impact of the head in the bedroom to be dulled by re-acquaintance; it was not. Though she struggled to capture its scale and detail as best she could, she knew the photographs would be at best a dim echo of its perpetual howl.

Much of its power lay in its context, of course. That such an image might be stumbled upon in surroundings so drab, so conspicuously lacking in mystery, was akin to finding an icon on a rubbish-heap: A gleaming symbol of transcendence from a world of toil and decay into some darker but more tremendous realm. She was painfully aware that the intensity of her response probably defied her articulation. Her vocabulary was analytic, replete with buzz-words and academic terminology, but woefully impoverished when it came to evocation. The photographs, pale as they would be, would, she hoped, at least hint at the potency of this picture, even if they couldn't conjure the way it froze the bowels.

When she emerged from the maisonette the wind was as uncharitable as ever, but the boy was waiting outside—the same child as had attended upon her yesterday—dressed as if for spring weather. He grimaced in his effort to keep the shudders at bay.

"Hello," Helen said.

"I waited," the child announced.

"Waited?"

"Anne-Marie said you'd come back."

"I wasn't planning to come until later in the week," Helen said. "You might have waited a long time."

The boy's grimace relaxed a notch. "It's all right," he said, "I've got nothing to do."

"What about school?"

"Don't like it," the boy replied, as if unobliged to be educated if it wasn't to his taste.

"I see." said Helen, and began to walk down the side of the quadrangle. The boy followed. On the patch of grass at the centre of the quadrangle several chairs and two or three dead saplings had been piled.

"What's this?" she said, half to herself.

"Bonfire Night," the boy informed her. "Next week."

"Of course."

"You going to see Anne-Marie?" he asked.

"Yes."

"She's not in."

"Oh. Are you sure"

"Yeah."

"Well, perhaps *you* can help me..." She stopped and turned to face the child; smooth sacs of fatigue hung beneath his eyes. "I heard about an old man who was murdered near here," she said to him. "In the summer. Do you know anything about that?"

"No."

"Nothing at all? You don't remember anybody getting killed?"

"No," the boy said again, with impressive finality. "I don't remember."

"Well; thank you anyway."

This time, when she retraced her steps back to the car, the boy didn't follow. But as she turned the corner out of the quadrangle she glanced back to see him standing on the spot where she'd left him, staring after her as if she were a mad-woman.

By the time she had reached the car and packed the photographic equipment into the boot there were specks of rain in the wind, and she was sorely tempted to forget she'd ever heard Anne-Marie's story and make her way home, where the coffee would be warm even if the welcome wasn't. But she needed an answer to the question Trevor had put the previous night. Do *you* believe it?, he'd asked when she'd told him the story. She hadn't known how to answer then, and she still didn't. Perhaps (why did she sense this?) the terminology of verifiable truth was redundant here; perhaps the final answer to his question was not an answer at all, only another question. If so; so. She had to find out.

Ruskin Court was as forlorn as its fellows, if not more so. It didn't even boast a bonfire. On the third floor balcony a woman was taking washing in before the rain broke; on the grass in the centre of the quadrangle two dogs were absent-mindedly rutting, the fuckee staring up at the blank sky.

13

As she walked along the empty pavement she set her face determinedly; a purposeful look, Bernadette had once said, deterred attack. When she caught sight of the two women talking at the far end of the court she crossed over to them hurriedly, grateful for their presence.

"Excuse me?"

The women, both in middle-age, ceased their animated exchange and looked her over.

"I wonder if you can help me?"

She could feel their appraisal, and their distrust; they went undisguised. One of the pair, her face florid, said plainly: "What do you want?"

Helen suddenly felt bereft of the least power to charm. What was she to say to these two that wouldn't make her motives appear ghoulish? "I was told..." she began, and then stumbled, aware that she would get no assistance from either woman. "...I was told there'd been a murder near here. Is that right?"

The florid woman raised eyebrows so plucked they were barely visible. "Murder?" she said.

"Are you from the press?" the other woman enquired. The years had soured her features beyond sweetening. Her small mouth was deeply lined; her hair, which had been dyed brunette, showed a half-inch of grey at the roots.

"No, I'm not from the press," Helen said, "I'm a friend of Anne-Marie's in Butts' Court." This claim of *friend* stretched the truth, but it seemed to mellow the women somewhat.

"Visiting are you?" the florid woman asked.

"In a manner of speaking—"

"You missed the warm spell—"

"Anne-Marie was telling me about somebody who'd been murdered here, during the summer. I was curious about it."

"Is that right?"

"—do you know anything about it?"

"Lots of things go on around here," said the second woman. "You don't know the half of it."

"So it's true," Helen said.

"They had to close the toilets," the first woman put in.

"That's right. They did," the other said.

"The toilets?" Helen said. What had this to do with the old man's death?

"It was terrible," the first said. "Was it your Frank, Josie, who told you about it?"

"No, not Frank," Josie replied. "Frank was still at sea. It was Mrs Tyzack."

The witness established, Josie relinquished the story to her companion, and turned her gaze back upon Helen. The suspicion had not yet died

14

from her eyes.

"This was only the month before last," Josie said. "Just about the end of August. It was August, wasn't it?" She looked to the other woman for verification. "You've got the head for dates, Maureen."

Maureen looked uncomfortable. "I forget," she said, clearly unwilling to offer testimony.

"I'd like to know," Helen said. Josie, despite her companion's reluctance, was eager to oblige.

"There's some lavatories," she said, "outside the shops—you know, public lavatories. I'm not quite sure how it all happened exactly, but there used to be a boy . . . well, he wasn't a boy really, I mean he was a man of twenty or more, but he was . . ." she fished for the words, ". . . mentally subnormal, I suppose you'd say. His mother used to have to take him around like he was a four-year-old. Anyhow, she let him go into the lavatories while she went to that little supermarket, what's it called?" she turned to Maureen for a prompt, but the other woman just looked back, her disapproval plain. Josie was ungovernable, however. "Broad daylight, this was," she said to Helen. "Middle of the day. Anyhow, the boy went to the toilet, and the mother was in the shop. And after a while, you know how you do, she's busy shopping, she forgets about him, and then she thinks he's been gone a long time . . ."

At this juncture Maureen couldn't prevent herself from butting in: The accuracy of the story apparently took precedence over her wariness.

"—She got into an argument," she corrected Josie, "with the manager. About some bad bacon she'd had from him. That was why she was such a time . . ."

"I see," said Helen.

"—anyway," said Josie, picking up the tale, "she finished her shopping and when she came out he still wasn't there—"

"So she asked someone from the supermarket—" Maureen began, but Josie wasn't about to have her narrative snatched back at this vital juncture.

"She asked one of the men from the supermarket—" she repeated over Maureen's interjection, "to go down into the lavatory and find him."

"It was terrible," said Maureen, clearly picturing the atrocity in her mind's eye.

"He was lying on the floor, in a pool of blood."

"Murdered?"

Josie shook her head. "He'd have been better off dead. He'd been attacked with a razor—" she let this piece of information sink in before delivering the *coup de grâce*, "—and they'd cut off his private parts. Just cut them off and flushed them down a toilet. No reason on earth to do it."

15

"Oh my God."

"Better off dead," Josie repeated. "I mean, they can't mend something like that, can they?"

The appalling tale was rendered worse still by the *sang-froid* of the teller, and by the casual repetition of "Better off dead."

"The boy," Helen said, "Was he able to describe his attackers?"

"No," said Josie, "he's pratically an imbecile. He can't string more than two words together."

"And nobody saw anyone go into the lavatory? Or leaving it?"

"People come and go all the time—" Maureen said. This, though it sounded like an adequate explanation, had not been Helen's experience. There was not a great bustle in the quadrangle and passageways; far from it. Perhaps the shopping mall was busier, she reasoned, and might offer adequate cover for such a crime.

"So they haven't found the culprit," she said.

"No," Josie replied, her eyes losing their fervour. The crime and its immediate consequences were the nub of this story; she had little or no interest in either the culprit or his capture.

"We're not safe in our own beds," Maureen observed. "You ask anyone."

"Anne-Marie said the same," Helen replied. "That's how she came to tell me about the old man. Said he was murdered during the summer, here in Ruskin Court."

"I do remember something," Josie said. "There *was* some talk I heard. An old man, and his dog. He was battered to death, and the dog ended up . . . I don't know. It certainly wasn't here. It must have been one of the other estates."

"Are you sure?"

The woman looked offended by this slur on her memory. "Oh, yes," she said, "I mean if it had been here, we'd have known the story, wouldn't we?"

Helen thanked the pair for their help and decided to take a stroll around the quadrangle anyway, just to see how many more maisonettes were out of operation here. As in Butts' Court, many of the curtains were drawn and all the doors locked. But then if Spector Street *was* under siege from a maniac capable of the murder and mutilation such as she'd heard described, she was not surprised that the residents took to their homes and stayed there. There was nothing much to see around the court. All the unoccupied maisonettes and flats had been recently sealed, to judge by a litter of nails left on a doorstep by the council workmen. One sight *did* catch her attention, however. Scrawled on the paving stones she was walking over—and all but erased by rain and the passage of feet— the same phrase she'd seen in the bedroom of number 14: *Sweets to the sweet*. The words were so benign; why did she seem to sense menace in them? Was it in their excess, perhaps, in the sheer overabundance of sugar upon sugar, honey upon honey?

She walked on, though the rain persisted, and her walkabout gradually led her away from the quadrangles and into a concrete no-man's-land through which she had not previously passed. This was—or had been—the site of the estate's amenities. Here was the children's playground, its metal-framed rides overturned, its sandpit fouled by dogs, its paddling pool empty. And here too were shops. Several had been boarded up now; those that hadn't were dingy and unattractive, their windows protected by heavy wire-mesh.

She walked along the row, and rounded a corner, and there in front of her was a squat brick building. The public lavatory, she guessed, though the signs designating it as such had gone. The iron gates were closed and padlocked. Standing in front of the charmless building, the wind gusting around her legs, she couldn't help but think of what had happened here. Of the man-child, bleeding on the floor, helpless to cry out. It made her queasy even to contemplate it. She turned her thoughts instead to the felon. What would he look like, she wondered, a man capable of such depravities? She tried to make an image of him, but no detail she could conjure carried sufficient force. But then monsters were seldom very terrible once hauled into the plain light of day. As long as this man was known only by his deeds he held untold power over the imagination; but the human truth beneath the terrors would, she knew, be bitterly disappointing. No monster he; just a wheyfaced apology for a man more needful of pity than awe.

The next gust of wind brought the rain on more heavily. It was time, she decided, to be done with adventures for the day. Turning her back on the public lavatories she hurried back through the quadrangles to the refuge of the car, the icy rain needling her face to numbness.

The dinner guests looked gratifyingly appalled at the story, and Trevor, to judge by the expression on his face, was furious. It was done now, however; there was no taking it back. Nor could she deny the satisfaction she took in having silenced the interdepartmental babble about the table. It was Bernadette, Trevor's assistant in the History Department, who broke the agonizing hush.

"When was this?"

"During the summer," Helen told her.

"I don't recall reading about it," said Archie, much the better for two hours of drinking; it mellowed a tongue which was otherwise fulsome in its self-coruscation.

"Perhaps the police are suppressing it," Daniel commented.

"Conspiracy?" said Trevor, plainly cynical.

"It's happening all the time," Daniel shot back.

"Why should they suppress something like this?" Helen said. "It doesn't make sense."

"Since when has police procedure made sense?" Daniel replied.

Bernadette cut in before Helen could answer. "We don't even bother to read about these things any longer," she said.

"Speak for yourself," somebody piped up, but she ignored them and went on:

"We're punch-drunk with violence. We don't see it any longer, even when it's in front of our noses."

"On the screen every night," Archie put in, "Death and disaster in full colour."

"There's nothing very modern about that," Trevor said. "An Elizabethan would have seen death all the time. Public executions were a very popular form of entertainment."

The table broke up into a cacophony of opinions. After two hours of polite gossip the dinner-party had suddenly caught fire. Listening to the debate rage Helen was sorry she hadn't had time to have the photographs processed and printed; the graffiti would have added further fuel to this exhilarating row. It was Purcell, as usual, who was the last to weigh in with his point of view; and—again, as usual—it was devastating.

"Of course, Helen, my sweet—" he began, that affected weariness in his voice edged with the anticipation of controversy "—your witnesses could all be lying, couldn't they?"

The talking around the table dwindled, and all heads turned in Purcell's direction. Perversely, he ignored the attention he'd garnered, and turned to whisper in the ear of the boy he'd brought—a new passion who would, on past form, be discarded in a matter of weeks for another pretty urchin.

"Lying?" Helen said. She could feel herself bristling at the observation already, and Purcell had only spoken a dozen words.

"Why not?" the other replied, lifting his glass of wine to his lips. "Perhaps they're all weaving some elaborate fiction or other. The story of the spastic's mutilation in the public toilet. The murder of the old man. Even that hook. All quite familiar elements. You must be aware that there's something *traditional* about these atrocity stories. One used to exchange them all the time; there was a certain *frisson* in them. Something competitive maybe, in attempting to find a new detail to add to the collective fiction; a fresh twist that would render the tale that little bit more appalling when you passed it on."

18

"It may be familiar to you—" said Helen defensively. Purcell was always so *poised*; it irritated her. Even if there were validity in his argument—which she doubted—she was damned if she'd concede it. "—*I've* never heard this kind of story before."

"Have you not?" said Purcell, as though she were admitting to illiteracy. "What about the lovers and the escaped lunatic, have you heard that one?"

"I've heard that . . ." Daniel said.

"The lover is disembowelled—usually by a hook-handed man—and the body left on the top of the car, while the fiancée cowers inside. It's a cautionary tale, warning of the evils of rampant heterosexuality." The joke won a round of laughter from everyone but Helen. "These stories are very common."

"So you're saying that they're telling me lies—" she protested.

"Not lies, exactly—"

"You said *lies*."

"I was being provocative," Purcell returned, his placatory tone more enraging than ever. "I don't mean to imply there's any serious mischief in it. But you *must* concede that so far you haven't met a single *witness*. All these events have happened at some unspecified date to some unspecified person. They are reported at several removes. They occurred at best to the brothers of friends of distant relations. Please consider the possibility that perhaps these events do not exist in the real world at all, but are merely titillation for bored housewives—"

Helen didn't make an argument in return, for the simple reason that she lacked one. Purcell's point about the conspicuous absence of witnesses was perfectly sound; she herself had wondered about it. It was strange, too, the way the women in Ruskin Court had speedily consigned the old man's murder to another estate, as though these atrocities always occurred just out of sight—round the next corner, down the next passageway—but never *here*.

"So why?" said Bernadette.

"Why what?" Archie puzzled.

"The stories. Why tell these horrible stories if they're not true?"

"Yes," said Helen, throwing the controversy back into Purcell's ample lap. "*Why?*"

Purcell preened himself, aware that his entry into the debate had changed the basic assumption at a stroke. "I don't know," he said, happy to be done with the game how that he'd shown his arm. "You really mustn't take me too seriously, Helen. *I* try not to." The boy at Purcell's side tittered.

"Maybe it's simply taboo material," Archie said.

"Suppressed—" Daniel prompted.

19

"Not the way you mean it," Archie retorted. "The whole world isn't politics, Daniel."

"Such naiveté."

"What's so *taboo* about death?" Trevor said. "Bernadette already pointed out: It's in front of us all the time. Television; newspapers."

"Maybe that's not close enough," Bernadette suggested.

"Does anyone mind if I smoke?" Purcell broke in. "Only dessert seems to have been indefinitely postponed—"

Helen ignored the remark, and asked Bernadette what she meant by 'not close enough'?

Bernadette shrugged. "I don't know precisely," she confessed, "maybe just that death has to be *near*; we have to *know* it's just round the corner. The television's not intimate enough—"

Helen frowned. The observation made some sense to her, but in the clutter of the moment she couldn't root out its significance.

"Do you think they're stories too?" she asked.

"Andrew has a point—" Bernadette replied.

"Most kind," said Purcell. "Has somebody got a match? The boy's pawned my lighter."

"—about the absence of witnesses."

"All that proves is that I haven't met anybody who's actually *seen* anything," Helen countered, "not that witnesses don't exist."

"All right," said Purcell. "Find me one. If you can prove to me that your atrocitymonger actually lives and breathes, I'll stand everyone dinner at *Appollinaires*. How's that? Am I generous to a fault, or do I just know when I can't lose?" He laughed, knocking on the table with his knuckles by way of applause.

"Sounds good to me," said Trevor. "What do you say, Helen?"

She didn't go back to Spector Street until the following Monday, but all weekend she was there in thought: Standing outside the locked toilet, with the wind bringing rain; or in the bedroom, the portrait looming. Thoughts of the estate claimed all her concern. When, late on Saturday afternoon, Trevor found some petty reason for an argument, she let the insults pass, watching him perform the familiar ritual of self-martyrdom without being touched by it in the least. Her indifference only enraged him further. He stormed out in high dudgeon, to visit whichever of his women was in favour this month. She was glad to see the back of him. When he failed to return that night she didn't even think of weeping about it. He was foolish and vacuous. She despaired of ever seeing a haunted look in his dull eyes; and what worth was a man who could not be haunted?

He did not return Sunday night either, and it crossed her mind the following morning, as she parked the car in the heart of the estate, that nobody even knew she had come, and that she might lose herself for days here and nobody be any the wiser. Like the old man Anne-Marie had told her about: Lying forgotten in his favourite armchair with his eyes hooked out, while the flies feasted and the butter went rancid on the table.

It was almost Bonfire Night, and over the weekend the small heap of combustibles in Butts' Court had grown to a substantial size. The construction looked unsound, but that didn't prevent a number of boys and young adolescents clambering over it and into it. Much of its bulk was made up of furniture, filched, no doubt, from boarded-up properties. She doubted if it could burn for any time: If it did, it would go chokingly. Four times, on her way across to Anne-Marie's house, she was waylaid by children begging for money to buy fireworks.

"Penny for the guy," they'd say, though none had a guy to display. She had emptied her pockets of change by the time she reached the front door.

Anne-Marie was in today, though there was no welcoming smile. She simply stared at her visitor as if mesmerised.

"I hope you don't mind me calling . . ."

Anne-Marie made no reply.

". . . I just wanted a word."

"I'm busy," the woman finally announced. There was no invitation inside, no offer of tea.

"Oh. Well . . . it won't take more than a moment."

The back door was open and the draught blew through the house. Papers were flying about in the back yard. Helen could see them lifting into the air like vast white moths.

"What do you want?" Anne-Marie asked.

"Just to ask you about the old man."

The woman frowned minutely. She looked as if she was sickening, Helen thought: Her face had the colour and texture of stale dough, her hair was lank and greasy.

"What old man?"

"Last time I was here, you told me about an old man who'd been murdered, do you remember?"

"No."

"You said he lived in the next court."

"I don't remember," Anne-Marie said.

"But you *distinctly* told me—"

Something fell to the floor in the kitchen, and smashed. Anne-Marie flinched, but did not move from the doorstep, her arm barring Helen's way into the house. The hallway was littered with the child's toys, gnawed and battered.

21

"Are you all right?"

Anne-Marie nodded. "I've got work to do," she said.

"And you don't remember telling me about the old man?"

"You must have misunderstood," Anne-Marie replied, and then, her voice hushed: "You shouldn't have come. Everybody *knows*."

"Knows what?"

The girl had begun to tremble. "You don't understand, do you? You think people aren't watching?"

"What does it matter? All I asked was—"

"I don't know *anything*," Anne-Marie reiterated. "Whatever I said to you, I lied about it."

"Well, thank you anyway," Helen said, too perplexed by the confusion of signals from Anne-Marie to press the point any further. Almost as soon as she has turned from the door she heard the lock snap closed behind her.

That conversation was only one of several disappointments that morning brought. She went back to the row of shops, and visited the supermarket that Josie had spoken of. There she inquired about the lavatories, and their recent history. The supermarket had only changed hands in the last month, and the new owner, a taciturn Pakistani, insisted that he knew nothing of when or why the lavatories had been closed. She was aware, as she made her enquiries, of being scrutinized by the other customers in the shop; she felt like a pariah. That feeling deepened when, after leaving the supermarket, she saw Josie emerging from the launderette, and called after her only to have the woman pick up her pace and duck away into the maze of corridors. Helen followed, but rapidly lost both her quarry and her way.

Frustrated to the verge of tears, she stood amongst the overturned rubbish bags, and felt a surge of contempt for her foolishness. She didn't belong here, did she? How many times had she criticized others for their presumption in claiming to understand societies they had merely viewed from afar? And here was she, committing the same crime, coming here with her camera and her questions, using the lives (and deaths) of these people as fodder for party conversation. She didn't blame Anne-Marie for turning her back; had she deserved better?

Tired and chilled, she decided it was time to concede Purcell's point. It *was* all fiction she had been told. They had played with her—sensing her desire to be fed some horrors—and she, the perfect fool, had fallen for every ridiculous word. It was time to pack up her credulity and go home.

One call demanded to be made before she returned to the car however: She wanted to look a final time at the painted head. Not as an anthropologist amongst an alien tribe, but as a confessed ghost train rider:

22

For the thrill of it. Arriving at number 14, however, she faced the last and most crushing disappointment. The maisonette had been sealed up by conscienctious council workmen. The door was locked; the front window boarded over.

She was determined not to be so easily defeated however. She made her way around the back of Butt's Court and located the yard of number 14 by simple mathematics. The gate was wedged closed from the inside, but she pushed hard upon it, and, with effort on both parts, it opened. A heap of rubbish—rotted carpets, a box of rain-sodden magazines, a denuded Christmas tree—had blocked it.

She crossed the yard to the boarded-up windows, and peered through the slats of wood. It wasn't bright outside, but it was darker still within; it was difficult to catch more than the vaguest hint of the painting on the bedroom wall. She pressed her face close to the wood, eager for a final glimpse.

A shadow moved across the room, momentarily blocking her view. She stepped back from the window, startled, not certain of what she'd seen. Perhaps merely her own shadow, cast through the window? But then *she* hadn't moved; it had.

She approached the window again, more cautiously. The air vibrated; she could hear a muted whine from somewhere, though she couldn't be certain whether it came from inside or out. Again, she put her face to the rough boards, and suddenly, something leapt at the window. This time she let out a cry. There was a scrabbling sound from within, as nails raked the wood.

A dog!—And a big one to have jumped so high.

"Stupid," she told herself aloud. A sudden sweat bathed her.

The scrabbling had stopped almost as soon as it had started, but she couldn't bring herself to go back to the window. Clearly the workmen who had sealed up the maisonette had failed to check it properly, and incarcerated the animal by mistake. It was ravenous, to judge by the slavering she'd heard; she was grateful she hadn't attempted to break in. The dog— hungry, maybe half-mad in the stinking darkness— could have taken out her throat.

She stared at the boarded-up window. The slits between the boards were barely a half-inch wide, but she sensed that the animal was up on its hind legs on the other side, watching her through the gap. She could hear its panting now that her own breath was regularizing; she could hear its claws raking the sill.

"Bloody thing..." she said. "Damn well stay in there."

She backed off towards the gate. Hosts of wood-lice and spiders, disturbed from their nests by moving the carpets behind the gate, were scurrying underfoot, looking for a fresh darkness to call home.

She closed the gate behind her, and was making her way around the front of the block when she heard the sirens; two ugly spirals of sound that made the hair on the back of her neck tingle. They were approaching. She picked up her speed, and came round into Butts' Court in time to see several policemen crossing the grass behind the bonfire and an ambulance mounting the pavement and driving around to the other side of the quadrangle. People had emerged from their flats and were standing on their balconies, staring down. Others were walking around the court, nakedly curious, to join a gathering congregation. Helen's stomach seemed to drop to her bowels when she realized *where* the hub of interest lay: At Anne-Marie's doorstep. The police were clearing a path through the throng for the ambulance men. A second police-car had followed the route of the ambulance onto the pavement; two plain-clothes officers were getting out.

She walked to the periphery of the crowd. What little talk there was amongst the on-lookers was conducted in low voices; one or two of the older women were crying. Though she peered over the heads of the spectators she could see nothing. Turning to a bearded man, whose child was perched on his shoulders, she asked what was going on. He didn't know. Somebody dead, he'd heard, but he wasn't certain.

"Anne-Marie?" she asked.

A woman in front of her turned and said: "You know her?" almost awed, as if speaking of a loved one.

"A little," Helen replied hesitantly. "Can you tell me what's happened?"

The woman involuntarily put her hand to her mouth, as if to stop the words before they came. But here they were nevertheless: "The child—" she said.

"Kerry?"

"Somebody got into the house around the back. Slit his throat."

Helen felt the sweat come again. In her mind's eye the newspapers rose and fell in Anne-Marie's yard.

"No," she said.

"Just like that."

She looked at the tragedian who was trying to sell her this obscenity, and said, "No," again. It defied belief; yet her denials could not silence the horrid comprehension she felt.

She turned her back on the woman and paddled her way out of the crowd. There would be nothing to see, she knew, and even if there had been, she had no desire to look. These people—still emerging from their homes as the story spread—were exhibiting an appetite she was disgusted by. She was not of them; would never *be* of them. She wanted to slap every eager face into sense; wanted to say: "It's pain and grief you're going to spy on. Why? Why?" But she had no courage left. Revulsion had drained her of all but the energy to wander away, leaving the crowd to its sport.

Trevor had come home. He did not attempt an explanation of his absence, but waited for her to cross-question him. When she failed to do so he sank into an easy *bonhomie* that was worse than his expectant silence. She was dimly aware that her dis-interest was probably more unsettling for him than the histrionics he had been anticipating. She couldn't have cared less.

She tuned the radio to the local station, and listened for news. It came surely enough, confirming what the woman in the crowd had told her. Kerry Latimer was dead. Person or persons unknown had gained access to the house via the back yard and murdered the child while he played on the kitchen floor. A police spokesman mouthed the usual platitudes, describing Kerry's death as an 'unspeakable crime', and the miscreant as 'a dangerous and deeply disturbed individual'. For once, the rhetoric seemed justified, and the man's voice shook discernibly when he spoke of the scene that had confronted the officers in the kitchen of Anne-Marie's house.

"Why the radio?" Trevor casually inquired, when Helen had listened for news through three consecutive bulletins. She saw no point in withholding her experience at Spector Street from him; he would find out sooner or later. Coolly, she gave him a bald outline of what had happened at Butts' Court.

"This Anne-Marie is the woman you first met when you went to the estate; am I right?"

She nodded, hoping he wouldn't ask her too many questions. Tears were close, and she had no intention of breaking down in front of him.

"So you were right," he said.

"Right?"

"About the place having a maniac."

"No," she said. "No."

"But the kid—"

She got up and stood at the window, looking down two storeys into the darkened street below. Why did she feel the need to reject the conspiracy theory so urgently? Why was she now praying that Purcell had been right, and that all she'd been told had been lies? She went back and back to the way Anne-Marie had been when she'd visited her that morning: Pale, jittery; *expectant*. She had been like a woman anticipating some arrival, hadn't she?—eager to shoo unwanted visitors away so that she could turn back to the business of waiting. But waiting for what, or *whom*?

25

Was it possible that Anne-Marie actually knew the murderer? Had perhaps invited him into the house?

"I hope they find the bastard," she said, still watching the street.

"They will," Trevor replied. "A baby-murderer, for Christ's sake. They'll make it a high priority."

A man appeared at the corner of the street, turned, and whistled. A large Alsatian came to heel, and the two set off down towards the Cathedral.

"The dog," Helen murmured.

"What?"

She had forgotten the dog in all that had followed. Now the shock she'd felt as it had leapt at the window shook her again.

"What dog?" Trevor pressed.

"I went back to the flat today—where I took the pictures of the graffiti. There was a dog in there. Locked in."

"So?"

"It'll starve. Nobody knows it's there."

"How do you know it wasn't locked in to kennel it?"

"It was making such a noise—" she said.

"Dogs bark," Trevor replied. "That's all they're good for."

"No . . ." she said very quietly, remembering the noises through the boarded window. "It didn't bark . . ."

"Forget the dog," Trevor said. "And the child. There's nothing you can do about it. You were just passing through."

His words only echoed her own thoughts of earlier in the day, but somehow—for reasons that she could find no words to convey—that conviction had decayed in the last hours. She was not just passing through. Nobody ever just *passed through*; experience always left its mark. Sometimes it merely scratched; on occasion it took off limbs. She did not know the extent of her present wounding, but she knew it more profound than she yet understood, and it made her afraid.

"We're out of booze," she said, emptying the last dribble of whisky into her tumbler.

Trevor seemed pleased to have a reason to be accommodating. "I'll go out, shall I?" he said. "Get a bottle or two?"

"Sure," she replied. "If you like."

He was gone only half an hour; she would have liked him to have been longer. She didn't want to talk, only to sit and think through the unease in her belly. Though Trevor had dismissed her concern for the dog—and perhaps justifiably so—she couldn't help but go back to the locked maisonette in her mind's eye: To picture again the raging face on the bedroom wall, and hear the animal's muffled growl as it pawed the boards

26

over the window. Whatever Trevor had said, she didn't believe the place was being used as a makeshift kennel. No, the dog was *imprisoned* in there, no doubt of it, running round and round, driven, in its desperation, to eat its own faeces, growing more insane with every hour that passed. She became afraid that somebody—kids maybe, looking for more tinder for their bonfire—would break into the place, ignorant of what it contained. It wasn't that she feared for the intruders' safety, but that the dog, once liberated, would come for her. It would know where she was (so her drunken head construed) and come sniffing her out.

Trevor returned with the whisky, and they drank together until the early hours, when her stomach revolted. She took refuge in the toilet—Trevor outside asking her if she needed anything, her telling him weakly to leave her alone. When, an hour later, she emerged, he had gone to bed. She did not join him, but lay down on the sofa and dozed through until dawn.

The murder was news. The next morning it made all the tabloids as a front page splash, and found prominent positions in the heavy-weights too. There were photographs of the stricken mother being led from the house, and others, blurred but potent, taken over the back yard wall and through the open kitchen door. Was that blood on the floor, or shadow?

Helen did not bother to read the articles—her aching head rebelled at the thought—but Trevor, who had bought the newspapers in, was eager to talk. She couldn't work out if this was further peace-making on his part, or a genuine interest in the issue.

"The woman's in custody," he said, poring over the *Daily Telegraph*. It was a paper he was politically averse to, but its coverage of violent crime was notoriously detailed.

The observation demanded Helen's attention, unwilling or not. "Custody?" she said. "Anne-Marie?"

"Yes."

"Let me see."

He relinquished the paper, and she glanced over the page.

"Third column," Trevor prompted.

She found the place, and there it was in black and white. Anne-Marie had been taken into custody for questioning to justify the time-lapse between the estimated hour of the child's death, and the time that it had been reported. Helen read the relevant sentences over again, to be certain that she'd understood properly. Yes, she had. The police pathologist estimated Kerry to have died between six and six-thirty that morning; the murder had not been reported until twelve.

She read the report over a third and fourth time, but repetition did not change the horrid facts. The child had been murdered before dawn. When she had gone to the house that morning Kerry had already been dead four hours. The body had been in the kitchen, a few yards down the hallway from where she had stood, and Anne-Marie had said *nothing*. That air of expectancy she had had about her—what had it signified? That she awaited some cue to lift the receiver and call the police?

"My Christ . . ." Helen said, and let the paper drop.

"What?"

"I have to go to the police."

"Why?"

"To tell them I went to the house," she replied. Trevor looked mystified. "The baby was dead, Trevor. When I saw Anne-Marie yesterday morning, Kerry was already dead."

She rang the number in the paper for any persons offering information, and half an hour later a police car came to pick her up. There was much that startled her in the two hours of interrogation that followed, not least the fact that nobody had reported her presence on the estate to the police, though she had surely been noticed.

"They don't want to know—" the detective told her. "You'd think a place like that would be swarming with witnesses. If it is, they're not coming forward. A crime like this . . ."

"Is it the first?" she said.

He looked at her across a chaotic desk. "First?"

"I was told some stories about the estate. Murders. This summer."

The detective shook his head. "Not to my knowledge. There's been a spate of muggings; one woman was put in hospital for a week or so. But no; no murders."

She liked the detective. His eyes flattered her with their lingering, and his face with their frankness. Past caring whether she sounded foolish or not, she said: "Why do they tell lies like that? About people having their eyes cut out. Terrible things."

The detective scratched his long nose. "We get it too," he said. "People come in here, they confess to all kinds of crap. Talk all night, some of them, about things they've done, or *think* they've done. Give you it all in the minutest detail. And when you make a few calls, it's all invented. Out of their minds."

"Maybe if they didn't tell you those stories . . . they'd actually go out and do it."

The detective nodded. "Yes," he said. "God help us. You might be right at that."

And the stories *she'd* been told, were they confessions of uncommitted crimes? Accounts of the worst-imaginable, imagined to keep fiction from becoming fact? The thought chased its own tail: These terrible stories still needed a *first cause*, a well-spring from which they leapt. As she walked home through the busy streets she wondered how many of her fellow citizens knew such stories. Were these inventions common currency, as Purcell had claimed? Was there a place, however small, reserved in every heart for the monstrous?

"Purcell rang," Trevor told her when she got home. "To invite us out to dinner."

The invitation wasn't welcome, and she made a face.

"Appollinaires, remember?" he reminded her. "He said he'd take us all to dinner, if you proved him wrong."

The thought of getting a dinner out of the death of Anne-Marie's infant was grotesque, and she said so.

"He'll be offended if you turn him down."

"I don't give a damn. I don't want dinner with Purcell."

"Please," he said softly. "He can get difficult; and I want to keep him smiling just at the moment."

She glanced across at him. The look he'd put on made him resemble a drenched spaniel. Manipulative bastard, she thought; but said: "All right, I'll go. But don't expect any dancing on the tables."

"We'll leave that to Archie," he said. "I told Purcell we were free tomorrow night. Is that all right with you?"

"Whenever."

"He's booking a table for eight o'clock."

The evening papers had relegated The Tragedy of Baby Kerry to a few column inches on an inside page. In lieu of much fresh news they simply described the house-to-house enquiries that were now going on at Spector Street. Some of the later editions mentioned that Anne-Marie had been released from custody after an extended period of questioning, and was now residing with friends. They also mentioned, in passing, that the funeral was to be the following day.

Helen had not entertained any thoughts of going back to Spector Street for the funeral when she went to bed that night, but sleep seemed to change her mind, and she woke with the decision made for her.

Death had brought the estate to life. Walking through to Ruskin Court from the street she had never seen such numbers out and about. Many were already lining the kerb to watch the funeral cortège pass, and looked to have claimed their niche early, despite the wind and the ever-present threat of rain. Some were wearing items of black clothing—a coat, a scarf— but the overall impression, despite the lowered voices and the studied frowns, was one of celebration. Children running around, untouched by reverence; occasional laughter escaping from between gossiping adults—

29

Helen could feel an air of anticipation which made her spirits, despite the occasion, almost buoyant.

Nor was it simply the presence of so many people that reassured her; she was, she conceded to herself, happy to be back here in Spector Street. The quadrangles, with their stunted saplings and their grey grass, were more real to her than the carpeted corridors she was used to walking; the anonymous faces on the balconies and streets meant more than her colleagues at the University. In a word, she felt *home*.

Finally, the cars appeared, moving at a snail's pace through the narrow streets. As the hearse came into view—its tiny white casket decked with flowers—a number of women in the crowd gave quiet voice to their grief. One on-looker fainted; a knot of anxious people gathered around her. Even the children were stilled now.

Helen watched, dry-eyed. Tears did not come very easily to her, especially in company. As the second car, containing Anne-Marie and two other women, drew level with her, Helen saw that the bereaved mother was also eschewing any public display of grief. She seemed, indeed, to be almost elevated by the proceedings, sitting upright in the back of the car, her pallid features the source of much admiration. It was a sour thought, but Helen felt as though she was seeing Anne-Marie's finest hour; the one day in an otherwise anonymous life in which she was the centre of attention. Slowly, the cortège passed by and disappeared from view.

The crowd around Helen was already dispersing. She detached herself from the few mourners who still lingered at the kerb and wandered through from the street into Butts' court. It was her intention to go back to the locked maisonette, to see if the dog was still there. If it was, she would put her mind at rest by finding one of the estate caretakers and informing him of the fact.

The quadrangle was, unlike the other courts, practically empty. Perhaps the residents, being neighbours of Anne-Marie's, had gone on to the Crematorium for the service. Whatever the reason, the place was eerily deserted. Only children remained, playing around the pyramid bonfire, their voices echoing across the empty expanse of the square.

She reached the maisonette and was surprised to find the door open again, as it had been the first time she'd come here. The sight of the interior made her light-headed. How often in the past several days had she imagined standing here, gazing into that darkness. There was no sound from inside. The dog had surely run off; either that, or died. There could be no harm, could there? in stepping into the place one final time, just to look at the face on the wall, and its attendant slogan.

Sweets to the sweet. She had never looked up the origins of that phrase. No matter, she thought. Whatever it had stood for once, it was transformed

30

here, as everything was; herself included. She stood in the front room for a few moments, to allow herself time to savour the confrontation ahead. Far away behind her the children were screeching like mad birds.

She stepped over a clutter of furniture and towards the short corridor that joined living-room to bedroom, still delaying the moment. Her heart was quick in her: A smile played on her lips.

And there! At last! The portrait loomed, compelling as ever. She stepped back in the murky room to admire it more fully and her heel caught on the mattress that still lay in the corner. She glanced down. The squalid bedding had been turned over, to present its untorn face. Some blankets and and a rag-wrapped pillow had been tossed over it. Something glistened amongst the folds of the uppermost blanket. She bent down to look more closely and found there a handful of sweets—chocolate and caramels— wrapped in bright paper. And littered amongst them, neither so attractive nor so sweet, a dozen razor-blades. There was blood on several. She stood up again and backed away from the mattress, and as she did so a buzzing sound reached her ears from the next room. She turned, and the light in the bedroom diminished as a figure stepped into the gullet between her and the outside world. Silhouetted against the light, she could scarcely see the man in the doorway, but she smelt him. He smelt like candy-floss; and the buzzing was with him or in him.

"I just came to look—" she said, "—at the picture."

The buzzing went on: The sound of a sleepy afternoon, far from here. The man in the doorway did not move.

"Well . . ." she said, "I've seen what I wanted to see." She hoped against hope that her words would prompt him to stand aside and let her pass, but he didn't move, and she couldn't find the courage to challenge him by stepping towards the door.

"I have to go," she said, knowing that despite her best efforts fear seeped between every syllable. "I'm expected . . ."

That was not entirely untrue. Tonight they were all invited to Appollinaires for dinner. But that wasn't until eight, which was four hours away. She would not be missed for a long while yet.

"If you'll excuse me," she said.

The buzzing had quietened a little, and in the hush the man in the doorway spoke. His unaccented voice was almost as sweet as his scent.

"No need to leave yet," he breathed.

"I'm due . . . due . . ."

Though she couldn't see his eyes, she felt them on her, and they made her feel drowsy, like that summer that sang in her head.

"I came for you," he said.

She repeated the four words in her head. *I came for you.* If they were

31

meant as a threat, they certainly weren't spoken as one.

"I don't. . .know you," she said.

"No," the man murmured. "But you doubted me."

"Doubted?"

"You weren't content with the stories, with what they wrote on the walls. So I was obliged to come."

The drowsiness slowed her mind to a crawl, but she grasped the essentials of what the man was saying. That he was legend, and she, in disbelieving him, had obliged him to show his hand. She looked, now, down at those hands. One of them was missing. In its place, a hook.

"There will be some blame," he told her. "They will say your doubts shed innocent blood. But I say—what's blood for, if not for shedding? And in time the scrutiny will pass. The police will leave, the cameras will be pointed at some fresh horror, and they will be left alone, to tell stories of the Candyman again."

"Candyman?" she said. Her tongue could barely shape that blameless word.

"I came for you," he murmured so softly that seduction might have been in the air. And so saying, he moved through the passageway and into the light.

She knew him, without doubt. She had known him all along, in that place kept for terrors. It was the man on the wall. His portrait painter had not been a fantasist: The picture that howled over her was matched in each extraordinary particular by the man she now set eyes upon. He was bright to the point of gaudiness: His flesh a waxy yellow, his thin lips pale blue, his wild eyes glittering as if their irises were set with rubies. His jacket was a patchwork, his trousers the same. He looked, she thought, almost ridiculous, with his blood-stained motley, and the hint of rouge on his jaundiced cheeks. But people were facile. They needed these shows and shams to keep their interest. Miracles; murders; demons driven out and stones rolled from tombs. The cheap glamour did not taint the sense beneath. It was only, in the natural history of the mind, the bright feathers that drew the species to mate with its secret self.

And she was almost enchanted. By his voice, by his colours, by the buzz from his body. She fought to resist the rapture, though. There was a *monster* here, beneath this fetching display; its nest of razors was at her feet, still drenched in blood. Would it hesitate to slit her own throat if it once laid hands on her?

As the Candyman reached for her she dropped down and snatched the blanket up, flinging it at him. A rain of razors and sweetmeats fell around his shoulders. The blanket followed, blinding him. But before she could snatch the moment to slip past him, the pillow which had lain on the blanket rolled in front of her.

It was not a pillow at all. Whatever the forlorn white casket she had seen in the hearse had contained, it was not the body of Baby Kerry. That was *here*, at her feet, its blood-drained face turned up to her. He was naked. His body showed everywhere signs of the fiend's attentions.

In the two heartbeats she took to register this last horror, the Candyman threw off the blanket. In his struggle to escape from its folds, his jacket had come unbuttoned, and she saw—though her senses protested— that the contents of his torso had rotted away, and the hollow was now occupied by a nest of bees. They swarmed in the vault of his chest, and encrusted in a seething mass the remnants of flesh that hung there. He smiled at her plain repugnance.

"Sweets to the sweet," he murmured, and stretched his hooked hand towards her face. She could no longer see light from the outside world, nor hear the children playing in Butts' Court. There was no escape into a saner world than this. The Candyman filled her sight; her drained limbs had no strength to hold him at bay.

"Don't kill me," she breathed.

"Do you believe in me?" he said.

She nodded minutely. "How can I not?" she said.

"Then why do you want to live?"

She didn't understand, and was afraid her ignorance would prove fatal, so she said nothing.

"If you would learn," the fiend said, "just a *little* from me . . . you would not beg to live." His voice had dropped to a whisper. "I am rumour," he sang in her ear. "It's a blessed condition, believe me. To live in people's dreams; to be whispered at street-corners; but not have to *be*. Do you understand?"

Her weary body understood. Her nerves, tired of jangling, understood. The sweetness he offered was life without living: Was to be dead, but remembered everywhere; immortal in gossip and graffiti.

"Be my victim," he said.

"No . . ." she murmured.

"I won't force it upon you," he replied, the perfect gentleman. "I won't oblige you to die. But think; *think*. If I kill you here—if I unhook you . . ." he traced the path of the promised wound with his hook. It ran from groin to neck. "Think how they would mark this place with their talk . . . point it out as they passed by and say: '*She* died there; the woman with the green eyes'. Your death would be a parable to frighten children with. Lovers would use it as an excuse to cling closer together . . ."

She had been right: This *was* a seduction.

"Was fame ever so easy?" he asked.

33

She shook her head. "I'd prefer to be forgotten," she replied, "than be remembered like that."

He made a tiny shrug. "What do they know?" he said. "Except what the bad teach them by their excesses?" He raised his hooked hand. "I said I would not oblige you to die and I'm true to my word. Allow me, though, a kiss at least..."

He moved towards her. She murmured some nonsensical threat, which he ignored. The buzzing in his body had risen in volume. The thought of touching his body, of the proximity of the insects, was horrid. She forced her lead-heavy arms up to keep him at bay.

His lurid face eclipsed the portrait on the wall. She couldn't bring herself to touch him, and instead stepped back. The sound of the bees rose; some, in their excitement, had crawled up his throat and were flying from his mouth. They climbed about his lips; in his hair.

She begged him over and over to leave her alone, but he would not be placated. At last she had nowhere left to retreat to; the wall was at her back. Steeling herself against the stings, she put her hands on his crawling chest and pushed. As she did so his hand shot out and around the back of her neck, the hook nicking the flushed skin of her throat. She felt blood come; felt certain he would open her jugular in one terrible slash. But he had given his word: And he was true to it.

Aroused by this sudden activity, the bees were everywhere. She felt them moving on her, searching for morsels of wax in her ears, and sugar at her lips. She made no attempt to swat them away. The hook was at her neck. If she so much as moved it would wound her. She was trapped, as in her childhood nightmares, with every chance of escape stymied. When sleep had brought her to such hopelessness—the demons on every side, waiting to tear her limb from limb—one trick remained. To let go; to give up all ambition to life, and leave her body to the dark. Now, as the Candyman's face pressed to hers, and the sound of bees blotted out even her own breath, she played that hidden hand. And, as surely as in dreams, the room and the fiend were painted out and gone.

She woke from brightness into dark. There were several panicked moments when she couldn't think of where she was, then several more when she remembered. But there was no pain about her body. She put her hand to her neck; it was, barring the nick of the hook, untouched. She was lying on the mattress she realized. Had she been assaulted as she lay in a faint? Gingerly, she investigated her body. She was not bleeding; her clothes were not disturbed. The Candyman had, it seemed, simply claimed his kiss.

She sat up. There was precious little light through the boarded window—and none from the front door. Perhaps it was closed, she reasoned. But no; even now she heard somebody whispering on the threshold. A woman's voice.

She didn't move. They were crazy, these people. They had known all along what her presence in Butts' Court had summoned, and they had *protected* him—this honeyed psychopath; given him a bed and an offering of bonbons, hidden him away from prying eyes, and kept their silence when he brought blood to their doorsteps. Even Anne-Marie, dry-eyed in the hallway of her house, knowing that her child was dead a few yards away.

The child! That was the evidence she needed. Somehow they had conspired to get the body from the casket (what had they substituted; a dead dog?) and brought it here—to the Candyman's tabernacle—as a toy, or a lover. She would take Baby Kerry with her—to the police—and tell the whole story. Whatever they believed of it—and that would probably be very little— the fact of the child's body was incontestable. That way at least some of the crazies would suffer for their conspiracy. Suffer for *her* suffering.

The whispering at the door had stopped. Now somebody was moving towards the bedroom. They didn't bring a light with them. Helen made herself small, hoping she might escape attention.

A figure appeared in the doorway. The gloom was too impenetrable for her to make out more than a slim figure, who bent down and picked up a bundle on the floor. A fall of blonde hair identified the newcomer as Anne-Marie: The bundle she was picking up was undoubtedly Kerry's corpse. Without looking in Helen's direction, the mother about-turned and made her way out of the bedroom.

Helen listened as the footsteps receded across the living room. Swiftly, she got to her feet, and crossed to the passageway. From there she could vaguely see Anne-Marie's outline in the doorway of the maisonette. No lights burned in the quadrangle beyond. The woman disappeared and Helen followed as speedily as she could, eyes fixed on the door ahead. She stumbled once, and once again, but reached the door in time to see Anne-Marie's vague form in the night ahead.

She stepped out of the maisonette and into the open air. It was chilly; there were no stars. All the lights on the balconies and corridors were out, nor did any burn in the flats; not even the glow of a television. Butts' Court was deserted.

She hesitated before going in pursuit of the girl. Why didn't she slip away now, cowardice coaxed her, and find her way back to the car? But if she did that the conspirators would have time to conceal the child's body. When she got back here with the police there would be sealed lips and shrugs, and she would be told she had imagined the corpse and the

Candyman. All the terrors she had tasted would recede into rumour again. Into words on a wall. And every day she lived from now on she would loathe herself for not going in pursuit of sanity.

She followed. Anne-Marie was not making her way around the quadrangle, but moving towards the centre of the lawn in the middle of the court. To the bonfire! Yes; to the bonfire! It loomed in front of Helen now, blacker than the night-sky. She could just make out Anne-Marie's figure, moving to the edge of the piled timbers and furniture, and ducking to climb into its heart. *This* was how they planned to remove the evidence. To bury the child was not certain enough; but to cremate it, and pound the bones— who would ever know?

She stood a dozen yards from the pyramid and watched as Anne-Marie climbed out again and moved away, folding her figure into the darkness.

Quickly, Helen moved through the long grass and located the narrow space in amongst the piled timbers into which Anne-Marie had put the body. She thought she could see the pale form; it had been laid in a hollow. She couldn't reach it however. Thanking God that she was as slim as the mother, she squeezed through the narrow aperture. Her dress snagged on a nail as she did so. She turned round to disengage it, fingers trembling. When she turned back she had lost sight of the corpse.

She fumbled blindly ahead of her, her hands finding wood and rags and what felt like the back of an old armchair, but not the cold skin of the child. She had hardened herself against contact with the body: She had endured worse in the last hours than picking up a dead baby. Determined not to be defeated, she advanced a little further, her shins scraped and her fingers spiked with splinters. Flashes of light were appearing at the corners of her aching eyes; her blood whined in her ears. But there! *There!* the body was no more a yard and a half ahead of her. She ducked down to reach beneath a beam of wood, but her fingers missed the forlorn bundle by millimetres. She stretched further, the whine in her head increasing, but still she could not reach the child. All she could do was bend double and squeeze into the hidey-hole the children had left in the centre of the bonfire.

It was difficult to get through. The space was so small she could barely crawl on hands and knees; but she made it. The child lay face down. She fought back the remnants of squeamishness and went to pick it up. As she did so, something landed on her arm. The shock startled her. She almost cried out, but swallowed the urge, and brushed the irritation away. It buzzed as it rose from her skin. The whine she had heard in her ears was not her blood, but the hive.

"I knew you'd come," the voice behind her said, and a wide hand covered her face. She fell backwards and the Candyman embraced her.

"We have to go," he said in her ear, as flickering light spilled between the stacked timbers. "Be on our way, you and I."

She fought to be free of him, to cry out for them not to light the bonfire, but he held her lovingly close. The light grew: Warmth came with it; and through the kindling and the first flames she could see figures approaching the pyre out of the darkness of Butts' Court. They had been there all along: Waiting, the lights turned out in their homes, and broken all along the corridors. Their final conspiracy.

The bonfire caught with a will, but by some trick of its construction the flames did not invade her hiding-place quickly; nor did the smoke creep through the furniture to choke her. She was able to watch how the children's faces gleamed; how the parents called them from going too close, and how they disobeyed; how the old women, their blood thin, warmed their hands and smiled into the flames. Presently the roar and the crackle became deafening, and the Candyman let her scream herself hoarse in the certain knowledge that nobody could hear her, and even if they had, would not have moved to claim her from the fire.

The bees vacated the fiend's belly as the air became hotter, and mazed the air with their panicked flight. Some, attempting escape, caught fire, and fell like tiny meteors to the ground. The body of Baby Kerry, which lay close to the creeping flames, began to cook. Its downy hair smoked, it back blistered.

Soon the heat crept down Helen's throat, and scorched her pleas away. She sank back, exhausted, into the Candyman's arms, resigned to his triumph. In moments they would be on their way, as he had promised, and there was no help for it.

Perhaps they would remember her, as he had said they might, finding her cracked skull in tomorrow's ashes. Perhaps she might become, in time, a story with which to frighten children. She had lied, saying she preferred death to such questionable fame; she did not. As to her seducer, he laughed as the conflagration sniffed them out. There was no permanence for him in this night's death. His deeds were on a hundred walls and ten thousand lips, and should he be doubted again his congregation could summon him with sweetness. He had reason to laugh. So, as the flames crept upon them, did she, as through the fire she caught sight of a familiar face moving between the on-lookers. It was Trevor. He had forsaken his meal at Appollinaires and come looking for her.

She watched him questioning this fire-watcher and that, but they shook their heads, all the while staring at the pyre with smiles buried in their eyes. Poor dupe, she thought, following his antics. She willed him to look past the flames in the hope he might see her burning. Not so that he could save her from death—she was long past hope of that—but because she pitied him in his bewilderment and wanted to give him, though he would not have thanked her for it, something to be haunted by. That, and a story to tell.

DREAMS MAY COME
H. Warner Munn

Illustration by Andrew Smith

Harold Munn, who died in 1981, was a regular Weird Tales *contributor from the 1920s onwards. Correspondence with H.P. Lovecraft inspired him to write* The Werewolf of Ponkert *in 1925, which led to several sequels later on. His Arthurian romance,* King of the World's Edge, *was published in 1939 and many years later he wrote its sequel,* The Ship from Atlantis, *both published in the 1970s as* Merlin's Godson *along with another novel in the sequence,* Merlin's Ring. *Publisher Donald M. Grant issued deluxe editions of* Tales of the Werewolf Clan *(illustrated by J.K. Potter) in two volumes in 1980, during a late revival of interest in the author's work. A haunting tale of lost desires, 'Dreams May Come' originally appeared in* Unknown Worlds *magazine in 1939 and received its first British publication in the sixth issue of* Fantasy Tales.*

P ARTIALLY shielded by the bridge abutment, the woman stared into the windy night. Sleet hid the farther shore and, except for the melancholy and distant lowing of a tug and the occasional grinding of wheels on the El far overhead, she could have fancied herself alone upon a barren seacoast.

But that, she knew, was only a fancy.

Beyond the scud lay the city, with lights, music and warmth to cheer

'But could the past be changed?'

the myriads of people it contained. Some were fortunate, most were con-tented, but every night a few sought lonely places, troubling no one, to do that which she soon must do.

However, a few moments could be spared to collect one's thoughts. She leaned back in the corner and closed her eyes. It was good that the wind had lost some of its sharpness.

If she could only have foreseen, she thought, that the dreams of her childhood were to have proved so brutally true! Could she have taken warning by them and avoided the actions which had inevitably brought her to this river bank on such a night?

Or had she merely possessed a gift of "seeing" denied to most people, but found it impossible to profit by her premonitions which, not heeded until now, had been almost forgotten?

There had been, she remembered, the young student of philosophy whose studies had made him sombre and despairing. They had discussed the matter at length. She could see him now, as he twisted his glass and eyed the dregs of the stale beer.

"You know, Madge," he said, "it was a fine and wise provision of nature which hid the future from mortals, for who, knowing all that was to befall him, would choose to live?"

'Perhaps," she had replied, "if one really did know , he could change his future."

"Not so. The reasoning is fallacious, for if the future could be changed, then his foreknowledge would have been wrong and the future he had foreseen would not have been his real future at all.

"No, Madge, a man could as easily change his past as his immutable future. Seeing his life as a whole, he would find that little unconsidered events in his past had caused deviations through the years, as a misplaced pebble on the watershed can change the course of the rivulet and eventually affect the strength of the river.

"Now, if a man could but return into his past, remove those distant causes and have his life to live again, what a desirable thing that would be! But the future cannot be changed and neither can the past—we have only the present."

But could the past be changed?

Only in memory did the past live now. Then let her go back in memory and search for the deviation which had caused her life to be what it had been.

She *must* find that deviation, the exact infinitesimal fraction of a second that, taken in the wrong way, had changed, beyond repair, all her possible unformed future and brought her down the years to this dark stairway leading to the river.

Skip then, the years of misery and degradation! Pass over the dirty alleys and byways. Back, farther back, to the stage doors and hotels of the little towns, with which she was so familiar. Forget them and press on—deeper into the past!

There was her name high in the lights of the city, but the moment of deviation was not there! Other stages, other hotels, champagne, pearls—nights of hectic living, days of restless sleep. Back, back, further back!

Back to a rose-perfumed night of June!

She opened her eyes and looked up into the dim face of the man who held her. She cuddled deeper into the nook of his arm, feeling his strength about her like a protecting wall. Shortly his life would be her life, his fortune her fortune. Years without drudgery, years with glamour, sparkle—LIFE!

She sighed happily and raised her lips to be kissed. Sweetly, distant from the dance pavilion, drifted strains of music.

She hummed:

"Margie, I'm always thinking of you, Margie."

"I'm always thinking of *you*, Margie!" and the impetuous, passionate kiss stopped both the humming and her breath.

"What a dear you are," she gasped, laughing. "Will you always be like that, Arnold?"

"Always and a day, honey. Don't you know it?"

"Perhaps. But suppose some day you say to yourself, quite quietly, of course, when I can no longer dance so well, when my voice is a little edgy—"Why, what *am* I doing here? She's passe!'

"I had a dream, I think, about this, when I was a little, little girl, a dream I couldn't understand. I was always dreaming such horrible dreams! For years and years I was so frightened! Almost every night I walked in my sleep, because of them. And some have since come true and brought me sorrow. I wish I could remember what I dreamed about you!"

The arm tightened about her.

"Maybe I have been a little wild, honey, but a man gets tired of wandering. You and I will go far. We'll be topnotchers, I tell you. We'll have the best act in the big time, but without all that, if you were lame, or couldn't sing a note, I'd love you."

"I wonder. I thought *I'd* always love Paul—"

"That clod? Forget him. You're with me tonight, tomorrow night and all the nights from now on."

She began to laugh hysterically. "How funny! Paul said that when he proposed to me! Just exactly those same words!"

He looked nervously out of the coupe's rear window. "Not so loud, honey, somebody might hear you."

"Afraid?" There was a slight tinge of scorn in the tone. "I'm giving up my home, my husband, my reputation. Everything I have, and you're afraid to be seen with me!"

With a little twist she freed herself from the encircling arm and sprang out of the car.

All at once, it seemed that a little warning bell jangled in her brain. *This* was the turning point of her life! In this second she could make the decision that would affect all her years to come. Should she re-enter the car and make up, or should she shut the door?

His hand was outstretched but not to seize, only to urge. Her choice was free. Should she?

"Get in, you little fool!" he said, rudely, harshly. "I'll have your name in lights on Broadway in six months. You'll never see a chance like this again. We'll coin money!"

Suddenly she saw with dreadful clarity what she had been about to do, what she must escape from. She slammed the door.

"No, Arnold, we're through, finished! I never want to see you again. I'd die before I'd go away with you. Find some other girl who can dance and sing! I'm going back to Paul!"

She ran sobbing through the dark woods towards the distant music that sang as though to mock her:

"Bought a home and ring and everything for Margie!"

After that one secret lapse, she was a faithful wife, but more than mere fidelity is needed for a happy home and her home life was not happy.

An atrocious housekeeper, her slovenliness drew constant cutting remarks from her not-too-patient husband. Sparks flew as her quick spirit clashed against the sullen flint of his determination to enjoy a neat and peaceful existence. Quarrels were followed by mutual repentance, and hidden illfeelings that would not, could not die.

A breach once begun, widens swiftly. There were times when each felt like a stranger to the other, as the home became only a house, and it seemed that any change would be better than to continue thus sordidly.

Yet for a long time there was no definite break. Children might in the end, have kept them together, but there were none and their interests in life also lay apart. "I gave up a career to marry you," she once wept. "I could have gone to business college and made something of my life. But I didn't, and look what I got! You'll never be anything but a dumb, flat-footed cop!"

He did not answer, but nowadays he seldom did. Soon he went quietly out to his beat and left her to another lonely day.

The depression brought its changes and economies, little privations, reduced wages—a cheaper apartment, then a tenement.

Still they clung together in a shifting, crashing world, united by despair, needing each other even as their different natures repelled. The small extravagances which alone had made her life bearable for her, were now no longer possible and temper was held in check even less often than before.

A chance word precipitated the final quarrel which ended when she said, calmly and deliberately: "I can understand now, how a woman can take an axe and finish off her whole family!"

The last words were shouted at a slamming door.

Returning late, he found her asleep. The words he had intended to speak were left unspoken. He would apologise tomorrow. With patient sympathy he bent and kissed her, then with a weary sigh, stripped off his wet clothing and went to bed. It was a bad night.

Long later when she was positive he was sound asleep, her hand stole beneath her pillow and found the staghorn handle of the carving knife she had secreted three hours before.

Then—Blood, Horror! Frenzied, fantastic, unconsidered, unplanned flight into the storm! Aimless walking, finally an empty taxi.

There was less than a dollar in her purse. She gave it all to the driver. "Take me north, as far as this will carry me. I want to get out of the city."

Immediately the words were spoken, she regretted them. Had she said the right thing? Would he suspect from her manner that something was wrong? Apparently not, for he touched his cap brim casually, flipped up the flag and started, threading through the occasional downtown traffic almost driven from the streets by the inclemency of the weather.

The warmth of the cab made her drowsy. He had to speak twice to rouse her. "This all right, lady?"

"Oh! Where are we?"

And then she knew—"Yes, quite all right. I have friends across the river."

"Give me the address and I'll take you there. This is a bad neighbourhood."

"No, I'll walk. The cold will clear my head. It's only a short distance." The cab door clicked behind her.

He called something after her, but the closed window and the wind in her ears muted the words below her hearing.

She hurried on, feeling his unbelieving eyes upon her back. Would he follow? Did he suspect that something was not as it should be?

No! Her purposeful manner had misled him. There was the mutter of the engine as he turned about. Yonder the red eye of the tailight vanished into the storm.

She had crossed the bridge and come to the spot before she consciously realised where she was. The driving sleet in her face and the harsh wind had combined with her distress to produce an effect like stupor. She moved more or less directly to her objective.

Now that she had arrived, her senses cleared. Before her were wet icy steps leading down, and beyond—darkness and oblivion for a lost soul.

She strained her eyes to peer into the watery dark. Was someone already there? Was that a huddled shape, crouched in wet rags, in the corner where the bridge abutment met the wall? She shook her head and dashed away the rime from her eyelashes. No, it was a trick of her vision. No one was there.

Lights fell upon her from a slowly moving car, rolling to a stop. Wet tires squealed upon the icy street. Cruisers, searching the city, searching for her? That taxi-driver! She *had* been recognised!

Steeling herself, she started down the slippery steps that led to the river—and rest.

Just for one last second she leaned, eyes closed, against the icy wall, near the bridge abutment.

"Oh, Lord!" she whispered passionately. "Why did I have to come to this? If only I hadn't married Paul! If only I had gone to business college and forgotten him.

"If I could live my life over again, live that *one second* over again, I would say,

"'No! No! No!'"

"No. I am so sorry, Paul, but I have to say it."

Her voice trembled just a little as she raised her eyelids and looked at him fairly. She hoped he would not notice the quaver. At least her will was firm and even his warm kiss, his strong clasp could not swerve her resolution. She was confident.

Yet, she fended him away when he sought to draw her close. The hammock swung gently—like a cradle, she thought, the cradle she would never rock.

"But why? Margaret, darling—why? We love each other?"

This was terrible, much worse than she had expected, yet she could not draw back now.

"I love life more, Paul. I want luxuries, excitement, adventure. I want knowledge. All those, Paul. I would never make you a good wife, I am too restless, too discontented."

"Well, I know I'm not much!"

Now his dignity was ruffled. He was like a small boy, she thought. She could not let him know she loved him. She must be hard, ruthless, if she was to turn aside her destiny. She must hurt him!

"That's just it, Paul, I want things that you can't give me."

"I can give you—love."

Now he was standing over her. She would not look up, she must not! Would he take her in his arms again and kiss her fears away? She knew this time resolution would break like spring ice.

Paul—Paul! Hold me close and mold my future for me! Paul!

Now he was going. He had not caught her agonized thought. He would never come back.

Paul!

She *could* call him, yet!

The gate clicked. Again there rushed over her the memory of that dream, that dreadful, torturing dream that was somehow realer than real.

A night of blood, of storm—Paul lying dead in blood-soaked sheets— blood on that knife! Ice in the air, in her heart—ice on the steps leading toward the black river.

He was gone beyond recall, yet she softly cried after him: "I did love you, Paul, so much! And I'll never marry anybody now, never in all my days."

Years followed years. There were years of study, of preparation. Years of secretarial work. Long, lonely years of adhering to her secret vow. Years of denying, of hurting others as she had hurt Paul, while her heart seemed to slowly wither, becoming dry, indurated.

Drab years spent at desks, her mind weary with business, drearily concerned with depressions, recessions, market quotations. Then feeling herself gray before her natural time, knowing herself respected, feared for her power by her underlings, distantly admired by her equals. Treated as a man among men in the world she had chosen, she lived a neutral life without other strong interests than her work.

The years passed slowly over her in their relentless march, bringing new honours. From secretary to head buyer was one step, on to district manager was second. Her savings brought her partnership; death and her business acumen made her head of the firm. Carmichael & Klein, Furriers, prospered.

Then at long last, on the Fifth Avenue windows, in Dun and Brad street's, in *Who's Who In America*, the name Carmichael meant a great deal.

She sat alone one night in a lighted office, thinking, after the books had been locked away. Somewhere in the warehouse, the watchman was making his rounds, but if he was anywhere at hand just at present, the sound of sleet against the window hid his movements.

Long ago she had regretted her weak moment of superstition and that dream so pregnant of omen had become overlaid by life and almost forgotten, but the driving patter of the sleet brought it vividly back to her now.

Would events have come about as she had imagined them, if she had said, "Yes" to Paul? Could a slight turning from the path bring one to such a different end as the way she had trod had brought her?

She looked at her turquoise incrusted Guren. Eleven-thirty. Stevens would be waiting in the Rolls. The work was done, it was only ennui which had brought her here at all.

She yawned, stretching like a man and threw her head back, to gaze straight up into the dark interior of a sack descending silently upon her head. Instantly, she rolled out of the chair to the floor. A crushing weight fell upon her legs, a harsh grip pinioned her hands behind her. She opened her mouth to call to the watchman and received in it a choking wad of waste as a gag.

It was then she knew it was useless to struggle or hope for aid. One of the men was the watchman, another a discharged employee, the third a man whom she did not know, but whom she felt she had seen before in a dream and could not in any conceivable circumstance, forget. A scarred cheek, and a missing lobe on his right ear would see to that!

46

The watchman tried to put the bag over her head again, but the stranger who obviously gave the orders, motioned him to desist.

"No use in that," he growled. "She knows you and she'll know me, if ever she sets eyes on me again—won't you, old lady?"

She could only mumble, but she did that much and managed to nod her head.

"Well, we'll have to see to it then, that you don't," he chuckled and they went out, closing the door behind them.

They were away for what seemed a long time, while she listened to the pecking sleet and wondered if Stevens would become alarmed and call for her. Finally the door opened again, but it was not Stevens who entered.

The watchman and the other subordinate picked her up and, preceded by the scarred man, they passed through the echoing warehouse toward the rear entrance.

Rage filled her, to see the many empty hooks where costly furs had swung, but she was hurried on, unable to remonstrate, at such a pace that even the watchman grumbled: "Slow down, will you, Arnold? We can't see!"

Then, out of the warehouse and into a large sedan. She was unceremoniously thrown, on bales and bags of furs—and so, off through the storm.

With her head below the level of the window, she could not guess at her route, but kept working with tongue and teeth at the gag which was suffocating her. At length she spat it out, just as the brakes were applied and the wet tires squealed on the icy street.

The driver, Arnold, looked back over his shoulder and snarled: "Come on, hurry it up! Let's get out of here."

They dragged her out, neck and heels, and she could see. The icy scud hid the lights of the distant city, but before her was the heavy railing of a bridge and the first steps of a flight leading down.

She thought she saw a dark figure standing below, looking back, nearly down the steps, almost beyond her range of vision. She could not be quite sure, yet she screamed, "Help! Help!"

A violent blow dazed her and she could feel warm wetness on her neck but she was not unconscious as they picked her up again.

"This must be a dream," she dazedly thought, "but I haven't had such a bad one since I was a little girl and scared my mother, because I walked in my sleep to get away from those dreams. How foolish these thugs will seem when I wake up!"

She chuckled quietly, as she felt herself being carried down the long icy stairway leading toward the river.

It was very dark in the corridor and a draft blew cold against her bare ankles and knees beneath her nightdress. By the very absence of the night light always burning in her bedroom, she knew instantly that she had climbed, yet again in her sleep, the five flights of stairs leading to the attic and had been wandering about, hag-ridden by a dream.

She could feel the tears wet upon her cheeks because of the dream. In the dreams she had first thoughts of blood, then sleet, which, melting upon her, was drenching her skin.

It must have been the storm outside which had caused the dream; and that was another odd thing, because every night that she had walked thus in her sleep, either raindrops, hail or sleet had resounded upon the unsheathed roof of the echoing attic as though she stood within an empty drum.

She felt weak and dizzy and she knew that even yet she was not fully awake, for tears still flowed. She could not, would not stand another of these dreams.

What if her mother did not come sometime? The landing was only four steps wide! Twice she had been two steps from the edge, once, the last time, teetering, rocking on the very brink, the last step—emptiness!

Yet—she gasped at the enormity of the swift thought, the awful blasphemy of it. Would it not be better if she had taken the last step? Suppose the dreams she had been having would some day come true? One little second of firm resolve would forever prevent the dreadful possibilities of the future from ever becoming real!

In the corridor, at a distance, she heard swift steps, searching frantically, running now. That would be her mother, she knew, hunting for her little sleep-walking daughter. Just as before, she would be found on the verge of the stairwell.

She would be drawn back if she did not hurry, drawn back to safety and to walk through the long years again. Turn and twist as she might, she would be directed unyieldingly to one inexorable end—the end of every dream.

She *must* hurry. This was the crucial factor of her life, the deciding second, the one deviation from which return would be impossible! A bright light fell upon her face!

How very, very strange! Mother was behind her in the corridor, calling, running—yet there she was before her, too, beckoning, smiling, her eyes full of love and understanding! And how her robes shone!

She stepped forward across the landing, to mother's embracing arms—three—four—She took the fifth step.

The wind was in her ears as she fell, and a sharp keen sound. It was her mother's agonized cry, it was the squeal of wet tires on an icy pavement, it was the mournful sound of a tugboat on the river—it was a policeman's whistle.

She was smiling, as she fell into the abyss of eternity. She would not be hurt, she would not strike—people never did in dreams—she would not wake from this dream.

The patrolman flashed his light into the corner again.

"Aye, it's Meg, right enough," he said to his companion, unfeelingly, "the end ye'd be expectin' for the auld rip."

"Was she a bad one, then?" the other queried.

"Hm-m-m." The grunt was eloquent. "Give us a hand with her, noo." His associate was a devout man and doffed his cap. "Faith then, I'll not be doubting your word, if you say it, but I hope I have as easy an hour of my passing as she had. Twenty years have I covered the water front and never before seen a face like yon.

"Why she looks as peaceful and contented as a baby asleep in the arms of her mother!"

THE DARK COUNTRY
Dennis Etchison

Illustration by David Lloyd

Dennis Etchison has been described as the best short story writer in the field today and indeed his work has the knack of getting under your skin—with a psychological razor blade! Also an accomplished novelist and screenwriter, he has recently finished a script for director John Carpenter, and other associations with the Carpenter stable include novelizations of Halloween II, Halloween III, *and* The Fog. *The first two books were written under the pseudonym 'Jack Martin' (the lead character in* The Dark Country), *who is also the author of the novel version of David Cronenberg's movie* Videodrome. *Dennis has had three major collections of his short fiction published,* The Dark Country, Red Dreams *and* Blood Kiss, *and in addition is the author of the novel* Darkside *and the editor of the anthologies* The Cutting Edge *and* Master of Darkness, *volumes I and II. The story we include here made quite a splash after it was first published in* Fantasy Tales 8: *it appeared in a U.S. magazine, was chosen for* The Year's Best Horror *anthology, became the title of Dennis' first collection and won both the British and World Fantasy Awards! Not bad for a story that couldn't find a market when we bought it...*

MARTIN sat by the pool, the wind drying his hair. A fleshy, airborne spider appeared on the edge of the book which he had been reading

'Two guys from next door cornered him outside our place'

there. From this angle it cast a long, pointed needle across the yellowing pages. The sun was hot and clean; it went straight for his nose. Overweight American children practised their volleyball on the bird-of-paradise plants. Weathered rattan furniture gathered dust beyond the peeling diving board.

Traffic passed on the road. Trucks, campers, bikes.

The pool that would not be scraped till summer. The wooden chairs that had been ordered up from the States. Banana leaves. Olive trees. A tennis court that might be done next year. A single colour TV antenna above the palms. By the slanted cement patio heliotrope daisies, speckled climbing vines. The morning a net of light on the water. Boats fishing in Todos Santos Bay.

A smell like shrimps Veracruz blowing off the silvered waves.

And a strangely familiar island, like a hazy floating giant, where the humpback whales play. Yesterday in Ensenada, the car horns talking and a crab taco in his hand, he had wanted to buy a pair of huaraches and a Mexican shirt. The best tequila in the world for three-and-a-half a litre. Noche Buena beer, foil labels that always peel before you can read them. Delicious con Filtros cigarettes.

Bottles of agua mineral. Tehuacan con gas. *No retornable.*

He smiled as he thought of churros at the Blow Hole, the maid who even washed his dishes, the Tivoli Night Club with Reno cocktail napkins, mescal flavoured with worm, eggs fresh from the nest, chorizo grease in the pan, bar girls with rhinestone-studded Aztec headbands, psychoactive liqueurs, seagulls like the tops of valentines, grilled corvina with lemon, the endless plumes of surf. . .

It was time for a beer run to the bottling factory in town.

"*Buenos días!*"

Martin looked up, startled. He was blinded by the light. He fumbled his dark glasses down and moved his head. A man and a woman stood over his chair. The sun was at their backs.

"*Americano?*"

"Yes, said Martin. He shielded his forehead and tried to see their faces. Their features were blacked in by the glare that spilled around their heads.

"I told you he was an American," said the woman. "What are you studying?"

"What?"

Martin closed the book self-consciously. It was a paperback edition of *The Penal Colony*, the only book he had been able to borrow from any of the neighbouring cabins. Possibly it was the only book in Quintas Papagayo. For some reason the thought depressed him profoundly, but he had brought it poolside anyway. It seemed the right thing to do. He could not escape the feeling that he ought to be doing something more than nursing a tan. And the magazines from town were all in Spanish.

He slipped his sketchbook on top of Kafka and opened it awkwardly.

"I'm supposed to be working," he said. "On my drawings. You know how it is." They didn't, probably, but he went on. "It's difficult to get anything done down here."

"He's an artist!" said the woman.

"My wife thought you were an American student on vacation," said the man.

"Our son is a student, you see," said the woman. Martin didn't, but nodded sympathetically. She stepped aside to sit on the arm of another deck chair under the corrugated green fiberglass siding. She was wearing a sleeveless blouse and thigh-length shorts. "He was studying for his Master's Degree in Political Science at UCLA, but now he's decided not to finish. I tried to tell him he should at least get his teaching credential, but—"

"Our name's Winslow," said the man, extending a muscular hand. "Mr. and Mrs. Winslow."

"Jack Martin."

"It was the books," said Mr. Winslow. "Our boy always had books with him, even on visits." He chuckled and shook his head.

Martin nodded.

"You should see his apartment," said Mrs. Winslow. "So many." She gestured with her hands as if describing the symptoms of a hopeless affliction.

52

There was an embarrassing lull. Martin looked to his feet. He flexed his toes. The right ones were stiff. For something further to do, he uncapped a Pilot Fineliner pen and touched it idly to the paper. Without realizing it, he smiled. This trip must be doing me more good than I'd hoped, he thought. I haven't been near a college classroom in fifteen years.

A wave rushed toward the rocks at the other side of the cabins.

"Staying long?" asked the man, glancing around nervously. He was wearing Bermuda shorts over legs so white they were almost phosphorescent.

"I'm not sure," said Martin.

"May I take a peek at your artwork?" asked the woman.

He shrugged and smiled.

She lifted the sketchbook from his lap with infinite delicacy, as the man began talking again.

He explained that they owned their own motor home, which was now parked on the Point, at the end of the rock beach, above the breakwater. Weekend auto insurance cost them $13.70 in Tijuana. They came down whenever they got the chance. They were both retired, but there were other things to consider—just what, he did not say. But it was not the same as it used to be. He frowned at the moss growing in the bottom of the pool, at the baby weeds poking up through the sand in the canister ash trays, at the separating layers of the sawed-off diving board.

Martin could see more questions about to surface behind the man's tired eyes. He cleared his throat and squirmed in his chair, feeling the sweat from his arms soaking into the unsealed wood. Mr. Winslow was right, of course. Things were not now as they once were. But he did not relish being reminded of it, not now, not here.

A small figure in white darted into his field of vision, near the edge of the first cabin. It was walking quickly, perhaps in this direction.

"There's my maid," he said, leaning forward. "She must be finished now." He unstuck his legs from the chaise longue.

"She has keys?" said the man.

"I suppose so. Yes, I'm sure she does. Well—"

"Does she always remember to lock up?"

He studied the man's face, but a lifetime of apprehensions were recorded there, too many for Martin to isolate one and read it accurately.

"I'll remind her," he said, rising.

He picked up his shirt, took a step toward Mrs. Winslow and stood shifting his weight.

Out of the corner of his eye, he saw the maid put a hand to the side of her face.

Mrs. Winslow closed the pad, smoothed the cover and handed it back. "Thank you," she said oddly.

Martin took it and offered his hand. He realized at once that his skin had become uncomfortably moist, but Mr. Winslow gripped it firmly and held it. He confronted Martin soberly, as if about to impart a bit of fatherly advice.

"They say he comes down out of the hills," said Winslow, his eyes unblinking. Martin half-turned to the low, tan range that lay beyond the other side of the highway. When he turned back, the man's eyes were waiting. "He's been doing it for years. It's something of a legend around here. They can't seem to catch him. We never took it seriously, until now."

"Is that right?"

"Why, last night, while we were asleep, he stole an envelope of traveller's cheques and a whole carton of cigarettes from behind our heads. Can you beat that? Right inside the camper! Of course we never bothered to lock up. Why should we? Everyone's very decent around here. We've never had any trouble ourselves. Until this trip. It's hard to believe."

"Yes, it is." Martin attempted to pull back as a tingling began in his stomach. But the man continued to pump his hand, almost desperately, Martin thought.

"The best advice I can give you, young man, is to lock your doors at night. From now on. You never know."

"Thanks, I will."

"He comes out after the sun goes down." He would not let go of Martin's hand. "I figure he must hit the beach three-four in the morning, when all the lights are out. Slips right in. No one notices. And then it's too late."

Martin pretended to struggle with the books so that he could drop his hand. "Well, I hope you're able to enjoy the rest of your vacation." He eyed the maid. "Now I'd better—"

"We're warning everybody along the beach," said Winslow.

"Maybe you should report it."

"That don't do no good. They listen to your story, but there's nothing they can do."

"Good luck to you, then," said Martin.

"Thank you again," said the woman peculiarly. "And don't forget. You lock your door tonight!"

"I will," said Martin, hurrying away. I won't, that is. Will, won't, what does it matter? He side-stepped the dazzling flowers of an ice plant and ascended the cracked steps of the pool enclosure. He crossed the paved drive and slowed.

The maid had passed the last of the beachfront houses and was about to intersect his path. He waited for her to greet him as she always did. I should at least pretend to talk to her, he thought, in case the Winslows are still watching. He felt their eyes, or someone's, close at his back.

"*Buenos días,*" he said cheerfully.

She did not return the greeting. She did not look up. She wagged her head and trotted past, clutching her uniform at the neck.

He paused and stared after her. He wondered in passing about her downcast eyes, and about the silent doorways of the other cabins, though it was already past ten o'clock. And then he noticed the scent of ozone that now laced the air, though no thunderhead was visible yet on the horizon, only a gathering fog far down the coastline, wisps of it beginning to striate the wide, pale sky above the sagging telephone poles. And he wondered about the unsteadiness in Mrs. Winslow's voice as she had handed back the sketchbook. It was not until he was back at the beach that he remembered: the pages he had shown her were blank. There were no sketches at all yet in the pad, only the tiny flowing blot he had made with his pen on the first sheet while they talked, like a miniature misshapen head or something else, something else, stark and unreadable on the crisp white sulfite paper.

He was relieved to see that the private beach had finally come alive with its usual quota of sun-bathers. Many of them had probably arisen early, shortly after he left for the quiet of the pool, and immediately swarmed to the surf with no thought of TV or the morning paper, habits they had left checked at the border sixty miles from here. A scattered few lagged back, propped out on their patios, sipping coffee and keeping an eye on the children who were bounding through the spume. The cries of the children and of the gulls cut sharply through the waves which, disappointingly, were beginning to sound to Martin like nothing so much as an enormous screenful of ball bearings.

There was the retired rent-a-cop on holiday with his girl friend, stretched out on a towel and intent on his leg exercises. There was the middle-aged divorcee from two doors down, bent over the tidepools, hunting for moonstones among jealous clusters of acquamarine anemones. And there was Will, making time with the blonde in the blue tank top. He seemed to be explaining to her some sort of diagram in the slicked sand between the polished stones. Martin toed into his worn rubber sandals and went down to join them.

"Want to go to a party?" Will said to him as he came up.

"When?"

"Whenever," said the blonde in the blue top. She tried to locate Martin's face, gave up and gazed back in the general direction of the southern bungalows.

There a party was still in progress, as it had been since last Wednesday, when Will and Martin had arrived. The other party, the one on the north side, had apparently been suspended for a few hours, though just now as Martin watched a penny rocket streaked into the sky from the bathroom window, leaving an almost invisible trail of powder-blue smoke in the air above the water. The skyrocket exploded with a faint report like a distant rifle and began spiraling back to earth. Martin heard hoarse laughter and the sudden cranking-up of stereo speakers inside the sliding doors. So the party there was also nearly in full swing again, or had never let up. Perhaps it was all one big party, with his cabin sandwiched like a Christian Science reading room between two pirate radio stations. He remembered the occasional half-dressed teenager staggering around the firepit and across his porch last night, grunting about more beer and did he know where those nurses were staying? Martin had sat outside till he fell asleep, seeing them piss their kidneys out on the steaming stones of the footpath.

"Bummer," said the girl seriously. Martin noticed that she was lugging around an empty twelve-ounce bottle. She upended it and a few slippery drops hit the rocks. "You guys wouldn't know where the Dos Equis's stashed, wouldjou?"

"*No es problema*, my dear," said Will, steering her toward the patio.

Martin followed. Halfway there the girl wobbled around and hurled the bottle as high as she could away from the shoreline. Unfortunately, her aim was not very good. Martin had to duck. He heard it whistle end-over-end over his head and shatter on the flat rocks. Will caught her under the arms and staggered her inside. Next door, a Paul Simon song was playing on the tape deck.

By the time Martin got there she was on her way out, cradling a bottle of Bohemia. Again she tried to find his eyes, gave up and began picking her way across the rocks.

"Take it slow," yelled Will. "Hey, sure you don't want to lie down for a while?"

Martin grinned at him and walked past into the high-beamed living room. The fireplace was not lighted, nor was the wall heater, but a faint but unmistakable odour of gas lingered in the corners.

"We better stock up on Dos Equis from now on," said Will.

"Is that her favourite?"

"She doesn't care. But we shelled out a deposit on the case of Bohemia. Dos Equis is no return."

Martin stood staring out at the island in the bay. The fishing boats were moving closer to shore. Now he could barely make out the details of the nearest one. He squinted. It wasn't a fishing boat at all, he realized. It was much larger than he had imagined, some kind of oil tanker, perhaps. "Guess what, Will? We're going to have to start locking the doors."

"Why? Afraid the *putas* are gonna OD on Spanish fly and jump our bones in the middle of the night?"

"You wish," said Martin. He sniffed around the heater, then followed the scent to the kitchen and the stove. "The gas pilots," he said. "It's the draft. You—we're—always going in and out. The big door's open all the time."

"Got a match, man?" Will took out a bent cigarette, straightened it and crumpled the pack. The table was littered with empty packs of cheap Mexican cigarettes, Negritos and Faros mostly. Martin wondered how his friend could smoke such garbage. He took out his Zippo. Will struck it with an exaggerated shaking of his hands, but it was out of fluid. He stooped over the gas stove and winked at Martin. He turned the knob. The burner lit. He inhaled, coughed and reached for the tequila. He poured himself a tall one mixed with grape-fruit juice. "Mmm. Good for the throat, but it still burns a little."

"Your system runs on alcohol, Willy. You know that, don't you?"

"Don't all machines?"

"Myself, I could go for some eggs right now. How about you? What've we got left?" Martin went to the sink. It was full of floating dishes. "Hey, what the hell is it with the maid? We did remember to leave her a tip yesterday. Didn't we?"

"One of us must have."

That was it, then. That was why she had skipped them, and then snubbed him this morning. That had to be it. Didn't it?

The tape deck next door was now blaring a golden oldie by Steely Dan. Martin slid the glass door closed. Then he snagged his trousers from the back of a chair and put them on over his trunks. Started to put them on. They did not feel right. He patted his back pocket.

Will slid the door back open halfway. "You're serious, aren't you? Look at it this way. Leave it like this and the gas'll just blow on outside. Relax, man. That's what you came down here for, isn't it? After what happened, you need . . ."

Martin checked the chair. On the table were a deck of playing cards from a Mission Bay savings and loan, the backs of which were imprinted with instructions about conserving energy, a Mexican wrestling magazine with a cover picture of the masked hero, El Santo, in the ring against a hooded character in red jumpsuit and horns, and an old mineral water bottle full of cigarette butts. On the floor, lying deflated between the table legs, was his wallet.

"There's another reason, I'm afraid." Martin twisted open the empty wallet and showed it to his friend.

"Who in the hell . . . ?"

57

"Well, it certainly wasn't the maid. Look at this place." Outside, a small local boy came trudging through the patios. He was carrying a leather case half as big as he was. He hesitated at the cabin on the south side, as three teenaged American boys, their hair layered identically and parted in the middle, called their girls out into the sun. "It must have happened during the night."

"Christ!" said Will. He slapped the tabletop. He reached for his own wallet. It was intact. "There. I was over there partying all night, remember? They must've passed every place where anybody was still up."

The small boy opened his case and the American girls began poring excitedly over a display of Indian jewellery, rings and belt buckles and necklaces of bright tooled silver and turquoise. From a distance, an old man watched the boy and waited, nodding encouragement.

"You should have gone with me," said Will. "I told you. Well, don't you worry, Jack. I've got plenty here for both of us."

"No, man. I can wire my agent or—"

"Look," said Will, "I can even kite a cheque if I have to, to cover the rental till we get back. They'll go for it. I've been coming here since I was a kid."

I've got to get away from here, thought Martin. No, that isn't right. Where else is there to go? I've come this far already just to get away. It's hopeless. It always was. You can run, he told himself, but you can't hide. Why didn't I realize that?

"Here," said Will. "Here's twenty for now."

"Are you sure?"

"Don't worry about it. I'd better go see if the nurses got hit, too. Saw a bunch of people in a huddle down the beach a while ago." He drained his glass. "Then I'll make another beer run. The hell with it. We're going to party tonight, God damn it! You going by the office, Jack?"

"Sure."

"Then you might as well report it to the old lady. I think she's got a son or a nephew in the federales. Maybe they can do something about it."

"Maybe," said Martin, cracking open a beer. He could have told Will that it wouldn't do any good. He stopped in at the office anyway. It didn't.

He wandered on up the highway to Enrique's Cafe. On the way he passed a squashed black cat, the empty skin of it in among the plants, the blood-red flowers and spotted adder's tongues and succulents by the roadside. The huevos rancheros were runny but good. When he got back, Will's four-wheel drive was still parked under the carport. He took the keys and made the beer run into town himself, police cars honking him out of the way to make left turns from right-hand lanes, zigzagging across the busy intersections of the city to avoid potholes. He bought a case of Dos Equis and, for forty cents more, a litre of soft, hot tortillas. As the afternoon wore on he found himself munching them, rolled with butter and later plain, even though he wasn't really hungry.

That evening he sat alone on a bench by the rocks, hearing but not listening to a Beatles song ('Treat Me Like You Did the Night Before'), the smoke from his Delicado wafting on the breeze, blending with wood smoke from the chimneys and rising slowly to leave a smear like the Milky Way across the Pleiades. It's time for me to leave this place, he thought. Not to run away, no, not this time; but to go back. And face the rest of it, my life, no matter how terrible things may have turned back home since I left.

Not Will, though; he should stay awhile longer if he likes. True, it was my idea; he only took the time off at my suggestion, setting it all up to make me comfortable; he knew I couldn't take any more last week, the way things were up there. He's my friend. Still, he was probably waiting for just such an excuse in order to get away himself.

So I'll call or wire the agency for a plane ticket, give them a cock-and-bull story about losing everything—the truth, in other words. It was the truth, wasn't it? I'll say the trip was part of the assignment. I had to come down here to work on some new sketches for the book, to follow a lead about headstone rubbings in, let's see, Guanajuato. Only I never made it that far. I stopped off for some local colour. Charge it against my royalty statement . . . I'll talk to them tomorrow. Yes, tomorrow.

Meanwhile, there's still tonight . . .

But I should tell Will first.

He resumed walking. There was a fire on the breakwater by the Point. He went toward it. Will would be in one of the cabins, partying with a vengeance. Martin glanced in one window. A slide show was in progress, with shots that looked like the pockmarked surface of another planet taken from space. He pressed closer and saw that these pictures were really close-ups of the faces of newborn seals or sea lions. Not that one, he thought, and moved on.

One of the parties he came to was in the big cabin two doors north of his own. That one was being rented, he remembered, by the producer of a show in the late seventies called *Starship Disco*. Martin had never seen it.

An Elvis Costello tape shook the walls. A young card hustler held forth around the living room table. A warm beer was pushed into Martin's hand by a girl. He popped the beer open and raised it, feeling his body stir as he considered her. Why not? But she could be my daughter, technically, he thought, couldn't she? Then: what a disgusting point of view. Then: what am I doing to myself? Then it was too late; she was gone.

Will was not in the back rooms. The shelf in the hallway held three toppling books. Well well, he thought, there are readers down here, after all. Then he examined them—*By Love Possessed* by Cozzens, *Invitation to Tea* by Monica Lang (The People's Book Club, Chicago, 1952), *The Foundling* by Francis Cardinal Spellman. They were covered with years of dust.

He ducked into the bathroom and shut the door, seeing the mirror and razor blade lying next to the sink, the roll of randomly-perforated crepe paper toilet tissue. There was a knock on the door. He excused himself and went out, and found Will in the kitchen.

"*Dos cervezas*, Juan!" Will was shouting. "Whoa. I feel more like I do now than when I got here!" With some prodding, he grabbed two cold ones and followed Martin outside, rubbing his eyes.

He seemed relieved to sit down.

"So," began Martin. "What did you find out? Did anyone else get popped last night?"

"Plenty! One, the nurses. Two, the bitch from San Diego. Three, the—where is it now? Ojai. Those people. The . . ." He ran out of fingers. "Let's see. Anyway, there's plenty, let me tell you."

The ships were now even nearer the shore. Martin saw their black hulls closing in over the waves.

"I was thinking," he said. "Maybe it's time to go. What would you say to that, man?"

"Nobody's running scared. That's not the way to play it. You should hear 'em talk. They'll get his ass next time, whoever he is. Believe it. The kids, they didn't get hit. But three of those other guys are rangers. Plus there's the cop. See the one in there with the hat? He says he's gonna lay a trap, cut the lights about three o'clock, everybody gets quiet, then bam! You better believe it. They're mad as hell."

"But why—"

"It's the dock strike. It happens every year when there's a layoff. The locals get hungry. They swoop down out of the hills like bats."

Just then a flaming object shot straight through the open front door and fizzled out over the water. There was a hearty "All r-r-ight!" from a shadow on the porch, and then the patio was filled with pogoing bodies and clapping hands. The night blossomed with matches and fireworks, 1000-foot skyrockets, bottle rockets and volleys of Mexican cherry bombs, as the party moved outside and chose up sides for a firecracker war. Soon Martin could no longer hear himself think. He waited it out. Will was laughing.

Martin scanned the beach beneath the screaming lights. And noticed something nearby that did not belong. It was probably a weird configuration of kelp, but. . .he got up and investigated.

It was only this: a child's broken doll, wedged half-under the stones. What had he supposed it was? It had been washed in on the tide, or deliberately dismembered and its parts strewn at the waterline, he could not tell which. In the flickering explosions, its rusty eye sockets appeared to be streaked with tears.

A minute after it had begun, the firecracker war was over. They sat apart from the cheering and breaking bottles, watching the last shot of a Roman candle sizzle below the surface of the water like a green torpedo. There was scattered applause, and then a cry went up from another party house down the beach as a new round of fireworks was launched there. Feet slapped the sand, dodging rocks.

"Do you really believe that?"

"What?"

"About someone coming down from the hills," said Martin. *Like bats.* He shuddered.

"Watch this," said Will. He took his bottle and threw it into the air, snapping it so it flew directly at a palm tree thirty feet away. It smashed into the trunk at the ragged trim line.

Instantly the treetop began to tremble. There was a high rustling and a shaking and a scurrying. And a rattling of tiny claws. A jagged frond dropped spearlike to the beach.

"See that? It's rats. The trees around here are full of 'em. You see how bushy it is on top? It never gets trimmed up there. Those rats are born, live and die in the trees. They never touch down."

"But how? I mean, what do they eat if—?"

"Dates. Those are palm trees, remember? And each other, probably. You've never seen a dead one on the ground, have you?"

Martin admitted he hadn't.

"Not that way with the bats, though. They have to come out at night. Maybe they even hit the rats. I never saw that. But they have mouths to feed, don't they? There's nothing much to eat up in the hills. It must be the same with the peasants. They have families. Wouldn't you?"

"I hate to say this. But. You did lock up, didn't you?"

Will laughed drily. "Come on. I've got something for you. I think it's time you met the nurses."

Martin made a quick sidetrip to check the doors at their place, and they went on. They covered the length of the beach before Will found the porch he was looking for. Martin reached out to steady his friend, and almost fell himself. He was getting high. It was easy.

As they let themselves in, the beach glimmered at their backs with crushed abalone shells and scuttling hermit crabs. Beyond the oil tankers, the uncertain outline of the island loomed in the bay. It was called Dead Man's Island, Will told him.

He woke with the sensation that his head was cracking open. Music or something like it in the other room, throbbing through the thin walls like the pounding of surf. Voices. An argument of some kind. He brushed at the cobwebs. He had been lost in a nightmare of domination and forced acquiescence before people who meant to do him harm. It returned to him in fragments. What did it mean? He shook it off and rolled out of bed.

There was the floor he had pressed with his hand last night to stop the room from spinning. There was the nurse, tangled in the sheets next to him. He guessed she was the nurse. He couldn't see her face.

He went into the bathroom. He took a long draught of water from the tap before he came out. He raised his head and the room spun again. The light from the window hurt his eyes—actual physical pain. He couldn't find his sock. He tottered into the other room.

A young man with blown-dry hair was playing the tape deck too loudly. The sound vibrated the bright air, which seemed thin and brittle, hammering it like beaten silver. There was the girl in the blue tank top, still seated next to the smouldering fireplace. An empty bottle of Damiana Liqueur was balanced against her thigh. Her eyes were closed and her face was stony. He wondered if she had slept that way, propped upright all night. On the table were several Parker Brothers-type games from stateside: *Gambler, Creature Features, The Game of Life*. A deck of Gaiety Brand nudie cards, with a picture on the box of a puppy pulling a bikini top out of a purse. Someone had been playing solitaire. Martin couldn't remember.

There was a commotion outside.

"What's that?" he said, shielding his eyes.

"Talking Heads," said the young man. He showed Martin the tape box. "They're pretty good. That lead guitar line is hard to play. It's so repetitious."

"No, I mean . . ."

Martin scratched and went into the kitchen. It was unoccupied, except for a cricket chirping somewhere behind the refrigerator. Breakfast was in process; eggs were being scrambled in a blender the nurses had brought with them from home. Martin protected his eyes again and looked outside.

There was Will. And there were three or four tan beach boys from the other party. And the cop. He wasn't doing his leg exercises this morning. They were having an argument.

Martin stumbled out.

"But you can't do that," one of them was saying.

"Stay cool, okay, motherfuck? You want the whole beach to know?"

"You think they don't already?"

"The hell they do! We drug him over out of the way. No one'll—"

"No one but the maids!"

"That's what I'm *saying*. You guys are a bunch of jack-offs. Jesus Christ! I'm about *this* close to kicking your ass right now, do you know that?"

"All right, all right!" said Will. "That kind of talk's just digging us in deeper. Now let's run through the facts. One—"

Martin came up. They shot looks at each other that both startled him and made him unreasonably afraid for their safety as well as his own. They stopped talking, their eyes wild, as if they had gobbled a jar of Mexican amphetamines.

Will took him aside.

"We've got to do something!" said the one with the souvenir hat. "What're you—?"

"Hold on," said Will. "We're all in this together, like it or—"

"I'm not the one who—"

"—Like it or not. Now just try to keep a tight asshole another minute, will you, while I talk to my friend Jack? It's his neck, too."

They started back up the beach. Will propelled him ahead of the others, as to a rendevous of great urgency.

"They got him," said Will.

"Who?"

"The thief, whoever he was. Poor bastard. Two guys from next door cornered him outside our place. Sometime around dawn, the way I get it. Apparently he fell on the rocks. He's dead. They found me here a little while ago. Now—"

"*What?*"

"—Now there's no use shitting bricks. It's done. What we have to do is think of a way to put ourselves in the clear—fast. We're the strangers here."

"We can make it look like an accident," said the one in the hat. "Those rocks are—"

"Accident, hell," said the security cop. "It was self-defense, breaking and entering. We caught him and blew him away. No court in—"

"This isn't the USA, you dumb shit. You know what greaser jails are like? They hate our guts. All they want's our money. This buddy of mine, he got . . ."

And so it went till they reached the porch, the surrounding beach littered with the casings of burntout rockets, vomit drying on the rocks, broken clam shells bleaching between the rocks, the rocks like skulls. And here blood, vivid beyond belief even on the bricks of the patio, great splotches and gouts of it, like gold coins burnished in the sun, a trail that led them in the unforgiving light of day to the barbecue pit and the pile of kindling stacked in the charcoal shade.

Martin knelt and tore at the logs.

And there.

The body was hidden inside a burlap sack. It was the body of the boy who had come by yesterday, the boy who had wanted to sell his jewellery.

He felt his stomach convulse. The small face was scraped raw, the long eyelashes caked and flaking, the dark skin driven from two of the ribs to show white muscle and bone. A great fear overtook Martin, like wings settling upon him, blocking out the sun. He folded under them momentarily and dry-heaved in the ashes.

Will was pacing the narrow patio like a prisoner in a cell, legs pumping out and back over the cracking cement, pivoting faster and faster at the edges until he was practically spinning, generating a hopeless rage that would not be denied but could not be released. His hands were shaking violently, and his arms and shoulders and body. He looked around with slitted eyes, chin out, lips drawn in, jaws grinding stone. From far down the beach by the Point an elderly man came walking, hesitating at each house and searching each lot. He was carrying a leather case.

Will said, "You kicked him to death, didn't you? You stomped this child until he was dead." Then, his voice a hiss, he began to curse them between his teeth with an unspeakable power and vileness. The one in the hat tried to break in. He started shouting.

"It was dark! He could've been anyone! What was he doing creepin' around here? He could've been—"

But Will was upon him, his arms corded, his fingers going for the throat. The others closed in. People on the beach were turning to stare. Martin saw it all as if in slow motion: himself rising at last to his full height, leaping into it a split-second before the others could grab hold, as he fell on their arms to stop the thumbs from Will's eyes, to break Will's hands from the other's throat. Everything stopped. Martin stepped between them as the young one fell back to the flagstone wall. Martin raised his right hand, flattened and angled it like a knife. With his left he cupped the back of the young man's neck, holding it almost tenderly. The young man's eyes were almost kind. They were eyes Martin had seen all his life, outside recruiting offices and Greyhound bus depots the years over, and they were a law unto themselves. He brought his right hand down sharp and hard across the face, again, again, three times, like pistol shots. The tan went white, then red where he had slapped it. For a moment nobody said anything. The old man kept coming.

They passed motorcycle cops, overheated VW's, Jeeps, Chevy Luvs, Ford Couriers with camper shells, off-road vehicles with heavy-duty shocks and, a mile outside of town, a half-acre of pastel gravestones by the main road. Martin fit as best he could among the plastic water jugs, sleeping bags and Instamatic cameras in the back seat. The boys from next door were piled in with him, the one in the hat in front and Will at the controls of the four-wheel drive.

The twenty-mile access road behind Ensenada wound them higher and higher, pummeling them continuously until they were certain that the tie rods or the A-frame or their bodies would shake loose and break apart at the very next turn. The lane shrank to a mere dirt strip, then to a crumbling shale-and-sand-stone ledge cut impossibly around the backs of the hills, a tortuous serpentine above abandoned farmland and the unchecked acreage between the mountains and the sea. Twice at least one of the wheels left the road entirely; they had to pile out and lay wild branches under the tires to get across fissures that had no bottom. Martin felt his kidneys begin to ache under the endless pounding. One of the boys threw up and continued to retch over the side until Will decided they had gone far enough, but no one opened his mouth to complain. After more than an hour, they set the hand brake at the start of a primitive downslope, blocked the wheels with granite chips and stumbled the rest of the way, numb and reeling.

The silence was overpowering. Nothing moved, except for the random scrabbling of lizards and the falling of individual leaves and blades of grass. As they dragged the sack down to the meadows, Martin concentrated on the ribbon of dirt they had driven, watching for the first sign of another car, however unlikely that was. A small, puddled heat mirage shimmered on the dust, coiled and waiting to be splashed. A squirrel darted across the road, silhouetted as it paused in stop-motion, twitched its pointed head and then ran on, disappearing like an escaped shooting gallery target. Great powdered monarch butterflies aimlessly swam the convection currents; like back home, he thought. Yes, of course; I should have known. Only too much like home.

"Dig here," said Will.

The old wound in Martin's foot was hurting him again. He had thought it would be healed by now, but it wasn't. He rocked back wearily on one heel. A withered vine caught at his ankle. It snapped easily with a dull, fleshy sound as he shook free. He took another step, and something moist and solid broke underfoot. He looked down.

He kicked at the grass. It was only a tiny melon, one of dozens scattered nearby and dying on the vine. He rolled it over, revealing its soft underbelly. Too much rain this season, he thought absently; too much or too little, nourishing them excessively or not enough. What was the answer? He picked it up and lobbed it over their heads. It splattered on the road in a burst of pink. Watermelons, he thought, while fully-formed seeds pale as unborn larvae slithered off his shoe and into the damp grass. Who planted them here? And who will return for the harvest, only to find them already gone to seed? He stooped and wiped his hand. There was a faint but unmistakable throb and murmur in the ground, as though through a railroad track, announcing an unseen approach from miles away.

"What are you going to do, Jackie?"

Martin stared back at Will. He hadn't expected the question, not now.

"It's like this," said Will, taking him to one side. "Michael, for one, wants to get back to his own van and head on deeper into Baja, lay low for a few days. He wasn't registered, so there's no connection. Some of the others sound like they're up for the same, or for going north right away, tonight Kevin's due to check out today, anyway."

"And you?"

"Don't know yet. I haven't decided. I'll probably stay on for appearances, but you do what you want. I wouldn't worry about the maid or anyone coming by to check up. Anyway, we hosed off the patio. Nobody else saw a thing, I'm sure. The girls don't know anything about it."

There was a grunt. The sack, being lowered, had split open at the seams. Hands hurried to reclose it.

"What's that?"

Will grabbed a wrist. A silver bracelet inlaid with polished turquoise glittered against a bronze tan in the afternoon light.

"I—I bought it."

"Sure you did," said Will.

"I brought it with me on the trip. Ask my girl. She—"

Will stripped it off the arm and flung it into the shallow grave. "You want to get out of this alive, kiddo? That kind of work can be traced. Or didn't you think of that? You didn't think, did you? What else did you steal from him while you were at it yesterday? Is that why he came back last night? Is it?"

"Lookit, man, where do you get off—"

"We all hang together," said Will, "or we all hang together. Get it?"

He got to his knees to close the sack. As an afterthought, he reached deep and rifled the dead child's pockets for anything that might tie in with Quintas Papagayo.

His hands stopped. He withdrew a wad of paper money which fell open, a flower on his palm. A roll of American dollars, traveller's cheques, credit cards.

"Hey, that's—"

"I had eighty bucks on me when—"

Martin joined him in examining the roll. The cheques were signed NORMAN & BERNICE WINSLOW. Two of the cards, embossed on the front and signed on the back, read JACK MARTIN.

"Knew I was right!" said the one in the felt hat. "Fuck if I wasn't! Lookit that! The little son of a bitch..."

Martin straight-armed the wheel, running in darkness.

He reminded himself of the five-dollar bill clipped to the back of his license. Then he remembered that his wallet was flat, except for the credit cards. Motorcycle cops passed him like fugitive Hell's Angels. He kicked on the lights of his rented car and thought of the last news tape of the great Karl Wallenda. He had been running, too, though in wind, not fog, toward or away from something.

Did he look back, I wonder? Was that why it happened?

...Heading for the end, his last that day was weak. Or maybe he looked ahead that once, saw it was the same, and just gave up the ghost. No, not Wallenda. For him the game was running while pretending not to— or the other way around. Was that his private joke? Even in Puerto Rico, for him the walk was all. *Keep your head clear*, he wanted to tell Wallenda. For that was how it finished, stopping to consider. But Wallenda must have known; he had been walking for years. Still he should have remembered...Martin put on his brights, gripped the steering wheel and made for the border.

He turned on the radio, found an American station.

It was playing a song by a group called The Tubes. He remembered the Tivoli Night Club, the elevated band playing 'Around the World' and 'A Kiss to Build a Dream On.' He remembered Hussong's Cantina, the knife fight that happened, his trip to the Blow Hole, policia with short hair and semiautomatic rifles. The housetrailers parked on the Point, the Point obscured by mist. The military guns with silencers...

The doll whose parts had been severed, its eyes opening in moonlight.

Shaking, he turned his mind to what lay ahead. He wanted to see someone; he tried to think of her face. Her eyes would find his there under the beam ceiling, the spider plants in the corners growing into the carpet, the waves on Malibu beach, the Pleiades as bright, shining on what was below: the roots between the rocks, the harbour lights like eyes, the anemones closed inward, the gourds and giant mushrooms, the endless pull of riptide, the seagulls white as death's-heads, the police with trimmed moustaches, the dark ships at anchor...

He came to a bridge on the tollway. Ahead lay the border.

To his right a sign, a turnoff that would take him back into Baja.

He sat with the motor running, trying to pick a direction.

DEAD TO THE WORLD
Allen Ashley

Illustration by Dave Carson

Allen Ashley is a part-time writer who has had stories published in various small press magazines, such as Space & Time *and* Fantasy Macabre. *'Dead to the World' is a claustrophobic horror yarn from* Fantasy Tales *that the readers voted runner-up for the best story in issue 11.*

Friday:

SOMETHING is happening to me. I am losing the sight in my left eye. In this itself there is nothing remarkable: there must surely be millions of blind or partially-sighted people in the world. Many of them must also have lost their sight at a younger age than my own, twenty-seven.

Where I feel that my case is different to all the others is that my impending blindness is merely a symptom of some greater illness, some malaise peculiar to myself, a sickness yet to be diagnosed and categorized by the doctors of the world.

Let me explain. I believe that the pores of my skin are sealing over. At the moment I have been unable to obtain access to a microscope so as to confirm or deny my opinion, but if I do I am sure an alarming sight will greet me. I do not know for certain when the process began, but I first became aware of it seven days ago. I am a keen sportsman and regularly play squash with some colleagues from work. Over the last two years I have improved my game tremendously and three months ago I

'I must look like a giant embryo'

won a local competition.

Last week I played for two hours, winning comfortably in the end after a shaky start.

Coming off the court my opponent, a man named Clive Cartwright, said, "You amaze me, Russ. You're not even sweating."

I ran the back of my left hand across my forehead and it was true. Two hours of highly energetic activity and I had not even perspired once. My skin was dry, dusty almost, but not salty. I shrugged and smiled blandly like a true champion, but began to worry internally.

Since then I have been running, I have sat for hours in an over-heated, stuffy room, I have over-dressed for the mild weather, but all I have managed is one tiny teardrop of perspiration. It seems that all areas of my body are equally affected. All the usually sweaty regions—the soles of my feet, my armpits, my forehead, my groin, the back of my neck— are as dry as the proverbial bone.

And now I am unable to properly focus my left eye, receiving only hazy impressions at best. I telephoned the optician this morning and spoke to an answering machine. I expect to receive notice of an appointment early next week.

Being unable to read properly, I was allowed to come home early from work. Someone there said it might simply be influenza or sinusitis. I do not think it is either. The manager told me to phone on Monday morning if I am not well enough to come in. I am beginning to wonder if I will ever work again.

Saturday:
Perhaps I should offer some background information. For posterity, so to speak.

I am white, male, twenty-seven years of age. My name is Russell Parkes. I have been married for three years to a woman named Judy, who is a year younger than myself. We have a child of eighteen months whose name is Jonathan, a pet budgie called Joey, and a dog known as Rusty. We are buying our own house.

I work for the Shulman Drug Company and have done so since I left university six years ago. I now hold an important administrative post and earn a high wage. My financial position is "comfortable."

In the early days with Shulman's, before I was promoted, before I married, before I became a father, I used to experiment with drugs. There were six of us in all, new recruits, ex-students, and having access to the testing labs was seen as a great boon. For two years, on and off, we produced some incredible mind-blowing concoctions. Occasionally we all became too wrecked to go home and had to sleep on the lab floor. It was a surreal time, and one I thought would never end.

Then one day one of our pillpopping group went too far. As far as he could possibly go, in fact. His death marked a watershed in my life and a warning for us all. It was pure chance which left Steve the victim; it could have been any of us. Two of my friends resigned, one went into hospital and the other was voluntarily transferred abroad. I alone remained, resolved to make something of my life and never again live dangerously.

Since then, some four years back, I have touched no drugs other than alcohol, the occasional aspirin, and the very occasional cigarette. It is tempting to see my current problems as the results of my previous chemical misadventures, but I am sure that if my drug experiments have severely damaged my health, symptoms would have become evident before now. Wouldn't they?

No one at Shulman's had ever mentioned my illegal activities but I have gradually ascertained that our little group was by no means the first to indulge in such things. It seems that the company is run along the same lines as a chocolate factory: let the workers try the product until they get sick of it.

Monday:
I made it into work this morning. My left eye is now almost totally closed

up: the lids are stuck together. I expect most people have experienced the feeling of waking up after a deep sleep and finding that one's eyelids are difficult to prise apart. In the case of my left eye it is impossible. I look like I am permanently winking.

I wore dark glasses at work and managed to deal with some urgent business before the manager called me in to see him.

"Russ," he said, "you're in no fit state to come to work. I'm sending you home on indefinite sick leave. We're under pressure of work at the moment and we can't really afford to do without you, but we've got to consider your long-term health. At the moment you look like death warmed up."

So, home I came, to find Judy sitting at the kitchen table reading *Cosmopolitan* while the dog barked and the baby cried. As I took my coat off she got up and opened a can of dogfood for Rusty. The baby continued to cry. The magazine carried a feature entitled, *How to Tell if Your Man's Having an Affair*.

"Maybe Jonathan's hungry," I suggested.

"I don't know. I don't think so," Judy replied. "I offered him some yoghurt and he didn't take it."

"Perhaps he doesn't like yoghurt."

I took a banana from the fruit bowl which seemed to do the trick. Half an hour later Jonathan went to sleep. I decided to take a bath. Judy was still reading.

Forty minutes later as the bathwater swirled down the plughole I received another shock to my battered system. As I rubbed the towel over my wet skin, great clumps of body hair fell out, black tufts littering the carpet, as my closing pores rejected their crop.

Thursday:
This morning I was examined by an optician. He was a middle-aged man of vaguely Germanic origin, with a tendency to mumble.

"Well, Mr. Parkes," he concluded, "I can't really say if there's anything wrong with your eye as I can't see into it. I would suggest that some muscle connection has simply gone awry, causing the lid to jam. You'll have to go into hospital, of course, for the operation, but I feel confident that we can restore you to full sight."

Good news, at last. Now I only need find a surgeon capable of reopening my pores and I will be a normal man again. The latter, however, will surely be a trickier job, although it may also be due to a synaptic slip-up.

News of a less pleasing nature is the fact that since I have been off sick, Judy and I have argued most of the time. It seems I have disturbed her routine. Or perhaps I have disturbed her in something else? No, I must

71

not be suspicious, I ought to have more trust.

Last night saw a big row. Reconciliation took place at approximately ten o'clock and we decided to go straight to bed. Try as I might, however, I could not bring myself to make love with Judy, although we both wished to. Maybe it was just one of those things that happen to everyone occasionally, or maybe it's another symptom of this mysterious illness. If the latter, then it's another good reason to push for a speedy cure.

Friday:
I am more perturbed than ever before. Tonight on television there was a repeat of the old James Bond film *Goldfinger*. I remembered that one of the ideas behind the movie was that of an immensely powerful man who had a beautiful woman painted golden all over her body, thus sealing the pores and preventing the skin from breathing. A slow method of murder.

The significance was not lost upon me.

Saturday:
This morning I received a lot of mail: a mixture of the usual bills and also a few get-well cards. There was a large card signed by most of my colleagues at work, as well as one from Clive, one from the manager, and one from a lady called Maggie, with whom I'd had an affair some four years ago. This last card was very sweet, picturing two little children—a girl with flowers and a boy in bed with a thermometer—drawn in pastel shades and with a dedication that was less corny than the rest. Things had not worked out between Maggie and I, and shortly after we parted I met and married. Judy. Maggie, although a very attractive woman, had never married. She now works in another department to my own and so it was especially nice to hear from her.

Judy, however, did not see it that way. Treating me like an invalid or someone prematurely senile, she opened all the letters before handing them over to me. Then she allowed me twenty minutes to leaf through them before laying into me.

" 'Love from Maggie'," she quoted. " 'Kiss, kiss'. So that's why you miss work so much!" I tried to protest but she continued relentlessly: "You said you'd given up hanging around with that little slut before you met me, but I don't believe you now. I bet you two have been sleeping together for years and I bet you think that I daren't leave you because of the baby. Well, we'll see about that!"

Those were roughly her words, as I remember them. I tried to interrupt, to tell her that I had never been unfaithful throughout our marriage, to tell her that I rarely saw Maggie nowadays, to tell her that putting love and kisses on a card was simply a gesture of friendship, not passion. But Judy would not listen. Consumed by jealousy she stormed upstairs, presumably to pack her bags. Sadly, I sat reflecting on how easily good intentions can be misconstrued.

Two hours passed and Judy did not descend the stairs so I presumed she had calmed somewhat and was not hell-bent on leaving me. I picked up the phone and rang Clive to thank him for his card. I must be getting a cold or influenza, for I couldn't hear him too well and my nose felt a bit bunged up. I changed the receiver to the other ear and this helped a little.

Despite the impediment to my hearing, however, I did not miss the most important part. After Clive had hung up I held the line for a few seconds and clearly heard my suspicious wife breathing into the extension.

Sunday:
I have hit an all-time low and believe I have passed the point of no return. This morning I failed to hear Jonathan crying, the phone ringing, the dog barking, and the doorbell chiming. Judy, having attended to all these things, came back to verbally lacerate me and accuse me of being a lazy, degenerate good-for-nothing. And worse. Until I raised my head from the pillow, however, I could not hear her at all clearly.

"I'm sorry," I muttered, "I'm not too well. I must see the doctor again tomorrow."

"God." she continued, her fire now well fuelled, "you're twenty-seven years old and you talk and act like an old man!"

"Have some sympathy, love."

"Sympathy! Yes, I've sympathy: for myself! What a fool I was to pick you out. I never realized I was marrying a cripple!"

I ought to have argued with her, replied that I didn't ask to become ill and that I'd still love her even if some malaise ruined her life. Surely that was the point of marrying someone? To love . . . in sickness and in health?

But I didn't argue with her. Instead I buried my head under the covers where the harsh, grating sound of her voice was even more muffled than before, and after a couple of minutes, during which I imagine she stood glaring at me, Judy left the room.

Another half an hour passed before I rose and went to the bathroom. A few exploratory forays with my fingers and careful study in the mirror confirmed my worst fears.

I should have realized long ago exactly what was happening. In fact, part of my mind probably did but hid the diagnosis from my consciousness, for it is such a hard thing to face.

73

I can no longer hide from the basic fact, however, that my every orifice is closing up.

Already my sight and hearing are impaired. Holding my head back and looking downwards into the mirror I can discern a thin membrane covering both nostrils. Feeling them with my thumb they have, at the moment, a quality akin to the fineness of a cobweb, but I am sure it is only a matter of time before they thicken and effectively plug up my nose.

My hair is receding from my forehead and falling out elsewhere. Even my toe and finger nails are suffering. They feel loose, as if the digits are attempting to smooth themselves over and be rid of the hard encumberance of chitin.

The process is in full swing now and I will see the doctor tomorrow but I do not believe this dreadful progress can be arrested. I have but a few days left to me, for when every bodily opening has sealed up I will surely die.

Monday:

This morning I contemplated suicide. I got as far as actually holding the sharpened razor blade to my throat but I could not bring myself to make the incision. I am not, it seems, the suicidal kind, believing naively that while there is life there is surely hope.

This afternoon Judy went out. I've no idea where she took off to. She left me to cope with Jonathan, Rusty, Joey, and myself. I struggled, giving the budgie some birdseed and my son some babyfood. Satisfied, Joey remained quiet apart from an occasional cheep. Jonathan continued to cry until at last he fell asleep, which was a relief for both of us. I was in no fit state to walk the dog and had to let him run about the streets on his own.

Later a junior doctor called, ringing the doorbell twice before I heard him. He roughly confirmed my own opinion, though he suggested that he ought to check with a specialist first. He also said that he would do his best to get me into hospital, but I may have to wait two weeks. Two weeks! I could be dead within seven days, let alone a fortnight.

Wednesday:

Judy left me today. I cannot really blame her for doing so: I am beyond any help she can offer me. Her reasoning is sound.

"I can't cope, Russ," she said. "It's too much of a strain. I can't look after you and Jonathan, it's too much. I'm going to my mother's until things sort themselves out." Then, showing the kinder side that has lately been repressed, she added: "Look, as soon as I get there I'll get on to the doctor and the hospital and make them take you in as an emergency case."

"Thanks, Judy," I muttered, and she was gone.

She took with her the baby, the dog, the budgie, and the car. I am alone in the house now, in the place that will surely witness my death.

That was this morning. This afternoon, in desperation, I phoned Maggie, receiver pressed firmly against my good ear, on the pretext of thanking her for the card but actually just to hear her warm, compassionate voice. But, as if in response to Judy's accusations, she was rather cold towards me, as if dealing with a business call rather than a personal one.

"Yeah, Russ, this is really bad luck," she said, "but I'm sure you'll pull through."

I mumbled a reply, wondering whether to tell her the full truth, hesitating.

"By the way," she continued, "I'm getting married next month. On the fifth. You're invited, if you're well enough, that is."

"I'll come if I can," I replied and hung up.

Thursday:

Things have moved apace. I am now totally deaf, both ears having closed up. If an ambulance arrives to take me to the hospital I will not be able to hear it. If Judy rings up to see how I am I will not know it.

All my hair has fallen out. I must look like a giant embryo, my skin now being completely smooth and soft, like an invertebrate's. Also I am badly constipated. The last time I managed to urinate was yesterday afternoon, and I think that may turn out to be the final occasion for yours truly.

As a result I am trying to eat and drink only what I consider to be absolutely necessary. As my nose is now blocked up I am forced to breathe through my mouth. Taking nourishment, therefore, also involves holding my breath for long periods of time.

My right eye is closing up, just as the left did two weeks ago. Cooking is now an impossibility and I must eat cold food from tins and packets. This afternoon I accidentally started on some dog biscuits. Spitting them out, I realized that taste is one of the few sensations left to me.

This evening I again considered the option of suicide but for a second time I decided against it. There is something of the pioneer about me. My affliction is, as far as I know, unique, I feel a certain obligation, a certain duty, to see it through to the bitter end in the hope of helping some future victim. I am, therefore, leaving this diary in an accessible place so that whoever may chance upon it may be able to put my words and case history to good use.

A naive belief, possibly, but a last shred of hope for me to cling onto.

Friday:

I am now completely blind. These last few words are being recorded on a cassette recorder. I apologize for the low volume but I cannot open my mouth too wide for my lips are growing together. My breathing is rapid and shallow.

This is it. This is the end of the line for yours truly, Russell Parkes.

How do I feel at the moment? Surprisingly, there is a strain of optimism in my thoughts. I am leaving one world, the world outside my body, and will very soon be totally isolated in another world, the one inside my sealed-up body.

I wonder what I will find.

THE GENERATION WALTZ
Charles L. Grant

Illustration by Andrew Smith

Charles L. Grant's latest novel is For Fear of the Night, *which makes it around thirty novels he's published, under a variety of bylines and in a number of different genres. In the field of dark fantasy we should mention* The Hour of the Oxrun Dead, The Last Call of Mourning, A Quiet Night of Fear, The Soft Whisper of the Dead, The Nesting, Night Songs *and* The Pet. *The author of over one hundred short stories, he has appeared in all the major fiction markets and anthologies and had his stories collected in* Tales from the Nightside, A Glow of Candles, Nightmare Seasons *and* The Orchard. *He is also a prolific editor of anthologies, the best-known being his acclaimed* Shadows *series. A winner of both the Nebula and World Fantasy Awards, Charles L. Grant is renowned for his quiet, dark, atmospheric terrors, of which 'The Generation Waltz' is a memorable example.*

R AIN; and the settling of leaves into sodden masses at the bases of trees, into dark flapping huddles around the bars of storm drains, into slaps of wet colour against windshields, against windows, against unsuspecting faces; it cleans the streets and fouls the gutters, washes the panes and muddies the sills; it rattles on the roof, hisses through branches, splashes in harsh applause on the uncertain pavement.

It comes without warning in spite of the clouds; it stays forever in spite

'He thought it a distortion in the glass'

of the sun.

The wind, what there was of it, kept the rain away from the Logans' front porch, and Edwin stood on the straw welcome mat and watched it turn twilight into full dark. He was shivering, but he would not fold his arms or put his hands into his pockets or tuck his chin a little closer to his chest. He felt nothing, in fact, of the cold that came with the mid-autumn storm; he would feel nothing at all as long as Gram Mannix was inside, in the parlour, lying in her coffin while the family kept watch.

And only once did he wonder if he knew what he was doing.

The door opened slowly, its top hinge rusted and sounding its age, the coil that pulled it to just strong enough to make it slam when the knob was released.

He shifted to one side, pushed a finger over the tip of his nose, and glanced sideways at his wife.

"You'll freeze out here," Laura said unconvincingly. She was thin in her black dress, pinched with her dark hair pulled away from her face.

He rubbed his nose again. "I'll live."

She gripped her upper arms as the wind gusted a spray of mist into her face. A quick turn of her head as if ducking a blow. "Think it'll be long?"

"How should I know?"

"Well, it was your idea, not mine," she reminded him. "She's your family, thank God."

He would have argued, but he would have lost. Just as he had lost when she'd managed to find the rationalizations that blamed him for what their son had become—a kidnapper, a murderer, and a dead young man in the middle of a police assault on his rented home two thousand bloodied miles away from the nest. The victim had been a twelve-year-old girl; the police moved in when Sean had thrown out her arm to prove his demands were serious.

No, he had said to the authorities and the reporters, *I don't know why he did it. He left when he was eighteen. He was what you might call a difficult boy. Yes, I guess you could say that. Headstrong. Like his grandmother. We never saw him again until we saw him on the news.*

Adversity, then, was supposed to pull the parents together, strengthen them and their commitments to each other. And for a while it did. For a while they stood back-to-back and fought off the world—until the question they were asked they began to ask in earnest of themselves: Which one of them was to blame for turning Sean into a monster?

Laura had finally left him, claiming she needed time, needed distance, needed. . .something. . .to give her the wherewithal to think, and to wonder why his family was tainted and hers had to suffer. Sean had been disowned; Ed's family, not hers.

But when she returned two months later, they had embraced, had made love, and had barely touched each other since. Neither wanted to face the hell alone, and someone was better than no one at all.

They didn't really love each other, but they knew each other, and that was much preferable to starting all over.

"Talk to your brother," she urged him softly. "You're only staying because he wanted this nonsense to go on."

Another opporunity to disagree; another pass. She was right. As long as Tan was willing to see this thing through, he was too; at least, he amended silently, until tomorrow morning. Then he was going to pack their bags, tell Tan he could keep the damned house, and the jewelry, and the safe deposit box, and the bank accounts, and he was going back home. With Laura.

"I don't know," he said.

"Oh, Edwin," she said gently, "you're too nice, you know that? You're just too nice."

He supposed he was, though he didn't think it was bad. "Tan," he said then, "well, he has a notion."

She laughed without a sound. "Tan always has a notion of some kind or other. And if you remember, the last time he did he nearly went bankrupt."

"It looks like he's doing all right now."

"That, my love, is because he is a walking, talking, but I'm not so sure about breathing, miracle. No matter what happens, he always lands on his feet. Maybe lawyers are like that, I don't know. But he's . . .well, damnit, Ed, he's a creep and he never loses."

And that too he imagined was right. All of it. Tan's setbacks were never as serious as he made them sound, and Ed had often wondered how they'd come from the same womb. Luck, it seemed, had been passed on to the younger son, while the elder had to fight for everything he had.

"Lord, I feel like I've been here forever," she said, "and this is only the first day." A sigh, and a shudder. "My God, and there are actually two more to go." When he said nothing, she watched the street, watched the rain. "I can't believe I really agreed to this. I must be nuts."

He shrugged with a lift of his shoulders, a tilt of his head. "No, I don't think so. We're just nosey. She's the one who was crazy."

She closed her eyes and moved closer. "We could be arrested for this, you know. There must be laws against it. Don't they have to be buried right away or something? Or embalmed? Something like that?"

He didn't know. He hadn't bothered to ask since it wasn't his house, only his grandmother. His brother, who had lived in Oxrun Station since the death of their parents, made no assurances one way or the other, and as long as a patrol car didn't come screeching up the curb with warrants and guns blazing, he had no real argument with what they were doing. After all, Gram was Gram, and even after her insides had turned to hell, he wasn't going to fight her.

Laura asked if he wanted a cup of coffee, and he nodded. After she returned inside, he moved closer to the railing and heard the gutters running, and the spill of water as it gushed out of the drainpipe onto the gravel lip. He seemed to recall a rain barrel there, but he could not summon much more than the idea. Just as he'd been unable to bring to mind more than an image of Gram as she lay dying in her room, up there on the third floor in the refurbished attic.

Eight years it had taken before she succumbed. Every day of it, every minute of it a battle. Heels dug into the mattress, nails into claws, pale lips drawn back and teeth bared. She dared hang on for all that time—making deals with God, making deals with the Devil, making deals with the ghosts she saw in the rafters—and only when his son was killed did she falter, and her bluff was called, and the call was made and Ed came home.

And the moment he saw her body lying on the white satin, he saw her in her bed, upstairs, the day he had left three years ago, when she had smiled and told him not to worry, she'd either die or beat it, and the way things were going in this horrible world it didn't make much difference to her one way or the other.

"Poor Sean," she had said in a voice much deeper than she'd had before the illness. A look up, apologetic. "He was my favourite, are you mad?"

"No, Gram," he'd told her truthfully. "Though I'll never understand it."

She had smiled and pulled the thick braid of grey hair over her shoulder to stroke it—her talisman, and her souvener. "Think I'll make another deal with God."

He waited, smelling lavender and flour and the faint scent of her dying.

"Think I'll ask Him to take me now and bring him back."

"A bad deal, Gram," he'd said without thinking.

She scowled. "That, boy, is a cruel and ungodly thing to say about your only son."

"My only son, Gram, was a bastard. A sadist. Why he turned out that way I don't know. But he did. And because he's my son, I miss him. And because he was what he was, though, I don't miss the bastard a bit."

She turned her head away, but he hadn't been dismissed. Gram always cleared her throat after saying all she had to say; in public or on the telephone, that was the period in her speeches.

"He was like me," she'd whispered then. "Too much like me. Too much

81

of me passed on. Skipped your folks, you and your brother, thank God. Sean got it all."

An argument would have been fruitless. Gram Mannix was hard, scornful, bitter about too many things, but she never as far as he knew took pleasure in hurting people the way his son had. She knew that, yet the boy was still her favourite, and only when he thought of his own childhood did Edwin resent it, and wonder how it could be.

Before he'd left, he had kissed her cheek. It was dry, but not brittle, and when she grabbed his hand and made him promise to be sure Tan gave her the wake she wanted, he'd nodded because her grip was breaking the bones in his fingers.

On the way home on the train that afternoon, he had prayed for the first time in a hundred years that she would beat the odds; and when she died, he blamed it on Sean.

The rain turned briefly to a sheeting that drowned the cars at the curb, and set the weathervane atop the roof to spinning so rapidly he could hear the creaking.

Like the bones of an old woman trying to waltz.

He swallowed, waited, but the tears didn't come. Maybe later, he thought; maybe later.

The door opened again, and Tan strode to the top of the steps. He was a head taller than Edwin, wider, his dark suit tailored and his black shoes polished high enough to reflect the lightning. A finger poked and dug into his ear, and was cleaned swiftly on a handkerchief that flashed in and out of his hip pocket.

"Brother," he said, "I don't think your wife approves."

"She doesn't approve of this town, much less what we're doing."

Tan didn't turn. "What's wrong with the Station?"

He didn't answer; it wasn't worth it. But he had felt it when he'd attended school on High Street, when he heard the wind in October, when he walked through the park and saw the dancing shadows. The Station wasn't normal, and as soon as he could, he had left for the world.

Tan loved it.

"No," Ed said again, "she doesn't approve. As a matter of fact, I'm not so sure I do, either."

His brother looked at him, indecisive—should he frown, or laugh at a joke he didn't get?

"She's not coming back, Tan, and neither is Sean."

Tan managed to squirm without moving.

"The cancer got her, and the police got my son, and the more I think about it, the more silly it all gets."

"But you're here," Tan told him. "You can't think it's that silly if you're here."

82

He leaned over the railing, and snapped back when a few drops landed on his neck. He smiled foolishly and dried himself with a palm. "You want to know the truth?"

Tan nodded.

"I'm afraid she might do it. She was certainly ornery enough. And if I'm not here, and she does, she'll kill me." His smile was meant to be embarrassed, but it wavered and faded when he saw the look on his brother's face. "Hey," he said, "don't tell me you really think—"

"Don't be a fool, brother," Tan snapped, and jammed his hands into his pockets. He stared at the rain, at the lights in the houses across the street, swivelling his head slowly when a mail truck hissed by. His shoulders rose, paused, lowered. "I made a promise on her deathbed."

"She's dead, Tan. She won't know."

"I keep my promises, brother. My word means something to me."

Edwin moved to the far end of the porch, shaking his head. He never would have given it credence had someone else told him, but Tan was actually afraid of the old lady—just as afraid as he was. All those years of sniping and friendly arguing, and the big bastard was afraid. He smiled. He arched an eyebrow. He turned and saw Gram through the living room window.

The coffin was set on a bier of brass and walnut. There was nothing so prosaic as candlesticks at each end, but the corner lamps were dim enough to give the illusion. The lid was open, lowered so he could see her face on the pillow, could see the top half of her white brocade dress with the high lace collar and the baby pearls sewn into the pattern. Her dancing dress, she called it, the one she waltzed in at her children's and her grandchildren's weddings.

And now, he thought, she wanted to do one more step.

But she was dead. She didn't look asleep in there, she looked dead. Ravaged. Untouched by undertakers, only a hasty application of what little makeup she wore when she was alive.

She was dead, the dancing dress a waste of good jewelry and good memory.

Then he saw Sean.

At first he thought it was a reflection of someone come up behind him; a fast, fearful look, and he was wrong.

Then he thought it a distortion in the glass. It was old, as old as the house, and he knew the panes had a tendency to settle, to ripple, to become marred with time. But when he shifted slightly, almost unaware he was trying not to make any noise, the boy was still there.

His mouth opened to call his brother, and closed again. This was one delusion he wasn't going to share, not if he wanted to stay out of the rest home.

The boy was standing beside the head of the coffin, dressed in a dark shirt, dark slacks, his dark hair curled down to his shoulders. As he had been when they'd buried him, only he and Laura attending. His face was shadowed by the lamp's uncertain light, but Edwin knew he was looking at Gram. Staring at her. Finally reaching out to touch the dead woman's cheek.

Edwin held his breath against a scream, and could hear Tan shifting and clearing his throat.

The corpse shuddered, the coffin trembled, and Sean lay his other hand to her other cheek; the corpse jumped in its satin bed and the coffin rocked on the bier, and Edwin stumbled back until he came up against the railing.

"Hey, brother, what's the matter?"

He shook his head.

"Jesus, are you all right?"

Then Sean drew back his hands, and looked up.

His eyes were dead, his lips pale, his forehead punctured still with the undertaker's clumsy attempts to hide the entry of the bullets. Five of them that had blown away the back of his skull.

He looked up, and saw his father, and he smiled.

"Ed, I'm going to get Laura. You look like hell."

"Shut up, Tan," he said.

"Hey, now wait a minute."

"Shut up."

Sean's lips moved, and bits of dead skin flaked onto Gram's face.

i was her favourite

"Sean," he whispered.

Tan grabbed his arm, and Edwin shook himself free.

in her will i get everything

"Ed—" Tan grabbed him again, and he whirled, his hand cocked for a punch. "Now hold it, Ed, hold it! It's a delayed reaction, that's all."

Everything, pop, i got it all

"Laura!" Tan called, backing away nervously. "Laura, come out here a minute, okay?"

everything

Edwin looked, and Sean was gone. The coffin was still and the lamps were still dim, and he staggered along the porch to throw open the door. Laura was hurrying out of the kitchen when he raced by her into the front room and looked down at the old woman.

"Tan?" Laura said.

Tan stood beside her, and cocked his head toward her husband. "I think he's . . . I don't know, but I think he's finally realized that Gram is really dead."

Edwin leaned closer. "The will, Tan. Gran's will."

"Yes? What about it?"

"Sean inherits the whole thing, right?"

"Right," Tan said. "But how did you . . . not that it matters, because it's moot, actually. She never bothered to change it since she knew it would go to us since the boy was—was dead."

Edwin frowned and leaned closer.

"Ed, what are you doing?" Laura said nervously.

"Us?" Ed said.

"Sure. You, me, Laura. Sole survivors."

His hands gripped the coffin's edge to balance him, and his lips were close enough to kiss the dead woman. On her right cheek were particles of dust, odd-shaped until he blew softly and they fluttered away to the satin. Not dust. Bits of skin.

from gram to me to you, pop; don't worry about them, you've got what's important

He straightened and looked at his wife who still blamed him for fate, looked at his brother who blamed him for leaving.

Everything, he thought, and walked out of the room.

Everything, he thought as he went to the kitchen and searched for a knife.

Everything, he thought, and he didn't mind a bit.

DON'T OPEN THAT DOOR
Frances Garfield

Illustration by Jim Pitts

Frances Garfield paid us the tribute of saying that Fantasy Tales *rekindled her interest in writing horror stories. During the late 1930s and early '40s she had a number of stories published in* Weird Tales *and* Amazing Stories, *although she was never prolific. She is of course better known as Frances Wellman, wife of author Manly Wade Wellman. She kept thinking up ideas for horror stories for her husband who dismissed them as 'women's stories' and suggested she write them herself. So Frances returned to the typewriter and over the past decade has contributed to such markets as* Whispers, Fantasy Book, Kadath *and* The Year's Best Horror Stories. *A regular contributor to* Fantasy Tales, *Frances revised her 1940* Weird Tales *story 'The Forbidden Cupboard' for our fifth issue.*

I PANTED up the two dark flights of stairs and gratefully set my heavy suitcase down. Father O'Neil stood smiling at the open door of my new flat. He was the very picture of chubby, priestly embarrassment.

"I came to check out your apartment. The place isn't ready yet, Miss Hampton," he protested gently. "We didn't expect you until tomorrow, you know."

"Yes, but I took an earlier train," I apologised. "And the expressman's on the way with my trunk. But don't worry, I'm not fussy."

'The closet must never be opened'

The good father looked at me thoughtfully. The dim light from inside barely lighted him. With his round belly, his black garments and comfortable warmth of nature, he reminded me of an old-fashioned depot stove. Even though his face was solemn just now, its rosy cheer was like a glow of friendly flame.

"Well, come in," he said at last. "I musn't keep you on your own doorstep," and he managed a smile. "I promised to look after you and I shall. I'm in charge here. You probably think this an odd arrangement."

"Oh, not at all," I made haste to say, though I burned with curiosity to know why a priest should double as landlord. It was through Lola Knesbec, my old professor of boarding-school English, that I had rented the flat. She knew that I hoped to live and write in New York, and that I wanted the cheapest of comfortable lodgings.

Her old friend, Father O'Neil, had been able to find this place in an ancient house on the border of Greenwich Village. There was an exchange of letters, careful consideration of my financial and character references—and here I was, at once happy and mystified by the whole thing.

I entered and almost squealed with delight.

"You like it," murmured Father O'Neil.

"Tremendously," I assured him, and I did. No tawdry stage set this, reminiscent of a crass Village studio with cushioned divans, batik hangings and busy colour; no, nor imitation Park Avenue, with mock oriental rugs and plush over-stuffings.

The huge living room was papered in fawn brown up to the lofty ceiling, with heavy carved mouldings, wide-boarded flooring, and an open fireplace. A beautiful one, with a white marble slab for mantel. The furniture, of massive wood with leather cushioning, looked the epitome of unfashionable comfort. A full-length mirror hung opposite the front door. The windows, set high in the front wall, were lined with varnished maple shutters. To such a room might Washington Irving once have come to tea, talking of headless horsemen to his crinolined hostess; while outside the half-open shutters, might have paced and shivered a beautiful, wretched man in unseasonable nankeen, hungry for the lunch he could not buy—Edgar Allan Poe.

"Miss Knesbec was sure you'd like it," smiled the priest. He was bathed from the knees up in grey light from the autumn sky, shimmering in from the window. His shanks looked darker and more indistinct in the shadows. And on the floor in a corner I saw a pile of dust and lint that had been swept up to be carried out. Someone had told me that in New York I would fight a constant battle with the dirt of the city, and I was glad that someone had tried to help me win that fight.

Father O'Neil caught my glance and smiled. "Where does it all come from? And where does it go?" he asked. "Do you mind if I smoke?"

"Please do."

The room was soon filled with the reassuring smell of good tobacco. And I remembered that I wanted to ask him about a fascinating tale that Lola Knesbec had not had time to finish.

"I understand that this house once belonged to Guilford Colt," I began, and waited for a response. It came and it was more intriguing than I had dared hope. Father O'Neil's face lost some of its jolly pinkness, and the hand that held the pipe seemed to quiver.

"What do you know about Guilford Colt?" he demanded.

"Only that he was an eccentric scholar of the middle Nineteenth Century," I replied, "Miss Knesbec told our class that his character had been used by Fitz-James O'Brien in that story about the wizard who brought evil little toys to life, and by Nathaniel Hawthorne for the alchemical genius in *The Birthmark*—"

"Miss Knesbec was right," said Father O'Neil; "only those tales did not do Guilford Colt grim enough justice."

"And didn't this house once belong to him?" I pursued.

"It did," the priest nodded. "Colt conducted many experiments here—experiments that escaped police notice because legal men scorn to believe such things. But he and his works were baleful. A group of citizens visited him one night in a very vengeful mood—he had made himself too dreadful a figure, even for the strange but tolerant community that was New York City a century ago. And in the morning he had vanished.

"I doubt if he could be frightened," continued Father O'Neil gravely. "He was the sort who had gone beyond fear. But—yes, he was driven away. And he had no heirs.

"This house remained closed until recently, when we of the Church, as trustees, were asked to put it to some profitable use. We had it cleaned up—though for some reason, it had never gotten terribly dirty—and prepared to rent the flats. After, I must add, taking certain precautions."

As he spoke this last word, his eyes wandered as if in spite of themselves, to a grey-painted door in the rear of the room. Then he spoke more brightly.

"I've laid a fire. Shall I light it?"

"Please," I said, slipping my arms out of my coat and putting it across my shoulders like a cape to keep me from shivering.

The grey door must be a clothes closet. I moved toward it and drew down the latch, but it would not open. A heavy chest of dark wood, that at first had seemed a great shadow, had been shoved against the bottom of the door.

"Wait. Don't open that door, my child," called Father O'Neil urgently. He had crouched down to light the fire, but now, moving quickly for so plump a little man, he was at my side. His pleasant face was strained, anxious.

"Not if you say so," I said, rather startled.

He smiled once more, in an obvious effort to reassure me. "The closet must never be opened. In fact it is to be plastered over—then it will be cut off permanently and can be forgotten."

"I doubt if I could move that chest, in any case," I smiled back.

"Please don't try."

I moved across to the little bedroom, and laid my coat upon a stout old walnut bed.

"Now I need to get at my work," I said, coming back into the parlor. "I'm racing a deadline as usual."

89

"Then I'll go. I, too, have work." Father O'Neil put his pipe into his mouth and picked up his broad, black hat. "I'd like to come back later, if you don't mind. I'm expecting some workmen. And I want to be sure you're comfortable. We'll try not to bother you—interrupt your writing."

"It's quite all right," I assured him. "Why don't you come have tea with me, around four o'clock?" I asked on impulse. "I feel that we've destined to be friends."

"Thank you. I'll be delighted" And he smiled himself out.

Almost immediately the expressman arrived with my trunk and suitcase and I set about arranging my few possessions.

I sat down to work. It was hardly an inspiring job. Merely ghost-writing the biography of a business man, even titled by his widow—*Truman Murdock, A Man's Man*. But I set out to make a good job of it, compromising between the canonizing desired by his heirs and my own idea of what a biography should be.

I had planned a good first chapter, at least—a widely imaginary pedigree. His patronymic suggested the dashing follower of Roderick Dhu. I might even quote a few lines of Walter Scott. His mother's name had been Blake—perhaps this made him a connection of Percy Blake, who is supposed to have sat for Frans Hals as the *Laughing Cavalier*.

Was that a rustling behind me? I ignored it.

I sat down to my typewriter drumming away at page after ambling page. "Each of us," I paraphrased something I had seen in *The Reader's Digest*, "is a great vehicle in which ride all the ghosts of his forefathers..."

What was it that stirred behind me?

I swung quickly around. No living thing was there. I saw only the room, the furniture, the fireplace in which the coals had died to a ruddy glow, the grey closet door spanned by the dark chest... There was the noise again—or was it?

I rose, crossed the floor, and stopped just beside the forbidden closet, listening with both my ears.

Silence now. I must have been mistaken. Nervous in a new house. Excited by Father O'Neil's air of mystery. Who, and in what stodgy book, has said that an imaginative mind is bad for the nerves? Standing beside the closet, I wished that Father O'Neil had not been so insistent and mysterious about my leaving that grey door shut.

My impulse to pry was natural, if extreme. How could I be otherwise? All the way back to the wife of Bluebeard, to Pandora and her box, women have found forbidden things fascinating.

I examined the heavy chest that did duty as obstacle. Heavy, dark, roughly carved, it looked like something out of the hold of a pirate ship, but undoubtedly it was only a modern imitation. The lock, for instance,

90

was a new automatic one, and fast. I could not lift the lid. The closet door, by contrast, was not locked, it did not even have a keyhole—only a heavy iron latch, painted dull grey like the rest of the panel, and once before I had lifted it.

Looking closely now, I saw that there was a mark in the paint above that latch, a line undoubtedly scraped when the paint had been fresh. A cross—no, it was more than a cross. At the upper end of the vertical bar was attached a sickle-like curve. I had seen such a device before, in my childhood, and an old Irish cook had called it the "God-have-mercy sign." Why was such a sign here?

I thought again of Guilford Colt. The legend, so skimmed over by Lola Knesbec and also by Father O'Neil, had suggested his belief, if not even power, in black magic. Did this closet have some connection with his tale? If so, why shouldn't the priest tell the truth about it instead of just plastering the door closed? The amateur-detective impulse, which I surely share with every human being, became strong and insistent.

I bent, seized the handle at the side of the chest, and tried to drag it away. Who could have helped but try? The tremendous weight baffled me. I tugged and tugged. Suddenly I straightened up guiltily as a sharp ringing filled the room.

The telephone—I hadn't even noticed it before. It rang again, and yet again, while I walked toward it. I was angered for a moment and I snatched up the instrument with a needlessly sharp, "Hello."

"Hello," said a high, drawling voice, hard to classify as male or female, young or old, "I want to order a ton of coal."

"You have the wrong number," I replied.

"But I bought coal there last year," protested the drawl. "Isn't this Chelsea 3-0036?"

The instrument's foot showed me that it was. But I could only repeat that I had no coal for sale.

"You used to sell coal," reproached the scratchy voice.

"There's some mistake," I said, feeling somehow guilty. "This is a private home." And I hung up.

Blasted telephone, I thought savagely, interrupting my work. But I hadn't been working. What I had been doing was what I was supposed not to do. I had been trying to get at that closet.

I walked back to the chest. The problem must be faced. Father O'Neil had warned me not to open the door. But I felt I must prove to myself that I did not fear that persistent little scratching noise—that I was probably imagining the whole thing. And I did need storage space.

I bent and pulled vigorously. This time I succeeded in pulling it slantwise back from the door.

91

Sound again. Shrill now, almost tuneful. It flowed in and filled the room, but from outside.

Mystified and intrigued, I hurried to the window. It was open a crack and I lifted it all the way and leaned out.

The shrill music came from a penny whistle and the ragged old man who played it was getting real melody out of his cheap little instrument. He was playing *Annie Laurie*, and as I peered out at him, he shifted to *Bonnie Doon*. Then he saw me. Taking the whistle from his mouth, he gazed up at my window.

"Please, kind lady!" he bawled winningly.

My purse lay on that very sill, and I quickly opened it and fumbled out a few coins. These I flung down to him. They fell in a little rain about my serenader, who quickly retrieved them with eagerly darting fingers. In thanks he doffed the filthiest tweed cap I ever saw, played me a little chirpy flourish on his whistle, and tramped away.

Another interruption from my attempt on the closet's secret—I frowned. Was something marshalling these telephones and whistles against me? Supporting Father O'Neil's orders? I toyed with the fancy for only a moment. Then I told myself that it sprang from a falsely guilty conscience. I went straight and purposefully to the chest, pushing away a little pile of sweepings with my foot. Once more I clutched the handle, and drew the chest away with a mighty heave. Straightening up, I pressed down the latch and opened the closet door.

I looked into absolute blackness, a formless and spacious cave. It was as though it had no sides or back. As though it were, instead, a vast and lightless valley, filled with a dusty atmosphere of nothingness. But close to me, so close that it must have dangled against the door when shut, there hung something.

An old garment, dirty old garment, I thought. I was about to step in and examine it when my eye caught some writing on the inner side of the door. It was crude, heavy writing, as though done with a coarse instrument—maybe even a human finger. What kind of ink could turn such a rusty brown? I began to read:

They are shutting me up in here to die. They think they are rid of me—but I'll live. Life, in some sort, will be mine forever. The rotting of my flesh and my bones will only set my spirit free.

I write this in my own blood. They left me nothing else. I'm not done with this world. Whenever this prison is opened—

I felt relieved and a bit amused. Was this the bizarre legend that Father O'Neil had considered so dreadful? Saying that it was written in human blood was enough to discredit it with me. Melodramatic stuff from paperback thrillers. I must chide him for thinking me a simple, credulous child. I moved back, smiling to myself.

The fabric-like dusty figure made a fluttery movement toward me.

I looked again.

There was a filmy openwork about it, like lace or cobwebs. Not a garment, after all—more probably a rotting grey curtain, stowed here and forgotten.

But does a curtain stand erect, to the width and height of a human figure, no hook or rod to support it? Does a curtain turn toward you a misshapen upper roundness like an ill-modeled head? Does it look at you with two black caverns like a mockery of eyes? And does it lift a pair of ragged trails that seem to gesture and grope like skinny arms?

Does a curtain drift slowly toward you, staring from its hollow eyes, stretching toward you, as if it meant to catch you and grapple with you?

I fell back, my face gone all frostily dry, and my legs drained of bone and blood. The thing left its grimy cave, pausing only an instant on the threshold.

I had a good view of it. Not a curtain—no honest fabric at all. The cloudy mass of it, like a concentration of lint and dust and smoke, stirred in all its particles. Yet it clung to a filmy shape-travesty of a human being. The dull black eye blotches narrowed themselves, as if the grey light hurt them. And then it drifted into the open, around the chest and moved meaningfully at me.

Its arms raised themselves to a level with the face. I saw, with increased horror, that its hands had no fingers—they flapped like dusty mittens, opening and extending, to take hold of me. I raised my hands to fight back. My heart had become a giant fist, trying to batter free my ribs. For, by some telepathy, I realised what the creature wanted.

He intended to don me, as a human, living garment. As if changing his clothes, to do his devil's doings in my human flesh. This was the thing that had been shut away from the world for so long—was now visiting its wrath and will upon me—once Guilford Colt, the sorcerer, now an entity made stronger and ghastlier by death's change.

Something blocked my retreat. I tried to scream. The wall beside my writing table was at my shoulder blades. Within reach lay my dictionary, bought last week for a dollar in a second hand bookstore. I clutched it, hurled it with all my strength. It struck square upon the cheek, or where the cheek should be. There was no noise, nor did the book stop in its flight. It flew through and past—into the inky blackness of the closet.

Where it had struck the creature, there gaped a ragged hole. I could see the wall through it. The shape neither paused nor faltered. It drifted closer. I felt its purposeful menace like a crushing weight.

The arms spread horizontally, to pin me against the wall. I tried to dodge away. Too late. I was caught in the angle of the wall and the table. The torn, musty head seemed to crinkle its eyes, as though it were smiling, although it had no mouth.

The window. Could I reach it, lift it, scream for help? Jump out? Too late for that now. The dirtfluff mittens were soaring before my face, fumbling to reach my neck. An aura of dust thickened in my nose and throat. A wave of cold passed over me like drifting snow. Dimness weighted my eyelids. My head lolled upon my shoulders as if it were improperly fastened there. The round head, the dull eye patches, were within inches of my face. I could not cry out.

All at once the creature shrank back. Suddenly. As frightened as I had been seconds before. Something was coming. There. A noise. A knock, loud and free, at the door. After a moment, a voice:

"Miss Hampton?"

Father O'Neil was outside. And the thing knew him.

I had no doubt the thing had been outfaced by Father O'Neil. And it feared him as an even more fearsome creature might. It fluttered back swiftly toward the closet, almost falling in its haste.

All at once I could breath again, could hold myself erect without leaning on the wall.

"Miss Hampton, may I come in?" called Father O'Neil.

The filmy grey creature had reached the open door, drooping limply in its eagerness to seek shelter there. It drew inside, becoming small and dark to merge with the shadows. I managed to hurry after, to throw myself against the chest, to push against the panel, swinging it shut with my weight.

My fingers groped with the latch. Let it fall into place.

"F-Father O'Neil." I found my voice at last. "Yes, please. Come in."

And my front door opened. Still sagging against the closet door, I turned to this blessedly welcome visitor, all hearty girth and churchly blackness and rosy, beaming face.

"I'm afraid that I'm just a few minutes early for tea," he began. Then broke off, staring at me. "Why, Miss Hampton, what are you doing at that door?"

He hurried across to me.

I moved from the chest and came toward him.

"You weren't going to open that closet?" He scolded me earnestly.

I shook my head mutely. Not all the publisher's gold, the critics' acclaim, the reading public's patronage, would ever tempt me to touch that latch again.

Father O'Neil pushed the chest back into its sentinel position with one quick, solid shove. It stood heavily on guard again.

"Once more, I urge you never to look into that closet, Miss Hampton," he said. "I've just talked to the plasterers and they are on their way now to guarantee that it won't be done. Meanwhile, though it will be plastered shut, I must ask you to promise never to try to open that door."

"I promise," I assured him with husky eagerness.

Helping me to set out the tea things, Father O'Neil noticed the shaking of my hands and apologised.

"I'm sorry to have frightened you, my child. But it is important—extremely important."

I nodded.

Father O'Neil had saved me without himself knowing how close a thing it had been. Now I made a silent decision. Why trouble him by confessing my narrow escape? I held his respect and friendship, so why worry him by letting him know what I had done? Already the memory was becoming blessedly unreal, dream-like, in the warmth of his presence.

"I was tempted for a moment to tell you the whole story, but I doubt if you'd believe it," he said.

"No," I agreed, as brightly as I could manage. "No, I might not."

THE FROLIC
Thomas Ligotti

Illustration by David Lloyd

Thomas Ligotti's select body of work has mainly appeared in the small press, which is a shame, because anyone who has read anything by this gifted craftsman will immediately recognise his distinctive and subtle style. A first collection was published a few years ago by Silver Scarab Press, Songs of a Dead Dreamer, *the title of which sums up the author's sometimes oblique, but ravishingly compelling prose. We are proud to present a slightly revised version of 'The Frolic' which is a real horror, mainly for its underplaying of the fears it so readily feeds us. The readers voted it the best story published in* Fantasy Tales 9.*

In a beautiful home in a beautiful part of town—the town of Nolgate, site of the state prison—Dr. Munck examined the evening newspaper while his young wife lounged on a sofa nearby, lazily flipping through the colorful parade of a fashion magazine. Their daughter Norleen was upstairs asleep, or perhaps she was illicitly enjoying an after-hours session with the new color television she'd received on her birthday the week before. If so, her violation of the bedtime rule went undetected due to the affluent expanse between bedroom and living room, where her parents heard no sounds of disobedience. The house was quiet. The neighbourhood and the rest of the town were also quiet in various ways, all of them slightly distracting to the doctor's wife. But so far Leslie had only dared complain of the town's social lethargy in the most joking fashion ("Another exciting evening at the Munck's monastic hideaway"). She knew her husband was quite dedicated to this new position of his in this new place. Perhaps tonight, though, he would exhibit some encouraging symptoms of disenchantment with his work.

"How did it go today, David?" she asked, her radiant eyes peeking over the magazine cover, where another pair of eyes radiated a glossy gaze. "You were pretty quiet at dinner."

"It went about the same," said David without lowering the small-town newspaper to look at his wife.

"Does that mean you don't want to talk about it?"

He folded the newspaper backwards and his upper body appeared. "That's how it sounded, didn't it?"

"Yes, it certainly did. Are you okay today?" she asked, laying aside the magazine on the coffee table and offering her complete attention.

"Severely doubting, that's how I am." He said this with a kind of far off reflectiveness.

"Anything particularly doubtful, Dr. Munck?"

"Only everything," he answered.

"Shall I make us drinks?"

"That would be much appreciated."

Leslie walked to another part of the living room and from a large cabinet pulled out some bottles and some glasses. From the kitchen she brought out a supply of ice cubes in a brown plastic bucket. The sounds of drink-making were unusually audible in the living room's plush quiet. The drapes were drawn on all windows except the one in the corner where an Aphrodite sculpture posed. Beyond that window was a deserted streetlighted street and a piece of moon above the opulent leafage of spring trees.

"There you go, doctor," she said, handing him a glass that was very thick at its base and tapered almost undetectably toward its rim. "We have a little lump of hash left over to go with that, if you like."

"Definitely no. The situation's borderline as it is," he replied.

"Why? Aren't things going well with your work?"

"You mean my work at the prison?"

"Yes, of course."

"You could say *at the prison* once in a while. Not always talk in the abstract. Overtly recognize my chosen professional environment, my—"

"All right, all right. How's things at the wonderful prison, dear? Is that better?" She paused and took a deep gulp from her glass, then calmed a little. "I'm sorry about the snideness, David."

"No, I deserved it. I'm blaming you for long realizing something I can't

97

'In the black foaming gutters and black alleys of Paradise.......

bring myself to admit."

"Which is?" she prompted.

"Which is that maybe it was not the wisest decision to move here and take this saintly mission upon my psychologist's shoulders."

This remark was an indication of even deeper disenchantment than Leslie had hoped for. But somehow these words did not cheer her the way she thought they would. She could distantly hear the moving vans pulling up to the house, but the sound was no longer as pleasing as it once was.

"You said you wanted to do something more than treat urban neuroses. Something more meaningful, more challenging."

"What I wanted, masochistically, was a thankless job, an impossible one. And I got it."

"Is it really that bad?" Leslie inquired, not quite believing she asked the question with such encouraging skepticism about the actual severity of the situation. She congratulated herself for placing David's self-esteem above her own desire for a change of venue, important as she felt this was.

"I'm afraid it is that bad. When I first visited the prison's psychiatric section and met the other doctors, I swore I wouldn't become as hopeless and cruelly cynical as they were. Things would be different with me. I overestimated myself by a wide margin, though. Today one of the orderlies

98

'my awe-struck little deer and I have gone frolicking'

was beaten up again by two of the prisoners, excuse me, 'patients.' Last week it was Dr. Valdman, that's why I was so moody on Norleen's birthday. So far I've been lucky. All they do is spit at me. Well, they can all rot in that hellhole as far as I'm concerned."

David felt his own words lingering atmospherically in the room, tainting the serenity of the house. Until then their home had been an insular haven beyond the contamination of the prison, an imposing structure outside the town limits. Now its psychic imposition transcended the limits of physical distance. Inner distance constricted, and David sensed the massive prison walls shadowing the cozy neighbourhood outside.

"Do you know why I was late tonight?" he asked his wife.

"No, why?"

"Because I had an overlong chat with a fellow who hasn't got a name yet."

"The one you told me about who won't tell anyone where he's from or what his real name is?"

"That's him. He's just an example of the pernicious monstrosity of that place. Worse than a beast, a rabid animal. Demented blind agression . . . and clever. Because of this cute name game of his, he was classified as unsuitable for the regular prison population and thus we in the psychiatric section ended up with him. According to him, though, he has

99

plenty of names, no less than a thousand, none of which he's condescended to speak in anyone's presence. From my point of view, he doesn't really have use for any human name. But we're stuck with him, no name and all."

"Do you call him that, 'no name'?"

"Maybe we should, but no, we don't."

"So what do you call him, then?"

"Well, he was convicted as John Doe, and since then everyone refers to him by that name. They've yet to uncover any official documentation on him, though. Neither his fingerprints nor photograph corresponds to any record of previous convictions. I understand he was picked up in a stolen car parked in front of an elementary school. An observant neighbor reported him as a suspicious character frequently seen in the area. Everyone was on the alert, I guess, after the first few disappearances from the school, and the police were watching him just as he was walking a new victim to his car. That's when they made the arrest. But his version of the story is a little different. He says he was fully aware of his pursuers and expected; even wanted, to be caught, convicted, and exiled to the penitentiary."

"Why?"

"Why? Why ask why? Why ask a psychotic to explain his own motivation, it only becomes more confusing. And John Doe is even less scrutable than most."

"What do you mean?" asked Leslie.

"I can tell you by narrating a little scene from the interview I had with him today. I asked him if he knew why he was in prison.

" 'For frolicking,' he said.

"What does that mean?' I asked.

His reply was: 'Mean, mean, mean. You're a meany.'

"That childish ranting somehow sounded to me as if he were mimicking his victims. I'd really had enough right then but foolishly continued the interview.

" 'Do you know why you can't leave here?' I calmly asked a poor variant of my original inquiry.

" 'Who says I can't? I'll just go when I want to. But I don't want to yet.'

" 'Why not?' I naturally questioned.

"'I just got here,' he said. 'Thought I'd take a rest after frolicking so hard. But I want to be in with all the others. Unquestionably stimulating atmosphere. When can I go with them, when can I?'"

"Can you believe that? It would be cruel, though, to put him in with the normal population, not to say he doesn't deserve this cruelty. The average inmate despises Doe's kind of crime, and there's really no predicting what would happen if we put him in there and the others found out what he was convicted for."

"So he has to stay in the psychiatric section for the rest of his term?" asked Leslie.

"He doesn't think so. He thinks he can leave whenever he wants."

"And can he?" questioned Leslie with a firm absence of facetiousness in her voice. This had always been one of her weightiest fears about living in this prison town, that every moment of the day and night there were horrible fiends plotting to escape through what she envisioned as rather papery walls. To raise a child in such surroundings was another of her objections to her husband's work.

"I told you before, Leslie, there have been very few successful escapes from that prison. If an inmate does get beyond the walls, his first impulse is usually one of practical self-preservation, and he tries to get as far away as possible from this town, which is probably the safest place to be in the event of an escape. Anyway, most escapees are apprehended within hours after they've gotten out."

"What about a prisoner like John Doe? Does he have this sense of 'practical self-preservation,' or would he rather just hang around and do damage to someone?"

"Prisoners like that don't escape in the normal course of things. They just bounce off the walls but not over them. You know what I mean?"

Leslie said she understood, but this did not in the least lessen the potency of her fears, which found their source in an imaginary prison in an imaginary town, one where anything could happen as long as it approached the hideous. Morbidity had never been among her strong points, and she loathed its intrusion on her character. And for all his ready reassurance about the able security of the state prison, David also seemed to be profoundly uneasy. He was sitting very still now, holding his drink between his knees and appearing to listen for something.

"What's wrong, David?" asked Leslie.

"I thought I heard . . . a sound."

"A sound like what?"

"Can't describe it exactly. A faraway noise."

He stood up and looked around, as if to see whether the sound had left some tell-tale clue in the surrounding stillness of the house, perhaps a smeary sonic print somewhere.

"I'm going to check on Norleen," he said, setting his glass down rather abruptly on the table beside his chair and splashing the drink. He walked across the living room, down the front hallway, up the three segments of the stairway, and then down the upstairs hall in the opposite direction he'd traveled downstairs. Peeking into his daughter's room he saw her tiny figure resting comfortably, a sleepy embrace wrapped about the form of a stuffed Bambi. She still occasionally slept with an in-animate companion, even though she was getting a little old for this. But her psychologist father was careful not to question her right to this childish comfort. Before leaving the room Dr. Munck lowered the window which was partially open on that warm spring evening.

When he returned to the living room he delivered the wonderfully routine message that Norleen was peacefully asleep. In a gesture containing faint overnotes of celebratory relief, Leslie made them two fresh drinks, after which she said:

"David, you said you had an 'overlong chat' with that John Doe. Not that I'm morbidly curious or anything, but did you ever get him to reveal very much about himself?"

"Sure," Dr. Munck replied, rolling an ice cube around in his mouth. His voice was now more relaxed.

"He told me everything about himself, and on the surface all of it was nonsense. I asked him in a casually interested sort of way where he was from.

" 'No place' he replied like a psychotic simpleton.

" 'No place?' I probed.

" 'Yes, precisely there, Herr Doktor.'

" 'Where were you born?' I asked in another brilliant alternate form of the question.

"'Which time do you mean, you meany?' he said back to me, and so forth. I could go on with this dialogue—"

"You do a pretty good John Doe imitation, I must say."

"Thank you, but I couldn't keep it up for very long. It wouldn't be easy to imitate all his different voices and levels of articulateness. He may be something akin to a multiple personality, I'm not sure. I'd have to go over the tape of the interview to see if any patterns of coherency turn up, possibly something the detectives could use to establish the man's identity, if he has one left. The tragic part is that this is all, of course, totally useless information as far as the victims of Doe's crimes are concerned. . . and as far as I'm concerned it really is too. I'm no aesthete of pathology. It's never been my ambition to merely study disease for its own sake, without effecting some kind of improvement, trying to help someone who would just as soon see me dead, or worse. I used to believe in rehabilitation, maybe with too much naiveté and idealism. But those people, those *things* at the prison are only an ugly stain on existence. The hell with them," he concluded, draining his glass until the ice cubes rattled.

"Want another?" Leslie asked with a smooth therapeutic tone to her voice.

David smiled now, the previous outburst having purged him somewhat. "Let's get drunk, shall we?"

Leslie collected his glass for a refill. Now there was reason to celebrate, she thought. Her husband was not giving up his work from a sense of ineffectual failure but from anger. The anger would turn to resignation, the resignation to indifference, and then everything would be as it had been before; they could leave the town and move back home. In fact, they could move anywhere they liked, maybe take a long vaction first, treat Norleen to some sunny place. Leslie thought of all this as she made the drinks in the quiet of that beautiful room. This quiet was no longer an indication of soundless stagnancy but a delicious lulling prelude to the formlessly promising days to come. The indistinct happiness of the future glowed inside her along with the alcohol; she was gravid with pleasant prophecies. Perhaps the time was now right to have another child, a little brother for Norleen. But that could wait just a while longer . . . a lifetime of possibilities lay ahead, awaiting their wishes like a distinguished and fatherly genie.

Before returning with the drinks, Leslie went into the kitchen. She had something she wanted to give her husband, and this was the prefect time to do it. A little token to show David that although his job had proved a sad waste of his worthy efforts, she had nevertheless supported his work in her own way. With a drink in each hand, she held under her left elbow the small box she had got from the kitchen.

"What's that? asked David, taking his drink.

"Something for you, art lover. I bought it at that little shop where they sell things the inmates at the penetentiary make—belts, jewelry, ashtrays, you know."

"I know," David said with an unusual lack of enthusiasm.

"I didn't think anyone actually bought that staff."

"I, for one, did. I thought it would help to support those prisoners who are doing something *creative*, instead of . . . well, instead of destructive things."

"Creativity isn't always an index of niceness, Leslie," David admonished.

"Wait'll you see it before passing judgement," she said, opening the flap of the box. "There—isn't that nice work?" She set the piece on the coffee table.

Dr. Munck now plunged into that depth of sobriety which can only be reached by falling from a prior alcoholic height. He looked at the object. Of course he had seen it before, watched it being tenderly molded and caressed by creative hands, until he sickened and could watch no more. It was the head of a young boy, discovered in grey formless clay and glossily glazed in blue. The face expressing a kind of ecstatic serenity,

103

the labyrinthine simplicity of a visionary's gaze.

"Well, what do you think of it?" asked Leslie.

David looked at his wife and said solemnly: "Please put it back in the box. And then get rid of it."

"Get rid of it? Why?"

"Why? Because I know which of the inmates did this work. He was very proud of it, and I even forced a grudging compliment for the craftmanship of the thing. It's obviously remarkable. But then he told me who the boy was. That expression of sky-blue peacefulness wasn't on the boy's face when they found him lying in a field about six months ago."

"No, David," said Leslie as premature denial of what she was expecting her husband to reveal.

"This was his last—and according to him most memorable—'frolic'."

"Oh my God," Leslie murmured softly, placing her right hand to her cheek. Then with both hands she gently placed the boy of blue back in his box. "I'll return it to the shop . . .," she said quietly.

"Do it soon, Leslie. I don't know how much longer we'll be residing at this address."

In the moody silence that followed Leslie briefly contemplated the now openly expressed and definite reality of their departure from the town of Nolgate, their escape. Then she said: "David, did he actually talk about the things he did. I mean about—"

"I know what you mean. Yes, he did," answered Dr. Munck with a professional seriousness.

"Poor David," Leslie sympathized.

"Actually it wasn't that much of an ordeal. The conversation we had could even be called stimulating in a clinical sort of way. He described his 'frolicking' in a kind of unreal and highly imaginative manner that wasn't always hideous to listen to. The strange beauty of this thing in the box here—disturbing as it is—somewhat parallels the language he used when talking about those poor kids. At times I couldn't help being fascinated, though maybe I was shielding my feelings with a psychologist's detachment. Sometimes you just have to distance yourself, even if it means becoming a little less human.

"Anyway, nothing that he said was sickeningly graphic in the way you might imagine. When he told me about his last and 'most memorable frolic,' it was with a powerful sense of wonder and nostalgia, shocking as that sounds to me now. It seemed to be a kind of homesickness, though his 'home' is a ramshackle ruin of his decaying mind. His psychosis has bred this blasphemous fairyland which exists in a powerful way for him, and despite the demented grandeur of his thousand names he actually sees himself as only a minor figure in this world—a mediocre courtier in a broken-down kingdom of horror. This is really interesting when you consider the egoistical magnificence that a lot of psychopaths would attribute to themselves given a limitless imaginary realm in which they could play any imaginary role. But not John Doe. He's a comparatively lazy demi-demon from a place, a No Place, where dizzy chaos is the norm, a state of affairs on which he gluttonously thrives. Which is as good a description as any of the metaphysical economy of a psychotic's universe.

"There's actually quite a poetic geography to his interior dreamland as he describes it. He talked about a place that sounded like the back alleys of some cosmic slum, an inner-dimensional dead end. Which might be an indication of a ghetto upbringing in Doe's past. And if so, his insanity has transformed these ghetto memories into a realm that cross-breeds a banal streetcorner reality with a psychopath's paradise. This is where he does his 'frolicking' with what he calls his 'awe-struck company,' the place possibly being an abandoned building of some kind or even an accomodating sewer somewhere. I say this based on his repeated mentioning of 'the jolly river of refuse' and 'the jagged heaps in shadows,' which are certainly mad transmutations of a literal wasteland. Less fathomable are his memories of a moonlit corridor where mirrors scream and laugh, dark peaks of some kind that won't remain still, a stairway that's 'broken' in a very strange way, though this last one fits in with the background of a dilapidated slum.

"But despite all these dream back-drops in Doe's imagination, the mundane evidence of his frolics still points to a crime of very familiar, down-to-earth horrors. A run-of-the-mill atrocity. Consistently enough, Doe says he made the evidence look that way as a deliberate afterthought, that what he really means by 'frolicking' is a type of activity quite different from, even opposed to the crime for which he was convicted. This term probably has some private associations rooted in his past."

Dr. Munck paused and rattled around the ice cubes in his empty glass. Leslie seemed to have drifted while he was speaking. She had lit a cigarette and was now leaning on the arm of the sofa with her legs up on its cushions, so that her knees pointed at her husband.

"You should really quit smoking someday," he said.

Leslie lowered her eyes like a child mildly chastised. "I promise that as soon as we move I'll quit. Is that a deal?"

"Deal," said David. "And I have another proposal for you. First let me tell you that I've definitely decided to hand in my resignation no later than tomorrow morning."

"Isn't that a little soon," asked Leslie, hoping it wasn't.

"Believe me, no one will be surprised. I don't think anyone will even care. Anyway, my proposal is that tomorrow we take Norleen and rent a place up north for a few days or so. We could go horseback riding. Remember how she loved it last summer? What do you say?"

"That sounds nice," Leslie agreed with a deep glow of enthusiasm. "Very nice, in fact."

"And on the way back we can drop off Norleen at your parents'. She can stay there while we take care of the business of moving out of this house, maybe find an apartment temporarily. I don't think they'll mind having her for a week or so, do you?"

"No, of course not, they'll love it. But what's the great rush? Norleen's still in school, you know. Maybe we should wait till the year ends. It's just a month away."

David sat in silence for a moment, apparently ordering his thoughts.

"David, what's wrong?" asked Leslie with just a slight quiver of anxiety in her voice.

"Nothing is actually wrong, nothing at all. But—"

"But what?"

"Well, it has to do with the prison. I know I sounded very smug in telling you how safe we are from prison escapes and I still maintain that we are. But the one prisoner I've told you about is very strange, as I'm sure you've gathered. He is positively psychotic . . . and then again he's something else."

Leslie quizzed her husband with her eyes. "I thought you said he just bounces off the walls, not—"

"Yes, much of the time he's like that. But sometimes, well . . ."

"What are you trying to say, David?" asked a puzzled and increasingly uneasy Leslie.

"It's something that Doe said when I was talking with him today. Nothing really definite. But I'd feel infinitely more comfortable about the whole thing if Norleen stayed with your parents until we can organize ourselves."

Leslie lit another cigarette. "Tell me what he said that bothers you so much," she said firmly. "I should know too."

"When I tell you, you'll probably just think I'm a little crazy myself. You didn't talk to him, though, and I did. The tone, or rather the many different tones of his voice; the shifting expressions on that lean face. Much of the time I talked to him I had the feeling he was beyond me in some way, I don't know exactly how: I'm sure it was just the customary behaviour of the psychopath—trying to shock the doctor. It gives them a sense of power."

"Tell me what he said," Leslie insisted.

"All right, I'll tell you. As I said, it's probably nothing. But toward the end of the interview today, when we were talking about those kids, and actually kids in general, he said something I didn't like at all. He said it

106

with an affected accent, Scottish this time with a little German flavor thrown in. He said: 'You wouldn't be havin' a misbehavin' laddie nor a little colleen of your own, now would you, Professor von Munck?' Then he grinned at me silently.

"Now I'm sure he was deliberately trying to upset me without, however, having any purpose in mind other than that."

"But what he said, David: 'nor a little colleen.'"

'Grammatically, of course, it should have been 'or' not 'nor', but I'm sure it wasn't anything except a case of bad grammar."

"You didn't mention anything about Norleen, did you?"

"Of course not. That's not exactly the kind of thing I would talk about with these patients," said Dr. Munck.

"Then why did he say it like that?"

"I have no idea. He possesses a very weird sort of cleverness, speaking much of the time with vague hints and suggestions, even subtle jokes. He could have heard things about me from people on the staff, I suppose. Then again, it might be just an innocent coincidence." He looked to his wife for comment.

"You're probably right," Leslie agreed with an ambivalent eagerness to believe in this conclusion. "All the same, I think I understand why you want Norleen to stay with my parents. Not that anything might happen—"

"Not at all. There's no reason to think anything would happen. Maybe this is a case of the doctor being out-psyched by his patient, but I don't really care anymore. Any reasonable person would be a little spooked after spending months upon months in the chaos and physical danger of that place . . . the murderers, the rapists, the dregs of the dregs. It's impossible to lead a normal family life while working under those conditions. You saw how I was on Norleen's birthday."

"I know. Not the best surroundings in which to bring up a child."

"David nodded slowly. "Yes. When I think of how she looked when I went to check on her a little while ago, hugging one of those stuffed security blankets of hers." He took a sip of his drink.

"It was a new one, I noticed. Did you buy it when you were out shopping today?"

Leslie glazed blankly. "The only thing I bought was that," she said, pointing at the box on the coffee table. "What 'new one' do you mean?"

"The stuffed Bambi. Maybe she had it before and I just never noticed it," he said, partially dismissing the issue.

"Well, if she had it before, it didn't come from me," Leslie said quite resolutely.

"Nor me."

"I don't remember her having it when I put her to bed," said Leslie.

"Well, she had it when I looked in on her after hearing..."

David paused with a look on his face of intense thought, an indication of some frantic, rummaging search within.

"What's the matter, David?" Leslie asked, her voice weakening.

"I'm not sure exactly. It's as if I know something and don't know it at the same time."

But Dr. Munck was beginning to know. With his left hand he covered the back of his neck, warming it. Was there a draft coming from somewhere, another part of the house? This was not the kind of house to be drafty, not a broken down place where the wind gets in through ancient attic boards and warped windowframes. There actually was quite a wind blowing now; he could hear it hunting around outside and could see the resltess trees through the window behind the Aphrodite sculpture. The goddess posed languidly with her flawless head leaning back, her blind eyes contemplating the ceiling and beyond. But beyond the ceiling? Beyond the hollow snoozing of the wind, cold and dead? And the draft? What?

"David, do you feel a draft?" asked his wife.

"Yes," he replied very loudly and with unusual force.

"Yes," he repeated, rising out of the chair, walking across the room, his steps quickening toward the stairs, up the three segments, then running down the second floor hallway. "Norleen, Norleen," he chanted before reaching the half-closed door of her room. He could feel the breeze coming from there.

He knew and did not know.

He groped for the light switch. It was low, the height of a child. He turned on the light. The child was gone. Across the room the window was wide open, the white translucent curtains flapping upwards on the invading wind. Alone on the bed was the stuffed animal, torn, its soft entrails littering the mattress. Now stuffed inside, blooming out like a flower, was a piece of paper, and Dr. Munck could discern within its folds a fragment of the prison's letterhead. But the note was not a typed message of official business: the handwriting varied from a neat italic script to a child's scrawl. He desperately stared at the words for what seemed an infinite interval without comprehending their message. Then, finally, the meaning sank heavily in.

Dr. Monk, read the note from inside the animal, *We leave this behind in your capable hands, for in the black-foaming gutters and back alleys of paradise, in the dank windowless gloom of some galactic cellar, in the hollow pearly whorls found in sewerlike seas, in starless cities of insanity, and in their slums... my awe-struck little deer and I have gone frolicking. See you anon. Jonathan Doe.*

"David?" he heard his wife's voice inquire from an infinite distance at the bottom of the stairs. "Is everthing all right?"

Then the beautiful house was no longer quiet, for there rang a bright freezing scream of laughter, the pefect sound to accompany a passing anecdote of some obscure hell.

THE SORCERER'S JEWEL
Robert Bloch

Illustration by Randy Broecker

Robert Bloch's name has become synonymous with his 1959 novel,
Psycho, and Alfred Hitchcock's famous movie adaptation. Of course
he'll need no further introduction to readers of horror stories, and since
his first appearance in Weird Tales *in 1935 he has written hundreds*
of short stories and novels—often combining his own unique blend of
psychological horror and black humour—as well as numerous film,
television and radio scripts. His most recent novels include Psycho
II, The Night of the Ripper *and and Twilight Zone, The Movie, while*
500,000 words comprising The Selected Stories of Robert Bloch *have*
appeared in three deluxe volumes. 'The Sorcerer's Jewel' originally
appeared in the February 1939 issue of Strange Stories *under the*
psuedonym 'Tarleton Fiske', where it languished until the thirteenth
issue of Fantasy Tales. *A further outing for this one, we think you will*
find, is well deserved.

BY RIGHTS, I should not be telling this story, David is the one to tell
it, but then, David is dead. Or is he?

  That's the thought that haunts me, the dreadful possibility that in some
way David Niles is still alive—in some unnatural, unimaginable way, alive.
That is why I shall tell the story; unburden myself of the onerous weight
which is slowly crushing my mind.

110

'They can extend their forces back through the jewel to suck you down'

But David Niles could do it properly. Niles was a photographer; he could give the technical terms, perhaps explain coherently many things that I do not pretend to understand. I can only guess, or hint.

Niles and I shared a studio together for several years. It was a true partnership—we were both friends and business associates. This was peculiar in itself, for we were dissimilar types, with widely divergent interests. We differed in almost every particular.

I am tall, thin, and dark. Niles was short, plump, and fair. I am naturally lazy, moody, inclined towards introspection. Niles was always tense with energy, high-spirited, volatile. My chief interests, in latter years, have leaned towards metaphysics and a study of occultism. Niles was a skeptic, a materialist, and above all, a scientist. Still, together, we formed an integrated personality—I, the dreamer; Niles, the doer.

Our mutual business association, as I have already intimated, lay in the field of photography.

David Niles was one of the most brilliant personalities in the domain of modern portrait photography. For several years prior to our association he had done salon work, exhibiting internationally and creating a reputation which brought him a considerable income from private sittings.

At the time of our meeting he had become dissatisfied with commercial work. Photography, he argued, was an art; an art best nourished by serious, solitary study unimpeded by the demands of catering to customers. He therefore determined to retire for a year or so and devote himself to experiment.

I was the partner he chose for the work. He had lately become a devotee of the William Mortensen school of photography. Mortensen, of course, is the leading exponent of fantasy in photography; his studies of monstrosities and grotesques are widely known. Niles believed that in fantasy, photography most closely approximated true art. The idea of picturing the abstract fascinated him; the thought that a modern camera could photograph dream worlds and blend fancy with reality seemed intriguing. That's where I came in.

Niles knew of my interest in the occult, knew that I had made a study of mythology. I was to serve as technical advisor on his subject matter. The arrangement pleased us both.

At first Niles limited himself to studies in physiognomy. With his usual thoroughness, he mastered the technique of photographic makeup and hired models whose features lent themselves to the application of gargoylian disguises. I handled the matter of checking over reference works, finding illustrations in old books of legends to use in devising suitable makeup.

112

Niles did a study of Pan, one of a satyr, and a Medusa. He became interested in demons, and we spent some time on his *Gallery of Fiends* series; Asmodeus, Azaziel, Sammael, and Beelzebub. They were surprisingly good.

But for some reason or other, Niles was not satisfied. The quality of the photographs was excellent, the posing effective, the characterization superb. And still Niles did not feel that he was achieving his goal.

"Human figures," he stormed. "Human faces are, after all, only human faces, no matter how much you cover them up with grease-paint and putty. What I want is the soul of Fantasy, not the outward aping."

He strode up and down the studio, gesticulating in his feverish manner. "What have we got?" he demanded. "A lot of stupid horror-movie faces. Amateur Karloffs. Kid stuff. No, we must find something else."

So the next phase was modelling clay. I was handy here, for I had a rudimentary knowledge of sculpture. We spent hours on composing scenes from an imaginary Inferno; constructing bat-winged figures that flew against bizarre, other-worldly backgrounds of fire, and great malignant demons that squatted and brooded on jagged peaks overlooking the Fiery Pit.

But here, too, Niles could not find what he was looking for.

One night he exploded again, after finishing a set. With a sweep of his arm he smashed the papier-maché set and its clay figures to the floor.

"Hokum," he muttered. "Peepshow, pennydreadful stuff."

I sighed, getting set to listen patiently to a further tirade.

"I don't want to be the Gustave Doré of photography, or the Sime, or even the Artzybasheff," he said. "I don't want to copy any style. What I'm after is something original, something I can claim as absolutely individual."

I shrugged. Wisdom had taught me to keep my mouth shut and let Niles talk himself out.

"I've been on the wrong track," he declared. "If I photograph things as they are, that's all I'm going to get. I build a clay set, and by Heaven, when I photograph it, all I can get is a picture of that clay set—a flat, two-dimensional thing at that. I take a portrait of a man in makeup and my result is a photo of a man in makeup. I can't hope to catch something with the camera that isn't there. The answer is—change the camera. Let the instrument do the work."

I saw his argument, and conceded its validity.

The following few weeks Niles' existence was a frenzy of experimental activity. He began to take montage shots. Then he worked with odd papers, odder exposures. He even reverted to the Mortensen principles and employed distortion—bending and twisting the negative so that prints showed elongated or flattened figures in nightmarish fashion.

An ordinary man's forehead, under these methods, would register as being hydrocephalic; his eyes might appear as bulging beacons illumined by insane lights. The perspective of nightmare, the nuances of oneirodynia, the hallucinative images of the demented were reproduced by distortion. Pictures were shadowed, shaded; portions blocked out or moulded into weird backgrounds.

And then came a night when Niles again paced the floor, tracing a restless path through piles of torn-up prints. "I'm not getting it," he murmured. "I can take a natural subject and distort it, but I can't actually change its content. In order to photograph the unreal, I must see the unreal. *See the unreal*—Good Lord, why didn't I think of that before?"

He stood before me, his hands twitching. "I studied painting once, you know. My instructor—old Gifford, the portrait man—hung a certain picture in his studio. It was the old boy's masterpiece. The painting was a water scene, in oils; a winter scene of a farmhouse.

"Now here's the point. Gifford had two pairs of spectacles; one sensitive to infra-red, the other to ultra-violet rays. He'd show a guest the winter scene, then ask him to try on the first pair of spectacles and look again. Through the glasses the picture showed the same farmhouse on a summer day. The second pair of lenses gave a view of the farmhouse in autumn. He had painted three layers, and the proper lenses each showed a different picture."

"So what?" I ventured.

Niles talked faster, his excitement increasing.

"So this. Remember the war? The Germans used to camouflage machine-gun nests and field batteries. They did it quite elaborately; painting the guns with leafy hues and using artificial plant formations to cover them up. Well, American observation posts employed ultra-violet lenses in field glasses to spot the camouflaging. Through the glasses the natural leaves showed up in entirely different colours in comparison to the artificially painted ones, which lacked ultra-violet pigment."

"I still don't see the point."

"Use ultra-violet and infra-red lenses in photography and we'll get the same effect," he almost shouted.

"But isn't that just an extension of the ordinary colour-filter principle?" I asked.

"Perhaps. But we can combine them with reground lenses of various types—lenses that will distort perspective in themselves. So far we've merely distorted form, shape. But with both colour and form distorted, we can achieve the type of photography I'm striving for—fantasy, pure

114

and simple. We'll focus on fantasy and reproduce it without tampering with any objects. Can you imagine what this room will look like with its colours reversed, some of them absent completely; with the furniture shapes altered, the very walls distorted?"

I couldn't, but I was soon privileged to actually see it. For Niles at once began another cycle; he experimented endlessly with the new lenses he brought in daily. He sent out special orders for grinding, spent time studying the physical laws of light, enmeshed himself in technicalities I cannot pretend to comprehend. The results were startling.

The *outré* views he had promised me materialized. After a final day of effort before the camera and in the dark-room, we gazed together on a wonderful new world created right here in our own studio. I marvelled at some of the effects Niles had created.

"Splendid," he gloated. "It all seems to tie in with the accepted scientific theories too. Know what I mean? The Einsteinian notions of coexistence; the space-time continuum ideas."

"The Fourth Dimension?" I echoed.

"Exactly. New Worlds all around us—within us. Worlds we never dream of exist simultaneously with our own; right here in this spot there are other existences. Other furniture, other people, perhaps. And other physical laws. New forms, new colour."

"That sounds metaphysical to me, rather than scientific," I observed. "You're speaking of the Astral Plane—the continuous linkage of existence."

We were back again at our perpetual squabbling point—science or occultism; physical versus psychical reality.

"The Fourth Dimension is Science's way of interpreting the metaphysical truths of existence," I maintained.

"The metaphysical truths of existence are the psychological lies of *dementia praecox* victims," he asserted.

"Your pictures don't lie," I answered.

"My pictures are taken by recognized scientific means," he said.

"Your pictures are taken by means older than science," I replied. "Ever hear of lithomancy? Divination by the use of jewels. Ever hear of crystal-gazing? For ages, men have peered into the depths of precious stones, gazed through polished, specially cut and ground glasses, and seen new worlds."

"Absurd. Any oculist can tell you that—"

"You don't have to finish that one," I cut in. "Any oculist will tell you that we really see everything upside down. Our minds alone interpret the retinal image as being right-side up. Any oculist will tell you that muscularly, a near-sighted person is really far-sighted, and a far-sighted, person is near-sighted."

I warmed to my theme. "Any oculist will tell you that the hand is quicker than the eye; that mirages and hallucinations are actually 'seen' by the brain, rather than by the actual retina. In fact, any oculist will tell you that the phenomenon of sight has very little to do with either perception or the true laws of light.

"Look at the cat—contrary to popular impression a nyctalops. Yet men can train themselves similarly. Reading, too, is a matter of the mind rather than of minute perception. And so I say to you, don't be too sure of your laws of optics, and your scientific theories of light. We see a lot no physical laws will ever explain. The Fourth Dimension can be approached only through angles—science must concede that in theorization. And your lenses are cut similarly. It all goes back to occultism in the end—occultism, not 'oculism' or ophthalmology."

It was a long speech for me, and it must have astonished Niles, who glowered at me, speechless for once.

"I'll prove it," I went on. "Let me cut you a lens."

"What?"

"I'll go down to a friend of mine and borrow a few stones from him. There are some Egyptian crystals there which were used by the seers for divination. They claimed that they could see other worlds through the angles of the jewels. And I'm willing to bet you that you'll get pictures through them that will make you forget experiments with Iceland spar and quartz and all the rest; pictures you and your scientific ideas won't so readily explain."

"All right. I'll call you on that," Niles snapped. Bring me the stones."

So the next day I went down to Issac Voorden's. I went with misgivings. The truth was that I had been half-bragging when I had spoken about the properties of jewels and glasses. I knew that such things were much used for prophecy and various forms of lithomancy; but as to whether I could procure one, and whether it could be ground into a camera lens, I was not at all certain.

Still, I spoke to Isaac Voorden. He was the logical person to go to. His antique shop down on South Kinnikinnic, pervaded by an aura of mysticism, was a little fortress that preserved the past. Issac Voorden made a profession of his hobby and a hobby of his profession; he lived on metaphysics and dabbled in antiques. He spent the greater portion of his time in the musty back rooms of his establishment, and left the care of his shop to a clerk.

Here in the rear of the place he had relics of other days which made his commercial antiques seem bright and new by contrast. The centuried symbols of magic, alchemy, and the secret sciences fascinated Voorden; he had gathered unto himself a collection of statuettes, talismans, fetiches and other paraphernalia of wizardry that would have been hard to match.

It was from Isaac, then, that I expected help in my quest, and he gave it to me. I told my story of Niles' photographic problems. The sallow-faced, thin-lipped little antique-dealer listened, his eyebrows crawling over his forehead like astonished black beetles.

"Very interesting," he said, when I had concluded. His rasping voice and preoccupied manner betokened the introverted pedant—Isaac always seemed to be delivering a lecture to himself.

"Very, very interesting," he repeated. "David Niles has had illustrious predecessors. The priests of Ishtar sought in their Mysteries to peer beyond the veil; and they looked through crystals. The first crude telescopes of Egypt were fashioned by men who sought to use them in seeing beyond the stars and unlocking the gates of the Infinite. The Druids contemplated pools of water, and the mad emperors sought the Heavenly Stairway in China, hoping to ascend by gazing at turning rubies whilst under the influence of drugs.

"Yes, your friend Niles has an age-old wish, and expresses it in a timeless fashion. It is the wish that animated Appolonius, and Paracelsus, and the absurd, posturing Cagliostro. Men have always sought to see the Infinite; to walk between the worlds—and sometimes that wish has been granted."

I cut in. Voorden was wound up for the afternoon, but I wanted my information.

"They say there are jewels that hold queer visions," I murmured. Unconsciously, I adopted Voorden's pomposity of speech. He smiled, slowly.

"I have them here," he replied.

"Niles does not believe that," I countered.

"Many do not believe. But there is a stone once used by Friar Bacon, and a set of crystals which intrigued Theophrastus, and divining-jewels that the Aztecs peered through before the blood-sacrifice. Jewels, you know, are mathematical figures of light—they reflect within their facets. And who knows but that in some way those angles impinge on other worlds? Perhaps they reach out and transmute poly-angularity so that gazing into their depths, we become aware of it three-dimensionally. The ancients used angles in magic; the moderns do the same thing and call it mathematics. De Sitter says—"

"The jewel for the camera lens," I interrupted.

"I am sorry, my friend. Of course. I think I have one that should prove eminently suitable. The Star of Sechmet. Very ancient, but not costly. Stolen from the crown of the Lioness-headed Goddess during a Roman

117

invasion of Egypt. It was carried to Rome and placed in the vestal girdle of the High-Priestess of Diana. The barbarians took it, cut the jewel into a rounded stone. The black centuries swallowed it.

'But it is known that Axenos the Elder bathed it in the red, yellow and blue flames, and sought to employ it as a Philosopher's Stone. With it he was reputed to have seen beyond the Veil and commanded the Gnomes, the Sylphs, the Salamanders, and the Undines. It formed part of the collection of Gilles De Rais, and he was said to have visioned within its depths the concept of *Homonculus*. It disappeared again, but a monograph I have mentions it as forming part of the secret collection of the Count St. Germain during his ritual services in Paris. I bought it in Amsterdam from a Russian priest whose eyes had been burned out by little grey brother Rasputin. He claimed to have divinated with it and foretold—"

I broke in again at this point. "You will cut the stone so that it may be used as a photographic lens, then," I repeated. "And when shall I have it?"

"You young men have no love for quiet conversation," he rebuked me. "Tomorrow, if you like. You understand, the jewel has only a great sentimental value to me; I have never experimented with it personally. All that I ask is that you report to me your findings with it. And I counsel you that if the camera reveals what I think it will, you promise to take care in using it. There is danger in invading the realms—"

He was still chattering away as I bowed out. Great character, Isaac.

The following afternoon I called and took the little package which he proffered me.

That evening I gave it to Niles.

Together we unwrapped the cloudy lens, I had given Voorden the specifications of the large camera we ordinarily employed in our later work—a reflex, with a reflecting mirror set inside so that we could easily peer through and view the focus. Voorden had done his work amazingly well—Niles gave a little snort of astonishment before he commented, "Nice job."

He lost no time in changing the lenses and inserting the Star of Sechmet. He bent over the camera—I shall never forget the sight of him there—and his plump body loomed large against the shadowed walls of the studio. I thought of a stooping alchemist peering into a crystal to seek instructions from the demons that danced within.

Niles jerked erect with a grunt. "The devil!" he muttered. "It's all cloudy. Can't make any adjustment. The whole thing's a fake."

"Let me try."

I took my place and stared through a grey mass. Yes, it was merely a dull lens. Or was it?

A hint of movement in the cloudy grey.

A swirling, as of parted mists. A dancing light. The fog was dispersing, and it seemed to be opening up—opening to a view that receded far into the distance. The wall it was focused on appeared faintly, very tiny, as though through the reverse end of binoculars. The wall began to fade, so that I thought of a ghost room, with ectoplasmic lines. Then it fled away, and something new loomed large before the camera. Something grew out of empty space. Abruptly—focus!

I think I shouted. Certainly a scream seared across my brain.

For I saw Hell.

At first only angles and angles, weaving and shifting in light that was of no colour, yet phosphorescent. And out of the angles, a flat black plain that stretched upward, endlessly, without horizon. It was moving, and the angles moved, and yet through the lurching roll as of a ship's deck in heavy seas, I saw cubes, triangles, mathematical figures of bewildering size and complexity. There were thousands of them, lines of light in the shape of polyhedrons. And as I gazed, they *changed*.

Changed into forms.

Those forms—they were spawned only in delirium; only in nightmare and dreams of the Pit. There were grinning demons that skulked on padding paws across the endless moving plain; there were shapeless toadstools with tentacles ending in Cyclopean eyes; there were fanged heads that rolled towards me, laughing; great hands that curled and crawled like mad spiders. Ghouls, monsters, fiends—the words sprang to my consciousness. And a moment ago they had been mathematical figures!

"Here," I gasped. "Look again, Niles."

He gazed, his face reflecting puzzlement at my agitation. "Still nothing," he grumbled. But watching him I saw the pallor come into his face as he stared more intently.

"Yes!" he hissed. "The mist parting. Yes! The room is smaller, fading. And now—something is rushing up or I'm rushing toward it—angles of light."

"Wait," I said in a low voice, yet triumphantly. "You haven't seen anything yet."

"I see geometrical shapes. Cubic shapes. Polyhedrons of luminance. They cover a plain and—Good God!"

His body shook over the camera.

"I see them!" he cried. "I see them. Dozens of tall, eyeless creatures with heads all hair. Knotted hair, it twists and weaves, and underneath the hair, little wrinkled pink-pulp mouths like the convolution slits of the human brain. And that—*the Goat with the Hands!*"

He made an indescribable sound, fell back shaking, and turned the adjusting device. His eyes were red, he looked as though he had awakened from a fever-sleep.

We each had a drink. We didn't trouble about glasses, we drank from the bottle.

"Well?" I said, when composure had been restored.

"Hallucination," he hazarded, somewhat weakly.

"Want to look again?" I countered. He gave me a wry smile.

"It can't be delusion," I went on. "I didn't see any goat, but we both saw the mists swirl, saw the same plane, the same geometric forms of living light."

"True. But the last—things—were different to each of us. I don't understand."

"I think I do," I said. "If Voorden is right. That jewel is a key. Its angles open to the Astral Plane. The Astral Plane—here, don't shake your head so—corresponds to the scientific conception of the Fourth Dimension, although metaphysicians believe it is an extension of third-dimensional life. That is, when men die their souls enter the Astral Plane and pass through it into another higher form of existence on a higher dimension. The Astral Plane is a sort of No Man's Land existing all about us, where lost souls, and lower entities that have never achieved life, wander forever in a sort of Limbo."

"Hooey."

"A modern criticism. But it's an ancient belief, mirrored in a thousand forms in scores of religions. And wait until you see what I'm getting at. Ever hear of Elementals?"

"Nothing, but a few mentions. Ghosts, aren't they?"

"No—forces. Entities not human, but linked with humanity. They are the *demons* and the *familiars* and the *incubaee* and the *genie* of all religions; the beings that exist invisibly around us and seek traffic with men. Organisms outside three-dimensional life, if you want it in more scientific terminology. They inhabit another space continuum that is nevertheless synchronized and co-existent with our own. They can be viewed, or reached, as ultra-dimensional inhabitants, only through angles. The angles, the facets of this jewel, enabled us to see through to them. They establish a focal point with infinity. What we saw, then, are Elementals."

"All right, *swami*, but why did we see different creatures?" he persisted.

"Because, my dear fellow, we have different brains. At first we both saw geometrical figures. That is the purest form of life they exist in.

"But our minds interpreted these figures into familiar shapes. I saw one type of monstrosity because of my background of mythological study. You received another impression—and I gather from your little comments (you look smug enough now, friend, but you were bleating pretty loudly a while ago and I know you were genuinely impressed) that you drew your images from past dreams and nightmares. I should imagine that a Hungarian peasant, peering through the lens, would see vampires and werewolves.

"It's psychological. In some way that jewel establishes a focal point in more than a visual way. It must also enable those creatures to become aware of us—and they *will* that we see them according to our mental concepts of such entities. In fact, that's how superstition probably originated; these beings at times communicated with men."

Niles made a gesture of impatience. "Dropping the psychological and the nut-house angle for a minute," he said, "I certainly must hand it to your friend Voorden. Whether his story about the jewel is hokum or not, and whether your rather naive explanation is accepted or disbelieved, I still can see that we've stumbled on something quite marvellous. I mean it. The pictures we can take with that camera will be unique in the field. I've never read of any experimental work that even approached this. It goes beyond the wildest Dadaistic or Surrealistic concepts. We'll get actual photographs—but of what, I'll be darned if I can foretell. Your so-called mental concepts were different from mine."

I shook my head as something that Voorden had said came back to me.

"Now look here, Niles. I know you don't believe me, but you believe what you saw in the lens. I saw you shudder; you must admit the horror of those creatures—whether you choose to think they originate in your imagination or in my theory of the Astral Plane, you must recognize the fact that they are a menace to any man's sanity.

"If you see too much of that sort of thing you'll go mad. I'm not being melodramatic. I wouldn't advise looking too closely into that lens now, or spending too much time before it."

"Don't be silly," Niles said.

"Elementals," I persisted, "—and you must believe this—yearn for life. They are cosmic ghouls, feeding on dead soul-bodies; but they long to lure a living man through the planes to them. Consider all legend—it's merely allegory. Stories of men disappearing, selling their souls to the devil, going to foreign worlds; all are founded on the idea of Elementals seeking human prey and dragging men down to their plane."

"Cut it out, it annoys me." Niles was colloquially common in his speech, but his eyes betokened a slight credulity that grew as I ignored his skepticism.

"You say it's superstition," I went on. "I say it's science. Witches, wizards, so-called wonder-workers; the wise men whose secrets built the pyramids—they all employed spells in which they used what? Geometrical figures. They drew angles and pentagons and cabalistic circles. Through the lines they summoned the forces from the Astral Plane—or the outer Dimensions. These forces granted them boons, and in turn they finally were drawn along the angles themselves into the Astral Plane, to pay for the boon with their lives. Witchcraft and geometry are strange bed-fellows, but it's historical fact.

"And so I warn you. You see creatures through the jewel lens, and they see, feel, are in some way aware, of you. They will seek your soul—and just as you can look through the lens at them, they can extend their forces back through the jewel to suck you down. Hypnotic force, of some sort psychology has not yet postulated. Magnetism, telepathy; these are the words psychologists use to describe things they do not fully understand; just as the ancients called such forces magic. Don't look too long or too closely through that jewel."

Niles laughed.

"Tomorrow I'll take the pictures," he declared. "And then we'll see just what your Elementals are like. If it makes you nervous, you can stay away."

"Frankly, I will," I said.

And I did.

The following afternoon I left the studio in Niles'hands.He was tremendously excited. He spoke of using new focusing adjustments to extend part of the field; he wondered what speeds to photograph with, what paper to use for printing. He also speculated as to whether or not the creatures he saw would appear on the finished negative, or merely the amazing light-figures. I left, for I felt growing nervousness and apprehension I did not wish him to see.

I went down to Voorden's.

The shop was open, but the clerk was not there when I passed through the front of the place, although the bell tinkled its usual warning of a customer's approach as I entered the door. I walked back through the gloom to the room where Isaac usually spent his time in study.

He was sitting there in the soft haze peculiar to the lightless chamber; his eyes glazed in rapt attention on the open pages of some old book.

"Isaac," I said. "That jewel has something. Niles and I used it last night, and I think it's a gateway to something incredible. Those divinators of ancient times were no fools. They knew what they were doing—"

Isaac never moved. Imperturbable, he sat and stared through the quiet dusk. There was a little smile on his sallow face.

122

"You promised to look up some more of the jewel's history," I went on. "Did you find anything? It's amazing, you know; quite amazing."

Isaac sat and stared and smiled. I bent forward.

Sitting bolt upright in his chair, hand clutching a pen, Isaac Voorden seemed a modern necromancer. And like many an ancient necromancer who had overstepped the pale, Isaac Voorden was dead.

Stone-dead.

"Isaac!" I shouted. Funny, isn't it, how people always shout the name of the departed upon discovery of death? It's a sort of despairing wail of disbelief at a friend's passing; an invocation, as though the echo of human voice can recall the soul of one that has passed beyond. Beyond— to the Astral Plane?

Quickly I bent over the cold body, stared at the crabbed scrawl covering the paper. I read the notes Voorden had been working on when his pale Visitor had arrived.

They blurred through my brain.

"The Star of Sechmet. Ptolemaic. Aug. Lulla, name of Roman who stole it. See note in Veno's *History*. Lulla died under curse for removing sacred jewel. Point one.

"Priestess of Diana who wore it in vestal girdle also died. For sacrilege. Again, see Veno. Point two. The pattern grows.

"Giles De Rais—his fate is known. He misused the jewel. Yes, it's the inevitable story of violation.

"See *Mysteries of the Worm* for Prinn's chapter on divination. Might be reference concerning jewel during its disappearance.

"Again, the Russian. Claims to have stolen jewel from Rasputin, who used it in prophecy. Rasputin dead. The Russian lost his eyes. And unless he lost his reason, his warnings concerning sacred character of the jewel are to be respected. Points three, four, and five. Whoever or whatever exists in the world opened up by the jewel is not anxious to have the gateway changed, or misused. Cutting the stone, transplanting it from one setting to another, misusing it—all result in death.

"And—I have done all three. God help this man Niles for what he must endure. They may get at him through the stone.

"God help me. There will be a price I must pay; soon.

"Why didn't I think before I gave up the jewel? Now I'm—"

That was all he had written. There was no scrawling off of the interrupted pen, no frozen look of horror, no 'mounting dread' in the text of the writing. Voorden had written it. One minute he was alive, and the next minute he was dead.

Of course it could have been heart-failure, thrombosis, or simply old age. Shock, excitement, anxiety might have brought it on; a stroke may

123

have done it.

But I didn't fool myself. I knew. I rose and ran from that shop as though fiends dogged my heels. And all the way my legs worked in rhythm to a single phrase racing through my brain. "God help Niles."

It was dusk when I unlocked the studio door. The studio was empty, the twilight room darkened. Had Niles gone out?

I prayed so. But where would he go? He wouldn't abandon work. I walked to where the camera loomed; noted the exposure of one film. He must have been called.

I restrained an impulse to peer again through the jewel lens, as I lit the light. No—I did not wish to see that plain again; see those horrible figures dwelling outside laws of space and time, yet—mocking thoughts!—actually existing here around me, in this very room. Worlds within worlds of horror. Where was Niles?

I couldn't brood like this. Why not develop the exposed film? Keep busy. I carried the camera into the dark-room. Ten minutes in darkness, then the regular process. I set the fans going as I hung the dark square up to dry.

My mind teemed with excited conjectures. Would we find a blank photograph? Would it show the angled figures of light? Or would—wonderful possibility—the creatures conjured up by our imaginations appear? Would our brains aid in taking the pictures, as a part of the focal point linked to the camera by the hypnotic jewel? It was a fascinating thought.

The fans hummed as the minutes fled. But where was Niles? Whatever had caused his hasty departure, surely he would have returned by now. And he had left no note.

The door had been locked from outside, and I had the only key.

The thought grinned at me through a wave of horror.

There was no way Niles could have left.

Only one way.

I jammed the dried negative into the printer, with a sheet of ordinary paper.

I pressed down, slipped the print into the developer; waited a moment.

I raced out into the light of the other room, held the finished print, wet and dripping, to the light.

Then I screamed, and smashed that camera, stamped on the jewel until I could control myself sufficiently to pick it up and hurl it through the open window at the further rooftops. I tore print and negative to shreds. And still I screamed, for I could not and never shall be able to erase the memory of what I had seen in that picture Niles had taken.

He must have clicked it off at a very fast speed. Very fast. And perhaps it was the actual working of the camera which accounted for what had happened. It might have established the focal point instantaneously— established it so that those things—forces, Elementals, call them what you will— could achieve their goal.

I saw the print. It was as Niles guessed it might be; a picture of a black endless plain. Only there were no lights visible, no figures, nothing except black shadows that seemed to blur around a central point. *They* did not photograph.

But *they* blurred around a print—a central point. *They* got through just as the picture must have snapped, yet faster than light itself. They got through and drew Niles along the angles as I had feared. Faster than light itself, as I have said. For it had to be faster, else I would not have seen—I would not have seen what I did see on that print. The central point . . .

The central point of that accursed picture; the only visible thing amidst the shadows—*was the dead and mangled body of David Niles!*

THE STRANGE YEARS
Brian Lumley

Illustration by Dave Carson

Brian Lumley, like Ramsey Campbell and numerous others, honed his writing skills in the H.P. Lovecraft tradition and published several books which updated Lovecraft's influential Cthulhu Mythos, including The Caller of the Black, The Horror at Oakdene, Beneath the Moors, The Burrowers Beneath, The Transition of Titus Crow, The Clock of Dreams *and the trilogy* Hero of Dreams, Ship of Dreams *and* Mad Moon of Dreams. *His other books include the fantasy* Khai of Ancient Khem *and the more contemporary terrors of* Psychomech, Psychosphere, Psychamock, Necroscope *and* Necroscope II: Wamphyri! *'The Strange Years' is an apocalyptic gem and first appeared in the ninth issue of* Fantasy Tales.

HE LAY face-down on the beach at the foot of a small dune, his face turned to one side, the summer sun beating down upon him. The clump of beachgrass at the top of the dune bent its spikes in a stiff breeze, but down here all was calm, with not even a seagull's cry to break in upon the lulling *hush, hush* of waves from far down the beach.

It would be nice, he thought; to run down the beach and splash in the sea, and come back dripping salt water and tasting it on his lips, and for the very briefest of moments be a small boy again in a world with a future. But the sun beat down from a blue sky and his limbs were leaden, and

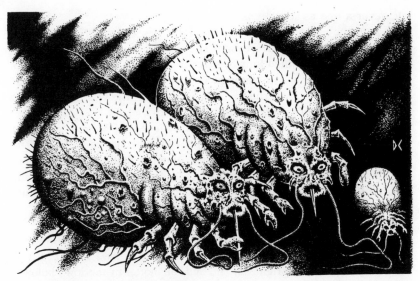

'They sucked the world to death'

a great drowsiness was upon him.

Then . . . a disturbance. Blown on the breeze to climb the far side of the dune, flapping like a bird with broken wings, a slim book—a child's exercise book, with tables of weights and measures on the back—flopped down exhausted in the sand before his eyes. Disinterested, he found strength to push it away; but as his fingers touched it so its cover blew open to reveal pages written in a neat if shaky adult longhand.

He had nothing else to do, and so began to read . . .

"When did it begin? Where? How? Why?'

"The Martians we might have expected (they've been frightening us long enough with their tales of invasion from outer space) and certainly there have been enough of threats from our Comrades across the water. But this?'

"Any ordinary sort of plague, we would survive. We always have in the past. And as for war: Christ!—when has there not been a war going on somewhere? They've irradiated us in Japan, defoliated us in Vietnam, smothered us in DDT wherever we were arable and poured poison into us where we once flowed sweet and clean—and we always bounced right back.'

"Fire and flood—even nuclear fire and festering effluent—have not appreciably stopped us. For 'They' read 'We,' Man, and for 'Us' read 'the world,' this Earth which once was ours. Yes, there have been strange years, but never a one as strange as this.'

"A penance? The ultimate penance? Or has Old Ma Nature finally decided to give us a hand? Perhaps she's stood off, watching us try our damnedest for so damned long to exterminate ourselves, and now She's sick to death of the whole damned scene. 'OK,' She says, 'have it your own way.' And She gives the nod to Her Brother, the Old Boy with the scythe. And He sighs and steps forward, and—'

"And it is a plague of sorts; and certainly it is DOOM; and a fire that rages across the world and devours all . . . Or will that come later? The cleansing flame from which Life's bright phoenix shall rise again? There will always be the sea. And how many ages this time before something gets left by the tide, grows lungs, jumps up on its feet and walks . . . and reaches for a club?'

"*When* did it begin?'

"I remember an Irish stoker who came into a bar dirty and drunk. His sleeves were rolled up and he scratched at hairy arms. I thought it was the heat. 'Hot? Damned right, sur,' he said, 'an' hotter by far down below—an' lousy!' He unrolled a newspaper on the bar and vigorously brushed at his matted forearm. Things fell onto the newsprint and moved, slowly. He popped them with a cigarette. 'Crabs, sur!' he cried. 'An' Christ—they suck like crazy!'"

"*When*?'

"There have always been strange years—plague years, drought years, war and wonder years—so it's difficult to pin it down. But the last twenty years . . . they have been *strange*. When, *exactly*? Who can say? But let's give it a shot. Let's start with the '70s—say, '76?—the drought.'

"There was so little water in the Thames that they said the river was running backwards. The militants blamed the Soviets. New laws were introduced to conserve water. People were taken to court for watering flowers. Some idiot calculated that a pound of excreta could be satisfactorily washed away with six pints of water, and people put bricks in their WC cisterns. Someone else said you could bathe comfortably in four inches of water, and if you didn't use soap the resultant mud could be thrown on the garden. The thing snowballed into a national campaign to 'Save It!'—and in October the skies were still cloudless, the earth parched, and imported rainmakers danced and pounded their tom-toms at Stonehenge. Forest and heath fires were daily occurrences and reservoirs became dustbowls. Sun-worshippers drank Coke and turned very brown . . .'

"And finally it rained, and it rained, and it rained. Wide-spread flooding, rivers bursting their banks, gardens (deprived all summer) inundated and washed away. Millions of tons of water, and not a pound of excreta to be disposed of. A strange year, '76. And just about every year since, come to think.'

"'77, and stories leak out of the Ukraine of fifty thousand square miles turned brown and utterly barren in the space of a single week. Since then the spread has been very slow, but it hasn't stopped. The Russians blamed 'us' and we accused 'them' of testing a secret weapon.'

"'79 and '80, and oil tankers sinking or grounding themselves left, right and centre. Miles-long oil slicks and chemicals jettisoned at sea, and whales washed up on the beaches, and Greenpeace, and the Japanese slaughtering dolphins. Another drought, this time in Australia, and a plague of mice to boot. Some Aussie commenting that 'The poor 'roos are dying in their thousands—and a few aboes, too . . .' And great green swarms of aphids and the skies bright with ladybirds.'

"Lots of plagues, in fact. We were being warned, you see?'

"And '84! Ah—1984! Good old George!'

"He was wrong, of course, for it wasn't Big Brother at all. It was Big Sister—Ma Nature Herself. And in 1984 She really started to go off the rails. '84 was half of India eaten by locusts and all of Africa down with a mutant strain of beriberi. '84 was the year of the poisoned potatoes and sinistral periwinkles, the year it rained frogs over wide areas of France, the year the cane-pest shot sugar beet right up to the top of the crops.'

"And not only Ma Nature but Technology, too, came unstuck in '84. The Lake District chemically polluted—permanently; nuclear power stations at Loch Torr on one side of the Atlantic and Long Island on the other melting down almost simultaneously; the Americans bringing back a 'bug' from Mars (see, even a *real* Martian invasion); oil discovered in the Mediterranean, and new fast-drilling techniques cracking the ocean floor and allowing it to leak and leak and leak—and even Red Adair shaking his head in dismay. How do you plug a leak two hundred fathoms deep and a mile long? And that jewel of oceans turning black, and Cyprus a great white tombstone in a lake of pitch. 'Aphrodite Rising From The High-Grade."

"Then '85 and '86; and they were strange, too, because they were so damned quiet! The lull before the storm, so to speak. And then—'

"Then it was '87, '88 and '89. The American space-bug leaping to Australia and New Zealand and giving both places a monstrous malaise. No one doing any work for six months; cattle and sheep dead in their millions; entire cities and towns burning down because nobody bothered to call out the fire services, or they didn't bother to come . . . And all the world's beaches strewn with countless myriads of great dead octopuses, a new species (or a mutant strain) with three rows of suckers to each tentacle; and their stink utterly unbearable as they rotted. A plague of great, fat seagulls. All the major volcanoes erupting in unison. Meteoric debris making massive holes in the ionosphere. A new, killer-cancer caused by sunburn. The common cold cured!—and uncommon leprosy spreading like wildfire through the Western World.'

"And finally—'

"Well, that was 'When.' It was also, I fancy, 'Where' and 'How.' As to 'Why'—I give a mental shrug. I'm tired, probably hungry. I have some sort of lethargy—the spacebug, I suppose—and I reckon it won't be long now. I had hoped that getting this down on paper might keep me active, mentally if not physically. But . . .'

"*Why?*'

"Well, I think I've answered that one, too.'

"Ma Nature strikes back. Get rid of the human vermin. They're lousing up your planet! And maybe *that's* what gave Her the idea. If fire and flood and disease and disaster and war couldn't do the trick, well, what else could She do? They advise you to fight fire with fire, so why not vermin with vermin?'

"They appeared almost overnight, five times larger than their immediate progenitors and growing bigger with each successive hatching; and unlike the new octopus they didn't die; and their incubation period down to less than a week. The superlice. All Man's little body parasites, all of his tiny, personal vampires, growing in the space of a month to things as big as your fist. Leaping things, flying things, walking sideways things. To quote a certain Irishman: 'An' Christ—they suck like crazy!'

"They've sucked, all right. They've sucked the world to death. New habits, new protections—new immunities and near—invulnerability—to go with their new size and strength. The meek inheriting the Earth? Stamp on them and they scurry away. Spray them with lethal chemicals and they bathe in them. Feed them DDT and they develop a taste for it. 'An' Christ—they suck like crazy!'

"And the whole world down with the creeping, sleeping sickness. We didn't even *want* to fight them! Vampires, and they've learned new tricks. Camouflage . . . Clinging to walls above doors, they look like bricks or tiles. And when you go through the door . . . And their bite acts like a sort of LSD. Brings on mild hallucinations, a feeling of well-being, a kind of euphoria. In the cities, amongst the young, there were huge gangs of 'bug-people!' My God!'

"They use animals, too; dogs and cats—as mounts, to get them about when they're bloated. Oh, they kill them eventually, but they know how to use them first. Dogs can dig under walls and fences; cats can climb and squeeze through tiny openings; crows and other large birds can fly down on top of things and into places . . .'

"Me, I was lucky—if you can call it that. A bachelor, two dogs, a parakeet and an outdoor aviary. My bungalow entirely netted in; fine wire netting, with trees, trellises and vines. And best of all situated on a wild stretch of the coast, away from mankind's great masses. But even so, it was only a matter of time.'

"They came, found me, sat outside my house, outside the wire and the walls, and they waited. They found ways in. Dogs dug holes for them, seagulls tore at he mesh overhead. Frantically, I would trap, pour petrol, burn, listen to them pop! But I couldn't stay awake for ever. One by one they got the birds, leaving little empty bodies and bunches of feathers. And my dogs, Bill and Ben, which I had to shoot and burn. And this morning when I woke up, Peter parakeet.'

"So there's at least one of them, probably two or three, here in the room with me right now. Hiding, waiting for night. Waiting for me to go to sleep. I've looked for them, of course, but—'

"Chameleons, they fit perfectly into any background. When I move, they move. And they imitate perfectly. But they do make mistakes. A moment ago I had two hairbrushes, identical, and I only ever had one. Can you imagine brushing your hair with something like *that*? And what the hell would I want with *three* fluffy slippers? A left, a right—and a centre?'

". . . I can see the beach from my window. And half a mile away, on the point, there's Carter's grocery. Not a crust in the kitchen. Dare I chance it? Do I want to? Let's see, now. Biscuits, coffee, powdered milk, canned beans, potatoes—no, strike the potatoes. A sack of carrots . . ."

The man on the beach grinned mirthlessly, white lips drawing back from his teeth and freezing there. A year ago he would have expected to read such in a book of horror fiction. But not now. Not when it was written in his own hand.

The breeze changed direction, blew on him, and the sand began to drift against his side. It blew in his eyes, glazed now and lifeless. The shadows lengthened as the sun started to dip down behind the dunes. His body grew cold.

Three hairy sacks with pincer feet, big as footballs and heavy with his blood, crawled slowly away from him along the beach . . .

RED
Richard Christian Matheson

Illustration by Allen Koszowski

*The son of genre giant Richard Matheson, Richard Christian Matheson
has over the past decade written more than 250 television shows as
diverse as* Knightrider, The Incredible Hulk *and* Three's Company. *He
has served as story editor on* The A-Team, Hardcastle & McCormick,
Quincy *and* Hunter, *and recently he wrote and produced the CBS-TV
series* Stir Crazy. *His, often very short, short fiction has appeared in
such magazines and anthologies as* Rod Serling's Twilight Zone
Magazine, Night Cry, Gallery, Shadows, Dark Forces *and* The Cutting
Edge, *while a collection entitled* Scars and Other Distinguishing Marks
*has recently appeared. His latest projects include films with his father,
Tobe Hooper, Dustin Hoffman, Barbara Striesand and Steven Speilberg
and a number of new TV series. 'Red' is one of the author's short, but
sharp, scares and originally appeared in the Summer 1986 issue of*
Night Cry *before being reprinted in* Fantasy Tales 16.

HE KEPT walking.
 The day was hot and miserable and he wiped his forehead. Up
another twenty feet, he could make out more. Thank God. Maybe he'd
find it all. He picked up the pace and his breathing got thick. He struggled
on, remembering his vow to himself to go through with this, not to stop
until he was done. Maybe it had been a mistake to ask this favour. But

' "But I'm not finished," the man cried'

it was the only way he could think of to work it out. Still, maybe it had been a mistake.

He felt an edge to his stomach as he stopped and leaned down to what was at his feet. He grimaced, lifted it into the large canvas bag he carried, wiped his hands, and moved on. The added weight in the bag promised more, and he somehow felt better. He had found most of what he was looking for in the first mile. Only a half mile more to go, to convince himself; to be sure.

To not go insane.

It was a nightmare for him to realise how far he'd gone this morning with no suspicion, no clue. He held the bag more tightly and walked on. Ahead, the forms who waited got bigger; closer. They stood with arms crossed, people gathered and complaining behind them. They would have to wait.

He saw something a few yards up, swallowed, and walked closer. It was everywhere and he shut his eyes, trying not to see how it must have been. But he saw it all. Heard it in his head. The sounds were horrible and he couldn't make them go away. Nothing would go away, until he had everything, he was certain of that. Then his mind would at last have some chance to find a place of comfort. To go on.

He bent down and picked up what he could, then walked on, scanning ahead. The sun was beating down and he felt his shirt soaking with sweat under the arms and on his back. He was nearing the forms who waited when he stopped, seeing something halfway between himself and them. It had lost its shape, but he knew what it was and couldn't step any closer. He placed the bag down and slowly sat crosslegged on the baking ground, staring. His body began to shake.

A somber-looking man walked to him and carefully picked up the object, placing it in the canvas bag and cinching the top. He gently coaxed the weeping man to stand and the man nodded through tears. Together, they walked toward the others who were glancing at watches and losing patience.

"But I'm not finished," the man cried. His voice broke and his eyes grew hot and puffy. "Please . . . I'll go crazy . . . just a little longer?"

The somber-looking man hated what was happening. He made the decision. "I'm sorry, sir. Headquarters said I could only give you the half-hour you asked for. That's all I can do. It's a very busy road."

The man tried to struggle away but was held more tightly. He began to scream and plead.

Two middle-aged women who were waiting watched uncomfortably.

"Whoever allowed this should be reported," said one, shaking her head critically. "The poor man is ready to have a nervous breakdown. It's cruel."

The other said she'd heard they felt awful for the man, whose little girl had grabbed on to the back bumper of his car when he'd left for work that morning. The girl had gotten caught and he'd never known.

They watched the officer approaching with the crying man whom he helped into the hot squad car. Then the officer grabbed the canvas bag, and as it began to drip red onto the blacktop, he gently placed it into the trunk beside the mangled tricycle.

The backed-up traffic began to honk, and traffic was waved on as the man was driven away.

EVER THE FAITH ENDURES
Manly Wade Wellman

Illustration by Alan Hunter

Manly Wade Wellman died in 1986. His long career in writing spanned mainstream novels to works on the American Civil War with a huge output of over seventy-five books and a couple of hundred short stories. Much of that material was in the field of horror and fantasy and, as can be imagined, Wellman's stories were widely published by all the major science fiction, horror and mystery pulps. His is fondly remembered for his classic collection of tales featuring John the Baladeer, Who Fears the Devil?, *and more recently for the fine collections from Carcosa,* Worse Things Waiting *and* Lonely Vigils. *It would take much more space than we have here to give more than a passing acknowledgement to Manly Wellman's long list of books and stories, or the numerous literary awards he received over the years. Always a good friend of* Fantasy Tales, *the sixth issue reprinted 'Ever the Faith Endures' from* The Year's Best Horror Stories VI. *We'll just let you read this yarn, written as a 'love letter' to England, a country he loved greatly and which he visited only a few times in his last years from his home in North Carolina.*

'When a god's overthrown, it becomes a devil'

HE'D SOMEHOW expected it to be like this. What else had he been looking for?

Though he'd never been here, had only wanted to be here. Had saved money for this journey overseas, then had puzzled and striven over railway timetables and guidebooks to get here. Here to the home his ancestors had left to go to America.

The place was swaddled in trees, there a couple of miles from the village where he'd left the train that noon, all among a landscape of tawny hills and softly grassed valleys, gatherings of sheep grazed here and there in the open, under the serene authority of black and white dogs. And no trees out there, only here, heavily marshalled beyond the quickset hedge with its June blossoms. There were yews, rowans, Scotch firs, two or three enormous oaks, with shrubs matted here and there underneath. It was like a solid chunk of forest taken from somewhere else and set here among the meadows and slopes and distant heights.

Wofford Belson stood opposite a driveway gap in the hedge. He was fifty-five, big but not soft, wearing the tweed suit he had bought in London. Gray stitched his heavy black hair. His face was square-jawed, vigorously seamed. He reminded himself that the Belsons had been American for three hundred years. Before that, British for how many thousands?

Movement among the trees, and a woman stepped into view. She was tall, slim, in dark blue slacks and a white blouse and a gray jacket. Her hair was a fine toss of syrupy brown. She wore broad spectacles. In one long hand she held a towel. She came toward him.

"Yes?" she said.

Belson wished he had a hat to take off.

"I wondered—" he began, stopped, and started again. "Does this house happen to be called Belstone?"

"Yes," she said again, clipping the syllable. "It happens to be called Belstone."

"Let me explain." He wondered if he could. "My name's Wofford Belson, but it used to be Belstone." Once more he stopped.

"Used to be?" she prompted. Behind the spectacles her watchful eyes were as blue as deep, clear water, and as calm. She was, he thought, perhaps forty-two or forty-three. And quite pretty.

"I'm American," he said unnecessarily. "The name got changed over there. Back in 1643, in Virginia." He smiled, white-toothed. "That's long ago in America, if it's not long ago here."

"And I daresay you're curious about your British origins, Mr. Belson," she said gently. "I am Anne Belstone, and we must be cousins, at a number of removes." She smiled, ever so slightly, and she had a dimple. "Forgive me if I seemed careful. I live here alone, you know, and I don't get many

137

callers." Her blue eyes appraised him. "But come into the yard if you like."

"Thank you, ma'am," he said. "I ought to say, I'm from North Carolina, a town called Chapel Hill. That's where the State university is."

"You are of the university?" she asked as he walked into the driveway and toward her. "You teach?"

"No, ma'am, but I graduated form there, and I have a book store in town. Now that I'm alone in the world—divorced, my children grown up—I wanted to come here. I always wanted to. Hoped to make it during the war, but they sent me to the Pacific theater." He felt that he was jabbering nervously, and wondered why. "I do know something, not much, about my family before the name got changed."

"Do you know why the name is Belstone?" she asked. "Do come and sit on the porch, I was going to have tea there. Would you care for a cup?"

"I thank you, ma'am, that's right good of you."

"Not at all."

They walked along the pebbled driveway. Overhead, the trees crossed stirring green branches. The driveway curved in around a gaunt, jagged rock, mottled gray in colour and almost as tall as Belson. He thought that Anne Belstone drew away from it as she walked, and would have looked at it closely, but there was the house.

He stopped in his tracks to look. It was what he had wanted, without knowing it.

The house was squarely and massively built, with lean windows in its two stories and dormers in the high slate roof. The stone of the walls was gray with a hint of rose. Up the two gable sides sprouted wide chimneys of the same rose—gray stone, built into the walls themselves and each crowned with a row of hatlike pots. Across the front sprawled a paved porch with sturdy posts of cut stones in dark mortar. Inside the windows behind the porch clung tawny curtains. Along the porch's edge stood flower pots with tufts of bloom.

"Is something wrong?" asked Anne Belstone at his shoulder.

"I was admiring the house."

"I suppose it's different from houses in the States."

"The chimneys," he tried to explain his feelings. "They're part of the house, of the walls. Not put on after the house was built, not tacked on as an afterthought."

She chuckled. It was a musical chuckle.

"Well, sir, generations of your forebears lived here. This house, or most of it, goes back to Elizabethan times. I think of it as utilitarian, old-fashioned. You make me wonder if it isn't more than that. But come up and sit on the porch."

They mounted the blocky steps. "Here," she said, and laid a hand on the back of a chair of weathered, solid wood. "Sit here and I'll fetch us out a tray."

Then she was gone. Belson sat in the chair. Next to it was a blocky table. He looked out into the trees of the yard.

Someone stood beside the driveway. No, it was the jagged rock. It was like an ill-proportioned human figure in the shadows. It seemed to have sloping shoulders and a knobby head. Eyes? But they were only scraps of shadow. The mouth-like crack was just a crack. Belson told himself that. For a moment he almost got out of the chair to step from the porch and walk down to examine the rough pillar. Then he lectured himself to wait and ask Anne Belstone about it first.

Behind him he fancied he heard a rustle. He turned in his chair, expecting to see his hostess. There was only a window behind him, and a stir in the stealthy curtains.

Then she came through the door, bringing a broad tray set with heaped dishes. He rose, took the tray from her and set it on the table.

"I hope you don't mind tea." she said, sitting in another chair. "I believe that most Americans prefer coffee."

"Tea suits me fine, ma'am," he said. "Don't fret about Americans not appreciating it. Some of them dumped a whole shipload of it into Boston harbour one time."

She laughed her musical laugh and poured him a cup. He declined cream and sugar and thanked her when she put a roll and a pat of butter on a plate for him. They ate and drank.

"That's a right interesting chunk of rock in your yard," he felt it was time to remark. "For a moment, sitting here, I thought it looked like somebody coming in."

She set down her cup, her eyes moody behind the spectacles. "I'd better tell you about that. That stone is named Belstone, too."

"It is?" he said, smiling, for he had begun to like her company. "Who named it that?"

"Nobody knows. It's been here, probably, since prehistoric times. And the name means a god. Baal."

She sipped tea. Belson gazed at the stone, disliking the fancy that it gazed back at him.

"Baal," he repeated. "That's out of the Bible."

"Out of many places," said Anne Belstone. "Baal was worshipped by Old Testament people, by European pagans, worshipped here in the British Isles. His name's on the land. Balquiddir and Balgonie in Scotland, Baltimore in Ireland—they hark back to Baal, worshipped by the Celts before the Romans."

"And we have the name too, Cousin Anne."

She smiled again when he called her that. "Yes, let's be cousinly. I'll call you Cousin—Wofford, you said?"

"That's my mother's family name. I've lots of Wofford kinfolk."

"Kinfolk," she said after him. "Not me. I was an only child, so was my father, and his father before him. Any cousins I have are almost as distant as you, Cousin Wofford. I don't keep in touch with them, and I have no friends you could call friends, not here. People don't come here."

"Not the milkman, the postman?"

"I get milk and letters and supplies yonder in the village. I've a little car out behind, to do my errands. I don't even try to keep up this house, so forgive me for not taking you inside. I live in just a bedroom and a kitchen."

He had a sense of movement at the window, but did not look. "We were talking about the Belstone," he reminded her.

"And I said the stone was always there where you see it. The Romans invaded and wanted to take it away, but some sort of disaster happened to anyone who tried, so they left it. When Saxon missionaries came along, they learned to let it alone, too."

"Was it that bad?" asked Belson, gazing at the rock.

"Bad enough that someone was told off, about a thousand years ago, to live here and guard it; and he took the name Belstone on account of his job."

"Baal's stone," said Belson, buttering a bit of roll. "Why Baal's stone? Was it an altar?"

Anne Belstone's shoulders drew up, in not quite a shudder. "You can say that. The old pagans had human sacrifices—that's why the Romans were so bitter about them. And where sacrifice has been, a spirit stays. It can't be exorcised."

"The missionaries tried, I reckon."

"Yes, and they failed. This must sound silly to you."

"It sounds fascinating, Cousin Anne."

She dimpled at the name. "Well, the stone's stayed where you see it, all those centuries. And the Belstones have lived here beside it, and sometimes got into trouble and then got out."

"One got to America," said Belson. "My ancestor Thomas."

"What do you know of him?"

"Almighty little," admitted Belson. "His name's in a book about persons of quality coming to America. He arrived at Jamestown in 1643, aboard a ship named *Bristol Venture*, and there's a note saying he had to take a special oath of allegiance to Charles the First. I've wondered about that."

"I can tell you," said Anne Belstone. "He was a younger son—the older son, Alan, was my ancestor. The records say that Thomas Belstone claimed magical powers. One day Matthew Hopkins arrived in this area. Do you know who he was?"

"A witch-hunter, wasn't he?"

"England's Witch-finder General. Thomas Belstone was one of twenty-three accused witches here, and the only one not hanged. He seems to have had money and friends to help him get more or less exiled instead."

"I'm glad he got to America," said Belson, smiling into her spectacled eyes. "He married a girl with Indian blood, and I'm glad for that, too. A drop of the Indian—that's really American."

She pondered that for a moment. Then:

"My ancestor Alan joined Cromwell—the winning side." Her soft voice had music in it. "He profited by that and he enlarged this house. We've lived here ever since, and I hope this much family history will content you, because I don't know much more."

"It's pleasant on this porch." He changed the subject.

"Sometimes, when I sit out here at night, I hear a nightingale sing in the trees."

"Nightingale," he said after her. "We don't have those in America. I've often wondered how they sounded."

But she did not invite him to stay and find out. He set down his teacup.

"You said you won't show me the house, but I'd like to walk out and look at that rock I'm named for."

"Well . . ." That was no permission, but no refusal, either.

He rose and walked into the yard. The gravelled way was bordered with shaggy moss, in which grew tiny red toadstools. He reached the rock. It stood as tall as himself. It was like the outline of a human shape, but if it had been hewn like that, the marks of hewing had long weathered away. Belstone studied the shadowed dints that looked like eyes, the crack that ran across like a mouth. That crack seemed to twist wryly.

"You're not pretty," he addressed it. "No wonder the old Romans wanted to put you away. What if I shoved you over?"

He lifted a hand, but he did not touch the rock. At that moment, it seemed to blur, as in a mist. He had a sensation of cold. And he heard the murmur of a voice.

That made him jump backward and turn around.

Anne Belstone had come silently out with him. Her hands clasped themselves in front of her. She whispered something. A prayer? But he did not know the words:

"*Sobrosto, ekkshilhai—pion fhanfhantisham—*"

She sidled away.

"What did you say?" he asked her.

"Old words I was taught when I was a girl."

"Some kind of spell?"

She did not answer that. "Come," she said, and turned to lead him back to the porch. He sat down and lifted his teacup, and silently cursed his hand for trembling.

"You had your wish, saw it at close quarters," she said. "Why did you make fun of it?"

He looked out at the silent rock. "You said human sacrifices."

"Only in those days before the Romans. Later on, blood sacrifices of animals." Her smooth cheek looked tense. "When a god's overthrown, it becomes a devil."

"And a devil must be bought off," he tried to fall in with her unhappy humour.

"Yes, he must be bought off."

"Let's talk about something else, Cousin Anne. Thanks, I'd like more tea."

She asked about his children. He talked proudly of his lawyer son who had two sons himself, and of his daughter who was finishing her studies for a doctorate in psychology. He told about his book store and how happily he kept it. He said he approved of old shoes and the novels of P. G. Wodehouse, and of vacations in the mountains and at the seaside.

She talked more briefly about herself. She had always lived at Belstone, except when she had gone to school as a girl. When her parents died, she had stayed there, quietly alone.

"Haven't men come visiting?" he teased her, smiling. "I'd think that any man who was a man would want to."

"I know very few men."

"You ought to come and visit in North Carolina."

"You make it sound perfect there," she said.

"Nothing's perfect, but most time things are good. Beautiful spring and summer and fall, and mild winters. And I have friends, some of them professors, scholars. You'd like them." He looked at her earnestly. "They'd like you, too."

At last her own smile came back. "Why do you think that?"

"They have to, because I like you so much myself."

"I wish I could come." She sounded as if she meant it. She rose and began to gather up the tea things.

"I hate to bring this to an end, Cousin Wofford."

"Why bring it to an end?" he protested.

Her eyes were blue, blue, behind the spectacles. "You have quite a walk to the village. You'll want to be there by sundown."

"It won't be sundown for quite a while. Look, come with me. We can

142

have dinner at the inn."

She stacked dishes on the tray. "I mustn't, really. But it's been good having you here. You're—well, so healthy, so cheerful."

"You don't look unhealthy, and you could be cheerful if you half tried," he said. "I want to help you to try."

"I might be cheerful if—"

She left it unfinished. He studied the sweet curve of her cheek as she bent over the tray.

"Look here, why didn't you ever marry?" he demanded suddenly, strong in the sense it was none of his business. "You ought to have a family, children."

"No," she said gently, "not for me. If you'll excuse me, I'll take these back to the kitchen."

She carried the tray to the door and turned the knob with her free hand. She stepped inside and closed the door behind her. He heard the click of the catch. Had she locked it from inside? Why?

Rising, he walked to the door and turned the big brass knob. It wasn't locked. He pushed it inward and stepped into the house.

Dim in there, a sort of sandy-brown light. That was from the curtains at the window. He took half a dozen steps along a hall and looked through an open arch into a broad, dim room.

It was walled with darkly aged wooden panels and set with upright timbers, like the ribs of a ship's hold. Furniture stood here and there, draped with dusty sheets. At the far end, a fireplace, and, though it was warm June outside, a nest of coals burned redly on the hearth. Belson felt its heat.

On the hob of the fireplace was built up a little cube of stones. Upon it, as upon an altar, lay what looked like shreds of raw meat.

Belson gazed at the hearth, wondering. Something moved on the far side of the room, beside a draped chair, something black and bulky. Belson turned his gaze upon it.

Only a particularly deep shadow, shifting perhaps in the light of the coals. Or a robe or coat of heavy dark fur, thrown there. Or—

But it stirred again. It rose slowly erect, like a black bear, gross and shaggy. But not a bear either, not with that broad flat face, those glowing pale eyes. Where the nose should be was a damp blob, like soggy brown leather, with staring nostrils. The mouth was a broad cleft. Upper and lower teeth jutted, like splinters of china.

Frozen, unbelieving, Belson looked. The glowing eyes looked back at him. Long, knobby arms lifted, spreading hands like hairy rakes. Talons glinted, as sharp and pale as the teeth. The mouth gaped, made a crooning snarl. It stepped toward him, on long flippers of feet.

143

"No, you don't!" Belson found his voice. "Stay away from me!"

He turned to run, and bumped into Anne Belstone. She pushed him into the hall. She raised her arms high.

"*Athe, pemeath.*" She was saying more strange words. "*Somiatoai, haliha.*"

It stood fast, its eyes flashed pale.

"*Ah jathos noio sattis,*" Belson heard her chant. "*Ishoroh.*"

He ran into the hall, leaving her alone there. He scrabbled the door open and was out on the porch, gasping for breath.

"*Selu, samhaiah,*" said her voice in the house behind him. "*Trinu, iamensaha.*"

He clung dizzily to the back of a chair. His knees wavered. Something made a noise behind him and he looked back in terror. Anne Belstone was on the porch, closing the door. She walked toward him. Her sweet face was as a pan of fresh milk.

"Now," she said gently. "Now you know why I didn't want to invite you into the house."

"That in there," he mouthed. "A man or an animal or what?"

"Not a man or animal." She was precise, informative. "I told you that the Belstones were ordered to look after him."

"A god, is that thing a god?"

"He used to be. Now he's what he is. Always hungry."

Belson grunted. "You said words to drive him back."

"I told you, my parents made me learn them." She shrugged. "I keep him here, so that he won't plague others—plague the world."

Something scraped inside the heavy door. She turned that way. "*Heriel aias stoch nahas,*" she pronounced. The scraping ceased.

"He's not wholly satisfied with pieces of butcher's meat or just rabbits or chickens," she said wearily. "Maybe he thought you were the sort of sacrifice he used to expect."

He blinked at her. "You worship him," he half accused.

"Yes," she agreed. "Yes I do. That way, I can keep him here. And now, you must go."

"Go?" He looked out at the jagged stone pillar.

"Probably he knows you're of the Belstone blood. That makes it bad for you, very bad. You must never come near this house again."

The drapes stirred at a window.

"How can you possibly live here?" cried Belson, wondering how steady her stance was, her voice was. "How can you?"

"Because I've always lived here," she replied, "I was brought up to live here, stay here, see that he stays here, too. It's what I'm on earth for."

"No!" he fairly shouted into her calm, pale face. He seized both her slim hands in his big ones. "Come with me."

"Come with you?" she said after him and stared.

"Come home to America with me, Anne. Don't even step back inside there for anything. We'll buy you clothes, whatever you need, in London. We'll go back together, back home. It'll be your home, too." He pressed her hands. "Come with me," he begged. "Please!"

"I can't. If you'll only stop to think, you'll know why I can't. It's for me to live here at Belstone and keep him here, too. Keep him here away from everyone else."

"But when you don't live to keep him any more?" he prodded at her. "When you die at last?"

"Who knows what will happen then?" Her voice rose, her hands gripped his. "Who can know that? I'll be dead. I'll be past knowing. But until I'm dead, I'll stay and keep him here."

Strongly she dragged her hands free of his grip.

"Now, this is my house," she said, "though just now it may not seem quite like that to you. This is my house, and I must tell you to leave."

"I won't leave," he tried to argue.

"Go this instant," she commanded. "If you don't, I'll open the door and let him out here."

Again, a stir at the drapes of the window.

"And you know that I mean what I say," she told him. "Go on, go away, and don't ever come back."

She pushed him towards the steps, with a power he had not expected in her slim body. He blundered down them to the gravel below.

"Go away!" she cried at him once more.

He walked along the driveway. As he came opposite the rock he heard a sound from it, like a sigh of wind. Its eye-patches shone suddenly, as bits of ice shine. The crack of a mouth seemed to twitch.

He quickened his steps. Out on the road, he turned toward the village. He dared not look back. He could not have seen her, anyway. Upon him rushed a grinding sense of loss, of defeat.

His breath shook in his throat. He felt a trickle of wet on his cheeks. He was in tears, for the first time since he had been a little, little boy.

145

EXTENSION 201
Cyril Simsa

Illustration by Russ Nicholson

Cyril Simsa has a degree in Zoology, and for some years has been earning a living as an academic editor. He has contributed to The Science Fiction Source Book, Foundation, Vector *and* The Anthology of Speculative Poetry *and has recently been researching the history of Czech fantasy and science fiction. Despite these SF credentials, we couldn't help being delighted to publish this old-fashioned style narrative of supernatural terror and mystery in* Fantasy Tales 5. *'Extension 201' remains Cyril's only professionally published story.*

"Now the serpent was more subtil than any beast of the field"
—Genesis iii 1

Dec. 11th, 1911.

TODAY, for the first time, we truly spent a day in the jungle. The journey upriver on the steamer from Manaos gives one only a partial idea of the nature of jungle existence; no matter how deep into the jungle one goes, one is living and sleeping on board an island, and views the jungle from a distance. A rotting wooden jetty is the last vestige of civilisation: the steamer's run ends there, and for all intents and purposes so does everything. I was quite surprised at how sorry I was to leave it behind; the canoes rounded a wide curve in the river, going slowly but steadily,

'The coiled snake was moving, moving'

and the steamer vanished behind a dead rubber tree (someone had been tapping it, without using much skill).

We have four canoes, each propelled by a team of natives; I am in the leading one with our half-caste guide, Lucio. He is very learned in the ways of the jungle, he points out many fascinating epiphytes which may be seen by skilful observation, though they be masked by the innumerable lianas and considerable quantities of Spanish moss. I will not go into details of finds, since those may be found in the official records of the Expedition, but will (as I have 'til now) confine entries to my personal experiences.

The Professor's craft ran afoul of a carcass; it was indistinguishable in its decay, but it smelled of the charnel-house. The Professor was almost dislodged into the water by the impact, for which he was not grateful, and he has been muttering oaths at the natives ever since. In ways, the Professor is an odd choice for leader; he is frequently petulant and impulsive, and yet he can be terribly stubborn in his opposition to an idea, if he sets his mind to it.

Later, I was talking to Lucio: he claims the corpse was the victim of a snake, since (he claims) the upper reaches of the river are infested with "serpents of vast size." When I asked him whether he meant anaconda, he replied: yes, but not so small(!) as the Colonel is accustomed to seeing. This is clearly one of those native legends, for when I asked him if he had seen these himself, he said: no, he would not be foolish enough to approach one, nor to go where they were believed to be. But he was not sure exactly where one could find such snakes. I would be inclined to dismiss this as nonsense, if I did not have it on the authority of so reputable an explorer as Major Percy Fawcett, that on his expedition of 1906-7 he shot an anaconda of 62 ft. length. I met Fawcett a couple of years after that, and he recounted to me the terrible difficulties his expedition experienced later on.

Kate Morrow frowned, pulled the wisps of hair from her cheeks as she raised her head, and looked round for Bill, the museum's telephone operator. He was plugging a call, but he came over when she spoke.

"What's happened to extension 201?" she asked.

"Eh?" he scratched his ribs through the white regulation shirt, and almost grudgingly looked down to where she was pointing.

The old directory lay open at a page listing numbers 170-211. Kate's narrow finger pointed to number 200, it was followed by number . . . by number 202?

"It *is* missing, isn't it?" he admitted. "I never noticed that before . . . probably it's been cancelled."

"But just look at the rest of the page," she had been expecting that sort of answer from Bill, and had prepared her line of argument: "Practically all of the names have been changed some time or another. All those extensions have been cancelled and re-allotted. Number 201 just wasn't there in the first place." She turned to the front of the directory—the earliest one she had been able to find; it gave the original date of compilation as 1936. Number 201 had been missing for over forty years.

"I'd better ask Vic," said Bill. "Vic...Vic, where are you? Come here, a minute."

Vic was even older than Bill, but without the beergut. He regarded Kate fondly, but clearly thought she ought to be settling down somewhere with a nice young man, getting ready to spend her life scraping carrots. She might have felt annoyed, if Vic hadn't been such a likeable old relic.

"Vic, there's an extension number missing."

"Oh, yes. Number 201," he paused. "I noticed it was missing when I was put in charge of compiling those ledgers...that was ages ago, let me see, now..."

"It says 1936 in here."

"Does it? It could well be, could well be. I asked about 201 at the time, but nobody seemed to know what had happened to it. It's one of those traditions."

"But there must have been an extension 201, once. I mean, they couldn't have left it out in the first place, could they?"

"I don't know. It's so easy to lose things in this museum, even to lose people. There was a visitor got lost once, and had to spend the night by an old mammoth skeleton. When they found him the next morning, they discovered it was a skeleton they'd been looking for for the past five months."

She looked at him disbelievingly, so he offered to let her go into the corridors of the museum.

"Don't go too far, unless you know how to get back," Vic warned her.

Kate smiled, shook her head kindly, and then turned into the corridor. She was amused by the old man, and she liked him too well to want to laugh openly. But sometimes he really took things so *seriously*... And then she began to see what he had meant.

The Museum of Nature that she knew was a comforting place—a cosily knowable place. After two visits you could find your way from anywhere to anywhere else—it gave the impression of being small, even though some of the halls were huge. That was the museum that opened to the public. The *real* museum was altogether different.

A labyrinth of small, narrow passageways; confused by the numberless storerooms, the intersections that could not be told apart; the old glass-fronted cabinets filled with little drawers, each bearing a faded label with an obscure Latin name; the lumpy shapes under grubby tarpaulins; fossil shells a yard-and-half across, blocking the corridor; there were even turnings that showed clearly the footprints of the last person to walk that way—as indentations in the dust. And then there were muddled additions to the buildings in later architectural styles. She came to understand how somebody or something could become lost in this . . . chaos, she almost laughed when she thought of that over—and mis-used word. This maze of boxed-in walkways gave the true impression of the sprawling confusion of the museum, much more so than exhibition halls an eighth of a mile long. And curiously, her awareness of the awesome profusion of hiding places made her only more keen to find the missing extension number.

She thought ruefully of how she had got the assignment: the editor announcing that he wanted a short feature on behind-the-scenes in a large museum at Christmas, with character sketches of people involved. She had thought he was fobbing her off with some pretty job-for-the-sake-of-keeping-the-newcomers-busy. She hadn't reacted exactly . . . well, fervently.

"It should be very exciting for you," he had said, scarcely concealing his grin (of delight at her being piqued?).

"Bloody thrilling," she had replied before stomping out.

But maybe she could find out something interesting after all, giving a bit of grubbing around in the archives.

Dec. 13th, 1911.
Last evening, we travelled after dark for the first time since leaving the steamer, and a most untoward occurrence resulted in near disaster for the lead canoe (in which Lucio and I were seated at the time). There was a swell on the river, and quite suddenly two green lights approached at speed, narrowly missing the boat. The object (whatever it may have been) must have emerged from one of those multitudinous watercourses that branch off from the mainstream periodically, and make navigation so confusing at times. The other boats reported seeing nothing, however.

I was inclined to think this a steamer's lights, until I remembered that no steamers venture this far upriver. Lucio started talking about his snakes once more—he claimed the lights were reflections from an anaconda's eyes, and that the creature submerged before reaching the other canoes. If anaconda it was, then I have never before seen anything whose eyes gave such a demoniac glare. It is a tempting theory, nevertheless, since it explains why the other members of the expedition saw nothing, without having to assume that I was asleep or deranged (I do not in any case

150

believe that both I and Lucio—a reliable and level-headed witness, even at the worst of times—dreamed the same thing). If only it were not for the inordinate size required for this thesis to be viable, I would believe it; I still find that great a length difficult to accept.

Lucio told me more about these snakes, later on. He said that they were never hunted, because even if one was to capture or slay one of the creatures, one would have to beware of its mate; anacondas, he said, always live in couples. He also claimed that they frequently seek to absorb warmth, and may be found coiled around the embers of a fire; this is by way of bare sustenance at times when they cannot draw the life-heat from a human victim.

The Professor, naturally, gives no credence to any of this; the natives obviously believe otherwise since no less than three of them have deserted us. I think that, in matters of the jungle, I would rather trust the natives than the Professor!

"Vic?" she asked, "Vic, aren't there any older directories like these anywhere?"

"Older ones? Y'know, there might be somewhere . . . I'm not sure where. The ones we've got here are all that were important when we moved in here . . ."

"Who moved where?"

"Us caretakers, the telephone exchange, all that sort of thing. When the old telephone exchange got too small to manage."

"The old telephone exchange?"

"Yes. There was an old office for the caretakers, I think it must have been Victorian. When telephones began to be installed, they set up a central exchange in that same office, but it was too small. So they promised to build a new office, but you know how these places work—it wasn't till the '50s, what with the war getting in the way, that we actually got this place. I think they kept the same wiring system—it would have cost too much to rewire a museum of this size—just re-routed the exchange through to here. Anyway, then we moved in, and took most of the stuff with us. But there may have been some things we left behind, or put into safe keeping in a cupboard somewhere."

"A cupboard somewhere?" Kate snorted in disappointment, "and how many miles of corridor are there?"

"Miles and miles. I don't think they've ever been counted."

"So I've got to search miles of corridor?"

"Oh, no. The old telephone exchange would be your best bet. I'd try looking there, I doubt it's been used for anything else."

Vic showed her the old telephone exchange, down in the basement.

"The first time I've been down here in twenty-five years," he commented.

They found a heap of ledgers. They were old and fragile, brown spots disfigured the paper of their pages. The edges were crumbling, and one or two had woodworm. The lights didn't work—or the power had been cut off—so they had to carry the find out into the corridor. She sat down on the floor, ignoring the mess she was gathering on her trousers. She checked their pages, looking for dates. And she found a directory—the thinnest of all—dated 1911.

Extension 201 was listed.

It belonged to Doctor Rudolf Baehr; and next to the name was added "*poste restante*, The Amazon Expedition."

The 1915 ledger still listed 201, but somebody had crossed out the name—and the extension number, too. It looked like an accident, but that accident had ensured that the 1922 ledger had no extension 201. Kate was awed that if it had not been for that one slip of the pen, she might never have known about this.

"Have you ever heard of an Amazon Expedition?" she asked Vic.

"No, never. Why don't you check the library? I'll phone through to tell them you're coming."

She found a reference to Rudolf Baehr in the museum records: he had been a herpetologist, employed by the museum during the early part of the century, presumed to have left the museum staff circa 1912, "but no record exists. It has probably been mislaid." Or maybe he got lost in the corridors, she thought sardonically. Trust the telephone exchange to be behind everyone else in scrubbing his name off the records.

With the Amazon Expedition, she was forced to rely on a newspaper cutting, dated 9th January 1913: "AMAZON EXPEDITION FAILS," it read. "Yesterday, the Museum of Nature announced that it believes its Amazon Expedition, under Professor James Winterton, to have failed, and its members to have perished. The expedition first set out in November of 1911, but returned to the port of Manaos early in 1912 following difficulties. It returned to the Amazon in March 1912, and has not been heard from since. Dr. Rudolf Baehr, the Expedition's contact at the Museum, could not be found for comment."

Dec. 17th, 1911.

I have been unable to write my journal for several days, and find time now only by neglecting certain duties allotted me by the Professor (he has been growing continually more demanding, as we make new discoveries). But I have several matters of considerable import, that need prompt recording lest I forget some detail.

Last night we played host to a pair of rubber hunters, and they made many references to a place named Rio de los Culebras (by their descrip-tions, a fascinating place indeed). They were retreating back to Manaos, not for fear of hostiles (though they say there is an increasing number of them, as more and more natives become angry at the failure of the rubber trade they had made their livelihood), but for fear of snakes, of which there are many and of abnormal size in that rio I mentioned earlier. Needless to say, I feel a great urge to visit that river myself, for Lucio's tales have fascinated me not a little.

The rubber hunters showed me an old map, which they obtained from a mulatto; it shows the general region we are exploring, and particularly an obscure tributary, the Rio de los Culebras. I cannot say that I have ever heard of it before, but they have visited it and do not ever wish to return (in truth, their desire is so strong that they have given me the map). The mouth of the river is guarded by a three-pointed symbol, a triangle with an eye in each vertex, and in the centre what I take to be a represen-tation of a predator's jaws. The rubber hunters were attracted to the place precisely because of this evil symbol; it was their experience that such maps with warnings of danger are a means of safeguarding the location of treasure. The rubber trade has been none too good this last year, and they were hoping that such a treasure might earn them the money they so badly needed.

Lucio tells me that the sign is a symbol of a mythical Indian deity, a three-eyed reptile that can only act through the medium of an anaconda. However, these deities (there are many of them) require the belief of their victim before they are able to attack them. I tried to catch him out at this point, by asking why these deities had not previously shown themselves to white men, since by doing so they could have gained a whole new race of believers. His reply shook me by its astuteness: "I think they are afraid of you white men, you would not believe in the way we do: you would come to the jungle to hunt them, you would want to make them your trophies." Only those that believe run any risk, so the expedi-tion should be safe so long as the Professor stays with it, unless something should happen to convert him (but that, surely, is unthinkable).

I find this idea of an intelligent reptile (not to mention a three-eyed one) wholly fascinating; reptiles have evolved away from intelligence (unless one counts the evolution of mammals from reptiles as an exam-ple of reptile intelligence, which I would not consider a true way of regar-ding matters). If some intelligent reptile species truly exists, and controls the anacondas of the Amazonian forest, it must have evolved by a thoroughly different line from the remainder of the reptiles. But here I am trying to rationalise a genuine example of a native myth (and rather feebly, at that), and by doing so I am removing its charm (not to mention the fact that I am bearing out Lucio's condemnation). I have a distinct weakness for such stories, for their almost-naive acceptance as fact some things which people like the Professor would dismiss as "poppycock". We white men lose many things of great beauty by our scepticism; sometimes I am tempted simply to believe.

The editor had been on the phone last night, asking where was that story, and why-the-hell hadn't she been in to the bloody office? She told him that she'd found something mysterious in the museum's records which nobody had spotted before, and that she was doing further research. He said okay-but: she was to be back at the office by today . . . some chance, she mocked silently, as she walked up the driveway to the museum.

Her boyfriend had rung her up last night, as well. He asked why he never saw her anymore. She said she was terribly busy. He said she was always busy, and hung up on her reply.

Her landlady wanted to see her about the rent, but Kate had rushed out without speaking to her. Come to think of it, she had hardly spoken to anybody for the past week except Vic—and that was only because he was so full of information (and so ready to give it, added a callous part of her). Somehow she felt that it didn't matter, she would start talking to them again when she had sorted out the missing extension 201 . . . she just *had* to find out what had happened. Just *had* to. The problem was that they didn't understand dedication . . . except perhaps the editor, but he forbade her to "waste" any more time. But she would show them it hadn't just been a waste of time—and as she thought it, she realised that she only half-believed it.

It had been raining during the night, and the brass statue in the driveway was covered with small drops of water, almost evenly spaced. And climbing up the polished surface—moist with the rainwarts—was a frog. The sculpture provided no grip for the frog's smooth skin, but the frog doggedly dragged itself up, placing one leg after another, its body swinging from side to side like a lizard's. For every three steps upwards, it slipped two steps down—but it *was* reaching the summit, slowly. Soon it would be there, soon. But the sun was out, warming the metal of the statue, and the teardrops were dying. If the frog didn't reach the top quickly, the sun-dried surface wouldn't let it.

She didn't even bother to talk to Vic this morning, but went straight to the old telephone exchange. The thin ledger still lay open with its entry, "201, Doctor Rudolf Baehr," provocatively conspicuous. She had found a name associated with the number, but she wanted to find the owner, to find the place where the extension number led. A name was not enough.

She started to search the old exchange, looking for a clue—anything—

to where she could find Dr. Baehr's office. And she found another old directory, listing the whereabouts of the employees, dated 1916. Baehr's name wasn't on it . . . but it did list a vacant post, in the field of Snakes & Lizards. She tried hard to find an earlier directory, searching the empty shelves, opening the cupboards—the first person to do so for a quarter of a century. She rummaged in the packing cases of old books that stood in obtrusive positions on the floor . . . and nowhere could she find a single clue. And then she suddenly thought of ringing him . . . of dialling extension 201, and waiting for his reply. Surely, if he was still there, he *would* reply.

She ran up the stairs to find Vic, arriving short of breath and panting. "Vic . . . Vic . . . I want . . . to . . . phone . . . exten- . . . sion 201, quick— . . . ly . . ."

"Slow down, there, girl, slow down," said Vic. "I can't understand a word you're saying."

She leaned against a wall, swallowing hard, brushing her hair back into place with her hands, waiting for the heat in her cheeks to go away: "Vic. Let's phone extension 201, see what happens."

"Yes," he mumbled, "that's a good idea." He dialled as he spoke, and handed her the receiver. It was ringing, they had got through!

She waited, expecting the waiting to finish after each pair of bell-tones, and each time she was disappointed. And after a time she realised that the ringing was somehow different from the sort she was used to hearing, it seemed more . . . archaic? She began to wonder what she had expected to happen if the phone really had been answered. She turned to Vic:

"Where could he be?"

"Who?"

"Doctor Rudolf Baehr. Nobody knows when he left, nobody has any idea where he worked. He might just as well not have existed. How could things get that way?"

"We get people like that working for us— they like to work alone, undisturbed. So they get themselves an office in an obscure corner of the museum. Nobody notices them coming in in the morning, nobody notices them when they leave at night. They might even *sleep* in their offices for all I know. We don't have so many of those now as we used to when I joined the staff as a boy."

"When was that?"

"1911, it was. I've been with the museum a good few years."

"1911? But then you must have known him. He was still here in 1911, that's about the only thing anybody agrees on . . ."

Vic shook his head sadly. "I wish I could help," it sounded empty.

Then Kate spoke again: "If you could put through a call to extension 201, I might be able to walk the corridors, listening."

Vic shook his head again. "No, it won't work. There are too many corridors, and too many phones—it needn't be his that you hear. Besides, we'd be blocking a line and someone might notice and complain . . . but I'll tell you what I *can* do, I can ring through occasionally, you could listen for that."

"What good is an occasional ringing? I might walk straight past his office in one of the periods when the phone has stopped."

"It's better than nothing, and I can give you an idea of roughly where to look: we used to shove these recluses in the west wing. It's not a wing anymore, it's had new halls built on either side of it, but I can show you the way."

He did, and Kate found herself wandering the west wing. It seemed dimmer and dirtier, even more cluttered than the parts she had visited previously. And distantly—just for a while—she thought she heard a phone ringing. It came from above her, the second floor.

The second floor had a pile of stuffed lizards. They had been discarded, and lay sprawled over each other in a miserable clump. And opposite the heap was a door, inside which a ringing abruptly started. The door had an old-fashioned knob on it—no trace of the modern handles she had seen nearer the exchange.

She reached out for the knob, grasped the cold metal firmly until her wrist hurt. She turned it slowly, and pushed. The ringing stopped.

When she looked into the office, she was reminded of a nursery rhyme: "And when she got there, the cupboard was bare." There was a desk facing her, with a large telephone. A few books were left on the shelves. A browning card lay on the floor by her feet. She picked it up and read the curviform handwriting, which had faded almost to the colour of the rust stain where a tack had once held it to the door: "I am moving to my new office behind the skeleton hall. I am off the telephone until I am given a new extension number." It was signed, "Rudolf Baehr, December 1912."

An office behind a skeleton hall. But *which* skeleton hall? There were so many of them, and it could be any one . . . She went over to the desk, and glanced at the phone. It was labelled 201. Then, amongst the drifts of dust that had been shaken up by the ringing, she saw an old book lying open, face down, as if it had been hastily consulted. The spine had cracked, but when she picked it up and blew, the print crawled out from under the blanket of filth. A passage was marked, and she read:

"The pineal eye of reptiles is an outgrowth at the top of the brain, corresponding to the pineal gland of mammals. It is best developed in

156

Sphenodon (the tuatara) where it has a lens and retina corresponding to those in a normal eye, and the skull is known to have a pineal apperture, allowing nervous linkage between this third eye and the brain. It is believed that the tuatara can react to light stimulation of this eye, but it is not capable of true sight, since the lens is covered with a layer of skin. Pineal appertures are found in a number of primitive fossil reptiles types, indicating that they, too, must have had a "third eye". However, the importance of the pineal eye becomes greatly reduced in more advanced reptiles, indicating that the general evolutionary trend had been for the pineal eye to degenerate into a mere hormonal gland, as found in the birds and mammals. One is led to speculate what might have happened, had the evolutionary trend been otherwise?"

Kate closed the book gently, and put it under her arm, marking the place with the card she had picked up earlier. Then she began to look over the shelves, but found nothing of interest except a dried and cracking specimen of lizard. It had been stuffed and mounted, once, but now it lay on its side, hidden behind two hefty volumes. It was marked *Sphenodon punctatum*.

She examined it for a third eye. It only had two. But that was what the book had said: the tuatara's third eye was internal, covered by unbroken skin. If only the tuatara, or something else like it, had evolved some other way...that might have produced some fascinating results.

Dec. 20th 1911.
I have decided that I believe Lucio: the anacondas, and perhaps even his deities exist. I woke up this morning feeling great anticipation, since I have persuaded the Professor to pitch camp at the mouth of the Culebras 'til after Christmas. This means that I may take a small party to explore the Culebras itself. Lucio was hesitant about accompanying me: he explains that the anacondas (or perhaps the deities, he was not very explicit) have some way of stupefying their intended victims. This is not an uncommon legend, I have heard similar things said of a snake's breath on many occasions in many countries, but when I asked Lucio about it he seemed to indicate he meant some other means. In either case, he is afraid that they will trance him if he goes up the Culebras.

I argued with him at some length, and he acquiesced. But he is not happy about travelling with me, and on the journey he told me doom-laden myths about how the anacondas (or anaconda-gods, again he seemed muddled) have powers of giving life to the dead, so long as their actions will result in the taking of a life. Soul for soul. (In this way is the count of the dead kept constant).

We have made camp on a sandy beach at the side of a great bend in

157

the river, with a small, fresh rivulet coming down from the hills at that point. The jungle opens out around the camp, giving a fine view of the river both up and down. Now we sit in camp and wait, for Lucio assures me that the anacondas will find us, and then I shall catch an anaconda of unprecedented size! Oh, what a Christmas present for the expedition!

Kate woke up with a feeling of expectation, as if something was perched over the back of her neck, ready to bite. She remembered the discussion she had had last night over the phone: the editor warned her that if she didn't come into the office today, she'd be fired. But she didn't worry about that, the quest for the missing extension had absorbed her— it was so much more important to her than a second-rate reporting job. And she realised now what had been escaping her the day before: it was perfectly obvious where Doctor Baehr's—Rudolf's?—new office was. He had referred to "*the* skeleton hall," therefore it had to be a reptile skeleton hall...and there couldn't be too many of them.

As she walked through the streets towards the museum, she realised with a shock that it was almost Christmas: holly and trees and synthetic snow covered the shopfronts, special offer Christmas puds in the food-shops, special offer Xmas cards in the stationers'...the whole razzmatazz as usual. And she had forgotten all about it...but that meant that the museum would be shutting for several days, and what would she do about her researches? She would have to finish them soon, or put them aside...No. No, that was impossible, perhaps she could lay in some supplies and shack up in the corridors over Christmas. Hadn't Vic said that some of their recluses did it?

The frog was still on the statue. It had reached the top...and the sun had baked it down. It was a small, black squirm...like dried apricots gone bad...a mess. Then she saw Vic:

"Don't you ever take a rest?" he asked half-jovially, half-worried. Perhaps her anxiety over finding that extension had been rather obvious, and Vic was getting concerned. Trust old Vic to do that, he was rather fatherly in his interest, but she didn't mind it from him—it seemed so appropriate.

"No," she tried to smile. "Look, I haven't got time to talk now, I've got to get to the library. I'll see you later," she knew it was a lie as she said it.

"I'll phone them that you're coming," he said, ever-obliging. She was touched that, despite her brusque disregard, he offered to help her.

But it was her search that mattered most, and she went to the library to check their plans of the building. She found what she was looking for without difficulty on a 1908 plan of the west wing: right at the top of the tower in which the wing ended, was a small display room grandly entitled the "Snake & Lizard Skeleton Hall." And at the back of it was marked a small office. She suppressed her thoughts of academics in ivory towers, and took the plan to be xeroxed. Then she set off for the west wing.

She almost got lost along the way—there had been additions since the plan had been drawn. She understood how something like this could have stayed hidden for so long.

Dec. 21st, 1911 (morning).
There must have been rains in the mountains, since the water is steadily rising, and I begin to fear that the camp is not pitched high enough above the water line. The natives have deserted, all except Lucio who would dearly like to go, but in some way feels loyalty to me and stays. He says that the reason for the natives' departure is that high water is a warning of an anaconda's approach; I find this hard to believe, since surely no single creature could displace sufficient water to raise the level of a *whole river*, unless it be very huge indeed. If what Lucio says is true, I am delighted at the magnitude of the discovery I am about to make! (Though God alone knows how such a carcass could be transported through this insect-infested jungle). And yet, I cannot help remembering Lucio's anaconda-gods, and I wonder whether they will allow mere science to take one of their kind.
(later)
I must add a note to the above; I was wandering along the river bank, and I found the remains of a simply gigantic snake. I jest not when I say that the remains of its rib-cage form a tunnel of my height, and that the portion I explored (and it most clearly *was* a portion, since it lacked both head and tail) was a good twenty paces (say fifty feet) in length. I now understand why Lucio believes a single creature sufficient to displace the water of a river.

I tried to lift one vertebra and to carry it away as proof of the existence of such snakes, but I could not manage to lift it. I have marked the site clearly with several red flags, and I hope that I may persuade the Professor to come and examine the find for himself.

She found the skeleton hall. It was ancient and neglected—like everything else she seemed to come across. All round the walls little snakes and lizards posed for ever in glass boxes, bare of everything but their bones. The weak afternoon sun dripped in through a pair of grimy windows, illuminating the specimens in three shades of white.

The centrepiece of the collection was a pair of high, polished oak podia, without glass covers. Each bore the label 'Anaconda. Shot, Rio Negro, 1897." And on one of them stretched a twenty-foot skeleton. It was the biggest snake Kate had ever seen. The second podium was empty, but she noticed that another large skeleton had been set up in a sleepy coil in a corner of the hall. It was wrapped up with itself in front of a flaking radiator that must have been cold for decades. And on her right, a door presented its blank face. She walked over towards it, her careful footfalls muffled by the thick dust on the floor.

She opened the door soundlessly.

A human skeleton sat at a table with its back to her. Pigeon droppings from a half-shut skylight covered its head. She shut the door, and in the draught the bones tumbled into a heap. Papers rustled on the desk.

She crossed the room and saw the bony hands which still lay on the table, clutching a leather-bound book. Sidestepping the pile on the floor, she picked up the book and shook away the hands, which clattered aside like a boxful of chessmen. Then she sat down in the vacated chair and read the first page. It was handwritten: "The Journal of Colonel Julian Harringforth, Amazon Expedition, 1911." She turned the page and continued.

Soon, she realised why Doctor Baehr must have run down to his old office to consult that particular text. And why, in his excitement, he must have broken the spine. Presently, she came to the final entry:

Dec. 21st , 1911 (evening).
I have got one! It came up the beach in late afternoon, and I shot it through the head. It was as simple as that. I am almost disappointed at the inefficiency of these anaconda-gods, but I cannot complain of my catch: the creature must be a full sixty feet in length (and that does not include the tail which remains in the water). The body is still undergoing spasms, and I rest well clear of it, awaiting the serpent's death. When it finally stops its motions, then I will have my trophy. And truly, it must have been rains which raised the level of the water, for it has not fallen appreciably, despite the near-death of its supposed cause.

I sit in my tent now, writing this by candlelight, for I cannot bear to wait 'til morning to place my experiences on record. Lucio is less delighted than I, he sits in a corner quavering.

And then the handwriting changed:
"Dear Baehr,
I am sending you this diary since I know you and Harringforth were once friends. I am sorry about his death (at least, we have assumed that was his fate, in the absence of any traces of him), and I consider it not a little my fault, since I am the expedition leader. I will tell you what we know of the incidents following those described:
"Early on the morning of the 22nd, we heard a salvo of shots from up

the Culebras, and we saw flocks of birds rising noisily from upstream. An hour later, a red flag floated down to us, and I dispatched a canoe to investigate, myself in command. When we reached Harringforth's camp, we found the tents torn down, and no trace of either Harringforth or that half-caste with whom he was wont to talk. The river banks were wet, and I can only conclude that there must have been some sort of flash flood that dissipated itself before reaching the main river, for we saw no sign of it at our position by the Culebras' mouth.

"I have read the last few entries, and consequently have searched for this skeleton of which he speaks. I found only a cavity in the sand, by the side of which was one solitary red flag. There were marks leading to the water, though obscured by the flooding, as if something heavy had been dragged away, but of the skeleton (assuming it existed; I have fears that Harringforth's mind was turned by that Lucio's native folktales) there was not one bone left.

"I am sending this to you in the hope it can be put to some use; you clearly share an interest in snakes with the late Harringforth; but I would not take it too seriously (that mumbo-jumbo *re* anaconda-gods points clearly to derangement).

"I remain yours & c.,
James Winterton,
3rd March 1912"

Kate felt she ought to be delighted at her discovery— it was a justification of all the work, it would get published, it would make her famous. She should be happy about that. But curiously, it made her sad that this book would get soiled in that way. She felt like St. Luke wilfully selling film rights to Hollywood, betraying this book that she believed in. Now that she had discovered what she had been seeking, she wanted to leave this garret in the tower as quickly as she could: it frightened her.

She picked up the book, and turned to go. But as she reached the door, she heard a noise in the hall, a rustle-and-clack. The coiled snake was moving, moving . . . shedding great clouds of dust, fixing her with balefully staring sockets. Closer, closer, it drew towards her. How prettily the polished bone shone . . . Lethally: she kicked out. A tinkling cascade of ribs was accompanied by the skull rattling ponderously up into the late afternoon sunlight. She choked on the thick air. Tears ran down her cheeks—she wasn't sure whether they were from relief or fright.

It had been so predictable, really. (*They have powers of giving life to the dead, so long as their actions will result in the taking of a life. Soul for soul*). But she had defeated it . . . She sat down cross-legged, to rest. Morbidly, she wondered: if something *had* happened to her, would Vic have come after her, to find the ghastly remains? Or would she have been left as another fifty-year-old mystery? She wanted to think that Vic would search the museum top to bottom—being realistic, his superiors probably wouldn't let him . . . but that hadn't stopped her in her search. She had followed through her quest, and triumphed at the end!

Her breathing had returned to normal and she began to rise, about to go, when she heard another noise behind her. The mate! She had forgotten about the mate . . . A cold descended on her legs, a cold that burned like acid. Pain . . . oh, the pain, the very pain that Doctor Baehr—that Rudolf—must have experienced here, in this place, over sixty years before . . . and then she realised what she was thinking, and she struggled. Something was making her enjoy the pain, the sucking-melting-tingling pain. A swarm of bedbugs lapped her body heat, a cold-compress . . . No, she wanted to live!

(A small, forgotten voice mocked her: *Snakes can live a long time without food, and when they cannot draw the life-heat from a human victim, they may be found coiled around the embers of a fire* . . . or a radiator?).

"No, I don't believe in you!" she shouted, but it wasn't the truth. As she turned her head to look behind her, she *knew* it wasn't true. She had seen—she believed. The other skeleton was entwined around her feet, and something was riding on its back. Something small and scaly and three-eyed.

Then something hit the little deity, and the bones peeled away leaving just the pain. Vic stood by the podium, wielding a shattered glass specimen box.

"I followed your footprints in the dust," he said lamely. "I was worried."

The third eye of the lacerated god stared at her, poking weakly through the wrinkled skin. Kate could almost imagine what it was thinking: the life it had taken was its own.

It hadn't occurred to it that some humans go around in pairs, too.

THE LAST WOLF
Karl Edward Wagner

Illustration by Jim Pitts

Karl Edward Wagner made a name for himself in the fantasy field during the 1970s with his highly original series of Heroic Fantasy books featuring Kane, The Mystic Swordsman: Darkness Weaves, Bloodstone, Death Angel's Shadow, Dark Crusade *and* Night Winds. *For some years now he has been displaying the talents of other writers in his annual series* The Year's Best Horror Stories, *and also through the massive collections he's published under his Carcosa imprint. But we shouldn't forget the growing brood of highly distinctive horror fiction that Karl has himself wrought over the past few years, some of which can be sampled in his two excellent collections,* In a Lonely Place *and* Why Not You and I? *'The Last Wolf' originally appeared in* Midnight Sun *2 (1975) and was reprinted in the second issue of* Fantasy Tales. *More poignant than gruesome, this atmospheric tale of literary ghosts has more than a hint of despairing terror to it.*

The last writer sat alone in his study.

There was a knock at his door.

But it was only his agent. A tired, weathered old man like himself. It seemed not long ago that he had thought the man quite young.

"I phoned you I was coming," explained his agent, as if to apologize for the writer's surprised greeting.

'A thousand phantoms drifted in his study'

Of course . . . he had forgotten. He concealed the vague annoyance he felt at being interrupted in his work.

Nervously the agent entered his study. He gripped his attaché case firmly before him, thrusting it into the room as if it were a shield against the perilously stacked shelves and shelves of musty books. Clearing a drift of worn volumes from the cracked leather couch, he seated himself amidst a puff of dust from the ancient cushions.

The writer returned to the chair at his desk, swivelling to face his guest. His gnarled fingers gripped the chairarms; his black eyes, bright beneath a craggy brow, bored searchingly into the agent's face. He was proud and wary as an aging wolf. Time had weathered his body and frosted his hair. No one had drawn his fangs.

The agent had shifted against the deep cushions and erased the dusty film on his attaché case. His palms left sweat smears on the vinyl. He cleared his throat, subconsciously striving to clear his thoughts from the writer's spell. It would be easier if he could see him just as another client, as nothing more than a worn out old man. Just another tired old man, as he himself had become.

"I haven't had any success with your manuscripts," he said softly. "No luck at all."

There was pain in his eyes, but the writer nodded stiffly. "No, it was obvious from your manner that you hadn't been successful this time." He added: "This time either."

"Your last seven novels," the agent counted. "Nothing."

"They were good books," the writer murmured, like a parent recalling a lost child. "Not great books, for all my efforts, but they were good. Someone would have enjoyed reading them."

His eyes fell upon the freshly typed pages stacked on his desk, the newest page just curling from his ancient mechanical typewriter. "This one will be better," he stated.

"That's not the problem," his agent wearily told him. He had told him before. "No one's saying that you haven't written well— it's just . . . Who's going to print them?"

"There are still one or two publishers left, I believe."

"Well, yes. But they don't publish books like this anymore."

"What do they publish then?" The writer's voice was bitter.

"Magazines, mostly—like these." The agent hurriedly drew a pair of flimsy periodicals from his case.

The writer accepted them with a wry smile and thumbed through the pages of bright photographs. He snorted. "Pretty pictures, advertisements mostly, and a few paragraphs of captions. Like the newspapers. Not even real paper anymore."

He gestured toward the shelves of age-yellowed spines. "Those are magazines. *Saturday Review. Saturday Evening Post. Playboy. Kenyon Review. Weird Tales. Argosy.* And the others that have passed. Do you remember them? They contained stories, essays, articles, criticism. A lot of garbage, and a lot of things worthwhile. They contained thoughts."

"Still, there's some writing in the few periodicals that we have left," the agent pointed out. "You could do that sort of thing."

"That sort of thing?' That's not writing! Since the learned journals all went to computerized tapes, the only excuse for a periodical that's left are these mindless picture brochures the ad companies publish. Damned if I'll write copy for Madison Avenue!"

"But what are you trying to get to?" he scowled.

The plastic pages of smiling young consumers fluttered back into the attaché case. "I'm trying to say it's impossible to sell your books. Any books. No one publishes them. No one reads this sort of thing anymore."

"What do they read instead?"

The agent waved his hands in a vague gesture. "Well, there's these magazines. One or two newspapers are still around."

"They're just transcripts of the television news," the writer scoffed. "Pieced together by faceless technicians, slanted and censored to make it acceptable, and then gravely presented by some television father image. What about books?"

"Well, there are a few houses that still print the old classics—for school kids and people who still go to libraries. But all that's been made into movies, put on television—available on cassettes to view whenever you like. Not much reason to read those—not when everybody's already seen it on tv."

The writer made a disgusted noise.

"Well, damn it, man!" the agent blurted in exasperation. "Marshall McLuhan spoke for your generation. You must have understood what was coming."

"He didn't speak for my generation," the writer growled. "What about those last three novels that did sell? Somebody must have read those."

"Well, maybe not," explained the other delicately. "It was pure luck I found a publisher for them anyway. Two of them the publisher used just as a vehicle for Berryhill to illustrate—he has quite a following, you know. Collectors bought them for his artwork—but maybe some read the books. And the last one I sold . . . Well, that was to a publisher who wanted it for the nostalgia market. Maybe somebody read it while that fad lasted."

Beneath his white mustache, the writer's lips clamped tightly over words that would be ill-bred to use to a guest.

"Anyway, both publishers are defunct now," his agent went on. "Printing

costs are just too high. For the price of half a dozen books, you can buy
a tv. Books just cost too much, take too much time, for what you get out
of them."

"So where does that leave me?"

There was genuine sympathy, if not understanding, in the agent's voice.
He had known his client for a long while. "There just doesn't seem to
be any way I can sell your manuscripts. I'm sorry—truly sorry. Feel free
to try another agent, if you want. I honestly don't know one to recom-
mend, and I honestly doubt that he'll have any better success.

"There just isn't any market for books in today's world. You're like a
minstrel when all the castles have fallen, or a silent film star after the
talkies took over. You've got to change, that's all."

More than ever the writer seemed a wolf at bay. The last wolf. They
were all gone too. Just the broken-spirited creatures born in cages to
amuse the gawking, mindless world on the other side of the bars.

"But I do have some other prospects for you," the agent announced,
trying to muster a bright smile.

"Prospects?" The writer's shaggy brows rose dubiously.

"Sure. Books may have outlived their day, but today's writers still have
plenty to keep them busy. I think a few of your crowd may even still
be around, writing for television and the movies."

The writer's face was dangerous.

"I've talked with the producers of two new shows—one of them even
remembered that best-seller you had years back. They both said they'd
take a close look at anything you have to show. Quite a break, consider-
ing you've never written a script before. Ought to be right in your line
though— both shows are set back in your salad days.

"One's a sitcom about a screwball gang of American soldiers in a POW
camp back in the Indo-China wars. Dorina Vallecia plays the comman-
dant's daughter, and she's a hot property right now. The other's a sitcom
about two hapless beatnik drug pushers back in the Love Generation days.
This one looks like a sure hit for next season. It's got Garry Simson as
the blundering redneck chief of police. He's a good audience draw, and
they've got a new black girl, Livia Stone, to play the bomb-throwing activist
girl friend."

"No," said the writer in a tight voice.

"Now wait a minute," protested the agent. "There's good money in this—
especially if the show hits it off. And it wasn't easy talking to these guys,
let me tell you!"

"No. It isn't the money."

"Then what is it, for Christ's sake! I'm telling you, there's a bunch of
old-time writers who've made it big in television."

"No."

"Well, there's an outside chance I can get you on the script team for a new daytime gothic soaper. You've always had a fondness for that creepy stuff."

"Yes. I always have had. No."

The agent grimaced unhappily. "I don't know what I can do for you. I really don't. I tell you there's no market for your stuff, and you tell me you won't write for the markets that are there."

"Maybe something will come up."

"I tell you, it's hopeless."

"Then there's nothing more to say."

The agent fidgeted with the fastenings of his attaché case. "We've been friends a long time, you know. Damn it, why won't you at least try a few scripts? I'm not wanting to pry, but the money must look good to you. I mean, it's been a long dry spell since your last sale."

"I won't say I can't use the money. But I'm a writer, not a hired flunky who hacks out formula scripts according to the latest idiot fads of a tasteless media."

"Well, at least the new social security guarantees an income for everyone these days."

The writer's lined face drew cold and white. "I've never bothered to apply for the government's dole. Turning my personal life over to the computers for a share of another man's wages seems to me a rather dismal bargain."

"Oh." The agent felt embarrassed. "Well, I suppose you could always sell some of these books—if things got tight, I mean. Some of these editions ought to be worth plenty to a rare book collector, wouldn't they?"

"Good night," said the writer.

Like a friend who has just discharged his deathbed obligations, the agent rose to his feet and shook hands with the writer. "You really ought to keep up with today's trends, you know. Like television—watch some of the new shows, why don't you? It's not so bad. Maybe you'll change your mind, and give me a call?"

"I don't think so."

"You even got a television in this house? Come to think, I don't remember seeing a screen anywhere. Does that antique really work?" He pointed to an ancient fishbowl Stromberg-Carlson, crushed in a corner, its mahogany console stacked with crumbling comic books.

"Of course not," the writer said, as he ushered him to the door. "That's why I keep it here."

The last writer sat alone in his study.

There was a knock at his door.

His stiff joints complained audibly as he left his desk, and the cocked revolver that lay there. He swung open the door.

Only shadows waited on his threshold.

The writer blinked his eyes, found them dry and burning from the hours he had spent at his manuscript. How many hours? He had lost all count of time. He passed a weary hand over his face and crossed the study to the bourbon decanter that stood, amber spirits, scintillant crystal, in its nook, as always.

He silently toasted a departed friend and drank. His gaze fell upon a familiar volume, and he pulled it down with affection. It was a tattered asbestos-cloth first of Bradbury's *Fahrenheit 451*.

"Thank God you're dead and gone," he murmured. "Never knew how close you were—or how cruelly wrong your guess was. It wasn't government tyranny that killed us. It was public indifference."

He replaced the yellowed book. When he turned around, he was not alone.

A thousand phantoms drifted about his study. Spectral figures in a thousand costumes, faces that told a thousand stories. Through their swirling ranks the writer could see the crowded shelves of his books, his desk, substantial.

Or were they? When he looked more closely, the walls of his study seemed to recede. Perhaps instead he was the phantom, for through the ghostly walls of books, he began to see strange cities rising. Pre-Babylonian towers washed by a silent sea. Medieval castles lost within thick forests. Frontier forts standing guard beside unknown rivers. He recognized London, New York, Paris—but their images shimmered in a constant flux of change.

The writer watched in silence, his black eyes searching the faces of the throng that moved about him. Now and again he thought he glimpsed a face that he recognized, but he could not call their names. It was like meeting the brother of an old friend, for certain familiar lines to these faces suggested that he should know them. But he had never seen their faces before. No one had.

A heavy-set man in ragged outdoor clothing passed close to him. The writer thought his virile features familiar. "Don't I know you?" he asked in wonder, and his voice was like speaking aloud from a dream.

"I doubt it," replied the young man. "I'm Ethan Blackdaw. You would know me only if you had read Jack London's *Spell of the Snows.*"

"I'm not familiar with that book, though I know London well."

"He discarded me after writing only a fragment."

The writer called to another visitant, a powerful swordsman in antediluvian armor: "Surely I've met you."

"I think not," the barbarian answered. "I am Cromach. Robert E. Howard would have written my saga, had he not ended his life."

A lean-faced man in dirty fatigues nodded sourly. "Hemingway doomed me to limbo in the same way."

"We are the lost books," murmured a Berber girl, sternly beautiful in medieval war dress. "Some writer's imagination gave us our souls, but none of us was ever given substance by his pen."

The writer stared in wonder.

A young girl in the dress of a flapper smiled at him wistfully. "Jessica Tilma wanted to write about me. Instead she married and forgot her dream to write."

"Ben Pruitt didn't forget about me," growled a tall black in torn fieldhand's overalls. "But no publishers wanted his manuscript. The flophouse owner tossed me out with the rest of Pruitt's belongings that night when he died."

A slim girl in hoopskirts sighed. "Barry Sheffield meant to write a sonnett about me. He had four lines completed when a Yankee bullet took him at Shiloh."

"I was Zane Grey's first book," drawled a rangy frontier marshall. "Or at least the first one he tried to write."

A bleary-eyed lawyer adjusted his stained vest and grumbled, "William Faulkner always meant to get started on my book."

"Thomas Wolfe died before he started me," commiserated a long-legged mountain girl.

The walls of his study had almost vanished. A thousand, ten thousand phantoms passed about him. Gothic heroines and brooding figures in dark cloaks. Cowboys, detectives, spacemen and superheroes in strange costumes. Soldiers of a thousand battles, statesmen and explorers. Fat-cheeked tradesmen and matrons in shapeless dresses. Roman emperors and Egyptian slaves. Warriors of an unhistoried past, children of a lost future. Sinister faces, kindly faces, comic and tragic, brave men and cowards, the strong and the weak. There seemed no end to their number.

He saw a fierce Nordic warrior—a companion to Beowulf, had a waraxe not ended his stave. There were countless phantoms of famous men of history—each subtly altered after the conception of a would-be biographer. He saw half-formed images of beauty, whose author had died heartbroken that his genius was insufficient to transform his vision into poetry. A stoneage hunter stalked by, gripping his flint axe—as if seeking the mammoth that had stolen from mankind his first saga.

And then the writer saw faces that he recognized. They were from his own imagination. Phantoms from uncounted fragments and forgotten ideas. Characters from the unsold novels that yellowed in his files. And from the unfinished manuscript that lay beside his typewriter.

"Why are you here?" the writer demanded. "Did you think that I, too, was dead?"

The sad-eyed heroine of his present novel touched his arm. "You are the last writer. This new age of man has forgotten you. Come join us instead in this limbo of unrealized creation. Let this ugly world that has grown about you sink into the dull mire of its machine imagination. Come with us into our world of lost dreams."

The writer gazed at the phantom myriads, at the spectral cities and forests and seas. He remembered the dismal reality of the faceless, plastic world he had grown old in. No one would mark his passing . . .

"No." He shook his head and politely disengaged her hand. "No, I'm not quite ready for limbo. Not now. Not ever."

And the book-lined walls of his study rose solid about him once more.

The last writer sits alone in his study.

His eyes glow bright, and his gnarled fingers labor tirelessly to transform the pictures of his imagination into the symbolism of the page. His muscles feel cold, his bones are ice, and sometimes he thinks he can see through his hands to the page beneath.

There will be a knock at his door.

Maybe it will be death.

Or a raven, knelling "Nevermore."

Maybe it will be the last reader.

TONGUE IN CHEEK
Mike Grace

Illustration by Mark Dunn

Mike Grace has combined his interest in computers and writing to produce three adventure games books for the micro, but we were pleased to be able to use 'Tongue in Cheek' in the thirteenth issue of Fantasy Tales. *We hope you enjoy this charming little piece of grue...*

THE car just seemed to die, quietly and very firmly. Annabel felt sudden panic as the lights flickered out, leaving her driving headlong into black silence, totally blind as the world outside vanished as if blinked out of existence, then her foot rammed the brake onto the floor. The tyres squealed protestingly as she slewed across the road to bounce onto the grass verge, almost topple, then settle still upright and unharmed. Her breath hissed between her teeth and she realised that she had both hands gripping the steering wheel so tight it would have been impossible to prise them loose had she crashed, and she relaxed.

"Oh, shit!" she said, to no-one in particular.

She forced herself to breathe again, deeply, and turned the ignition key in an automatic gesture which she knew would be hopeless. Nothing.

"And just what the hell do I do now?" she asked, her voice sounding too loud in the utter quiet of the night.

It had been such a perfect day, she should have known it couldn't last. First the audition (she'd performed at her best, she knew), then she'd gone

172

'It began to move, to slither further and further out'

to Heal's to browse among the easy luxury, and window-shopped down Oxford Street. Hamburger lunch had been followed by a Stanley Kubrick film she'd missed in one of those tiny cinemas off Leicester Square (surprisingly, she'd been able to concentrate on the film, almost as if she had known the outcome of the day), and when she'd phoned her agent at seven he had confirmed that she had the part. She'd expressed surprise and joy, (after all, it *was* expected), but she'd known as if she was taking part in a story she'd read before and knew the ending. He'd taken her to dinner at a little Greek restaurant and they'd talked about the film and how, if she was lucky, she'd get at least three numbers (although she'd be lucky to have two left when the film was finished), and how rehearsals would begin in six weeks.

She'd nodded, and smiled, and laughed, but her mind was a thousand miles away in a place of mists and dreams and magic. At twelve she walked along the Embankment feeling as if she was a million dollars' worth, and stopped to gaze at the lights reflected in the Thames. Dimpled in the soft water they became romanticised in her imagination, transforming into footlights, and she was singing before a huge audience that stretched away and away into the far distance—so far it was just a blur of faces in the moonlight, all shouting her name, all applauding her as she poured her very soul into the words, as the music flowed through her . . . She felt so wonderful that she didn't want the magic of that evening to end, not just yet.

It had though, along a tiny country lane somewhere near Dorking at about three in the morning, in utter silence and complete blackness. The

173

car had just cut out, everything had stopped completely—no lights, no power, nothing at all. And she was furious.

"I told Chris we should have had it serviced sooner," she muttered to herself.

Outside, the night seemed to mock her, the dark to press in on her. On impulse she flicked the radio, but that too was dead. She could have been almost anywhere in the world. She opened the door . . .

There was a soft breeze with a undertone of chill. She had no coat (it *was* June), and her sleeveless arms goose-pimpled as she turned to see where she was. The car was sitting in the middle of a dirt lay-by so that only the offside corner projected over the road. Damn lucky not to have gone into the ditch, she reflected, pushing it off the road. She stood in the stillness and squinted up ahead to try and spot lights, houses, any sign of life at all. She'd passed a couple of houses about a mile back, she remembered, and she firmed her lips as she made the decision to walk back and knock them up, ask to use the phone.

After five minutes she wasn't so sure she'd made the right decision. She felt helpless, more frightened than she'd thought she would, and dark shadows seemed to be watching her from both sides of the road. It was impossible, but the trees seemed to be following her with black eyes, the branches creaking as they waved in the breeze, beckoning. She was walking on the white line, dead centre, her car a forgotten shape in the greyness of the distance, but a shape holding safety and warmth compared with the unseen terrors that might lie in the unknown ahead. Perhaps she should have stayed where she was, locked inside the car, warm and safe until the security of morning light. But she thought of Chris, of how he might soon start to worry because she'd said she would be back by two-thirty, and how much she wanted to hear his voice thick with sleep on the other end of the phone. God, she wanted that so much.

Annabel shivered and began to walk briskly, her shoes clicking defiantly. Something rustled in the bush to her right—her heart jumped, (it *really* did feel like it jumped into your mouth!) and she froze, one foot just touching the road on the heel. She was aware of a hammering in her ears and realised with surprise it was her pulse. It must be possible to hear it half a mile away. Her breath waited, waited in the silence outside, in the closeness of the night. It must be her imagination, but the trees on her right seemed to be moving, so slowly. She could hear a wet slithering noise, like roots being dragged over mud, like a spider scuttling through the grass, coming now from both sides of the road. She seemed to be paralysed, her whole attention on that impossible noise shuffling nearer, her head not daring to move, not daring to betray her presence, as if her very stillness would fool whatever was moving toward her. Her blood began to congeal—she could feel it slowing . . . Damn it, those trees *were* moving, she was sure . . .

She became aware of the stiffness in her body as she held herself rigid. She had to turn her head, had to look. She had to know if she was going insane, if her mind was really making a fool out of her, if there was *something*. She forced her head to turn.

The trees were back in their original places and the rustling came again, louder and nearer. It must be a bird, or a rabbit. It sounded very close.

"Shoo!" she shrieked harshly, the word almost ripped from vocal cords that constricted, and relief fell like a curtain over her as a tiny black rabbit detached itself from the darker blackness of the bushes and loped across the road. It had only been a rabbit. Slowly she relaxed, shoulders drooping and her breath sighing so that she didn't hear the imperceptible rattle of dry twigs above her head, feel the trees seem to grin to one another. They could afford to wait. It was still a long way to those houses.

She began to walk again, breathing the air deep into her lungs in an attempt to wash out the fear that was niggling at the back of her throat. Her feet crunched on the dry road. Ahead, the trees seemed to loom up, arms reaching out toward her. A drip of water splashed on her forehead. Christ! she thought, all I need now is for it to rain! The smell of the damp earth beneath her seemed peaceful and sweet, denying the existence of the evil shapes that she felt shifting in the shadows beside her. A bush touched her face. With a start she realised she'd drifted from the centre of the road and quickly she moved back. Somewhere in the distance she could hear a car, but it was moving away from her and might as well have been in another world. Another drip of rain on her bare shoulder and she felt the water trickle slowly down her arm.

She increased her step a little, as if in hope to outdistance whatever was keeping pace with her beside the road. She didn't know why, but she knew something was moving beside her, watching her with slitty eyes, something large. She stopped again, not wanting to walk on in case the sound of her steps would attract it.

Jesus Christ Almighty—those trees really *were* moving. A minute ago they'd been several yards away, yet now they were standing on the edge of the road, waving silently in the cool night air, branches grotesquely dancing in jazz-jagged rhythm in front of her face. Unbelievably—they were reaching down towards her.

Annabel moved on, quickly down the road, away from the impossible horror. It *must* be imagination! She cursed the day she'd ever read any of Stephen King's, any book of ghost stories. Gentle rain was now beginning to fall, a few drops kissed her face and hair, one fell down the back of her neck like a jolt of cold ice. She knew, suddenly she knew, that there was something in the middle of the road—behind her. Following her, matching step for step. And she knew that she couldn't turn around, she had to keep going, she had to keep walking, she daren't turn around and see what it was that was following her.

She screamed as a twig cut her cheek, drawing blood, and another hooked into her hair and twined, tugged, pulling her head back.

Above her the tree cackled a dusty dry chatter of triumph as it bent her head back, sticklike fingers gripping her hair and forcing tears of sharp pain into her eyes, blinding her. A whiplike blow sliced into her arm as if someone had held a branch aside for her to pass, then released it too soon, and she felt her legs give way as another, heavier log seemed to roll into her from behind, toppling her off balance. This can't be happening, her mind screamed out, but her neck cracked at the strain as she fell and the reality of agony told her the truth.

Annabel kicked out instinctively, sending the grasping shape into retreat with a sizzle of anger, and suddenly rolled free of the twigs still in her hair, hands blindly knocking them away. On the other side of the road blurred leafy limbs twittered dryly, like dusty mouths opening to receive her, and she screamed again as another branch caught her cheek, opening the first wound. Then she was up, twisting and dodging in a forest of snake-like fingers, tearing herself free and running, running as if a pack of mad hounds were baying at her heels, running back the way she had come, away from the houses, back toward her car. A low mocking laugh seemed to drift through the wall of terror (had she imagined it all?), then her world was filled with her rasping breath as she pounded down the centre of the road again, eyes staring unseeing, feet slapping the hard tarmac until each step brought a sting shooting up her leg, chest heaving with the exertion, not caring what lay ahead, not seeing what lay ahead.

Once she ran off the road and shrieked anew as she blundered into a bush, and fell, scraping her hands and knees badly. Then she collapsed, exhausted, spent, unable to draw in air, not even if the trees were still close behind, were even now reaching down again with their grasping, spiderlike claws. . .

And that was when the Mini came.

"Can I help you, dear? Are you hurt?" The voice seemed far away, distorted like a voice on a radio that hasn't been tuned properly, then it seemed to settle and she was aware of concern and age blended into a surprisingly gentle sound. Annabel looked up, suddenly remembering the sound of the car as it pulled up alongside and the engine died and the door opened. . . remembering as if the events hadn't really happened to her but were part of a memory of long ago. . . something that had lain dormant inside her for a timeless period to be reawakened by the sudden sound of the voice, an unexpectedly soft voice.

At that time of night she would have expected a man, perhaps a salesman or a secret lover, even a couple coming back from a party, in fact almost anyone except the little old lady in a blue plastic mac (her summer coat no doubt), who looked more as if she should be motoring back from Sunday Church instead of alone in a Mini at three-thirty in the morning. For a second the figure seemed to shimmer and lose shape and Annabel blinked some of the fear out of her eyes as a leather-gloved hand reached across the seat toward her.

"Climb in out of the rain, my dear. You look absolutely terrified, and wet through." The warmth in the voice washed over her. She was suddenly aware that it was raining quite hard, and that she was soaked and shivering and cold. Thankfully she accepted the hand and hauled herself in to slump into the passenger seat. The door clicked shut silently after her, and she found herself thinking that the old duck must keep the car in very good condition, and that made her angry at herself because if she and Chris had looked after her own car then she wouldn't be in the mess she was in now.

As the car started off again, the memory of the trees began to fade a little, and she wondered if she had imagined it all, had somehow blundered into the bushes and scratched herself and just thought that the branches were reaching for her . . . Her hand went to the warm tackiness on her cheek that was beginning to harden . . .

"Does it hurt much, my dear?"

Annabel shook her head. She still felt unsure, almost a little afraid, disorientated at the way events were taking control over her. She'd always hated that, she'd always wanted to have total control over her life so that she knew what was happening and why, and that she'd made it happen to please herself. But now the world was slipping away from her grasp, shooting down a helter skelter that steepened as it went, so that she was sliding faster and faster until it would be too late, she'd be unable to grip the sides and slow herself, stop, regain her touch with reality and things she could understand again . . . And even as she felt it, she wondered why she was still feeling it now that she was warm and safe and could get to a phone.

"I had a slight accident," she said, trying to sound bright and brave. "If you could just drop me at a phone and I'll call my husband and he'll get a taxi or something . . ."

"Whatever you say, whatever you say," said the old lady, peering ahead through the windscreen that was now being soaked by the rain.

Annabel pulled out her cigarettes (miraculously she had kept hold of her handbag) and offered one to her driver. Although she declined it was obvious there was no objection in the manner of her reply, so gratefully letting the first few inhalations calm her still-shattered nerves, Annabel lapsed into a thoughtful silence. Thank God it had been a women, she reflected.

Between puffs she watched the road unwind ahead of them like a tunnel of light created by the headlights. It was raining so hard now it was difficult to see, and the windscreen wipers flicked futilely back and forth in an attempt to keep pace with the torrents cascading down outside. She wondered what would have happened if the car had not come along, and she was lying drenched as the trees had closed for the kill.

That they would have killed her seemed a foregone conclusion, and she found herself thinking back to her incredible experience and peering out at the woodland at the fringe of the light cast by the car's headlamps at full beam. Was it imagination? Tree branches leaned hungrily forward as the car whizzed underneath to snatch at the space where they'd been. She shuddered. Suppose—just suppose—that the trees really were waiting to grab you at night! Childlike memories of Walt Disney's Snow White running from the huntsman surfaced to haunt her, fill her with as much dread as they had when she'd first seen the film, except that this time the reality of her recent experience added a new dimension to the terror. Suppose trees had always been able to, ever since time began, able to snatch up unwary lovers or naughty children once dusk fell, to wrap their strong branches round you and squeeze your body until ribs cracked and blood spurted. After all, people do disappear—are never heard of again!

The idea began to take on a fearsome attraction the more she thought about it. Suppose it were all true, that for centuries the trees had contained some evil life force that allowed them to move, to slither along at night until they could trap an unwary animal or, even better, an unsuspecting human. And now, with the advent of the car and less and less people walking alone at night, they were having to get bolder, to come to the side of the road, to actually start to hunt their prey . . .

"You're out late," the old lady said with a suddeness that made Annabel jump. "Unusually late, for a married lady, don't you think? And she turned to look at Annabel with a gleam in her eye that spoke of dark mischief and unease. "A lover, perhaps?"

Annabel gave her a hard look. Nosey old cow, she thought, and said nothing. After all, why should I tell the bitch anything, when she says something like that? After what seemed an unnaturally long time the old lady gave a hard laugh, in amusement at the reaction she'd provoked, and turned back to look at the road.

As she did so something cold started to prickle at the back of Annabel's neck, and she realised with horror that she could feel the hairs standing up. She could really feel them.

She tried to speak, and it came out harshly, forcing her to clear her throat. "How far. . .uh, how much farther before we come to a house or something?" It suddenly seemed very important to get out of the car, she wasn't sure why, but there was a strangeness in the woman's remark that had worried her.

"Don't know, dearie, but it won't be long, I expect."

Annabel stole a glance at her. Neat grey hair, rather wispy, pinned under a soft felt hat. Eyes of jet black that had twinkled merrily when she'd first seen them, but were now cold and flat and disturbed her when she looked straight into them. She looked harmless enough, but there was something . . .

Annabel looked at her watch. God! It was four-fifteen! Chris would be worried stiff by now.

"Look, have you got a map or something? I must find a phone. My husband will be worried."

There was no reply. The old lady ignored her, squinting out at the road ahead that wound on and on with an almost-hypnotic endlessness. Had she heard? Annabel was about to ask again when she caught herself, and paused. Suppose her request had been heard, and really ignored? For several reasons that was more terrible than not knowing, than trying to reassure herself that the old lady just hadn't heard. Because. . .because if she had been ignored, it implied a reason. And there was no obvious reason for it. In fact, no reason at all, unless something sinister was happening to her, and she didn't want to know, didn't want to think about that.

A stiff silence fell over them again. Ahead, the road seemed to straighten and Annabel felt a leap of hope. A town perhaps? She looked sideways at the driver again, and felt a shock of incredible fear jolt her so completely that she lost all sense of everything, felt the stench of sickness rise into her throat and her head swim toward oblivion. She clutched at consciousness, unable to believe her eyes, for sitting beside her now in the driving seat was a large man dressed in a black suit, a man with huge hairy hands hiding the steering wheel, hunching himself in the seat because he was too tall to sit straight.

Rigid, an ice-cold poker stretching the length of her spine and a stickyness between her legs, she just stared. The normal world counted for nothing the second time that night. She was very, very frightened. And, as if he knew, the man turned his head to stare back coldly at her, his face filled with a moon-shaped smile of teeth like some hulking Hallowe'en mask, an expression of cold hate and evil lust intermingled in his pits of eyes that were no longer flat, but deep and shining.

179

"Jesus bloody Christ," She mouthed, "this is a dream. This has got to be a dream . . ." But she knew it wasn't a dream, that reality had deserted her and she had fallen into the grip of some supernatural nightmare. The man took his hands from the wheel and she tore her gaze away from his own to watch those hands. The car thundered on with a life of its own, straight as an arrow down the endless road, and a part of her mind noted that the windscreen wipers were still whipping back and forth as she watched those hands reaching out for her. She squirmed back into her seat, yanking at the door handle. Better to jump from a speeding car than face the monstrosity before her. But the handle just spun uselessly. She'd known it would.

The creature before her grinned wider, splitting its face, and in that smile lay the evils of perversion. She began to go insane, she began to crack.

"Too late for that now, dearie," said the man in the old woman's voice, as if to taunt her. "Too late for that now"

And she looked again into those piglike eyes and was lost. He held her as securely as if he was holding her physically. The Mini drove on madly, like some charade that completed the tableau, and the gaping grin in that ballooning face creaked even wider to let a tongue emerge. Annabel sat, paralysed, most of her mind frigid, just a tiny part she could still call her own, looking, seeking for escape. She'd be damned if she'd let him take her, she thought, and was enough of herself to realise wryly how true that thought was. What he was, how he had come along, what he wanted, all was irrelevant to the horror of being with him. And perhaps worse, to the horror of what was surely to come . . .

His tongue slipped out between yellow-stained teeth like a snake leaving its nest to caress his lips. Her gaze fell from his icy stare to watch the tongue, she didn't know why it was so important, but it fascinated as well as repelled. The tongue turned, to look at her. Her flesh crawled. It began to move, to slither further and further out, impossibly further and further out, wavering across the space between them like some distorted worm blindly seeking its prey. Her eyes bulged, disbelieving its length. Christ, it must be all of two feet now and still coming, curling out like someone unreeling a hosepipe, reaching for her. Her breath jerked out—in again—out— like jolts of electricity being fed into her by necessity to keep her alive, alive until he had finished and could discard her . . . The tongue touched her face, cold and wet, smelling of gangrene and dank earth, slimy and shuddering.

It rasped along her cheek, tasting the thickly dried blood, travelled down to her own mouth, kissed her lips, softly sought an entrance. I'm being raped, she thought, raped by a tongue. And she laughed, a harsh unbelieving sound, and the tongue entered serpentlike. It probed between her teeth. I could clamp down on it, squish it, crush it, *hurt* it!

And a far-off part of her mind cried out, because she knew she wouldn't, she'd let it slide down her throat, into her, into her body, penetrating down past her throat, twining itself down to seek out her soul and it would drink deep of her, slaking an unholy thirst. And there was nothing she could do to stop it.

Her heart cried out for help.

The man-thing laughed at her cry, and his hands began to move toward her again.

'Annabel, what the hell did you do with the car last night? I can't see it anywhere."

She came up our of sleep like she was clawing for handholds of dirt in a deep, dark pit. Chris was staring out of the bedroom window, and she'd never been so glad to see anyone in her life. Christ! What a bastard of a dream! Feeling like death, she wriggled up on one elbow as he turned to face her.

"What did you do with the car, love? You were damn late last night, I must have dozed off waiting for you. What time did you get home?"

Was there just a hint of accusation? She tried to remember, but all she got was this awful dream, about trees, and tongues. She shuddered, and put up her hand to rub some sleep out of her eyes, wincing as her hand caught her cheek.

"Cut yourself?" He was beside her on the bed, concerned.

"Yes, I . . . No!"She shouted the last, denying the dream. Fear clutched her. "I don't think so," she ended lamely, and implored him to reassure her with his eyes, suddenly loving him more than she ever had—as if he seemed suddenly precious.

But the cut was there. She could see it in the mirror. A desire welled up in her for his touch, the gentleness of his voice, just to have him near. She needed him to help her, because she wasn't certain she could help herself anymore.

"Chris, what happened last night?"

"God, you have had a night, haven't you? You mean, you've left the car in town? How did you get home? Taxi?"

She nodded weakly, unsure. Yes, that must be it. Too much to drink, had to get a taxi home. But she could remember driving to Dorking, then the car had died on her. No, that was the dream, that was the dream.

"You should have phoned me," he chided, touching her softly. I'd have picked you up. I gather you got the part."

"But I did try to ring you but I couldn't find a phone," she murmured. "God, it's all so confused. You see, the car broke down, so I had to walk, and then..." She stopped, looking at him. He wouldn't believe her anyway, and it must have been a dream.

She stumbled out of bed and looked into the mirror more closely. Her shoulders were scratched, as if cut by branches or scratched by brambles. Her cheek was throbbing now. She could taste something nasty in her mouth. Perhaps she was ill. She didn't want to think about it, and turned back to the bed and smiled weakly.

"Kiss me," she said, for no real reason, feeling strangely cold and helpless as she said it. He smiled, stood up, and part of her wanted to suddenly scream at him to go, escape while there was time, get out of the room, the house. And part of her wanted him, wanted to feel his hardness coming down on her, feel his lips on hers...

He touched her, held her gently. His tongue pushed between her lips. (Get out now—run from him!) She smiled, returning his kiss. Her eyes seemed to glow. (It's too late, stop it now, there's still time!) Her tongue pushed his own aside. (If you really love him—don't) And with a satisfaction spawned within her she saw his eyes pop in surprise as her tongue probed down to the back of his throat, down, down, down inside him, slithering into him, and she began, very slowly and with newfound anticipation, to drink.

And then it really was too late.

IN THE X-RAY
Fritz Leiber

Illustration by Tom Campbell

*No introduction is really needed here for one of the finest genre writers
around, be it fantasy, supernatural horror or science fiction. Fritz
Leiber sold his first story to* Unknown *in 1939 and has subsequently
won almost every major award going. His recent collection* The Ghost
Light *included his revealing autobiographical essay 'Not Much
Disorder and Not So Early Sex' and he contributes a regular column
to the SF newspaper,* Locus. *He is also writing further adventures of
Fafhrd and the Gray Mouser for a seventh book in the famous heroic
fantasy series. In fact,* Weird Tales *refused to publish any of these sword
& sorcery adventures and so Fritz came up with a number of medical
horror tales instead. 'In the X-Ray' appeared in the renowned pulp
in July 1949 and was reprinted in the fifteenth issue of* Fantasy Tales.

D O THE dead come back?" Dr. Ballard repeated the question
puzzledly. "What's that got to do with your ankle?"

"I didn't say that," Nancy Sawyer answered sharply. "I said: 'I tried an
ice pack.' You must have misheard me."

"But . . ." Dr. Ballard began. Then, "Of course I must have," he said
quickly. "Go on, Miss Sawyer."

The girl hesitated. Her glance strayed to the large, gleaming window
and the graying sky beyond. She was a young woman with prominent

183

'Dr. Ballard was staring incredulously at the x-ray'

eyes, a narrow chin, strong white teeth, reddish hair, and a beautiful, doe-like figure which included legs long and slim—except for the ankle of the one outstretched stockingless on the chair before her. That was encircled by a hard, white, somewhat irregular swelling.

Dr. Ballard was a man of middle age and size, with strong, soft-skinned hands. He looked intelligent and as successful as his sleekly-furnished office.

"Well, there isn't much more to it," the girl said finally. "I tried the ice pack but the swelling wouldn't go down. So Marge made me call you."

"I see. Tell me, Miss Sawyer, hadn't your ankle bothered you before last night?"

"No. I just woke up from a nightmare, frightened because something had grabbed my foot, and I reached down and touched my ankle— and there it was."

"Your ankle didn't feel or look any different the day before?"

"No."

"Yet when you woke up the swelling was there?"

"Just as it is now."

"Do you think you might have twisted your foot while you were asleep?"

"No."

"And you don't feel any pain in it now?"

"No, except a feeling of something hard clasped snugly around it and every once in a while squeezing a bit tighter."

"Ever do any sleepwalking?"

"No."

"Any allergies?"

"No."

"Can you think of anything else—anything at all—that might have a bearing on this trouble?"

Again Nancy looked out the window. "I have a twin sister," she said after a moment, in a different voice. "Or rather, I had. She died more than a year ago." She looked back quickly at Dr. Ballard. "But I don't know why I should mention that," she said hurriedly. "It couldn't possibly have any bearing on this. She died of apoplexy."

There was a pause.

"I suppose the X-ray will show what's the matter?" she continued.

The doctor nodded. "We'll have it soon. Miss Snyder's getting it now."

Nancy started to get up, asked, "Is it all right for me to move around?" Dr. Ballard nodded. She went over to the window, limping just a little, and looked down.

"You have a nice view, you can see half the city," she said. "We have the river at our apartment. I think we're higher, though."

185

"This is the twentieth floor," Dr. Ballard said.

"We're twenty-three," she told him. "I like high buildings. It's a little like being in an airplane. With the river right under our windows I can imagine I'm flying over water."

There was a soft knock at the door. Nancy looked around inquiringly. "The X-ray?" He shook his head. He went to the door and opened it.

"It's your friend Miss Hudson."

"Hi, Marge," Nancy called. "Come on in."

The stocky, sandy-haired girl hung in the doorway. "I'll stay out here," she said. "I thought we could go home together though."

"Darling, how nice of you. But I'll be a bit longer, I'm afraid."

"That's all right. How are you feeling, Nancy?"

"Wonderful, dear. Especially now that your doctor has taken a picture that'll show him what's inside this bump of mine."

"Well, I'll be out here," the other girl said and turned back into the waiting room. She passed a woman in white who came in, shut the door, and handed the doctor a large, brown envelope.

He turned to Nancy. "I'll look at this and be back right away."

"Dr. Myers is on the phone," the nurse told him as they started out. "Wants to know about tonight. Can he come here and drive over with you?"

"How soon can he get here?"

"About half an hour, he says."

"Tell him that will be fine, Miss Snyder."

The door closed behind them. Nancy sat still for perhaps two minutes. Then she jerked, as if at a twinge of pain. She looked at her ankle. Bending over, she clasped her hand around her good ankle and squeezed experimentally. She shuddered.

The door banged open. Dr. Ballard hurried in and immediately began to re-examine the swelling, swiftly exploring each detail of its outlines with gentle fingers, at the same time firing questions.

"Are you absolutely sure, Miss Sawyer, that you hadn't noticed anything of this swelling before last night? Perhaps just some slight change in shape or feeling, or a tendency to favour that ankle, or just a disinclination to look at it? Cast your mind back."

Nancy hesitated uneasily, but when she spoke it was with certainty. "No, I'm absolutely sure."

He shook his head. "Very well. And now, Miss Sawyer, that twin of yours. Was she identical?"

Nancy looked at him. "Why are you interested in that? Doctor, what does the X-ray show?"

186

"I have a very good reason, which I'll explain to you later. I'll go into details about the X-ray then, too. You can set your mind rest on one point, though, if it's been worrying you. This swelling is in no sense malignant."

"Thank goodness, Doctor."

"But now about the twin."

"You really want to know?"

"I do."

Nancy's manner and voice showed some signs of agitation. "Why, yes," she said, "we were identical. People were always mistaking us for each other. We looked exactly alike, but underneath . . ." Her voice trailed off. There was a change hard to define. Abruptly she continued, "Dr. Ballard, I'd like to tell you about her, tell you things I've hardly told anyone else. You know, it was she I was dreaming about last night. In fact, I thought it was she who had grabbed me in my nightmare. What's the matter, Dr. Ballard?"

It did seem that Dr. Ballard had changed colour, though it was hard to tell in the failing light. What he said, a little jerkily, was: "Nothing, Miss Sawyer. Please go ahead." He leaned forward a little, resting his elbows on the desk, and watched her.

"You know, Dr. Ballard," she began slowly, "most people think that twins are very affectionate. They think stories of twins hating each other are invented by writers looking for morbid plots."

"But in my case the morbid plot happened to be the simple truth. Beth tyrannized me, hated me, and . . . wasn't above expressing her hate in a physical way." She took a deep breath.

"It started when we were little girls. As far back as I can remember, I was always the slave and she was the mistress. And if I didn't carry out her orders faithfully, and sometimes if I did, there was always a slap or a pinch. Not a little-girl pinch. Beth had peculiarly strong fingers. I was very afraid of them."

"There's something terrible, Dr. Ballard, about the way one human being can intimidate another, crush their will power, reduce to mush their ability to fight back. You'd think the victim could escape so easily—look, there are people all around, teachers and friends to confide in, your father and mother—but it's as if you were bound by invisible chains, your mouth shut by an invisible gag. And it grows and grows, like the horrors of a concentration camp. A whole inner world of pain and fright. And yet on the surface—why, there seems to be nothing at all."

"For of course no one else had the faintest idea of what was going on between us. Everyone thought we loved each other very much. Beth especially was always being praised for her 'sunny gaiety'. I was supposed

187

to be a little 'subdued'. Oh, how she used to fuss and coo over me when there were people around. Though even then there would be pinches on the sly—hard ones I never winced at. And more than that, for . . ."

Nancy broke off. "But I really don't think I should be wasting your time with all these childhood gripes, Dr. Ballard. Especially since I know you have an engagement for this evening."

"That's just an informal dinner with a few old cronies. I have lots of time. Go right ahead. I'm interested."

Nancy paused, frowning a little. "The funny thing is," she continued, "I never understood why Beth hated me. It was as if she were intensely jealous. She was the successful one, the one who won the prizes and played the leads in the school shows and got the nicest presents and all the boys. But somehow each success made her worse. I've sometimes thought, Dr. Ballard, that only cruel people can be successful, that success is really a reward for cruelty . . . to someone."

Dr. Ballard knit his brows, might have nodded.

"The only thing I ever read that helped explain it to me," she went on, "was something in psychoanalysis. The idea that each of us has an equal dose of love and hate, and that it's our business to balance them off, to act in such a way that both have expression and yet so that the hate is always under the control of the love."

"But perhaps when the two people are very close together, as it is with twins, the balancing works out differently. Perhaps all the softness and love begins to gather in the one person and all the hardness and hate in the other . And then the hate takes the lead, because it's an emotion of violence and power and action—a concentrated emotion, not misty like love. And it keeps on and on, getting worse all the time, until it's so strong you feel it will never stop, not even with death."

"For it did keep on, Dr. Ballard, and it did get worse." Nancy looked at him closely. "Oh, I know that what I've been telling you isn't supposed to be so unusual among children. 'Little barbarians', people say, quite confident that they'll outgrow it. Quite convinced that wrist-twisting and pinching are things that will automatically stop when children begin to grow up."

Nancy smiled thinly at him. "Well, they don't stop, Dr. Ballard. You know, it's very hard for most people to associate actual cruelty with an adolescent girl, maybe because of the way girls have been glorified in advertising. Yet I could write you a pretty chapter on just that topic. Of course a lot of it that happened in my case was what you'd call mental cruelty. I was shy and Beth had a hundred ways of embarrassing me. And if a boy became interested in me, she'd always take him away."

"I'd hardly have thought she'd have been able to," remarked Dr. Ballard.

"You think I'm good-looking? But I'm good-looking in an odd way, and in any case it never seemed to count then. It's true, though, that twice there were boys who wouldn't respond to her invitations. Then both times she played a trick that only she could, because we were identical twins. She would pretend to be me—she could always imitate my manner and voice, even my reactions, precisely, though I couldn't possibly have imitated her—and then she would . . . do something that would make the boy drop me cold."

"Do something?"

Nancy looked down. "Oh, insult the boy cruelly, pretending to be me. Or else make some foul, boastful confession, pretending it was mine. If you knew how those boys loathed me afterwards . . ."

"But as I said, it wasn't only mental cruelty or indecent tricks. I remember nights when I'd done something to displease her and I'd gone to bed before her and she'd come in and I'd pretend to be asleep and after a while she'd say—oh, I know, Dr. Ballard, it sounds like something a silly little girl would say, but it didn't sound like that then, with my head under the sheet, pressed into the pillow, and her footsteps moving slowly around the bed—she'd say: 'I'm thinking of how to punish you.' And then there'd be a long wait, while I still pretended to be asleep, and then the touch . . . oh, Dr. Ballard, her hands! I was so afraid of her hands! But . . . what is it, Dr. Ballard?"

"Nothing. Go on."

"There's nothing much more to say. Except that Beth's cruelty and my fear went on until a year ago, when she died suddenly—I suppose you'd say tragically—of a blood clot on the brain. I've often wondered since then whether her hatred of me, so long and cleverly concealed, mightn't have had something to do with it. Apoplexy's what haters die of, isn't it, doctor?"

"I remember leaning over her bed the day she died, lying there paralyzed, with her beautiful face white and stiff as a fish's, one eye bigger than the other. I felt pity for her (You realize, doctor, don't you, that I always loved her?) but just then her hand flopped a little way across the blanket and touched mine, although they said she was completely paralyzed, and her big eye twitched around a little until it was looking almost at me and her lips moved and I thought I heard her say: 'I'll come back and punish you you for this,' and then I felt her fingers moving, just a little, on my skin, as if they were trying close on my wrist, and I jerked back with a cry.

"Mother was very angry with me for that. She thought I was just a selfish, thoughtless girl, afraid of death and unable to repress my fear even for my dying sister's sake. Of course I could never tell her the real reason.

189

I've never really told that to anyone, except you. And now that I've told you I hardly know why I've done it."

She smiled nervously, quite unhumorously.

"Wasn't there something about a dream you had last night?" Dr. Ballard asked softly.

"Oh yes!" The listlessness snapped out of her. "I dreamed I was walking in an old graveyard with gnarly grey trees, and overhead the sky was grey and low and threatening, and everything was weird and dreadful. But somehow I was very happy. But then I felt a faint movement under my feet and I looked down at the grave I was passing and I saw the earth falling away into it. Just a little cone-shaped pit at first, with the dark sandy earth sliding down its sides, and a small black hole at the bottom. I knew I must run away quickly, but I couldn't move an inch. Then the pit grew larger and the earth tumbled down its sides in chunks and the black hole grew. And still I was rooted there. I looked at the gravestone beyond and it said 'Elizabeth Sawyer, 1926-48.' Then out of the hole came a hand and arm, only there were just shreds of dark flesh clinging to the bone, and it began to feel around with an awful, snatching swiftness. Then suddenly the earth heaved and opened, and a figure came swiftly hitching itself up out of the hole. And although the flesh was green and shrunken and eaten and the eyes just holes, I recognized Beth—there was still the beautiful reddish hair. And then the ragged hand touched my ankle and instantly closed on it and the other hand came groping upward, higher, higher, and I screamed . . . and then I woke up."

Nancy was leaning forward, her eyes fixed on the doctor. Suddenly her hair seemed to bush out, just a trifle. Perhaps it had 'stood on end.' At any rate, she said, "Dr. Ballard, I'm frightened."

"I'm sorry if I've made you distress yourself," he said. The words were more reassuring than the tone of voice. He suddenly took her hand in his and for a few moments they sat there silently. Then she smiled and moved a little and said, "It's gone now. I've been very silly. I don't know why I told you all I did about Beth. It couldn't help you with my ankle."

"No, of course not," he said after a moment.

"Why did you ask if she was identical?"

He leaned back. His voice became brisker again. "I'll tell you about that right now—and about what the X-ray shows. I think there's a connection. As you probably know, Miss Sawyer, identical twins look so nearly alike because they come from the same germ cell. Before it starts to develop, it splits in two. Instead of one individual, two develop. That was what happened in the case of you and your sister." He paused. "But," he continued, "sometimes, especially if there's a strong tendency to twin births in the

190

family, the splitting doesn't stop there. One of the two cells splits again. The result—triplets. I believe that also happened in your case."

Nancy looked at him puzzledly. "But then what happened to the third child?"

"The third sister," he amplified. "There can't be identical boy-and-girl twins or triplets, you know, since sex is determined in the original germ cell. There, Miss Sawyer, we come to my second point. Not all twins develop and are actually born. Some start to develop and then stop."

"What happens to them?"

"Sometimes what there is of them is engulfed in the child that does develop completely—little fragments of a body, bits of this and that, all buried in the flesh of the child that is actually born. I think that happened in your case."

Nancy looked at him oddly. "You mean I have in me bits of another twin sister, a triplet sister, who didn't develop?"

"Exactly."

"And that all this is connected with my ankle?"

"Yes."

"But then how—?"

"Sometimes nothing happens to the engulfed fragments. But sometimes, perhaps many years later, they begin to grow—in a natural way rather than malignantly. There are well-authenticated cases of this happening—as recently as 1890 a Mexican boy in this way 'gave birth' to his own twin brother, completely developed though of course dead. There's nothing nearly as extensive as that in your case, but I'm sure there is a pocket of engulfed materials around your ankle and that it recently started to grow, so gradually that you didn't notice it until the growth became so extensive as to be irritating."

Nancy eyed him closely. "What sort of materials? I mean the engulfed fragments."

He Hesitated. "I'm not quite sure," he said. "The X-ray was . . . oh, such things are apt to be odd, though harmless stuff—teeth, hair, nails, you never can tell. We'll know better later."

"Could I see the X-ray?"

He hesitated again. "I'm afraid it couldn't mean anything to you. Just a lot of shadows."

"Could there be . . . other pockets of fragments?"

"It's not likely. And if there are, it's improbable they'll ever bother you."

There was a pause.

Nancy said, "I don't like it.

"I don't like it," she repeated. "It's as if Beth had come back. Inside me."

191

"The fragments have no connection with your dead sister," Dr. Ballard assured her. "They're not part of Beth, but of a third sister, if you can call such fragments a person."

"But those fragments only began to grow after Beth died. As if Beth's soul... And was it my original cell that split a second time?—or was it Beth's?—so that it was the fragments of half her cell that I absorbed, so that..." She stopped. "I'm afraid I'm being silly again."

He looked at her for a while, then, with the air of someone snapping to attention, quickly nodded.

"But doctor," she said, also like someone snatching at practicality, "what's to happen now?"

"Well," he replied, "in order to get rid of this disfigurement to your ankle, a relatively minor operation will be necessary. You see, this sort of foreign body can't be reduced in size by heat or X-ray or injections. Surgery is needed, though probably only under local anaesthetic. Could you arrange to enter a hospital tomorrow? Then I could operate the next morning. You'd have to stay about four days."

She thought for a moment, then said, "Yes, I think I could manage that." She looked distastefully at her ankle. "In fact, I'd like to do it as soon as possible."

"Good. We'll ask Miss Snyder to arrange things."

When the nurse entered, she said, "Dr. Myers is outside."

"Tell him I'll be right along," Dr. Ballard said. "And then I'd like you to call Central Hospital. Miss Sawyer will take the reservation we got for Mrs. Phipps and were about to cancel." And they discussed details while Nancy pulled on stocking and shoe.

Nancy said goodbye and started for the waiting room, favouring her bad leg. Dr. Ballard watched her. The nurse opened the door. Beyond, Nancy's friend got up with a smile. There was now, besides her, a dark, oldish man in the waiting room.

As the nurse was about to close the door, Dr. Ballard said, "Miss Sawyer." She turned. "Yes?"

"If your ankle should start to trouble you tonight—or anything else—please call me."

"Thank you, doctor, I will."

Dr. Ballard nodded. Then he called to his friend, "Be right with you." The dark, oldish man flapped an arm at him.

The door closed. Dr. Ballard went to his desk, took an X-ray photograph out of its brown envelope, switched on the light, studied the photograph incredulously.

He put it back in its envelope and on the desk. He got his hat and over-coat from the closet. He turned out the light. Then suddenly he went back and got the envelope, stuffed it in his pocket, and went out.

The dinner with Dr. Myers and three other old professional friends proved if anything more enjoyable than Dr. Ballard had anticipated. It led
to relaxation, gossip, a leisurely evening stroll, a drink together, a few final
yarns. At one point Dr. Ballard felt a fleeting impulse to get the X-ray
out of his overcoat pocket and show it to them and tell his little yarn
about it, but something made him hesitate, and he forgot the idea. He
felt very easy in his mind as he drove home about midnight. He even
hummed a little. This mood was not disturbed until he saw the face of
Miss Willis, his resident secretary.

"What is it?" he asked crisply.

"Miss Nancy Sawyer. She. . ." For once the imperturbable, greying
blonde seemed to have difficulty speaking.

"Yes?"

"She called up first about an hour and a half ago."

"Her ankle had begun to pain her?"

"She didn't say anything about her ankle. She said she was getting a
sore throat."

"What!"

"It seemed unimportant to me, too, though of course I told her I'd inform
you when you got in. But she seemed rather frightened, kept complaining of this tightness she felt in her throat. . ."

"Yes? Yes?"

"So I agreed to get in touch with you immediately. She hung up. I called
the restaurant, but you'd just left. Then I called Dr. Myers' home, but didn't
get any answer. I told the operator to keep trying."

"About a half hour ago Miss Sawyer's friend, a Marge Hudson, called.
She said Miss Sawyer had gone to bed and was apparently asleep, but
she didn't like the way she was tossing round, as if she were having a
particularly bad dream, and especially she didn't like the noises she was
making in her throat, as if she were having difficulty breathing. She said
she had looked closely at Miss Sawyer's throat as she lay sleeping, and
it seemed swollen. I told her I was making every effort to get in touch
with you and we left it at that."

"That wasn't all?"

"No." Miss Willis' agitation returned. "Just two minutes before you
arrived, the phone rang again. At first the line seemed to be dead. I was
about to hang up. Then I began to hear a clicking, gargling sound. Low
at first, but then it grew louder. Then suddenly it broke free and whooped
out in what I think was Miss Sawyer's voice. There were only two words,
I think, but I couldn't catch them because they were so loud they stopped

193

the phone. After that, nothing, although I listened and listened and kept saying 'hello' over and over. But, Dr. Ballard , that gargling sound! It was as if I were listening to someone being strangled, very slowly, very, very . . . "

But Dr. Ballard had grabbed up his surgical bag and was racing for his car. He drove rather well for a doctor and, tonight, very fast. He was about three blocks from the river when he heard a siren, ahead of him.

Nancy Sawyer's apartment hotel was at the end of a short street terminated by a high concrete curb and metal fence and, directly below, the river. Now there was a fire engine drawn up to the fence and playing a searchlight down over the edge through the faintly misty air. Dr. Ballard could see a couple of figures in shiny black coats beside the searchlight. As he jumped out of his car he could hear shouts and what sounded like the motor of a launch. He hesitated for a moment, then ran into the hotel.

The lobby was empty. There was no one behind the counter. He ran to the open elevator. It was an automatic. He punched the twenty-three button.

On that floor there was one open door in the short corridor. Marge Hudson met him inside it.

"She jumped?"

The girl nodded. "They're hunting for her body. I've been watching. Come on."

She led him to a dark bedroom. There was a studio couch, its covers disordered, and beside it a phone. River air was pouring in through a large, hinged window, open wide. They went to it and looked down. The circling launch looked like a toy boat. Its searchlight and that from the fire engine roved across the dark water. Shouts and chugging came up faintly.

"How did it happen?" he asked the girl at the window.

"I was watching her as she lay in bed," Marge Hudson answered without looking around. "About twenty minutes after I called your home, she seemed to be getting worse. She had more trouble breathing. I tried to wake her, but couldn't. I went to the kitchen to make an ice pack. It took longer than I'd thought. I heard a noise that at first I didn't connect with Nancy. Then I realized that she was strangling. I rushed back. Just then she screamed out horribly. I heard something fall—I think it was the phone—and footsteps and the window opening. When I came in she was standing on the sill in her nightdress, clawing at her throat. Before I could get to her, she jumped."

"Earlier in the evening she'd complained of a sore throat?"

"Yes. She said, jokingly, that the trouble with her ankle must be spreading to her throat. After she called your home and couldn't get you,

194

she took some aspirin and went to bed."

Dr. Ballard switched on the lamp by the bed. He pulled the brown envelope from his coat pocket, took out the X-ray and held it up against the light.

"You say she screamed at the end," he said in a not very steady voice. "Were there any definite words?"

The girl at the window hesitated. "I'm not sure," she said slowly. "They were suddenly choked off, exactly as if a hand had tightened around her throat. But I think there were two words. 'Hand' and 'Beth.'"

Dr. Ballard's gaze flickered toward the mocking face in the photograph on the chest of drawers, then back to the ghostly black and whites of the one in his hands. His arms were shaking.

"They haven't found her yet," Marge said, still looking down at the river and the circling launch.

Dr. Ballard was staring incredulously at the X-ray, as if by staring he could make what he saw go away. But that was impossible. It was a perfectly defined and unambiguous exposure.

There, in the X-ray's black and greys, he could see the bones of Nancy Sawyer's ankle and, tightly clenched around them, deep under skin and flesh, the slender bones of a human hand.

THE BAD PEOPLE
Steve Rasnic Tem

Illustration by Jim Pitts

Steve Rasnic Tem's first sale was to Ramsey Campbell's innovative anthology, New Terrors, *and since then he's gone on to sell more than eighty stories to such publications as* Rod Serling's Twilight Zone Magazine, Weirdbook, Whispers, *and numerous anthologies, including:* Shadows, Night Visions, Halloween Horrors I and II, The Cutting Edge, Tropical Chills *and* Tales By Moonlight II. *1987 saw the publication of Steve's first novel,* Excavation, *to be followed by a second,* Deadfall Hotel. *His style is very contemporary as you'll see from the obliquely sinister 'The Bad People', first published in* Fantasy Tales 13.

SOMETHING cold and heavy had gotten on to the bus.

It was a silly thought. He knew that if he hadn't been having another one of those senseless arguments with Bob the perception would never have occurred to him. As it was, Bob and the intense Mexican heat were pushing him right to the edge. Perhaps that sudden, strange fantasy had been a mental defense, a pressure-release valve.

But he didn't feel relieved. He felt as if he had just done something profoundly evil.

It had been a typical argument with the eight-year-old; he was tired and hot. He wanted to stop now; he didn't want to ride the bus anymore. He was hungry. He had an upset stomach. They never visited the places *he*

'There was an old Mexican folk remedy for people talking bad about you'

wanted to see. He wished they had never gone to Mexico for the summer.

"I'm *bored!*" Bob pushed the thick black hair out of his eyes with a savage movement of his hand, stretched back against the worn bus seat, puffed out his cheeks, then blew out the air hard in ill-concealed anger. Lately, rather than shouting or crying as he had done when Marion was alive, he blew instead.

"I've just about *had it*, Bob." Cliff leaned over and whispered harshly into his ear, looking around at the other passengers, feeling watched. "You have no choice. We're going on to Tlaxcala tonight. You don't have to like it, but that's what we're doing. I'm not going to stop every time you feel like it, *son*."

Cliff felt a sudden drop in his stomach, a cold, hard sensation creeping in, making his chest tight. He really hadn't meant to put the nasty inflection on 'son'; it just came out that way. He hadn't called Bob 'son' the whole time his wife had been alive. Bob had been her brother's son. He couldn't use the word; it went too far. He'd felt bad about that.

He turned around in his seat. A man was watching him from the back of the bus, a tall man with dull black hair—no highlights at all—wearing a dark, soiled poncho. Cliff thought at first the man had been smiling at him, but then noticed that what he had mistaken for a smile was an odd scar across the entire upper lip, curving up at the ends like a wide, shallow 'U'. The man's complexion was a deep amber, almost chocolate, but his hands seemed almost impossibly pale, a white man's hands, a golden Scandinavian's. Cliff fantasised the man keeping the hands in ice to bleach out the colour. He pictured mountains full of snow, travellers lost in the cold and dark, frozen bodies recovered months later from beneath the steep cliffs.

The bus stopped briefly at almost every village in the central highlands, most consisting of nothing but a small arrangement of adobe huts. At each of these stops the villagers warned of the *mala gente*, the bad people, who were reported to occupy the next village down the road. He heard the same thing at each succeeding village. "Oh, no, senor; not this village. It is the *next* village. Mala gente. Mala gente!"

There was an old Mexican folk remedy for people talking bad about you: Sew a toad's mouth up with green thread, then leave it on the person's doorstep. Cliff wondered how the local toad population was holding up. Bob thought it was a wonderful idea.

The afternoon was sweltering; Cliff had stripped down to a T-shirt by noon. He tried to convince Bob to remove his heavy knit shirt; the boy was stubborn, and embarrassed as only an eight-year-old can be. The boy's obstinacy unaccountably infuriated Cliff.

At each stop the Mexican villagers tried to sell the tourists something through the bus windows: Small crafts and souvenirs, mangos, tacos. Bob had had three tacos so far that day; Cliff was at a loss about controlling his eating. He'd tried, but nothing seemed to work. Cliff took Bob's compulsive eating to be a personal attack. The boy didn't have to say a word to get back at him.

Cliff had watched the dark stranger at each of their stops. The man always remained in his seat, staring straight ahead. None of the other passengers seemed to want to have anything to do with him. At first Cliff thought they were just ignoring him completely, but then noted the way people subtly edged from his vicinity. No obvious reaction to him; they just physically backed away. Despite the fact that the bus was quite crowded, there were vacant seats all around the man. Local villagers selling their wares also stayed away from him.

But most disturbing of all, the man seemed so overdressed. Cliff could see at least two sweaters beneath the heavy wool poncho. Yet the man wasn't perspiring at all. The stranger didn't seem to be affected by anything.

"Mala gente! Mala gente!" The old Indian woman babbled to herself as she delivered their linen. Cliff started to reply but the woman had already headed down the walk. He wondered if any of the tourists had done something to offend her.

Bob sat outside their motel room, "bored" again. Cliff had tried to ignore him: Unpacking, rearranging his shirts in the small bureau, looking through the small stack of souvenir Spanish publications he could but half-comprehend. But he always found himself returning to the front window, pulling back the curtains and staring at the boy.

He'd never have agreed to taking Bob in if he hadn't felt safe. Until Marion, he had never found anyone ready to accept him, and even in his most distant, taciturn moments. "It shows character," she'd laugh, poking his stomach with her forefinger.

He had discovered he could only love a child in the abstract. Bob was every bit as distant, as taciturn as he, maybe more so, and Cliff didn't find the boy very likeable.

'Good People' loved and cared for children; he supposed that was what it had come down to. And he had always wanted to be a "good" person. But he had begun to realise that perhaps Marion was a fluke. She was the only one who seemed to know he was *not* a *cold* man, no, not really. Perhaps no one else was going to make him love. When she died, she'd taken that possibility with her.

Cliff had thought he could love Bob after a time, but it hadn't happened.

199

Maybe it never would. That fact was making him angry, frustrated, and still more irritated with Bob's petty childishness. He went to his bureau to pull out a warmer shirt; the room had suddenly felt much colder to him.

That night he found himself staying up watching Bob sleep. After a few hours Bob's snoring became visible to Cliff, cold puffs clouding the air above the boy's face.

The first person Cliff saw the next morning was the stranger. The man was sitting in an open-air, run-down little restaurant with oil-cloth covered tables and brown Indian waitresses. Flies were buzzing around outside the place and most of the patrons were drenched in sweat. But the stranger was cool, felt cold to the eye. Sitting in the grey shade of the cafe in his dark poncho he seemed like an arctic shadow.

As he watched Cliff approach him from the plaza, only his eyes showed any signs of light, like sun reflected off twin orbs of ice.

Cliff was exhausted from only two hours' sleep the previous night, and he was in a bit of a hurry, worried that Bob would wake up soon and come looking for him. For some reason he did not understand, Cliff took a chair at the stranger's table. But then he found he could hardly look at the man, and found it necessary to watch the other patrons, the passersby, even the dogs wandering the streets.

The stranger seemed a black sculpture. He leaned forward, as if to say something, tilted his head back, as if signalling Cliff to move closer. But Cliff could not let himself get any closer; his body would not allow it. What was he doing here anyway?

The man stared, eyes unblinking, and passed his left hand in front of Cliff's face, as if he were waving "hello."

Cliff's face seemed suddenly numb with cold, his eyes squinted shut, instinctively protecting themselves as if they'd been blasted by a winter gust. Cliff thought it must be some sort of anxiety attack, a nervous effect. Then he felt a sensation as if a sheet had been lifted from his face, his skin again being exposed to the Mexican heat. Water dripped down out of his eyebrows; he pictured hairs losing their coatings of frost.

The stranger settled back in his chair, looking past Cliff, into the distant mountain peaks.

"Is there . . . something I can do for you, sir?" Cliff stammered, unable to take his eyes off the stranger's blank-looking face.

But the stranger didn't answer.

"I'm . . . I'm afraid I don't understand what's going on here. Do you speak English?"

One of the emaciated stray dogs wandered closer to their table, obviously seeking some scraps. Cliff watched the stranger shift his eyes a fraction to register this new presence.

Cliff started to pet the dog, then stopped in mid-reach, feeling a sensation near his fingertips, as if they were dipping into cool butter. He watched, spell-bound, as the dog sank first onto his haunches, then, his front legs collapsing, onto his snout. The oddest thing, as if the dog were winding down in slow motion, running out of gas.

He touched the dog with his foot; there was no response.

Cliff looked up at the man, squinting, because suddenly the sun seemed to be in his eyes; he couldn't make out the man's features because of the glare. The man's head was a solid black oval. But then Cliff discovered he could see the man's mouth, and the wide shallow U of the scar making the false smile over the man's unsmiling lips.

The cafe owner was standing over Cliff moments later, alternately apologizing for the dead dog beneath the table, screaming at everyone within earshot for allowing such a thing to happen at his establishment, and suggesting pointedly that perhaps Cliff, after all, had something to do with the animal's presence. Soon a crowd had gathered, all arguing tangental points-of-view in rapid-fire Spanish.

When things had quieted down, Cliff couldn't find the stranger anywhere.

Cliff sat in a Mexican cowhide chair, looking past the bed where Bob was napping, and out the window at the rain clouds piling up in the sky, the gold and red sunset turning the distant mountains into black cut-outs. The clouds themselves, then the trees, people passing in the street outside had all become silhouettes before he finally broke out of his reveries, stood, and began moving around in the room.

Cliff had tried to ignore the stranger on the bus today, but had felt him watching, the dark eyes cooling the back of his neck. Bob was unusually quiet this day, and it made him vaguely uneasy. Cliff was afraid of being exposed now, afraid that Bob would discover how he really felt. The silence made him wonder if Bob already suspected. But it didn't make sense; Cliff had always acted, at least, "fatherly" around Bob; he was sure of it.

This leg of the trip had been essentially dull. Miles of pine trees baking in the hot sun; why didn't they just curl up and die? As the bus swung around the mountain curves they could look back on the hazy, dusty Mexican valley, and above the haze, in the clear upper air, the snow cap of Popocatepetl. The driver had shut off the engine and coasted part of the way, an unnerving habit of his, since he'd had to round some of those curves at high speed in order to mount the short rises. Cliff had found himself gasping in the mountain air. Occasionally they passed ruins of old haciendas and Cliff had been reminded of the age of the place, the history marked here, where Zapata had ridden with the Indians, and where

Cortez had traversed the highlands.

The natives seemed unimpressed, and the tourists too washed-out from the heat to pay much attention. Most of them, Cliff and Bob included, were scheduled to be in Cuernavaca the next day; they were saving their enthusiasm.

The boy was unhappy, always had been. Just look at him now, Cliff mused, tossing and turning in the clinging sheets, struggling with any number of demons he could only guess at, since Bob certainly wasn't one to share his dreams, or anything else, with anyone. Marion had just begun making progress with him, getting him to open up a little with her, when she was killed in the accident.

The drunk simply jumped the median; how could he have foreseen? It could have happened to anyone. But when he looked over at her, the blood streaming from her nose, her hair, matting above that dark place . . . Bob was screaming, crying in the back seat. He'd yelled at him, cursed; he could have *killed* him right then. Why should *he* be alive?

And looking at her, beginning to scream himself, he knew that he had been daydreaming at the time—Marion had always been amused by his little trances—but *damn*, he'd been *daydreaming!* The drunk hadn't been travelling that fast. They could have made it.

Bob knew that too; Cliff was sure of it. He'd been living with them long enough to know Cliff's habits, his funny lapses of attention. But he wasn't saying anything, expressing the blame. He was keeping it all locked up. It made Cliff want to wring that anger out of him so they might confront it directly. Bob was just killing him slowly this way.

The boy had finally settled down, his thumb at his lips in a peaceful, babyish gesture, the rising moon turning his dark hair almost silver, and bleaching out his face so that he looked more like an old man lying there twisted up in the bright sheets. Cliff could hold him, if only Bob could be like that all the time. He yearned to be able to hold the boy tightly against his own body, inseparable. But awake it was impossible; the boy would anger him. But Cliff remembered the times those barriers had frayed a bit: Bob leaning against him as they climbed aboard the bus, asking him for help picking out clothes, wanted Cliff to do things for him he already knew how to do. They were the same about a lot of things; it alternately hurt and enraged Cliff to be reminded of that. The shrunken old man in the bed there might be Cliff himself in thirty years, or thirty years ago.

Cliff had lived alone most of his life. He hadn't even been used to the marriage yet when they adopted Bob. He still woke up mornings believing he was single again until he rolled over and found Marion there, and he realised at her funeral that he never *had* become used to her presence in his life. He wasn't likely to get used to Bob either; it would continue like this, unfinished, as long as they both lived.

He was outside walking briskly away from the inn before he realised he'd even made some sort of decision. The night air felt somehow strange to him, as if the air itself were warm, but too thin, too spread-out to transfer any of its heat to his body. The back of his neck began to shiver, the hairs on his arms prickling.

The stranger was sitting on a bench in the darkness; even though only his profile was visible, Cliff recognised him immediately. It was almost as if the man had been waiting for Cliff to leave the room.

Cliff stopped, momentarily startled by the stranger's sharp silhouette: The hooked nose, the pouting lips, double chin, Cliff had had his own silhouette cut before, several years ago. And that was how it had looked, he was sure of it. He giggled nervously; it was as if the man had stolen his very shadow.

"*cold . . .*"

The word came from the direction of the bench, although he hadn't actually seen the man's lips move. Cliff wondered if the man was referring to the weather, or something more personal. He stepped impulsively closer to the bench. The man had turned his face slightly and the resemblence to his own profile was gone.

The man made no move to rise, and Cliff didn't have any intention of stepping closer to the negative-like figure.

"*You want me to do something . . .*"

"I don't think . . ." Cliff wasn't sure if that last had been a question, or a statement.

"*You want me to do something about . . . Bob . . .*"

"What? How did you know my son's name? You couldn't know . . ." Cliff halted, tried to catch his breath. The man just sat there unmoving, his dark form not even wavering against the light. "I don't understand. This . . . this *has* to stop!" Cliff said, suddenly on the verge of tears.

Someone was laughing in one of the bars down the dusty street. A man on a bicycle passed between them, but neither Cliff nor the stranger lost concentration, Cliff's gaze and the stranger's imagined gaze locked, unbreakable.

"*cold . . .*"

"Stop it, dammit!" Cliff began walking away, following the cyclist down towards the village, already thinking about getting drunk. "Oh, just do it! Do it, for God's sake! he said, almost absentmindedly, not thinking about the words, just wanting this apparition to go away, Bob to go away. Then, whispering back over his shoulder, "*please . . .*"

Cliff stopped halfway down the road and turned around. He watched as the stranger rose slowly to his feet and began moving steadily towards the inn and the room where Bob was sleeping. The wind was beginning to pick up; a small dust devil of leaves, grit, and small pebbles swung past the stranger and down the road a few feet from where Cliff was standing. But the stranger's poncho did not stir, but hung draped like clothing on a sculpture. Cliff turned and ran to catch the cyclist, unaccountably wondering how he might beat the rickety bicycle in the race to the village.

Cliff didn't return to the inn until the next dawn. He walked into a sunny, well-kept room. The maid had been there, the beds made, bureau straightened. There was no sign of his son. The boy's clothes were missing from the closet. It was as if the boy had never existed.

What had the man done? But Cliff wouldn't allow himself to think about the logistics involved.

If the other tourists on the bus to Cuernavaca noticed Bob's absence thay said nothing to him. Cliff looked everywhere for the stranger, not only on the bus, but in the crowds along the highway, in the small towns, even trying to imagine the man in other clothes, in false beards and moustaches. But there was no sign of him. By the time they'd reached the outskirts of the city he had begun to relax, almost ready to actually enjoy his vacation. He began daydreaming of moving, finding a new job, perhaps even dating again. For the first time since her death Cliff began to wonder if perhaps there *might be* another woman for him out there, perhaps even someone like Marion.

The Estrelle de Oro bus dropped him off at the terminal on Ave. Morelos at Calle Veracous. He caught a red and white city bus on Morelos, riding down to Aragon y Leon, where he registered at Casa Marilu, Aragon y Leon, number twelve, plain, but clean just as the guidebook had described.

He ate a late lunch at the restaurant Mary & San Miguel: Soup, omelette, frijoles, and salad—twenty pesos.

He spent the afternoon wandering the streets, visiting the square Jardon Juarez, vowing to return Sunday evening for the regular band concert held there, shopped the markets, passed Rajon, then Hidelgo, stopping at each dealer in pre-Columbian art, both the authentic and the faked antiques.

He had always been fascinated by the freakish look of these figures, the hysterical eyes and protruding tongues, the fearsome gods in their stiff headdresses. If spirits did live in this world, Cliff was convinced this would be how they looked.

It was strange how many times the new 'antiques' would cost just as much as the genuine, old ones. But then, they were made in the same way by the same kinds of people. And it made an ironic sense too, that new gods would be valued the same as the old.

The old woman wore several shawl rebozos in a rainbow of colour, no doubt selling them to tourists right off her back. But her main line were the artifacts, old and new arranged side by side on her little table.

Cliff felt gregarious. "So, how's business, senora?" he grinned.

"Mucho trabajo, poco diners, senor."

His face went blank momentarily. He knew *Mucho* meant *much*, and that last phrase was *little money*, but he couldn't remember the meaning of *trabajo*.

"Much work, little money, mister."

Cliff looked down gratefully at the small boy who had walked up beside him, then shivered involuntarily as he caught just a glimpse of the boy's profile. *You want me to do something about Bob . . .* The dark hair, the fleshy face . . .

The little Mexican boy stared up at Cliff quizically, blinking his dark eyes. He had several boxes of 'Chiclets' thrust forward in one grimy little hand.

Cliff shakily pulled out a coin, accepted a box of Chiclets, and stood there staring at it as the boy ran down the street.

"Mala gente! Mala gente!" the old woman screamed.

Cliff looked up at her, startled. She seemed to be looking slightly passed him, her lips tight, the cords standing in her neck.

He swung around in time to see a shadowy figure turning into the crowd, disappearing almost immediately. The faces of the people were bright, the colours in their clothing standing out distinctly. How could the one figure have been in shadow?

And Cliff was sure he recognised the clothing. No, that couldn't be. How could he be sure at all?

He held the woman's arm so she would not bolt from him. "What did he *look* like?"

She stared at him in bewilderment.

"Mala gente . . . that means more than one. Were there more than one?"

She opened her mouth soundlessly.

"*Woman*, were there *two*?"

The old woman pulled loose, stumbled back against the adobe behind her, then began scrambling up the street muttering hoarsely, *mala gente . . . mala gente . . . mala gente . . .*

For two days he wandered bar to bar drinking, watching out for the dark stranger, checking out carefully every small beggar who happened to stumble his way. He developed a cold which threatened to evolve into something worse, giving him an excuse to try the old Mexican cure of Mescal drunk hot with lemons. He seemed to have developed a taste for pulque as well, a milky fermented drink made from the juice of the agave. It had an unpleasant smell and sour taste, but it provided a sensory distraction.

He tried the herb seller at one of the street markets, hoping the men might sell him some tree bark, plant, or seed from ancient times designed to cure what was ailing him. After all, the man had herbs for headaches, bleeding, love and lost virginity, why not a herb for him, for "sons, shadows, and cold," as he had explained to the man, gesturing wildly.

The man had looked frightened, stammered "Ahorita," *right away*, then left through a curtain behind his stand. Cliff had become angry, confused, knowing that here "Ahorita" could mean hours. *Ahorita, Senor; I'll bring it. Ahorita, this very afternoon.* He heard it all the time.

Cliff slipped away when he saw the herb seller coming back around the corner, a member of the state police in tow, police who consider you guilty until you prove otherwise, especially a drunken, unshaven gringo. Cliff secreted himself within the fast-moving crowd.

Mala gente... mala gente... mala gente...

He felt a little better the fourth day, enough to dress up and treat himself to a small excursion to the Jardin Borda, the Borda Gardens, at Morelos and Hidalgo, the former summer retreat of the Emperor Maximilian and the Empress Carlotta. Fifteen pesos to enter the small preserve of the gardens proper.

Afterwards he had a drink at one of the fanciest restaurants in the city, Las Mananitas, a Spanish colonial house doubling as a hotel and restaurant. Behind the building were tropical gardens stocked with peacocks, toucans, macaws, cranes, and parrots. Here he could sit on the lawn among all the birds and sip a cool drink. Forty-five pesos.

He picked up a prostitute on the way back to his hotel. Twenty-five pesos. It was dark by the time they arrived at the front of the building. She seemed nervous, anxious to get upstairs and away from him, it seemed.

"Mala gente..." she whispered hoarsely.

"What!" He turned and grabbed her by the wrists. "What do you mean by *that*?" His voice shook, tears welling up in his eyes.

"The *people* here, senor," she wheezed, eyes darting fitfully. "See? How do you say... the criminal element?"

Cliff turned his head slowly, taking in the dark figures on the street-corners, grouped in alleys, lounging in front of buildings. He sighed and dropped her hands, "Sorry... I didn't mean to do that... please, please let's just go up now."

He had been halfway between waking and sleeping, drifting... somwhere

206

out in the snow? No, it had been sand, hot desert. Was he sure which? He half-remembered a dream about his father's death, the old man lying there, scowling in his stiff headress, his eyes wild, tongue protruding, and God forgive him, Cliff just didn't care, it wasn't in him to care at all. The old man had starved all the caring out of him a long time ago.

"Do you want me to do something?"

His eyes went open immediately.

"You want me to do something..."

Cliff jerked up in bed and screamed when he saw the dark, sharp-featured silhouette bending over him. He pushed it away with frantic fingers, scrambling up on his knees in the bed.

"You did not seem interested! I was just trying to *help*; I didn't know what you *wanted*!" The prostitute shouted at him. Cliff sat quietly, rubbing his eyes like a sleepy child.

She was slipping rapidly into her clothes, muttering in unintelligible Spanish, coughing, when he began to cry.

"I've tried...I really have."

The prostitute stopped and stared defiantly at Cliff as he continued to cry in loud, choked-off sobs. "Malvada!" she spat, then turned on her heels and left through the already open door.

Cliff looked around at the darkness in the room, the dim light from the hall filling his open door, and continued to talk, continued to cry, "I always wanted to be a *good* man; I knew that was important, and I really tried."

The door closed slowly until only a thin crack of light remained.

"I tried not to think only of myself, but of others too..." Cliff collapsed back onto the bed. His eyes, even through his tears, were slowly becoming accustomed to the semi-darkness, the crack of light through the door striping the humped forms of the room's furniture, the streetlight filtered through the thin shade behind him turning the sheets a dingy, pale yellow colour.

"It hasn't been easy for me," he said as he turned his head side to side as if addressing an entire crowd in his room, "...it has never been easy..." and he saw the tall shadow figure at the foot of his bed.

"I..." he sobbed, wide-eyed, watching the figure as it moved around the bed, toward his night-table, his pillow, "I know there is powerful love within me, deep down," brushing back its heavy poncho from arms which were long, angular, "...if I'd only reached far...cuh..." he choked, as the arms, ended with thin bony fingers were reaching out to his chest, "...enough, oh dear God, if I'd just touched that *love* in *me*!" he shouted, as the hard, steely, icy fingers touched him, that touch spreading throughout his body, freezing the brain, icing over the skin, spiking the heart. And, for the moment, stopping everything.

"*cold . . .*" the shadow whispered.

He could not move, just stare into the face of the stranger, whose profile now, indeed was his, but changed so quickly, even before the recognition had quite registered, and then the stranger's face was blank again, devoid of meaning, expressionless.

But behind the stranger another shadow moved, came around beside the figure, a small head beside the stranger's broad shoulders. Then the small shadow crept into the dim light from the door, and Cliff saw that it was his own son, the face striped across one eye and the nose by the crack of light, the other eye impassive, the lips smooth, together, untroubled. A beautiful child's face.

As the heavy weight of cold crept through his body, every pore, every extremity filling with the mass of the ice, Cliff thought of his own face, permanently marked by the glistening trails of frozen over tears.

A PLACE OF NO RETURN
Hugh B. Cave

Illustration by Dave Carson

Hugh B. Cave sold a staggering 800 stories to the pulp magazines during their heyday and he's still hard at work writing. After the Second World War he moved to Haiti and wrote a book on voodoo, Haiti: Highroad to Adventure, *and twenty more books were inspired by his move to Jamaica and the coffee plantation be bought there. His best horror stories were collected in Carcosa's hefty 1977 volume* Murgunstrumm and Others *and he returned to the genre with a string of modern horror novels, including* Legion of the Dead, The Nebulon Horror, The Evil, Shade of Evil, Disciples of Dread *and* The Lower Depths. *A new collection,* The Corpse Maker, *has recently appeared along with a long-overdue biography. 'A Place of No Return' is an atmospheric little chiller with a voodoo theme which originally appeared in* Fantasy Tales 8.

A S PROFESSOR Leslie Carter understood it, there were two kinds of zombies in the Republic of Haiti, and he didn't believe in either.

Accepted even by some of the educated elite was a theory that zombies could be produced through the use of poison. Formula: admister one of several potions known to be capable of inducing a physical condition resembling death. Remove the body from its grave immediately after burial. Revive it. And you had a living creature with a damaged mind who

209

'You believe there is no such creature as zombi, eh?'

could be trained as a canefield labourer, a household servant, et cetera.

The barefoot peasant believed in zombies of another kind, however, in dead persons brought back to life by a kind of sorcery practised by *bocors*, whose services were always for sale if one had sufficient money.

"So what I want you to do for me, Dieudonne," said Carter to the old black man standing before him on the pension veranda, "is take me to where I can see some zombies and talk to them. Do you understand?"

The old man hesitated.

"I am a learned man," Carter continued patiently. "I teach anthropology, the science of man and his beliefs, in a renowned American university. And though I am here in your country on a vacation, I look upon my visit as an opportunity to determine once and for all whether zombies really exist." Smilingly he repeated his favourite phrase: "Do you understand?"

Dieudonne Malfam solemnly nodded. Having worked for years for a Catholic priest in the village of his birth, he understood Carter's words. All but the hard ones, anyway. He was not sure, however, that he understood what was meant by them.

"Do you have time enough, *m'sieu*, to go with me into the mountains?"

"How much time will it require?"

"Well, if we leave now, we can be in Furcy by mid-afternoon. There we must leave the jeep and walk awhile. You are not against walking?"

Carter had to smile. he was at least twenty years younger than the man who seemed to be questioning his fitness, and at the Ivy League university where he taught he had been jogging at least five miles a day for the past two years. "I can walk."

"These will be difficult mountain trails, *m'sieu*."

"No more so for me than for you. Where will we be sleeping?"

"I will arrange a bed for you. Have no fear."

"All right," Carter said. "Just give me a few minutes to make ready." And, striding boldly through the pension's drawing room to show the old peasant how well he could walk, he leaped up the stairs two at a time to go to his room.

In the upper hall he encountered the pension's Haitian proprietor, round little Claude Jeannot, and Jeannot said, beaming, "Ah, Professor Carter. Will the man I obtained for you be satisfactory, do you think?"

"It was not simple, you know," the proprietor said. "With you speaking no Creole, you had to have someone who spoke English well enough to understand you. Also someone with a vehicle, for you said you did not wish the expense of a separate car and driver, remember."

"Dieudonne came in a jeep."

"He owns it."

"How could such a man afford to buy a jeep, Jeannot?"

"He has ways of acquiring things, it seems. At any rate, he makes a living with it."

"How?"

"Well, you are paying him for his services, are you not?"

"We've agreed on two hundred dollars."

"A thousand *gourdes*, eh? For that he should certainly find you some zombies, *m'sieu*."

"He'd better," Carter said darkly. "Will he, do you think?"

"Do you doubt it?"

"It's just that he seems—well, not too bright." But then, Carter thought, no one he had yet encountered in this Caribbean land of voodoo, sorcery and zombies had seemed really bright. Perhaps he was expecting too much.

In his room Carter tossed into a small overnight bag the few items he thought he might need, added his camera, then counted the money in his billfold. He had a little more than the two hundred American dollars required for Dieudonne. The rest of his money, in traveller's cheques, was locked in the pension safe.

Returning to the ground floor, he found his guide waiting outside in the jeep. The vehicle had seen better days, he observed as he climbed into it. Still, it was probably as clean as some small boy with a rag and a bucket of water had been able to make it. Depositing his bag in the back, he said, "Aren't you taking anything, Dieudonne?"

"I need nothing, *m'sieu*."

"These people know you? The ones we're going to?"

"They know me."

"Well, then," Carter said loudly, unable to suppress his excitement, "let's get going, man!"

From the sweltering August heat of Port-au-Prince they first climbed the steep, curving road to Petionville, then the even steeper one to the mountain village of Kenscoff. On the unpaved, almost vertical ladder from there to Furcy, Carter found himself fiercely clinging to various parts of the vehicle as though he were riding a bucking horse.

He had not been to Furcy before. After the shock of the road, which left him nearly breathless, came the awesome view from the height his guide told him was called La Decouverte—The Discovery. "*Deye morne ge morne*," the old man murmured, quoting an old Haitian proverb. "Beyond the mountains are mountains." These, in range after misty range, filled a wilderness extending all the way to the Caribbean Sea.

Now began the walking.

212

It was not, after all, quite the same as jogging through an Ivy League campus. True, the sea-level heat of Port-au-Prince was gone now, but the trail they follwed was demanding. it descended so steeply at times that Carter had to cling to anything his fingers could reach. Then it invariably reversed itself to climb so steeply that he had to crawl.

The old man plodded on without comment, but looked back occasionally to make sure he was being followed. After an hour or so he indicated they should rest.

"You are all right, *m'sieu*?"

"Of course. I'm not used to this kind of hiking, that's all. How much farther have we to go?"

"Two three hours."

"Well, don't worry about me. I can do anything you can."

When they stopped again, Carter prolonged the resting time by probing a little into his companion's background. "How," he asked, "did you happen to be given that odd name Dieudonne? It means God-given, doesn't it?"

The old fellow nodded. "My mother had wanted a child for many years. When it finally happened, she called me that to show her gratitude."

"Where do you live?"

"Oh, here and there in these mountains. Or in the capital. Or elsewhere, when it suits me."

"You have no real home, you mean?"

"My home, *m'sieu*, is where I happen to be at the moment."

Feeling the mountain stillness like a spell, Carter looked about him and said, frowning, "Doesn't anyone live in these hills?"

"A few, *m'sieu*. Not many."

"We haven't seen a single village."

"There are none. Only—well, you will see. Very few visitors come here, of course."

That must be true, Carter thought with satisfaction. No more tourist would ever do what he was doing. It would be something for him to talk about when he returned to the States. He must instruct his wife to organize an evening for him to tell about it. His colleagues, her friends among the faculty wives. He would show his colour slides. With luck he would have some pictures of "zombies"—to prove they were not zombies at all.

He spoke about them to this guide when they stopped again to rest—a badly needed halt this time for Carter who was nearing exhaustion. "Tell me, Dieudonne—what does a zombi look like?"

The old man sat on a fallen pine tree and picked his nose. "Like you and me, *m'sieu*."

"Are they dead?"

"Dead but alive."

"If they look like living persons, how can you know they're zombies?"

"There are signs, *m'sieu*. A lostness in the eyes. A foul smell about them. The way they walk and talk."

"They can talk."

"In their own way. Not our way."

"From the boulder onto which he had gratefully lowered his aching body Carter said, "I think you're putting me on, old man."

"Pardon, *m'sieu*?"

"There is no such thing as a zombi. We both know it."

"Would you also say, *m'sieu*, there is no such thing as a *bocor*?"

"Oh, there are sorcerers. I believe that. But their powers are vastly exaggerated. They can't make zombies."

"Should we turn back, then, *m'sieu*?" Dieudonne asked softly.

"No, no. We've come this far; we'll see it through."

Half-an-hour later they arrived.

As the old man had warned, it was not a village. The trail wriggled down to a patch of almost level mountainside about two acres in extent, and on the level stood a dozen widely separated huts with wattle-and daub walls and thatch roofs. Most of the ground not given up to the huts was used for growing vegetables. "These people carry produce to the Iron Market in Port-au-prince," Dieudonne explained. "Beyond the houses, where the land is less level, the gardens are larger."

"And that is where the zombies are employed?"

"I see that you know more about my people than you have led me to believe, *m'sieu*."

I warned you I was a man of learning," Carter retorted as they trudged side by side toward the largest hut.

"Ah, yes, so you did."

"And let me warn you now not to try deceiving me about these zombies, friend. if they are not the real thing, you won't be paid, I promise you."

The old Haitian shot him a sidelong glance out of eyes resembling black opals, but offered no retort.

Outside the hut Dieudonne halted. The door was open but he rapped on it with his bony black knuckles. "*Honneur, compere*," he called out. "It is Dieudonne."

A tall, muscular man of middle age appeared in the doorway, blending with the gloom behind him because the hut had no windows. "*Respect, compere*," he murmured, then offered Carter a smile of hospitality and spoke in Creole.

Dieudonne answered in the same peasant tongue and, turning to Carter, explained in English, "Ti-Jean asked who you are, and I have told him you are a man of great learning from America. I said you are here to talk to his zombies and take some photographs."

"Good. Is he the one who owns the zombies?"

"He is the leader here."

"Where does he find them? I want to know that, too."

The old man's shoulders eloquently rose and fell. "Such a question is not to be asked *m'sieu.*"

"From some local *bocor*, I suppose," Carter persisted with a smile that was half smirk.

"Perhaps. But let me talk to him now about a place for you to sleep tonight." Again Dieudonne addressed the muscular man in Creole.

The reply came without hesitation, and the old man was obviously pleased. "There is an empty house you may use," he said. "The man and woman who live there went to the capital with produce yesterday and will not return till Monday. Come, please."

The hut in question was smaller than Ti-Jean's and had for furniture only a table, two chairs and a bed, all crudely handmade of the Carribbean pine that grew in these mountains. Carter examined the bed and was not happy with its grass-filled mattress and soiled blanket, but was at this point too tired to reject it. "I believe I'll just rest a little before we do anything else, Dieudonne."

"Of course, *m'sieu.*"

"Don't let me sleep too long, now, I want to see those zombies at work!"

"I doubt they are working this late, *m'sieu.*"

"What do you mean, late? They work all the time, I've read."

"Perhaps on moonlit nights, *m'sieu.* But there will be no moon tonight, and the day is already dying."

Seated on the bed, Carter paused in the act of removing his shoes to look out the open door. Seen through tall pines on a western ridge, the setting sun was a fiery crimson ball that bloodied all in its reach. The day *was* a nearly over, he realized. They had walked for an eternity to get here. No wonder he felt an irresistible yearning to sleep.

He lay back and closed his eyes, and knew no more until a sound of drumming awoke him.

The glowing hands of the watch on his wrist said midnight.

Having fallen asleep fully dressed except for his shoes, he had only to put the shoes back on before angrily jerking the hut door open to look for the source of the drumming. He hadn't far to look. In an open space among the peasant houses, glowing lanterns hung from the horizontal branches of a solitary mapou—a tree supposed to possess magical powers, he knew from his extensive reading. Among the mapou's buttressed roots,

215

on a low stool, sat the drummer.

It was the man who, according to Dieudonne, owned the zombies.

In the space lit by the lanterns some twenty persons were dancing, if one could properly call it dancing. They moved in procession very slowly with their knees bent and their shoulders undulating. A voodoo thing? He had read about certain voodoo dances—the *yanvalou*, for instance— but had no way of knowing what this was. At any rate, it was damned inconsiderate of them to be holding such a noisy affair at midnight when they had an important guest so badly in need of sleep.

As Dieudonne had predicted, there was no moon in the black-velvet sky. He was not noticed as he left his doorway and strode toward the dancers. Only when he marched into the lanternlight were they aware of his intrusion.

The drumming dribbled away to silence. The dancing slowed and stopped. Carter went straight to the drummer, in such a way that some of the performers had to stumble out of his path.

"Do you *have* to do this tonight?" he demanded. The fellow spoke no English, of course, but perhaps the anger in his voice . . .

Sunddenly old Dieudonne appeared at his side. "Something is wrong, *m'sieu*?"

"Of course something is wrong! If I'm to pay these people for a night's sleep here, I want to *sleep*! Tell him that!"

M'sieu," the old man gently protested, "this is a thing they do at times to insure that the crops—"

"I know that, I know it! At least, I can guess. But let them do it after I'm gone!"

Dieudonne gazed at him in silence for a few seconds, perhaps attempting to decide just how resolute he might be. Then, with a shrug, he turned to the man at the drum. Squatting, which made him no taller than the drum itself, he spoke almost inaudibly into Ti-Jean's ear.

Ti-Jean, too, regarded Carter in silence. Then he rose, swung the drum up under an arm, and with a command in Creole to the dancers, walked off toward his hut.

The dancers drifted away in to the darkness.

Carter, satisfied, returned to his hut and slept undisturbed until daybreak.

At dawn he washed his face in a basin of water that had been placed on the table while he slept. It would be a nice day for what he had to do, he observed. The sky was clear, the mountain air crisp and clean. Opening his overnight bag, he took out his camera and checked it. Now if Dieudonne could produce some zombies . . .

But, of course, they would not be zombies. He already knew what they

216

would be, in a remote clan community such as this. Even his students at the university could be expected to know.

Dieudonne came with some breakfast for him—a white enamelled dish containing what appeared to be roasted yams and boiled green plantains; a cup of some sort of bush tea.

"Thanks," Carter said, "but if you don't mind, I'd like to get on with what we came here for. I'm not hungry." Nor was he—for a breakfast such as that.

"You wish to visit the zombies now, *m'sieu?*"

"That's the idea."

"Very well. Come." And Dieudonne led him through the settlement to the mountain-slope fields beyond.

Carter was surprised at the extent of these. In carefully constructed terraces they descended for what seemed a good half mile: fields of cabbages, turnips, carrots, sweet potatoes, scallions, yam vines climbing forests of slender poles. Far down near the bottom a dozen or so figures could be seen at work, spread out in a line. The bright early sunlight flashed on tools of some sort that rose and fell in unison.

"This path will take us down to them," Dieudonne said. "Come."

Bare feet had worn the path almost as smooth and hard as troweled concrete, Carter observed as he descended through the switchbacks. Years of labour must have gone into these fields. But, of course, when the produce was headed down to the capital it must bring in a handsome return. Don't underestimate these people, he told himself, even though they seem to live in a world apart.

Suddenly he became aware of the smell.

It was like . . . well, what was it like? The first thing that came to mind was the acrid stench of bat guano in a wild Kentucky cave he had once explored. Next, the stink of a pig farm near his sister's rural home in Vermont. A distressing odour, it rode the light breeze here like a chemical cloud, assailing not only his nostrils but his mind.

Halting, he said to his guide, "My God, man, don't they ever wash?

"They see no need to."

"Oh, come on. You know as well as I do they're not dead men!"

"If you wish to go closer, *m'sieu*, the smell must be endured."

Negotiating the last switchback, they reached the level on which the men were working. Still in a row, the toilers in unison lifted huge, heavy hoes above their heads and brought them down to send the reddish earth flying in clods. All were barechested. The sole garment of each was a pair of black trousers, earth-stained and worn.

And that awful stench!

"How do they stand one another?" he demanded. "Where do they sleep at night?"

"There," the old man said, pointing to a long, thatch-roofed shelter where the cleared part of the mountainside became forest. It had no walls.

"Don't they feel the cold? It must be really cold up here at times."

"They have few feelings." Dieudonne seemed a trifle impatient. Perhaps you can take your pictures now, *m'sieu*?"

"No! I must go closer."

"As you wish."

Carter would not let the smell stop him. Not until he stood within three feet of the nearest worker did he halt. About twenty years old, with a face that was not black but oddly grey and wore an expression of eternal sadness, the creature paid him absolutely no attention.

Carter studied him and then, trying not to inhale too much of that abominable odour, moved on down the line to scrutinize the others. He took pictures, changed the film, took more. Old Dieudonne resignedly waited for him. Then in silence they toiled back up the mountainside.

In the clearing some of the inhabitants of that lost-world community stood in their doorways watching. Wondering, Carter decided, how he would react to having been made a fool of. Well . . . he would show them.

Inside the hut in which he had spent the night he angrily confronted his guide. "All right, Dieudonne. I was stupid to come here—all this way for nothing. But you were even more stupid to bring me, if you expect to be paid!"

Dieudonne eyed him in apparant surprise. "*M'sieu*?"

"Zombies, ha! I'm an anthropologist, not a gullible tourist! Those men in the fields aren't dead; they're just a result of the inbreeding that's been going on in this place. They're idiots, morons, imbeciles, without any intelligence. What's needed here is some new *blood*."

"*M'sieu*," Dieudonne said, his dark eyes seeming to smoulder, "I say those men are zombies, and I brought you here in good faith."

"You're a liar."

"I am a truthful man, *m'sieu*."

"Oh, all right, I'll pay you somthing for your trouble. Not the two hundred we agreed on, but something."

"Thank you, *m'sieu*."

"I'll give you twenty."

"What, *m'sieu*?"

"You ought to be grateful! You know damned well you've played me for a dupe!"

"Very well," Dieudonne said, turning away. "I will get us something to eat, and then we can start back." At the door he paused to fix his gaze on the American's face for a moment. "I am sorry you think me dishonest, *m'sieu.* In time you will believe otherwise."

He disappeared, but in fifteen minutes was back with food and drink on a wooden tray. Transferring the dishes to the table, he motioned Carter to begin. The food this time was chicken and sweet potatoes. The drink was again some kind of tea.

"What's in this?" Carter demanded, tapping his cup with a fingernail.

"We make it from leaves of the corossol tree, *m'sieu.* The soursop. It is good." To show how good it was, the old man drank some of his own.

"I dislike bush teas," Carter said. And at the moment also distrust them, he added mentally. Rejecting the sweet potatoes too, he attacked the chicken, discovering he was ravenous.

Finished, he rose and looked about the room to make certain he had forgotten nothing. Opened his overnight bag on the bed to be sure it contained his camera. Glancing at the old man, who was still leisurely eating, he said irritably, "Well, are you ready?" He was not looking forward to the long walk back to the jeep.

"Yes, *m'sieu,* I am ready," Dieudonne said, pushing away his plate with his portion of the chicken untouched.

"Let's get out of here, then," Carter grumbled, and turned to the door.

Something happened to the doorway as he went toward it. Its outlines blurred. From a rectangle of brilliant sunlight it became one of swirling mist, then of total darkness. He felt himself falling but had no sensation of reaching the floor. The fall simply continued, as into a bottomless black pit.

Time passed—unmeasurable—and he was on the bed. The room was the same but blurred, as though seen through thick green glass. He was naked. There was no feeling in his hands, his feet—none, really, in his entire body. Near by stood the old man on whom a grateful mother had bestowed the name Dieudonne, holding in his hands a pair of trousers and lifting from them a billfold. "Thief!" Carter silently screamed. Now the old man was removing money from the billfold and counting it. And again, "Thief!" Carter shouted, but knew he was only thinking the word, not voicing it.

Into the hut came the man they had first spoken with in this terrible place. He and Dieudonne conversed but their talk was in Creole and Carter could not understand it, was not even sure he was hearing it. A wad of paper money was thrust into old Dieudonne's hand—Haitian money this time, not American—and the old man stuffed it into his pocket along with what he had removed from the billfold. "*Merci*, Ti-Jean," he said, and then, "*Adieu.*" The two solemnly shook hands.

Turning then, Dieudonne came to the bed and looked down at Carter, who saw him only through veiled eyes. "And *adieu* to you also, *m'sieu,*"

219

he said. "You believe there is no such creature as a zombi, eh? And that your belief makes it right for you to cheat a poor old *bocor*. Oh, but I forget—the powers of a sorcerer are greatly exaggerated, you said. And, of course, you know because you are a man of learning."

With a nod to the man who had paid him, he walked out of the hut. The other stepped to the doorway after him but halted there and spoke to someone outside.

The two men who shuffled into the hut then were naked except for black, earth-stained trousers, and they stank. They lifted Carter from the bed and set him on his feet. With a muttered command that sounded like "*Vini!*" they walked him to the door, then across the compound, then down the hard, red-earth path he had travelled earlier with Dieudonne to take pictures of them and their companions.

Holding him between them, they escorted him to the thatched shelter in which , according to Dieudonne, the workers were housed at night. The floor was a bed of dried grass. They pushed him and he sprawled face first onto it and once more felt himself falling, falling, falling into a pit of blackness that had no bottom.

When he awoke this time, or drifted into what passed for wakefulness, dawn was breaking over the mountains.

Full of despair, he sat up and looked about him and saw he was not alone. More than a dozen others shared the shelter with him. The muscular peasant leader called Ti-Jean stood there making pistolshot sounds with a bullwhip and snarling commands. Some of the men who had been dancing last night flanked him.

With the other workers Carter staggered to his feet. Someone had handed him a wooden bowl filled with grey, watery gruel from a black iron pot. Taking his cue from his companions, he lifted it to his mouth with both hands and drained it. The gruel had no taste.

Those being fed with him did not have that hellish odour now, either. Perhaps he had become used to it?

Discarding the empty bowls, they formed a line. The man with the whip pushed Carter into it and someone thrust a hoe at him. He was no longer naked, he realized vaguely. He wore ill-fitting black trousers that seemed strangely funeral on his dead-white body. The whip cracked and the line trudged out of the shelter, along a path to the fields.

As it halted at the work site Carter looked about him, aware that his mind was slowly becoming incapable of thought. He was receiving only impressions, and even those were now fragile and fleeting. In the golden dawn light the mountains all around him were part of a terrifying world in which he was a prisoner or slave. *Deye morne ge morne.* He was uncountable miles away from the home he would never see again.

By tomorrow would he even remember it?

THE TERMINUS
Kim Newman

Illustration by Jim Pitts

Kim Newman is a freelance writer, film critic and broadcaster. His features and reviews regularly appear in City Limits, Monthly Film Bulletin, Sight & Sound *and* Shock Xpress. *He is the author of* Nightmare Movies, *an acclaimed critical history of the horror film since 1968, and co-compiler of* Ghastly Beyond Belief, *the book of science fiction and fantasy quotations. His short fiction has appeared in both the* Interzone *anthologies, and although he has not been prolific in this particular area, we were pleased to be able to use 'The Terminus' in the fifteenth issue of* Fantasy Tales.

THEY had me spend my first month out of training processing statements. It was more like public relations than police work. Nobody the desk sergeant passed on to me was ever going to see any action arising from their complaint. It was my job to give them a polystyrene cup of coffee and politely explain that playing in a public playground was not an offence. The desk sergeant didn't approve of the Metropolitan Police Graduate Entry scheme which had given me the rank of inspector over him; so I had to deal with all the nutters in Holborn. They felt more comfortable surrounded by blue serge and had vintage stories about martians in the plumbing. Most were satisfied just to get their loony notions on police notepaper. I filed all the statements, but they might as well have

'The sweetness was stronger, soft yet slowing'

been shredded.

By the time Judyth Staines was sent to my strip-lit cubicle the novelty had gone. I'd learned all the pigeon holes: She was an Overly Nervous Missing Persons Reporter. She wore her hair in purple tentacles, insisted on the 'y', and had a cheery *Kill a Pig Today* patch on her jump suit. The disappearee was Robert Webb, the bass guitarist of a band called Slug Death. Ms. Staines had last seen Webb in Goodge Street underground station at about a quarter past ten the previous night. He had bought (I wrote 'purchased' in the statement) a ticket for Belsize Park and vanished into the lifts. Ms. Staines had stayed in town 'to see someone' (cockney rhyming slang for 'buy drugs') and had later taken the tube to Belsize Park herself. She'd arrived at eleven and found the rest of Slug Death, still waiting for Webb. "And since then he hasn't been back to our place, or rung up, or anything."

Ms. Staines had been up all night. Her charcoal eyeshadow had trickled, giving her that zombie look. She was not happy in a police station. She kept looking around nervously, like the leading lady of a psycho movie exploring an old dark house where, fifteen years before, an entire girls' basketball team had been fed into a giant kitchen blender by a family of demented fast food freaks. I gave her the Telly Savalas speech about calming down, waiting a few days, and not being too worried because: Although people sometimes disappear they usually turn up with a perfectly logical explanation.

"It's hard to explain without you knowing him. Bobby wasn't just about to disappear. We were going to party. He had the bottle. He wasn't strung out, or hung up, or anything. He was just normal."

I asked if she could give a description.

"You can't miss him. He has blue horns."

I thought of a funny remark, but kept it to myself.

"He had most of his hair off, and the rest shaped like horns. He dyed them blue."

After another month of statement processing I would have let Webb disappear on his own, but I still had a perverse feeling that being a policeman was all about kicking doors in and getting results. During the next martian cease fire I asked around, and ended up at New Scotland Yard. I found Eric Verdon, the liaison between the Metropolitan Police and the London Transport Police, in the smaller of his two offices. The other was filled with eighteen tons of documentation, all the way back to horse-drawn trams.

"Oh yes," Verdon told me, "disappearances from the underground are not uncommon. Every once in a while some unfortunate wanders off where he shouldn't and meets with an accident. Sometimes our staff doesn't come across the remains for years. Some people never do turn up. Those are the most interesting, I think. This pile.

It was an impressive stack of manila folders. On the night of October the ninth, 1872 (which I like to think of as appropriately foggy) Mr. Julian Selwyn-Pitt, a landscape painter, walked into Oxford Street station and was never seen again. Since 1872 fifteen thousand, eight hundred and twenty-four people had followed Mr. Selwyn-Pitt into Verdon's files. The figure was exclusive of all those whose disappearance was never reported and those, like Robert Webb, whose folders had not yet drifted down to settle in Verdon's office.

"So there are nearly sixteen thousand people lying around the tube somewhere?"

"Presumably. Over the years whole sections have been closed off, reopened, caved in or forgotten. Even our maps are nowhere near complete. There are plenty of nooks and crannies that could comfortably accommodate a missing person. I often think of sardines."

"Pardon?"

"The game. You must have played it as a child. It's like hide-and-seek, only when you find someone you have to hide with them. I always found it unnerving somehow. You'd start with a house full of children, and then one by one they'd vanish. Finally you'd pull back the curtain and there they all would be, packed in like sardines, waiting for you. I'm sure it's like that down there. Somewhere there's a hidey-hole full of all those people."

All my deductive prowess could make of that was that Verdon had been filed away for too long and faded out himself. The Singular Case of the Blue-Horned Vanisher remained unsolved. The traditional next step was an inspection of the scene of the crime. After the evening shift I had a couple of shorts to nerve me for my first foray into independent detection.

Goodge Street tube station is one of the deepest in London. It has polite robot lifts whose vocabulary is limited to "please stand clear of the doors," and a rude nightwatchman whose speech is limited to an incomprehensible Jamaican patois. I used my police identification to borrow a lantern, but the nightwatchman's presence was required elsewhere for some important swearing and snoozing. I suspected that he did not want to slip into Verdon's fifteen thousand, eight hundred and twenty-seventh manila folder. The lifts had shut off for the night. I had to go down a spiral staircase, lit by off-white Christmas tree bulbs.

I was conducting my search on the Whinnie the Pooh principle of looking for a thing lost by losing myself and thus ending up next to the original object. When I passed the third PUBLIC NOT ALLOWED BEYOND THIS POINT notice I decided to chuck it in. Ms. Staines would finally wash her hair and marry an accountant anyway.

I was a couple of levels below the actual railway tunnel and had succeeded in getting lost. Here were the catacombs where broken spades, long-handled brooms, buckets of sand, mops, antiquated ticket machines, lost uniform caps, and stray umbrellas drag themselves to die.

I found a locker full of tin hats and gas masks. A rusted 1930s sandwich box, complete with a green hairy lunch wrapped in pre-cellophane tracing paper. And quiet, no rumbling trains at night. Only the inevitable underground ear-cracking drip. It was a standing tap steadily leaking onto a bale of the *Chronicle*. Prams, bedsteads, army blankets, enamel basins, a rocking horse. After the public library tiling gave way to bare bricks there wasn't even any Persian graffiti or football propaganda. Everything terminated here.

The damp kept the air clean. Verdon's files had been musty, but here the chilly air had a sweet afterscent. I sucked in a lungful, drawing the wind over my tongue, but couldn't catch the taste. I meandered without urgency in search of an EXIT. The drip was gone. The corridors were smooth and empty. The calm of a sea bed during a storm. Nothing mattered. Through tunnels, down corkscrew stairs, past uninteresting junctions, at random into empty storerooms. I opened a brassbound door.

The hall was lit blue. The sweetness was stronger, soft yet slowing. There were more of them than I could count. Some pale faces turned without interest. An old man in a frock coat and a wing collar, a stocky type in a khaki sergeant's uniform, a girl in a miniskirt and stiletto heels. Ulsters, bustles, Norfolk jackets, overalls, flat caps, pinstripes, kaftans, black leather jackets, denims. They weren't dead or alive. Just waiting.

THE GREEN MAN
Kelvin Jones

Illustration by Dave Carson

Kelvin Jones is a student of Sir Arthur Conan Doyle and a couple of years back, Gaslight Publications released his book Sherlock Holmes and the South Eastern, *an illustrated guide to the Holmes stories in the Kent region and Doyle's origins for his story ideas. His articles on Holmes, including a study of the myth and folklore origins of* The Hound of the Baskervilles, *have been published in British and American journals. His own stories, Holmes pastiches and tales reflecting his interest in folklore and Mr.R. James, have appeared in various small press magazines. This interest is strongly felt in 'The Green Man', originally published in* Fantasy Tales 12 *and also selected by editor Charles L. Grant for his anthology* Midnight.

A S THE Reverend Bear opened the stout door to the west entrance, a gust of wind swept inwards. He stepped back, startled by this sudden intrusion of the elements. Past the porch he could see the dark shapes of the cedars, their branches laid bare, against the black sky. He had forgotten how late it was.

He drew the heavy brass key from the ring attached to his belt and inserted it into the door. As the lock engaged, he had a sudden image of the church's interior, the solid round pillars ranged either side of the nave, the great hammerbeam roof shadowing everything beneath it. St

'Something glimpsed when the sleeper breaks from his nightmare'

Helen's was not a church he liked to linger in, especially in the winter months. Not only was it difficult to heat, but its Norman builders had allowed little light to penetrate the dark interior, even on a day of brilliant sunshine. The deeply recessed windows gave a cloistered feeling to the interior and no amount of polish or ventilation eradicated the cloying fustiness of the central tower. It was not, to his mind, the most suitable of places for Christians to worship in.

He shivered, suddenly aware of the chill night wind. A procession of thoughts wound its way through his tired mind, ecclesiastical obligations, each more dreary than the last. His sermon was not due until tomorrow, yet he had not even the faintest idea of his subject.

Not that it mattered, he thought cynically. He could always choose a ready-made one from his countless volumes. Besides, of late his mind had been otherwise preoccupied. Workmen had been carrying out extensive restoration in the clerestory, stripping away the layers of whitewash, the legacy of sober Victorians and their Cromwellian ancestors.

Already they had revealed a series of remarkable wall paintings, patterns of interwoven flowers; their colours fresh and vivid as the day they were painted over eight hundred years before. The Reverend Bear paused at the entrance to the porch. It was almost unbelievable that Christian worship had been practised here for such a period. What would the subject of tomorrow's sermon have been then? The seven deadly sins, perhaps?

He shut the outer door and looked upwards. Against the pale halo of the city lights, three distorted gargoyles jutted from the central tower, their faces grimacing at him. He turned, rather more swiftly than usual, and began walking at a brisk pace down the long drive towards the main road.

There was a narrow footpath linking the old vicarage with the main south circular and it was his habit in the summer months to take a short cut along this route. Of late he had avoided the path since the way was poorly illuminated, a thick wood skirting much of its length. But tonight was an exception. Whether it was the thought of his cosy fireside that directed his footsteps this way or maybe some unconscious desire for excitement he could never afterwards determine. But he strode purposefully ahead, plunging into an indeterminate well of darkness where all that was visible was the dim strip of the chalk path.

Half-way along the path he stopped. He had no reason to do this. He told himself as much, for he had work to prepare before the evening was spent and already a sense of fatigue was starting to settle uncomfortably on his mind.

Nevertheless, he surprised himself by stopping and lighting his pipe, an action that could only suggest confidence in his surroundings. This was curious, for the Reverend Bear was nothing if not timid and darkness of any kind had always seemed to him to be a facet of that alarming world conjured by the medieval mind in which the souls of the departed languished in everlasting perdition.

He stood at the edge of the path, conscious of the wind biting angrily at the trees. It was odd to think that in the middle of the great city there were places like this wood, sealed off from the world, still much the same as it would have appeared in the Dark Ages. Only then, he reasoned, it would have been a place of wild beasts and nameless fears. Now it was something else; it represented that border of the conscious mind where vague shapes flitted . . .

Suddenly, something broke in on his train of thought. He listened. There it was again. The sound of a voice. Something between a sigh and a gasp. A curious sense of excitement began to rise within him. Should he not investigate? What if someone had injured himself and lay there in the darkness in need of assistance? He could not, in all conscience, pass by without offering help.

He began to make his way through the bracken, stopping every so often to listen. Embarrassment prevented him from calling out lest the sound be the product of his own imagination. No, there is was again, to the left of him, this time much closer, more sustained. He began to wish he had a torch. But slowly his eyes began to adjust to the darkness and he could discern the outlines of the tree trunks.

By the edge of a clearing he stopped. He peered into the gloom. He could hear it distinctly now. The breathing was rapid, but was it not more than one voice that he could hear?

The shadow of a suspicion began to cloud his mind. Then, as his eyes scanned the ground in front of him, realization dawned. Through the bare branches of the trees, a skein of moonlight fell on naked limbs, locked in a tight embrace. Slowly the body of the man rose and fell above that of his companion. The sighing of the woman grew faster, more ecstatic. The sight repelled him, yet he could not turn and bolt. He remained there, behind the tree, fascinated, frozen with anticipation . . .

"It is a truly remarkable piece of sculpture," said the Reverend John Waldon.

"Remarkable, yes, but I find it hideous."

They were standing in the clerestory. It was eleven o'clock. Above them, beyond the hammerbeam roof, the sun poured down on St Helens, but only a fraction of its power penetrated the length of the nave beneath.

Up here in the clerestory there was a smell compounded of age and disuse which made the Reverend Bear slightly nauseous. He looked again at the huge carving. It was, as his companion pointed out, remarkable. The workmen had discovered it only this morning, hidden away behind three inches of plaster. It was a large motif, probably dating from the 13th century, consisting of a grotesque head encompassed by a thick webbing of intertwined leaves and foliage.

The Reverend Bear felt slightly incensed by his friend's obvious pleasure in the piece. To him there was something altogether loathsome about the face. Its high cheekbones, curled saturnine nose and the cruel twist to the mouth gave it a suggestion of menace.

"What on earth does it represent?"

"It is certainly not a Christian image," replied his companion, a man steeped in the architectural trappings of early churches. "I remember seeing something similar in a church in Berkshire. There they called it the Green Man."

"The Green Man? Jack of the Green?"

He recalled a curious figure, clothed in a bush, in a mummer's play he had once seen. It had made little sense to him.

"The same. I imagine that to our pagan ancestors he was like a Roman silvanus, a creature of venery and of the wild hunt."

"All the same, I dislike it."

The Reverend John Waldon gave his companion an odd look. There was something in the clergyman's manner, a suggestion of unease, that had never manifested itself before. His normally pallid complexion and watery grey eyes seemed drained of life.

"The restoration work certainly has lightened much of the church's interior," he said, changing the subject.

The Reverend Bear managed a smile. As they turned and walked away from the scaffolding he felt a sense of inward relief. It was always so cold up here in the clerestory.

"The sun was risen upon the earth when Lot entered into Zoar. Then the Lord rained upon Sodom and Gomorrah brimstone and fire from the Lord out of heaven. And he overthrew those cities, and that which grew upon the ground. But his wife looked back from behind him, and she became a pillar of salt. And Abraham got up early in the morning to the place where he stood before the Lord. And he looked toward Sodom and Gomorrah and toward all the land of the plain, and beheld and lo, the smoke of the country went up as the smoke of the furnace. Here endeth the second lesson."

The Reverend Bear rose from a velvet cushion, bordered with golden tassles and inscribed with the initials INRI. To the left of him the gold-plated eagle which served as a lectern shone, distorting the features of the reader.

"We will now sing Hymm number fifty-two, *O God Our Help in Ancient Times.*"

The congregation droned into life. He looked about him. *Men, women and children, all in white and their faces as pale as moonlight.* His grip tightened on the brass rail. He made a conscious effort to concentrate on the words of the hymm. When he came to the words "In ancient times," he stopped abruptly and looked up.

It seemed as if the dark shadows of the clerestory had dispersed, giving way to a yellow effulgence. Although he was some sixty feet away, the head appeared almost brilliantly outlined among the scrolled leaves, the blank eyes bulging, the nose sharp as a razor edge. He looked down quickly at the hymm book but he was hopelessly lost.

He coughed to cover his embarrassment. He thought of Lot's wife, turning to view the forbidden city, her body turning to salt. A glimpse of unbelievable perversions, bodies articulated in death at their moment of ecstasy. Beads of perspiration broke on his brow . . .

When the service was concluded, he hurriedly changed out of his vestments and left the church. Outside the sun was streaming down, throwing the dazzling greens and browns of the late autumn into startling relief. Compared with the stale air of the church's interior, the excursion came as a pleasant contrast. Outside, standing beneath the tower, was the Reverend John Waldon. He approached rapidly, his face beaming.

"I must congratulate you. That was a most excellent sermon."

"You thought so?"

"I have rarely heard a better one. Such force. And such conviction."

Bear smiled gently. He felt strangely displaced. For the life of him he could not recall the contents of his sermon.

"Good. You must visit us again in the near future."

"Now, if you'll excuse me, I promised to see the members of the Mother's Union at twelve. Good luck with the restoration."

The Reverend Waldon made his way out of the churchyard with firm, unwavering steps. He was a man whose faith never faltered. Bear watched him go, then turned towards the driveway. He was looking forward to his lunch. Certainties of that type gave an added dimension to his life. The sound of the beef as it dropped sizzling onto the plate, the pungent aroma of white cabbage, these things comforted him.

The main road was particularly busy this Sunday morning. Several parishioners nodded to him as he made his way towards the railway bridge. He was beginning to feel like his old self again. Perhaps I should take a holiday, he thought. Maybe the work is beginning to get on top of me. He disliked doctors. He felt distinctly uneasy in their presence. It was the fear of being analysed that put him on edge.

At the corner of the bridge he stopped and looked about him. It was a beautiful day, sharp but vivid, the perfect weather for walking. Then he encountered the footpath which he had taken the previous night. He recalled the experience there that had so disturbed him. Still, it was unavoidable. It could not be helped. Today it was a different path, a different setting, he consoled himself.

He made the plunge. Soon he was halfway down the track, walking at a brisk pace. There was no one else about, which surprised him a little. It was such an obvious choice for a morning constitutional.

Half way along he stopped to sit down on the sawn bole of a tree. To his left, across an open field, a flock of black crows circled silently. He took out his pipe and lit it. Soon the pungent tobacco was swirling about him. His mind felt sharp and vigorous, full of distant thoughts and half-remembered phrases. He tried to recall some of his sermon but found the exercise dull and unedifying.

He was about to reach for his box of matches when suddenly he heard a sound behind him. He turned sharply, expecting to see a stranger there, but he could see nothing except the long line of trees stretching back towards the railway track.

He stood still for some moments, listening intently. There it was again, the sound of a voice, calling. But it was indistinct. He could not tell if it were a woman's or a man's. He stood up, irritated by his uncertainty, and knocked the bowl of his pipe against the tree stump. He moved towards the edge of the wood. There it was again. A sound like laughter this time, a woman's voice.

He felt an urge to continue his route, yet there was a part of him which pushed him over the bracken between the thick tree trunks into the shade of the wood. He moved silently, not wishing to disturb whoever it was who had penetrated the interior, desiring only to remain unseen.

From the depths of his brain words formed, a meaningless pattern, a rhyme he had heard as a child. But now they revived in his consciousness, flew hither and thither about his expectant mind:

"Fly then quickly, make no stay

For Herne the Hunter rides this way."

The words took on a magical force. They would not disperse, would not shift from his thoughts. He felt puzzled, confused by his own behaviour. What was he doing here? Why had he stepped across this threshold into the shade of the wood?

He stopped. It was the same clearing, but now brighter because of the sunlight that filtered through the branches. It was the same couple, he could swear to it. The voices were identical. Even their positions had not altered.

But now the act appeared even more brazen, daringly explicit. The woman lay with her back to him, her knees drawn up almost to her breasts. Above her the man rose and fell, his broad back moving with uninterrupted ease, his face suffused with pleasure. With each stroke the woman clenched her fists, then relinquished them, gasping as she did so. The man increased his speed, lengthening his strokes. Perspiration began to drip from his brow onto the woman's neck.

Bear shut his eyes, trying to blot out the picture, but the sounds continued, penetrating the barrier. His mind whirled chaotically but he knew that he dare not move; that he was an unwilling witness to the act. Slowly the words filtered back into his tortured mind:

"Fly then quickly, make no stay
For Herne the Hunter rides this way . . ."

He saw himself as if from far above the wood: a silent figure, petrified, cut off from the spectacle that took place before him. Then, from beyond the trees came a sound like none that he had ever heard before.

Like a cloud of darkness it crashed upon him, heavy and stifling, a nebula of chaos bearing with it the voices of the long dead. High in the air broke the frenzied neighing of stallions, their teeth champing, their eyes staring and mad, and beneath this was the unleashed anger of the beast, tearing at the ground, rooting up trees and bushes, rending flesh.

The Reverend staggered back, stunned and confused by the appalling sounds which had broken about him. His eyes were now wide open. No lingering doubts remained in his mind as to the meaning of this place. Whatever had sought to lure him here, whatever had lulled him into a false sense of security was now revealing its purpose with unchecked ferocity.

He looked about him. The wood, formerly so tranquil, was now plunged in unutterable gloom. The branches of the trees crashed wildly, locked with each other in a frenzied parody of the act of coition he had just witnessed. The man and woman, their embrace broken by the sudden change, sat staring about them, clutching at their clothes. Leaves whirled into their faces, flung by angry gusts of wind and above all this the sound of a horn, cold and shrill, as ancient as time itself. It was the summons of the Hunter.

Over the clearing a dark shape fell. From its centre there was fashioned a face, something glimpsed when the sleeper breaks from his nightmare, shaking the presence from him.

Burning eyes set in a halo of green and over all this there was the smell of decay, the acrid odour of death. He turned and fled from the wood. Behind him the storm still raged. But now there was another sound, a long sustained screaming. He dare not turn. He must not watch.

The Reverend Francis Bear dried his hands on the red towel that hung behind the bathroom door. He sighed. It had been a long day. But it had been an enjoyable day.

He padded along the corridor that led to his Italiante bedroom in his fur-lined carpet slippers, smiling to himself. Sodom and Gomorrah. It had been an excellent theme. It had fired the imagination of the congregation. He turned the gleaming brass door knob and opened the bedroom door. Inside, the heavy brown wood panelling was barely discernable in the light of the flickering embers of the coal fire. The landlady must have drawn the heavy velvet curtains in his prolonged absence, for the darkness in the room had a close, suffocating texture to it that he found almost overpowering.

He went to the curtains to draw them back then thought better of it. The room was snug. Why disturb things? He sat on the coverlet of the bed, staring into the fire. The red coals shimmered with a baleful intensity, sending up occasional flames of an orange hue into the chimney. He looked about him at the objects in the room. Somehow their familiar shapes appeared distorted. The mahogany bureau lay huddled by the bed, its scrolled feet scarcely visible in the shadow. They were like the feet of a giant bird of prey. Above them, the two brass handles glinted in the firelight.

He moved to the fireside and, picking up the poker, began to move the glowing coals into fresh life. He wondered if he should turn on the light. But what reason had he, a man of the cloth, to fear from a room he had lived in for nearly twenty years? He was tired, he told himself, and in that condition his imagination lay open to the suggestible.

Putting down the poker, he changed position so that the majority of the room's furniture lay to his left. He sank back into the Georgian armchair, feeling the protection of its enormous sides, and smiled to himself. His mind began to wander in the direction of the day's events. He wondered what it was that destroyed the cities of Sodom and Gomorrah. A nuclear explosion perhaps? Was God capable of that? Of course. God transcended moral or immoral actions. God was eternal. He pictured the earth, blasted bare, the trees torn from their roots, legs and arms and broken faces sticking out from beneath the rubble.

Suddenly his hands tightened on the arms of the chair. Barely perceptible, just out of the corner of his left eye he detected a movement. He turned his head, but that area of the room to which his attention was now drawn seemed quite still. Could it have been the reflection of a car in the street outside? Then he remembered that the curtains were drawn. Their heavy texture permitted no light. He sat staring at the corner of the room in the vague dread that something would moved there again. The corner, which had a potted plant on a small oak table and a low bookcase, lay silent as the grave.

He tried to concentrate on God, but God seemed remote and disinterested in the heavy Italiante room with its heavy furniture. He said the name out loud to himself: "God," but the word had lost its meaning and once uttered it was instantly lost in the enormity of the room.

He looked at his hands. Across the backs broad streaks of red still spread their tell-tale stain.

He had tried everything but not even the strongest bleach could remove the marks. And now there was something else, something that puzzled him, a deformity that he had never noticed before. He held his left hand in front of the flames and curled the fingers towards the palm. It was undeniable. In the course of a day the fingernails had grown to twice their length. And there was a faint greenish tinge to them.

He sat in the darkened room, thinking of the clerestory and the image on the wall there. What had he said to Waldon? That he found it hideous? What a peculiar remark. And then there was something else, some other memory. It frustrated him not to be able to locate it. Yet as he grasped for it, the imprint evaded him. What had he done today? Very little. The sermon, the walk along the footpath, the traditional Sunday lunch.

He looked back again into the fire and the flames leapt up at him like accusing fingers. The flames were scarlet now, like the colour of blood, like the colour of Babylon's whore in Revelations. The fingers of flame pinned him to the chair, daring him to move and be damned.

He would never be alone.

Not again.

THE VOICE OF
THE BEACH
Ramsey Campbell

Illustration by David Lloyd

In 1987 Ramsey Campbell celebrated twenty-five years of chilling spines with a bumper collection of his short fiction, Dark Feasts. *Ramsey made a name for himself during the 1970s, soon becoming a prolific short story writer and Britain's finest exponent of the weird fiction tradition. His subsequent novels, collections and anthologies have marked him as one of the most unique and respected voices in the genre. A winner of both the British and World Fantasy Awards, his numerous books include* The Doll Who Ate His Mother, The Nameless, The Face That Must Die, Incarnate, Obsession, The Hungry Moon, The Influence, Claw, New Terrors, Scared Stiff, Fine Frights *and* Ancient Images. *A regular contributor to* Fantasy Tales *since the first issue, Ramsey describes* The Voice of the Beach *as his 'last' Cthulhu Mythos tale. It was first published in the tenth issue of the magazine and was voted by the readers, not unsurprisingly as you'll no doubt agree, the best story in that number.*

I MET Neal at the station. Of course I can describe it, I have only to go up the road and look, but there is no need. That isn't what I have to get out of me. It isn't me, it's out there, it can be described. I need

236

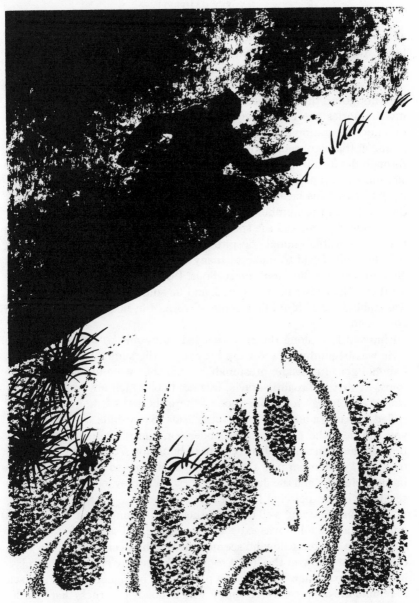

'Stranded objects, elaborate symbols composed of something like flesh, writhed on its paralyzed margin.'

all my energy for that, all my concentration, but perhaps it will help if I can remember before that, when everything looked manageable, expressible, familiar enough—when I could bear to look out of the window.

Neal was standing alone on the small platform, and now I see that I dare not go up the road after all, or out of the house. It doesn't matter, my memories are clear, they will help me hold on. Neal must have rebuffed the station-master, who was happy to chat to anyone. He was gazing at the bare tracks, sharpened by June light, as they cut their way through the forest—gazing at them as a suicide might gaze at a razor. He saw me and swept his hair back from his face, over his shoulders. Suffering had pared his face down, stretched the skin tighter and paler over the skull. I can remember exactly how he looked before.

"I thought I'd missed the station," he said, though surely the station's name was visible enough, despite the flowers that scaled the board. If only he had! "I had to make so many changes. Never mind. Christ, it's good to see you. You look marvellous. I expect you can thank the sea for that." His eyes had brightened, and he sounded so full of life that it was spilling out of him in a tumble of words, but his handshake felt like cold bone.

I hurried him along the road that led home and to the

He was beginning to screw up his eyes at the sunlight, and I thought I should get him inside; presumably headaches were among his symptoms. At first the road is gravel, fragments of which always succeed in working their way into your shoes. Where the trees fade out as though stifled by sand, a concrete path turns aside. Sand shifts over the gravel; you can hear the gritty conflict underfoot, and the musing of the sea. Beyond the path stands this crescent of bungalows. Surely all this is still true. But I remember now that the bungalows looked unreal against the burning blue sky and the dunes like embryo hills; they looked like a dream set down in the peircing light of June.

"You must be doing well to afford this." Neal sounded listless, envious only because he felt it was expected. If only he had stayed that way! But once inside the bungalow he seemed pleased by everything— the view, my books on show in the living room bookcase, my typewriter displaying a token page that bore a token phrase, the Breughel prints that used to remind me of humanity. Abruptly, with a moody eagerness that I hardly remarked at the time, he said: "Shall we have a look at the beach?"

There, I've written the word. I can describe the beach, I must describe it, it is all that's in my head. I have my notebook which I took with me that day. Neal led the way along the gravel path. Beyond the concrete turn-off to the bungalows the gravel was engulfed almost at once by sand, despite the thick ranks of low bushes that had been planted to keep back the sand. We squeezed between the bushes, which were determined to close their ranks across the gravel.

Once through, we felt the breeze whose waves passed through the marram grass that spiked the dunes. Neal's hair streamed back, pale as the grass. The trudged dunes were slowing him down, eager as he was. We slithered down to the beach, and the sound of the unfurling sea leapt closer, as though we'd wakened it from dreaming. The wind fluttered trapped in my ears, leafed through my notebook as I scribbled the image of wakening and thought with an appalling innocence: perhaps I can use that image. Now we were walled off from the rest of the world by the dunes, faceless mounds with unkempt green wigs, mounds almost as white as the sun.

Even then I felt that the beach was somehow separate from its surroundings: introverted, I remember thinking. I put it down to the shifting haze which hovered above the sea, the haze which I could never focus, whose distance I could never quite judge. From the self-contained stage of the beach the bungalows looked absurdly intrusive, anachronisms rejected by the geomorphological time of sand and sea. Even the skeletal car and the other debris, half-engulfed by the beach near the coast road, looked less alien. These are my memories, the most stable things left to me, and I must go on. I found today that I cannot go back any further.

Neal was staring, eyes narrowed against the glare, along the waste of beach that stretched in the opposite direction from the coast road and curved out of sight. "Doesn't anyone come down here? There's no pollution, is there?"

"It depends who you believe." Often the beach seemed to give me a headache, even when there was no glare—and then there was the way the beach looked at night. "Still, I think most folk go up the coast to the resorts. That's the only reason I can think of."

We were walking. Beside us the edge of the glittering sea moved in several directions simultaneously. Moist sand, sleek as satin, displayed shells which appeared to flash patterns, faster than my mind could grasp. Pinpoint mirrors of sand gleamed, rapid as Morse. My notes say this is how it seemed.

"Don't your neighbours ever come down?"

Neal's voice made me start. I had been engrossed in the designs of shell and sand. Momentarily I was unable to judge the width of the beach: a few paces, or miles? I grasped my sense of perspective, but a headache was starting, a dull impalpable grip that encircled my cranium. Now I know what all this meant, but I want to remember how I felt before I knew.

"Very seldom," I said. "Some of them think there's quicksand." One old lady, sitting in her garden to glare at the dunes like Canute versus

239

sand, had told me that warning notices kept sinking. I'd never encountered quicksand, but I always brought my stick to help me trudge.

"So I'll have the beach to myself."

I took that to be a hint. At least he would leave me alone if I wanted to work. "The bungalow people are mostly retired," I said. "Those who aren't in wheelchairs go driving. I imagine they've had enough of sand, even if they aren't past walking on it." Once, further up the beach, I'd encountered nudists censoring themselves with towels or straw hats as they ventured down to the sea, but Neal could find out about them for himself. I wonder now if I ever saw them at all, or simply felt that I should.

Was he listening? His head was cocked, but not toward me. He'd slowed, and was staring at the ridges and furrows of the beach, at which the sea was lapping. All at once the ridges reminded me of convolutions of the brain, and I took out my notebook as the grip on my skull tightened. The beach as a subconscious, my notes say: the horizon as the imagination—sunlight set a ship ablaze on the edge of the world, an image that impressed me as vividly yet indefinably symbolic—the debris as memories, half-buried, half-comprehensible. But then what were the bungalows, perched above the dunes like boxes carved of dazzling bone?

I glanced up. A cloud had leaned toward me. No, it had been more as though the cloud were rushing at the beach from the horizon, dauntingly fast. Had it been a cloud? It had seemed more massive than a ship. The sky was empty now, and I told myself that it had been an effect of the haze—the magnified shadow of a gull, perhaps.

My start had enlivened Neal, who began to chatter like a television wakened by a kick. "It'll be good for me to be alone here, to get used to being alone. Mary and the children found themselves another home, you see. He earns more money than I'll ever see, if that's what they want. He's the head-of-the-house type, if that's what they want. I couldn't be that now if I tried, not with the way my nerves are now." I can still hear everything he said, and I suppose that I knew what had been wrong with him. Now they are just words.

"That's why I'm talking so much," he said, and picked up a spiral shell, I thought to quiet himself.

"That's much too small. You'll never hear anything in that."

Minutes passed before he took it away from his ear and handed it to me. "No?" he said.

I put it to my ear and wasn't sure what I was hearing. No, I didn't throw the shell away, I didn't crush it underfoot; in any case, how could I have done that to the rest of the beach? I was straining to hear, straining to make out how the sound differed from the usual whisper of a shell. Was it that it seemed to have a rhythm that I couldn't define, or that it sounded shrunken by distance rather than cramped by the shell? I felt expectant, entranced—precisely the feeling I'd tried so often to communicate in my fiction, I believe. Something stooped toward me from the horizon. I jerked, and dropped the shell.

There was nothing but the dazzle of sunlight that leapt at me from the waves. The haze above the sea had darkened, staining the light, and I told myself that was what I'd seen. But when Neal picked up another shell I felt uneasy. The grip on my skull was very tight now. As I regarded the vistas of empty sea and sky and beach my expectancy grew oppressive, too imminent, no longer enjoyable.

"I think I'll head back now. Maybe you should as well," I said, rummaging for an uncontrived reason, "just in case there is quicksand."

"All right. It's in all of them," he said, displaying an even smaller shell to which he'd just listened. I remember thinking that his observation was so self-evident as to be meaningless.

As I turned toward the bungalows the glitter of the sea clung to my eyes. After-images crowded among the debris. They were moving; I strained to make out their shape. What did they resemble? Symbols— heiroglyphs? Limbs writhing rapidly, as if in a ritual dance? They made the debris appear to shift, to crumble. The herd of faceless dunes seemed to edge forward; an image leaned toward me out of the sky. I closed my eyes, to calm their antics, and wondered if I should take the warnings of pollution more seriously.

We walked toward the confusion of footprints that climbed the dunes. Neal glanced about at the sparkling of sand. Never before had the beach so impressed me as a complex of patterns, and perhaps that meant it was already too late. Spotlighted by the sun, it looked so artificial that I came close to doubting how it felt underfoot.

The bungalows looked unconvincing too. Still, when we'd slumped in our chairs for a while, letting the relative dimness soothe our eyes while our bodies guzzled every hint of coolness, I forgot about the beach. We shared two litres of wine and talked about my work, about his lack of any since graduating.

Later I prepared melon, salads, water ices. Neal watched, obviously embarrassed that he couldn't help. He seemed lost without Mary. One more reason not to marry, I thought, congratulating myself.

As we ate he kept staring out at the beach. A ship was caught in the amber sunset: a dream of escape. I felt the image less deeply than I'd experienced the metaphors of the beach; it was less oppressive. The band around my head had faded.

When it grew dark Neal pressed close to the pane. "What's that?" he demanded.

I switched out the light so that he could see. Beyond the dim humps of the dunes the beach was glowing, a dull pallor like moonlight stifled by fog. Do all beaches glow at night? "That's what makes people say there's pollution," I said.

"Not the light," he said impatiently. "The other things. What's moving?"

I squinted through the pane. For minutes I could see nothing but the muffled glow. At last, when my eyes were smarting, I began to see forms thin and stiff as scarecrows, jerking into various contorted poses. Gazing for so long was bound to produce something of the kind, and I took them to be after-images of the tangle, barely visible, of bushes.

"I think I'll go and see."

"I shouldn't go down there at night," I said, having realised that I'd never gone to the beach at night and that I felt a definite, though irrational, aversion to doing so.

Eventually he went to bed. Despite all his travelling, he'd needed to drink to make himself sleepy. I heard him open his bedroom window, which overlooked the beach. There is so much still to write, so much to struggle through, and what good can it do me now?

I had taken the bungalow, one of the few entries in my diary says, to give myself the chance to write without being distracted by city life—the cries of the telephone, the tolling of the doorbell, the omnipresent clamour—only to discover, once I'd left it behind, that city life was my theme. But I was a compulsive writer: if I failed to write for more than a few days I became depressed. Writing was the way I overcame the depression of not writing. Now writing seems to be my only way of hanging on to what remains of myself, of delaying the end.

The day after Neal arrived, I typed a few lines of a sample chapter. It wasn't a technique I enjoyed—tearing a chapter out of the context of a novel that didn't yet exist. In any case, I was distracted by the beach, compelled to scribble notes about it, trying to define the images it suggested. I hoped these notes might build into a story. I was picking at the notes in search of their story when Neal said: "Maybe I can lose myself for a bit in the countryside."

"Mm," I said curtly, not looking up.

"Didn't you say there was a deserted village?"

By the time I directed him I would have lost the thread of my thoughts. The thread had been frayed and tangled, anyway. As long as I was compelled to think about the beach I might just as well be down there. I can still write as if I don't know the end, it helps me not to think of

"I'll come with you," I said.

The weather was nervous. Archipelagos of cloud floated low on the hazy

242

sky, above the sea; great Rorschach blots rose from behind the slate hills, like dissolved stone. As we squeezed through the bushes, a shadow came hunching over the dunes to meet us. When my foot touched the beach a moist shadowy chill seized me, as though the sand disguised a lurking marsh. Then sunlight spilled over the beach, which leapt into clarity.

I strode, though Neal appeared to want to dawdle. I wasn't anxious to linger; after all, I told myself, it might rain. Glinting mosaics of grains of sand changed restlessly around me, never quite achieving a pattern. Patches of sand, flat, shapeless elongated ghosts, glided over the beach and faltered, waiting for another breeze. Neal kept peering at them as though to make out their shapes.

Half a mile along the beach the dunes began to sag, to level out. The slate hills were closing in. Were they the source of the insidious chill? Perhaps I was feeling the damp; a penumbra of moisture welled up around each of my footprints. The large wet shapes seemed quite unrelated to my prints, an effect which I found unnerving. When I glanced back, it looked as though something enormous was imitating my walk.

The humidity was almost suffocating. My head felt clamped by tension. Wind blundered booming in my ears, even when I could feel no breeze. Its jerky rhythm was distracting because indefinable. Grey cloud had flooded the sky; together with the hills and the thickening haze above the sea, it caged the beach. At the edge of my eye the convolutions of the beach seemed to writhe, to struggle to form patterns. The insistent sparkling nagged at my mind.

I'd begun to wonder whether I had been blaming imagined pollution for the effects of heat and humidity—I was debating whether to turn back before I grew dizzy or nauseous—when Neal said: "Is that it?"

I peered ahead, trying to squint the dazzle of waves from my eyes. A quarter of a mile away the hills ousted the dunes completely. Beneath the spiky slate a few uprights of rock protruded from the beach like standing stones. They glowed sullenly as copper through the haze; they were encrusted with sand. Surely that wasn't the village.

"Yes, that's it," Neal said, and strode forward.

I followed him, because the village must be further on. The veil of haze drew back, the vertical rocks gleamed unobscured, and I halted bewildered. The rocks weren't encrusted at all; they were slate, grey as the table of rock on which they stood above the beach. Though the slate was jagged, some of its gaps were regular: windows, doorways. Here and there walls still formed corners. How could the haze have distorted my view so spectacularly?

Neal was climbing rough steps carved out of the slate table. Without warning, as I stood confused by my misperception, I felt utterly alone.

243

A bowl of dull haze trapped me on the bare sand. Slate, or something more massive and vague, loomed over me. The kaleidoscope of shells was about to shift; the beach was ready to squirm, to reveal its pattern, shake off its artificiality. The massive looming would reach down, and

My start felt like a convulsive awakening. The table was deserted except for the fragments of buildings. I could hear only the wind, baying as though its mouth was vast and uncontrollable. "Neal," I called. Dismayed by the smallness of my voice, I shouted "Neal."

I heard what sounded like scales of armour chafing together—slate, of course. The grey walls shone lifelessly, cavitied as skulls; gaping windows displayed an absence of faces, of rooms. Then Neal's head poked out of half a wall. "Yes, come on," he said. "It's strange."

As I climbed the steps, sand gritted underfoot like sugar. Low drifts of sand were piled against walls; patches glinted on the small plateau. Could that sand have made the whole place look encrusted and half-buried? I told myself that it had been an effect of the heat.

Broken walls surrounded me. They glared like stormclouds in lightning. They formed a maze whose centre was desertion. That image stirred another, too deep in my mind to be definable. The place was—not a maze, but a puzzle whose solution would clarify a pattern, a larger mystery. I realized that then; why couldn't I have fled?

I suppose I was held by the enigma of the village. I knew there were quarries in the hills above, but I'd never learned why the village had been abandoned. Perhaps its meagreness had killed it—I saw traces of less than a dozen buildings. It seemed further dwarfed by the beach; the sole visible trace of humanity, it dwindled beneath the gnawing of sand and the elements. I found it enervating, its lifelessness infectious. Should I stay with Neal, or risk leaving him there? Before I could decide, I heard him say amid a rattle of slate: "This is interesting."

In what way? He was clambering about an exposed cellar, among shards of slate. Whatever the building had been, it had stood furthest from the sea. "I don't mean the cellar," Neal said. "I mean that."

Reluctantly I peered where he was pointing. In the cellar wall furthest from the beach, a rough alcove had been chipped out of the slate. It was perhaps a yard deep, but barely high enough to accommodate a huddled man. Neal was already crawling in. I heard slate crack beneath him; his feet protruded from the darkness. Of course they weren't about to jerk convulsively—but my nervousness made me back away when his muffled voice said: "What's this?"

He backed out like a terrier with his prize. It was an old notebook, its pages stuck together in a moist wad. "Someone covered it up with slate," he said as though that should tempt my interest.

Before I could prevent him he was sitting at the edge of the beach and peeling the pages gingerly apart. Not that I was worried that he might be destroying a fragment of history—I simply wasn't sure that I wanted to read whatever had been hidden in the cellar. Why couldn't I have followed my instincts?

He disengaged the first page carefully, then frowned. "This begins in the middle of something. There must be another book."

Handing me the notebook, he stalked away to scrabble in the cellar. I sat on the edge of the slate table, and glanced at the page. It is before me now on my desk. The pages have crumbled since then—the yellowing paper looks more and more like sand—but the large writing is still legible, unsteady capitals in a hand that might once have been literate before it grew senile. No punctuation separates the words, though blotches sometimes do. Beneath the relentless light at the deserted village the faded ink looked unreal, scarcely present at all.

FROM THE BEACH EVERYONE GONE NOW BUT ME ITS NOT SO BAD IN DAYTIME EXCEPT I CANT GO BUT AT NIGHT I CAN HEAR IT REACHING OUT FOR (a blot of fungus had consumed a word here) AND THE VOICES ITS VOICE AND THE GLOWING AT LEAST IT HELPS ME SEE DOWN HERE WHEN IT COMES

I left it at that; my suddenly unsteady fingers might have torn the page. I wish to God they had. I was on edge with the struggle between humidity and the chill of slate and beach; I felt feverish. As I stared at the words they touched impressions, half-memories. If I looked up, would the beach have changed?

I heard Neal slithering on slate, turning over fragments. In my experience, stones were best not turned over. Eventually he returned. I was dully fascinated by the shimmering of the beach; my fingers pinched the notebook shut.

"I can't find anything," he said. "I'll have to come back." He took the notebook from me and began to read, muttering "What? Jesus!" Gently he separated the next page from the wad. "This gets stranger," he murmured. "What kind of guy was this? Imagine what it must have been like to live inside his head."

How did he know it had been a man? I stared at the pages, to prevent Neal from reading them aloud. At least it saved me from having to watch the antics of the beach, which moved like slow flames, but the introverted meandering of words made me nervous.

IT CANT REACH DOWN HERE NOT YET BUT OUTSIDE IS CHANGING OUTSIDES PART OF THE PATTERN I READ THE PATTERN THATS WHY I CANT GO SAW THEM DANCING THE PATTERN IT WANTS ME TO DANCE ITS ALIVE BUT ITS ONLY THE IMAGE BEING PUT TOGETHER

245

Neal was wide-eyed, fascinated. Feverish disorientation gripped my skull; I felt too unwell to move. The heat-haze must be closing in: at the edge of my vision, everything was shifting.

WHEN THE PATTERNS DONE IT CAN COME BACK AND GROW ITS HUNGRY TO BE EVERYTHING I KNOW HOW IT WORKS THE SAND MOVES AT NIGHT AND SUCKS YOU DOWN OR MAKES YOU GO WHERE IT WANTS TO MAKE (a blotch had eaten several words) WHEN THEY BUILT LEWIS THERE WERE OLD STONES THAT THEY MOVED MAYBE THE STONES KEPT IT SMALL NOW ITS THE BEACH AT LEAST

On the next page the letters are much larger, and wavery. Had the light begun to fail, or had the writer been retreating from the light—from the entrance to the cellar? I didn't know which alternative I dislike more.

GOT TO WRITE HANDS SHAKY FROM CHIPPING TUNNEL AND NO FOOD THEYRE SINGING NOW HELPING IT REACH CHANTING WITH NO MOUTHS THEY SING AND DANCE THE PATTERN FOR IT TO REACH THROUGH

Now there are very few words to the page. The letters are jagged, as though the writer's hand kept twitching violently.

GLOW COMING ITS OUT THERE NOW ITS LOOKING IN AT ME IT CANT GET HOLD IF I KEEP WRITING THEY WANT ME TO DANCE SO ITLL GROW WANT ME TO BE

There it ends. "Ah, the influence of Joyce," I commented sourly. The remaining pages are blank except for fungus. I managed to stand up; my head felt like a balloon pumped full of gas. "I'd like to go back now. I think I've a touch of sunstroke."

A hundred yards away I glanced back at the remnants of the village—Lewis, I assumed it had been called. The stone remains wavered as though striving to achieve a new shape; the haze made them look coppery, fat with a crust of sand. I was desperate to get out of the heat.

Closer to the sea I felt slightly less oppressed—but the whispering of sand, the liquid murmur of the waves, the bumbling of the wind, all chanted together insistently. Everywhere on the beach were patterns, demanding to be read.

Neal clutched the notebook under his arm. "What do you make of it?" he said eagerly.

His indifference to my health annoyed me, and hence so did the question. "He was mad," I said. "Living alone there—is it any wonder? Maybe he moved there after the place was abandoned. The beach must glow there too. That must have finished him. You saw how he tried to dig himself a refuge. That's all there is to it."

"Do you think so? I wonder," Neal said, and picked up a shell.

As he held the shell to his ear, his expression became so withdrawn and unreadable that I felt a pang of dismay. Was I seeing a symptom of his nervous trouble? He stood like a fragment of the village—as though the shell was holding him, rather than the reverse.

Eventually he mumbled "That's it, that's what he meant. Chanting with no mouths."

I took the shell only very reluctantly; my head was pounding. I pressed the shell to my ear, though I was deafened by the storm of my blood. If the shell was muttering, I couldn't bear the jaggedness of its rhythm. I seemed less to hear it than to feel it deep in my skull.

"Nothing like it," I said, almost snarling, and thrust the shell at him.

Now that I'd had to strain to hear it, I couldn't rid myself of the muttering; it seemed to underlie the sounds of wind and sea. I trudged onward, eyes half shut. Moisture sprang up around my feet; the glistening shapes around my prints looked larger and more definite. I had to cling to my sense of my own size and shape.

When we neared home I couldn't see the bungalows. There appeared to be only the beach, grown huge and blinding. At least Neal heard a car leaving the crescent, and led me up the path of collapsed footprints.

In the bungalow I lay willing the lights and patterns to fade from my closed eyes. Neal's presence didn't soothe me, even though he was only poring over the notebook. He'd brought a handful of shells indoors. Occasionally he held one to his ear, muttering: "It's still there, you know. It does sound like chanting." At least, I thought peevishly, *I* knew when something was a symptom of illness—but the trouble was that in my delirium I was tempted to agree with him. I felt I had almost heard what the sound was trying to be.

Next day Neal returned to the deserted village. He was gone for so long that even amid the clamour of my disordered senses, I grew anxious. I couldn't watch for him; whenever I tried, the white-hot beach began to judder, to quake, and set me shivering.

At last he returned, having failed to find another notebook. I hoped that would be the end of it, but his failure had simply frustrated him. His irritability chafed against mine. He managed to prepare a bedraggled salad, of which I ate little. As the tide of twilight rolled in from the horizon he sat by the window, gazing alternately at the beach and at the notebook.

Without warning he said: "I'm going for a stroll. Can I borrow your stick?"

I guessed that he meant to go to the beach. Should he be trapped by darkness and sea, I was in no condition to go to his aid. "I'd rather you didn't," I said feebly.

"Don't worry, I won't lose it."

My lassitude suffocated my arguments. I lolled in my chair and through the open window heard him padding away, his footsteps muffled by sand. Soon there was only the vague slack rumble of the sea, blundering back and forth, and the faint hiss of sand in the bushes.

After half an hour I made myself stand up, though the ache in my head surged and surged, and gaze out at the whitish beach. The whole expanse appeared to flicker like hints of lightning. I strained my eyes. The beach looked crowded with debris, all of which danced to the flickering. I had to peer at every movement, but there was no sign of Neal.

I went out and stood between the bushes. The closer I approached the beach, the more crowded with obscure activity it seemed to be—but I suspected that much, if not all, of this could be blamed on my condition, for within five minutes my head felt so tight and unbalanced that I had to retreat indoors, away from the heat.

Though I'd meant to stay awake, I was dozing when Neal returned. I woke to find him gazing from the window. As I opened my eyes the beach lurched forward, shining. It didn't look crowded now, presumably because my eyes had had a rest. What could Neal see to preoccupy him so? "Enjoy your stroll?" I said sleepily.

He turned, and I felt a twinge of disquiet. His face looked stiff with doubt; his eyes were uneasy, a frown dug its ruts in his forehead. "It doesn't glow," he said.

Assuming I knew what he was talking about, I could only wonder how badly his nerves were affecting his perceptions. If anything, the beach looked brighter. "How do you mean?"

"The beach down by the village—it doesn't glow. Not any more."

"Oh, I see."

He looked offended, almost contemptuous, though I couldn't understand why he'd expected me to be less indifferent. He withdrew into a scrutiny of the notebook. He might have been trying to solve an urgent problem.

Perhaps if I hadn't been ill I would have been able to divert Neal from his obsession, but I could hardly venture outside without growing dizzy; I could only wait in the bungalow for my state to improve. Neither Neal nor I had had sunstroke before, but he seemed to know how to treat it. "Keep drinking water. Cover yourself if you start shivering." He didn't mind my staying in—he seemed almost too eager to go out alone. Did that matter? Next day he was bound only for the library.

My state was crippling my thoughts, yet even if I'd been healthy I couldn't have imagined how he would look when he returned: excited, conspiratorial, smug. "I've got a story for you," he said at once.

Most such offers proved to be prolonged and dull. "Oh yes?" I said warily.

He sat forward as though to infect me with suspense. "That village we went to—it isn't called Lewis. It's called Strand."

Was he pausing to give me a chance to gasp or applaud? "Oh yes," I said without enthusiasm.

"Lewis was another village, further up the coast. It's deserted too."

That seemed to be his punch line. The antics of patterns within my eyelids had made me irritable. "It doesn't seem much of a story," I complained.

"Well, that's only the beginning." When his pause had forced me to open my eyes, he said "I read a book about your local unexplained mysteries."

"Why?"

"Look, if you don't want to hear—"

"Go on, go on, now you've started." Not to know might be even more nerve-racking.

"There wasn't much about Lewis," he said eventually, perhaps to give himself more time to improvise.

"Was there much at all?"

"Yes, certainly. It may not sound like much. Nobody knows why Lewis was abandoned, but then nobody knows that about Strand either." My impatience must have showed, for he added hastily "What I mean is, the people who left Strand wouldn't say why."

"Someone asked them?"

"The woman who wrote the book. She managed to track some of them down. They'd moved as far inland as they could, that was one thing she noticed. And they always had some kind of nervous disorder. Talking about Strand always made them more nervous, as though they felt that talking might make something happen, or something might hear."

"That's what the author said."

"Right."

"What was her name?"

Could he hear my suspicion? "Jesus *Christ*," he snarled, "I don't know. What does it matter?"

In fact it didn't, not to me. His story had made me feel worse. The noose had tightened round my skull, the twilit beach was swarming and vibrating. I closed my eyes. Shut up, I roared at him. Go away.

"There was one thing," he persisted. "One man said that kids kept going on the beach at night. Their parents tried all ways to stop them. Some of them questioned their kids, but it was as though the kids couldn't stop themselves. Why was that, do you think?" When I refused to answer he said irrelevantly: "All this was in the 1930s."

I couldn't stand hearing children called kids. The recurring word had

249

made me squirm: drips of slang, like water torture. And I'd never heard such a feeble punch line. His clumsiness as a storyteller enraged me; he couldn't even organize his material. I was sure he hadn't read any such book.

After a while I peered out from beneath my eyelids, hoping he'd decided that I was asleep. He was poring over the notebook again, and looked rapt. I only wished that people and reviewers would read my books as carefully. He kept rubbing his forehead, as though to enliven his brain.

I dozed. When I opened my eyes he was waiting for me. He shoved the notebook at me to demonstrate something. "Look, I'm sorry," I said without much effort to sound so. "I'm not in the mood."

He stalked into his room, emerging without the book but with my stick. "I'm going for a walk," he announced sulkily, like a spouse after a quarrel.

I dozed gratefully, for I felt more delirious; my head felt packed with grains of sand that gritted together. In fact, the whole of me was made of sand. Of course it was true that I was composed of particles, and I thought my delirium had found a metaphor for that. But the grains that floated through my inner vision were neither sand nor atoms. A member, dark and vague, was reaching for them. I struggled to awaken; I didn't want to distinguish it shape, and still less did I want to learn what it meant to do with the grains—for as the member sucked them into itself, engulfing them in a way that I refused to perceive, I saw that the grains were worlds and stars.

I woke shivering. My body felt uncontrollable and unfamiliar. I let it shake itself to rest—not that I had a choice, but I was concentrating on the problem of why I'd woken head raised, like a watchdog. What had I heard?

Perhaps only wind and sea: both seemed louder, more intense. My thoughts became entangled in their rhythm. I felt there had been another sound. The bushes threshed, sounding parched with sand. Had I heard Neal returning? I stumbled into his room. It was empty.

As I stood by his open window, straining my ears, I thought I heard his voice, blurred by the dull tumult of waves. I peered out. Beyond the low heads of the bushes, the glow of the beach shuddered toward me. I had to close my eyes, for I couldn't tell whether the restless scrawny shapes were crowding my eyeballs or the beach; it felt, somehow, like both. When I looked again, I seemed to see Neal.

Or was it Neal? The unsteady stifled glow aggravated the distortions of my vision. Was the object just a new piece of debris? I found its shape bewildering; my mind kept apprehending it as a symbol printed on the whitish expanse. The luminosity made it seem to shift, tentatively and jerkily, as though it was learning to pose. The light, or my eyes, surrounded it with dancing.

Had my sense of perspective left me? I was misjudging size, either of the beach or of the figure. Yes, it was a figure, however large it seemed. It was moving its arms like a limp puppet. And it was half-buried in the sand.

I staggered outside, shouting to Neal, and then I recoiled. The sky must be thick with a stormcloud; it felt suffocatingly massive, solid as rock, and close enough to crush me. I forced myself toward the bushes, though my head was pounding, squeezed into a lump of pain.

Almost at once I heard plodding on the dunes. My blood half deafened me; the footsteps sounded vague and immense. I peered along the dim path. At the edge of my vision the beach flickered repetitively. Immense darkness hovered over me. Unnervingly close to me, swollen by the glow, a head rose into view. For a moment my tension seemed likely to crack my skull. Then Neal spoke. His words were incomprehensible amid the wind, but it was his voice.

As we trudged back toward the lights the threat of a storm seemed to withdraw, and I blamed it on my tension. "Of course I'm all right," he muttered irritably. "I fell and that made me shout, that's all." Once we were inside I saw the evidence of his fall; his trousers were covered with sand up to the knees.

Next day he hardly spoke to me. He went down early to the beach, and stayed there. I didn't know if he was obsessed or displaying pique. Perhaps he couldn't bear to be near me; invalids can find each other unbearable.

Often I glimpsed him, wandering beyond the dunes. He walked as though in an elaborate maze and scrutinized the beach. Was he searching for the key to the notebook? Was he looking for pollution? By the time he found it, I thought sourly, it would have infected him.

I felt too enervated to intervene. As I watched, Neal appeared to vanish intermittently; if I looked away, I couldn't locate him again for minutes. The beach blazed like bone, and was never still. I couldn't blame the aberrations of my vision solely on heat and haze.

When Neal returned, late that afternoon, I asked him to phone for a doctor. He looked taken aback, but eventually said: "There's a box by the station, isn't there?"

"One of the neighbours would let you phone."

"No, I'll walk down. They're probably all wondering why you've let some long-haired freak squat in your house, as it is."

He went out, rubbing his forehead gingerly. He often did that now. That, and his preoccupation with the demented notebook, were additional reasons why I wanted a doctor: I felt Neal needed examining too.

251

By the time he returned, it was dusk. On the horizon, embers dulled in the sea. The glow of the beach was already stirring; it seemed to have intensified during the last few days. I told myself I had grown hypersensitive.

"Dr. Lewis. He's coming tomorrow." Neal hesitated, then went on: "I think I'll just have a stroll on the beach. Want to come?"

"Good God no. I'm ill, can't you see?"

"I know that." His impatience was barely controlled. "A stroll might do you good. There isn't any sunlight now."

"I'll stay in until I've seen the doctor."

He looked disposed to argue, but his restlessness overcame him. As he left, his bearing seemed to curse me. Was his illness making him intolerant of mine, or did he feel that I'd rebuffed a gesture of reconciliation?

I felt too ill to watch him from the window. When I looked I could seldom distinguish him or make out which movements were his. He appeared to be walking slowly, poking at the beach with my stick. I wondered if he'd found quicksand. Again his path made me think of a maze.

I dozed, far longer than I'd intended. The doctor loomed over me. Peering into my eyes, he reached down. I began to struggle, as best I could: I'd glimpsed the depths of his eye-sockets, empty and dry as interstellar space. I didn't need his treatment. I would be fine if he left me alone, just let me go. But he had reached deep into me. As though I was a bladder that had burst, I felt myself flood into him; I felt vast emptiness absorb my substance and myself. Dimly I understood that it was nothing like emptiness—that my mind refused to perceive what it was, so alien and frightful was its teeming.

It was dawn. The muffled light teemed. The beach glowed fitfully. I gasped: someone was down on the beach, so huddled that he looked shapeless. He rose, levering himself up with my stick, and began to pace haphazardly. I knew at once that he'd spent the night on the beach.

After that I stayed awake. I couldn't imagine the state of his mind, and I was a little afraid of being asleep when he returned. But when, hours later, he came in to raid the kitchen for a piece of cheese, he seemed hardly to see me. He was muttering repetitively under his breath. His eyes looked dazzled by the beach, sunk in his obsession.

"When did the doctor say he was coming?"

"Later," he mumbled, and hurried down to the beach.

I hope he would stay there until the doctor came. Occasionally I glimpsed him at his intricate pacing. Ripples of heat deformed him; his blurred flesh looked unstable. Whenever I glanced at the beach it leapt forward, dauntingly vivid. Cracks of light appeared in the sea. Clumps of grass seemed to rise twitching, as though the dunes were craning to watch Neal. Five minutes' vigil at the window was as much as I could bear.

The afternoon consumed time. It felt as lethargic and enervating as four in the morning. There was no sign of the doctor. I kept gazing from the front door. Nothing moved on the crescent except windborne hints of the beach.

Eventually I tried to phone. Though I could feel the heat of the pavement through the soles of my shoes, the day seemed bearable; only threats of pain plucked at my skull. But nobody was at home. The bungalows stood smugly in the evening light. When I attempted to walk to the phone box, the noose closed on my skull at once.

In my hall I halted startled, for Neal had thrown open the livingroom door as I entered the house. He looked flushed and angry. "Where were you?" he demanded.

"I'm not a hospital case yet, you know. I was trying to phone the doctor."

Unfathomably, he looked relieved. "I'll go down now and call him."

While he was away I watched the beach sink into twilight. At the moment, this seemed to be the only time of day I could endure watching— the time at which shapes become obscure, most capable of metamorphosis. Perhaps this made the antics of the shore acceptable, more apparently natural. Now the beach resembled clouds in front of the moon; it drifted slowly and variously. If I gazed for long it looked nervous with lightning. The immense bulk of the night edged up from the horizon.

I didn't hear Neal return; I must have been fascinated by the view. I turned to find him watching me. Again he looked relieved—because I was still here? "He's coming soon," he said.

"Tonight, do you mean?"

"Yes, tonight. Why not?"

I didn't know many doctors who would come out at night to treat what was, however unpleasant for me, a relatively minor illness. Perhaps attitudes were different here in the country. Neal was heading for the back door, for the beach. "Do you think you could wait until he comes?" I said, groping for an excuse to detain him. "Just in case I feel worse."

"Yes, you're right." His gaze was opaque. "I'd better stay with you."

We waited. The dark mass closed over beach and bungalows. The nocturnal glow fluttered at the edge of my vision. When I glanced at the beach, the dim shapes were hectic. I seemed to be paying for my earlier fascination, for now the walls of the room looked active with faint patterns.

Where was the doctor? Neal seemed impatient too. The only sounds were the repetitive ticking of his footsteps and the irregular chant of the sea. He kept staring at me as if he wanted to speak; occasionally his mouth twitched. He resembled a child both eager to confess and afraid to do so.

Though he made me uneasy I tried to look encouraging, interested in whatever he might have to say. His pacing took him closer and closer to the beach door. Yes, I nodded, tell me, talk to me.

His eyes narrowed. Behind his eyelids he was pondering. Abruptly he sat opposite me. A kind of smile, tweaked awry, plucked at his lips. "I've got another story for you," he said.

"Really?" I sounded as intrigued as I could.

He picked up the notebook. "I worked it out from this."

So we'd returned to his obsession. As he twitched pages over, his feet shifted constantly. His lips moved as though whispering the text. I heard the vast mumbling of the sea.

"Suppose this," he said all at once. "I only said suppose, mind you. This guy was living all alone in Strand. It must have affected his mind, you said that yourself—having to watch the beach every night. But just suppose it didn't send him mad? Suppose it affected his mind so that he saw things more clearly?"

I hid my impatience. "What things?"

"The beach." His tone reminded me of something—a particular kind of simplicity I couldn't quite place. "Of course we're only supposing. But from things you've read, don't you feel there are places that are closer to another sort of reality, another plane or dimension or whatever?"

"You mean the beach at Strand was like that?" I suggested, to encourage him.

"That's right. Did you feel it too?"

His eagerness startled me. "I felt ill, that's all. I still do."

"Sure. Yes, of course. I mean, we were only supposing. But look at what he says." He seemed glad to retreat into the notebook. "It started at Lewis where the old stones were, then it moved on up the coast to Strand. Doesn't that prove that what he was talking about is unlike anything we know?"

His mouth hung open, awaiting my agreement; it looked empty, robbed of sense. I glanced away, distracted by the fluttering glow beyond him. "I don't know what you mean."

"That's because you haven't read this properly." His impatience had turned harsh. "Look here," he demanded, poking his fingers at a group of words as if they were a Bible's oracle.

WHEN THE PATTERNS READY IT CAN COME BACK. "So what is that supposed to mean?"

"I'll tell you what I think it means—what he meant." His low voice seemed to stumble among the rhythms of the beach. "You see how he keeps mentioning patterns. Suppose this other reality was once all there was? Then ours came into being and occupied some of its space. We didn't

254

destroy it—it can't be destroyed. Maybe it withdrew a little, to bide its time. But it left a kind of imprint of itself, a kind of coded image of itself in our reality. And yet that image is itself in embryo, growing. You see, he says it's alive but it's only the image being put together. Things become part of its image, and that's how it grows. I'm sure that's what he meant."

I felt mentally exhausted and dismayed by all this. How much in need of a doctor was he? I couldn't help sounding a little derisive. "I don't see how you could have put all that together from that book."

"Who says I did?"

His vehemence was shocking. I had to break the tension, for the glare in his eyes looked as unnatural and nervous as the glow of the beach. I went to gaze from the front window, but there was no sign of the doctor. "Don't worry," Neal said. "He's coming."

I stood staring out at the lightless road until he said fretfully "Don't you want to hear the rest?"

He waited until I sat down. His tension was oppressive as the hovering sky. He gazed at me for what seemed minutes; the noose dug into my skull. At last he said "Does this beach feel like anywhere else to you?"

"It feels like a beach."

He shrugged that aside. "You see, he worked out that whatever came from the old stones kept moving toward the inhabited areas. That's how it added to itself. That's why it moved on from Lewis and then Strand."

"All nonsense, of course. Ravings."

"No. It isn't." There was no mistaking the fury that lurked, barely restrained, beneath his low voice. That fury seemed loose in the roaring night, in the wind and violent sea and looming sky. The beach trembled wakefully. "The next place it would move to would be here," he muttered. "It has to be."

"If you accepted the idea in the first place."

A hint of a grimace twitched his cheek; my comment might have been an annoying fly—certainly as trivial. "You can read the pattern out there if you try," he mumbled. "It takes all day. You begin to get a sense of what might be there. It's alive, though nothing like life as we recognize it."

I could only say whatever came into my head, to detain him until the doctor arrived. "Then how do you?"

He avoided the question, but only to betray the depths of his obsession. "Would an insect recognize us as a kind of life?"

Suddenly I realized that he intoned "the beach" as a priest might name his god. We must get away from the beach. Never mind the doctor now. "Look, Neal, I think we'd better ·"

He interrupted me, eyes glaring spasmodically. "It's strongest at night. I think it soaks up energy during the day. Remember, he said that the quicksands only come out at night. They move, you know— they make you follow the pattern. And the sea is different at night. Things come out of it. They're like symbols and yet they're alive. I think the sea creates them. They help make the pattern live."

Appalled, I could only return to the front window and search for the lights of the doctor's car—for any lights at all. "Yes, yes," Neal said, sounding less impatient than soothing. "He's coming." But as he spoke I glimpsed, reflected in the window, his secret triumphant grin.

Eventually I managed to say to his reflection "You didn't call a doctor, did you?"

"No." A smile made his lips tremble like quicksand. "But he's coming."

My stomach had begun to churn slowly; so had my head, and the room. Now I was afraid to stand with my back to Neal, but when I turned I was more afraid to ask the question. "Who?"

For a moment I thought he disdained to answer; he turned his back on me and gazed toward the beach—but I can't write any longer as if I have doubts, as if I don't know the end. The beach was his answer, its awesome transformation was, even if I wasn't sure what I was seeing. Was the beach swollen, puffed up as if by the irregular gasping of the sea? Was it swarming with indistinct shapes, parasites that scuttled dancing over it, sank into it, floated writhing to its surface? Did it quiver along the whole of its length like luminous gelatin? I tried to believe that all this was an effect of the brooding dark—but the dark had closed down so thickly that there might have been no light in the world outside except the fitful glow.

He craned his head back over his shoulder. The gleam in his eyes looked very like the glimmering outside. A web of saliva stretched between his bared teeth. He grinned with a frightful generosity; he'd decided to answer my question more directly. His lips moved as they had when he was reading. At last I heard what I'd tried not to suspect. He was making the sound that I'd tried not to hear in the shells.

Was it meant to be an invocation, or the name I'd asked for? I knew only that the sound, so liquid and inhuman that I could almost think it was shapeless, nauseated me, so much that I couldn't separate it from the huge loose voices of wind and sea. It seemed to fill the room. The pounding of my skull tried to imitate its rhythm, which I found impossible to grasp, unbearable. I began to sidle along the wall toward the front door.

His body turned jerkily, as if dangling from his neck. His head laughed, if a sound like struggles in mud is laughter. "You're not going to try to get away?" he cried. "It was getting hold of you before I came, he was. You haven't a chance now, not since we brought him into the house,"

256

and he picked up a shell.

As he levelled the mouth of the shell at me, my dizziness flooded my skull, hurling me forward. The walls seemed to glare and shake and break out in swarms; I thought that a dark bulk loomed at the window, filling it. Neal's mouth was working, but the nauseating sound might have been roaring deep in a cavern, or a shell. It sounded distant and huge, but coming closer and growing more definite—the voice of something vast and liquid that was gradually taking shape. Perhaps that was because I was listening, but I had no choice.

All at once Neal's free hand clamped his forehead. It looked like a pincer desperate to tear something out of his skull. "It's growing," he cried, somewhere between sobbing and ecstasy. As he spoke, the liquid chant seemed to abate not at all. Before I knew what he meant to do, he'd wrenched open the back door and was gone. In a nightmarish way, his nervous elaborate movements resembled dancing.

As the door crashed open, the roar of the night rushed in. Its leap in volume sounded eager, voracious. I stood paralyzed, listening, and couldn't tell how like his chant it sounded. I heard footsteps, soft and loose, running unevenly over the dunes. Minutes later I thought I heard a faint cry, which sounded immediately engulfed.

I slumped against a chair. I felt relieved, drained, uncaring. The sounds had returned to the beach, where they ought to be; the room looked stable now. Then I grew disgusted with myself. Suppose Neal was injured, or caught in quicksand? I'd allowed his hysteria to gain a temporary hold on my sick perceptions, I told myself—was I going to use that as an excuse not to try to save him?

At last I forced myself outside. All the bungalows were dark. The beach was glimmering, but not violently. I could see nothing wrong with the sky. Only my dizziness, and the throbbing of my head, threatened to distort my perceptions.

I made myself edge between the bushes, which hissed like snakes, mouths full of sand. The tangle of footprints made me stumble frequently. Sand rattled the spikes of marram grass. At the edge of the dunes, the path felt ready to slide me down to the beach.

The beach was crowded. I had to squint at many of the vague pieces of debris. My eyes grew used to the dimness, but I could see no sign of Neal. Then I peered closer. Was that a pair of sandals, half-buried? Before my giddiness could hurl me to the beach, I slithered down.

Yes, they were Neal's, and a path of bare footprints led away toward the crowd of debris. I poked gingerly at the sandals, and wished I had my stick to test for quicksand—but the sand in which they were partially engulfed was quite solid. Why had he tried to bury them?

I followed his prints, my eyes still adjusting. I refused to imitate his path, for it looped back on itself in intricate patterns which made me dizzy and refused to fade from my mind. His paces were irregular, a cripple's dance. He must be a puppet of his nerves, I thought. I was a little afraid to confront him, but I felt a duty to try.

His twistings led me among the debris. Low obscure shapes surrounded me: a jagged stump bristling with metal tendrils that groped in the air as I came near; half a car so rusty and misshapen that it looked like a child's fuzzy sketch; the hood of a pram, within which glimmered a bald lump of sand. I was glad to emerge from that maze, for the dim objects seemed to shift; I'd even thought the bald lump was opening a crumbing mouth.

But on the open beach there were other distractions. The ripples and patterns of sand were clearer, and appeared to vibrate restlessly. I kept glancing toward the sea, not because its chant was troubling me—though, with its insistent loose rhthym, it was—but because I had a persistent impression that the waves were slowing, sluggish as treacle.

I stumbled, and had to turn back to see what had tripped me. The glow of the beach showed me Neal's shirt, the little of it that was left unburied. There was no mistaking it; I recognised its pattern. The glow made the nylon seem luminous, lit from within.

His prints danced back among the debris. Even then, God help me, I wondered if he was playing a sick joke—if he was waiting somewhere to leap out, to scare me into admitting I'd been impressed. I trudged angrily into the midst of the debris, and wished at once that I hadn't. All the objects were luminous, without shadows.

There was no question now: the glow of the beach was increasing. It made Neal's tracks look larger; their outlines shifted as I squinted at them. I stumbled hastily toward the deserted stretch of beach, and brushed against the half-engulfed car.

That was the moment at which the nightmare became real. I might have told myself that rust had eaten away the car until it was thin as a shell, but I was past deluding myself. All at once I knew that nothing on this beach was as it seemed, for as my hand collided with the car roof, which should have been painfully solid, I felt the roof crumble—and the entire structure flopped on the sand, from which it was at once indistinguishable.

I fled toward the open beach. But there was no relief, for the entire beach was glowing luridly, like mud struggling to suffocate a moon. Among the debris I glimpsed the rest of Neal's clothes, half absorbed by the beach. As I staggered into the open, I saw his tracks ahead—saw how they appeared to grow, to alter until they became unrecognizable, and then to peter out at a large dark shapeless patch on the sand.

I glared about, terrified. I couldn't see the bungalows. After minutes I succeeded in glimpsing the path, the mess of footprints cluttering the dune. I began to pace toward it, very slowly and quietly, so as not to be noticed by the beach and the looming sky.

But the dunes were receding. I think I began to scream then, scream almost in a whisper, for the faster I hurried, the further the dunes withdrew. The nightmare had overtaken perspective. Now I was running wildly, though I felt I was standing still. I'd run only a few steps when I had to recoil from sand that seized my feet so eagerly I almost heard it smack its lips. Minutes ago there had been no quicksand, for I could see my earlier prints embedded in that patch. I stood trapped, shivering uncontrollably, as the glow intensified and the lightless sky seemed to descend—and I felt the beach change.

Simultaneously I experienced something which, in a sense, was worse: I felt myself change. My dizziness whirled out of me. I felt light-headed but stable. At last I realized that I had never had sunstroke. Perhaps it had been my inner conflict—being forced to stay yet at the same time not daring to venture onto the beach, because of what my subconscious knew would happen.

And now it was happening. The beach had won. Perhaps Neal had given it the strength. Though I dared not look, I knew that the sea had stopped. Stranded objects, elaborate symbols composed of something like flesh, writhed on its paralyzed margin. The clamour which surrounded me, chanting and gurgling, was not that of the sea: it was far too articulate, however repetitive. It was underfoot too—the voice of the beach, a whisper pronounced by so many sources that it was deafening.

I felt ridges of sand squirm beneath me. They were firm enough to bear my weight, but they felt nothing like sand. They were forcing me to shift my balance. In a moment I would have to dance, to imitate the jerking shapes that had ceased to pretend they were only debris, to join in the ritual of the objects that swarmed up from the congealed sea. Everything glistened in the quivering glow. I thought my flesh had begun to glow too.

Then, with a lurch of vertigo worse than any I'd experienced, I found myself momentarily detached from the nightmares. I seemed to be observing myself, a figure tiny and trivial as an insect, making a timid hysterical attempt to join in the dance of the teeming beach. The moment was brief, yet felt like eternity. Then I was back in my clumsy flesh, struggling to prance on the beach.

At once I was cold with terror. I shook like a victim of electricity, for I knew what viewpoint I'd shared. It was still watching me, indifferent as outer space—and it filled the sky. If I looked up I would see its eyes, or eye, if it had anything that I would recognize as such. My neck shivered

259

as I held my head down. But I would have to look up in a moment, for I could feel the face, or whatever was up there, leaning closer—reaching down for me.

If I hadn't broken through my suffocating panic I would have been crushed to nothing. But my teeth tore my lip, and allowed me to scream. Released, I ran desperately, heedless of quicksand. The dunes crept back from me, the squirming beach glowed, the light flickered in the rhythm of the chanting. I was spared being engulfed—but when at last I reached the dunes, or was allowed to reach them, the dark massive presence still hovered overhead.

I clambered scrabbling up the path. My sobbing gasps filled my mouth with sand. My wild flight was from nothing that I'd seen. I was fleeing the knowledge, deep-rooted and undeniable, that what I perceived blotting out the sky was nothing but an acceptable metaphor. Appalling though the presence was, it was only my mind's version of what was there—a way of letting me glimpse it without going mad at once.

I have not seen Neal since—at least, not in a form that anyone else would recognize.

Next day, after a night during which I drank all the liquor I could find to douse my appalled thoughts and insights, I discovered that I couldn't leave. I pretended to myself that I was soing to the beach to search for Neal. But the movements began at once; the pattern stirred. As I gazed, dully entranced, I felt something grow less dormant in my head, as though my skull had turned into a shell.

Perhaps I stood engrossed by the beach for hours. Movement distracted me: the skimming of a windblown patch of sand. As I glanced at it I saw that it resembled a giant mask, its features ragged and crumbling. Though its eyes and mouth couldn't keep their shape, it kept trying to resemble Neal's face. As it slithered whispering toward me I fled toward the path, moaning.

That night he came into the bungalow. I hadn't dared go to bed; I dozed in a chair, and frequently woke trembling. Was I awake when I saw his huge face squirming and transforming as it crawled out of the wall? Certainly I could hear his words, though his voice was the inhuman chorus I'd experienced on the beach. Worse, when I opened my eyes to glimpse what might have been only a shadow, not a large unstable form fading back into the substance of the wall, for a few seconds I could still hear that voice.

Each night, once the face had sunk back into the wall as into quicksand, the voice remained longer—and each night, struggling to break loose from the prison of my chair, I understood more of its revelations. I tried to believe all this was my imagination, and so, in a sense, it was. The glimpses of Neal were nothing more than acceptable metaphors for what Neal had become, and what I was becoming. My mind refused to perceive the truth more directly, to learn what that truth might be.

For a while I struggled. I couldn't leave, but perhaps I could write. When I found that however bitterly I fought I could think of nothing but the beach, I wrote this. I hoped that writing about it might release me, but of course the more one thinks of the beach, the stronger its hold becomes.

Now I spend most of my time on the beach. It has taken me months to write this. Sometimes I see people staring at me from the bungalows. Do they wonder what I'm doing? They will find out when their time comes— everyone will. Neal must have satisfied it for a while; for the moment it is slower. But that means little. Its time is not like ours.

Each day the pattern is clearer. My pacing helps. Once you have glimpsed the pattern you must go back to read it, over and over. I can feel it growing in my mind. The sense of expectacny is overwhelming. Of course that sense was never mine. It was the hunger of the beach.

My time is near. The large moist prints that surround mine are more pronounced—the prints of what I am becoming. Its substance is everywhere, stealthy and insidious. Today, as I looked at the bungalows, I saw them change; they grew like fossils of themselves. They looked like dreams of the beach, and that is what they will become.

The voice is always with me now. Sometimes the congealing haze seems to mouth at me. At twilight the dunes edge forward to guard the beach. When the beach is dimmest I see other figures pacing out the pattern. Only those whom the beach has touched would see them; their outlines are unstable—some look more like coral than flesh. The quicksands make us trace the pattern, and he stoops from the depths beyond the sky to watch. The sea feeds me.

Often now I have what may be a dream. I glimpse what Neal has become, and how that is merely a fragment of the imprint which it will use to return to our world. Each time I come closer to recalling the insight when I wake. As my mind changes, it tries to prepare me for the end. Soon I shall be what Neal is. I tremble uncontrollably, I feel deathly sick, my mind struggles desperately not to know. Yet in a way I am resigned. After all, even if I managed to flee the beach, I could never escape the growth. I have understood enough to know that it would absorb me in time, when it becomes the world.

AFTERWORD
Stephen Jones
and David Sutton

Just over a decade ago, a small 'teaser' campaign announced a new magazine of 'the weird and unusual'. *Fantasy Tales* was created as a much-needed market for short stories of fantasy and terror, but it was more than just that. Although providing an additional marketplace was in itself an admirable sentiment, *Fantasy Tales* was aimed to recreate the look and, more importantly, the entertainment value of the most famous of the old pulp magazines from the 1930s and '40s. The logo, lettering style and contents were designed, not to mimic, but strongly suggest *Weird Tales*, that most nostalgically respected of the pulps. In the summer of 1977, our first issue appeared with the presumption of 'volume 1' on the contents page. It turned out to be no presumption though, and ten years and a string of awards later, *Fantasy Tales* is still going from strength to strength.

In the history of small press magazines, it is the common thing for up-and-coming writers and artists to hone their skills in the pages of the 'little' magazines—there are precious few other outlets for their creative talents. Numerous science fiction and fantasy authors and illustrators who have gone on to become well-known professionals began their humble origins in such a manner. However, the years have changed things

263

dramatically. When *Fantasy Tales* was conceived, it and a small pool of—mostly American—amateur magazines then being published, had become a respected and legitimate market for professionals in their own right, often complementing the bigger and sometimes more erratic outlets of anthologies and newsstand magazines. That situation continues today, with the small presses acting as a rich storehouse for fantasy fiction and artwork, a source from which the professional outlets often draw and, of course, a ready marketplace for the newer and younger fantasists to achieve recognition in.

Visually a homage to the pulps, *Fantasy Tales* went one better, attracting a small number of writers (some of whom have sadly since died) who themselves were contributors to *Weird Tales* and its companion titles: Robert Bloch, Manly Wade Wellman, Hugh B. Cave, H. Warner Munn, Frances Garfield and Fritz Leiber, whose work appear in this book, were all regularly featured in the pages of those early fantasy magazines. We have also managed to attract a wide range of new and established artists to complement the written material: Jim Pitts, Alan Hunter, Dave Carson, Stephen E. Fabian, J.K. Potter, Russ Nicholson, John Stewart, David Lloyd, Jim Fitzpatrick, Andrew Smith, Randy Broecker and Allen Koszowski have all regularly embellished our pages, and once again, many are featured in this volume.

Looking back over ten years, we appreciate the strength and loyalty of our readership and the judgement of our peers in the genre, since *Fantasy Tales* has won The British Fantasy Award in the Best Small Press category no less than seven times, and been nominated for the prestigious World Fantasy Award in the Special Award category five times, winning in 1985. Stories we've published have often been reprinted elsewhere, but we are probably most proud of Dennis Etchison's 'The Dark Country', which won both the British Fantasy Award and the World Fantasy Award in short fiction category in the same year.

This volume presents a sampling of twenty of *Fantasy Tales'* best stories of dark fantasy and horror, selected from the ten-year output of the magazine. There is some traditional storytelling from veterans Robert Bloch, Manly Wade Wellman, Fritz Leiber and others, and there is a contemporary baring of the mind in disturbing, psychological forays into urban horror from such modern masters as Clive Barker, Ramsey Campbell, Charles L. Grant and Thomas Ligotti. Whatever your taste in terror, we are certain that you'll be suitably entertained and chilled as you explore these fictional slices of the half-glimpsed world of horror.

March 1988